I0785081

PINNED DOWN

FORBIDDEN GOALS BOOK

REBECCA RATHE

For all of us.

As many times as life and circumstances tried to pin us down, we're still here and we're still fighting.

AUTHOR'S NOTE

All of the books in the Forbidden Goals series are written with care and understanding, with the guidance of sensitivity readers and members of the communities that are represented throughout the series. That being said, these books contain forbidden and sometimes dark themes that might trigger discomfort in some readers. Please continue with the following advisories in mind, with the understanding that content warnings may contain spoilers.

CONTENT WARNINGS

PINNED DOWN is a contemporary sports romance that takes place between two consenting adults. This story contains themes that some readers may find triggering, including but not limited to: homophobia from peers and family, internalized homophobia, bullying and hazing, humiliation, degradation, feminization, dubious consent and coercion, mentions of drug and alcohol abuse, addiction, and recovery, death of a parent due to alcohol related circumstance, classism/class discrimination, dementia, scenes that may contain questionable or dubious use of proper lubrication, pain or injury during sex, toxic relationship dynamics, and of course strong language and graphic on-page sex.

Instances of sexist, homophobic, and ableist language may be present throughout this book. This language does not reflect the author's beliefs or ideals, but are a realistic portrayal of lived experiences.

Wrestling is a sport of control, but the hardest opponent
to control is yourself.

ANONYMOUS

World

CHAPTER 1
BECK

My head swivels as I walk into the Howlers Wrestling Club main floor, checking every face that files in for the first team meeting of the new season.

I push my bickering roommates to go find their seats and make my way over to the bleachers and my co-captains. I'm usually always early for a team meeting, almost pathologically so, but not today. It's been a weird morning, and I'm feeling a little out of sorts.

I'm seeing things.

I have to be seeing things. But why is my brain conjuring a memory of someone I make a point to never think about? A memory I've buried deep, deep down.

"Bullshit you haven't noticed!" Cade exclaims, stopping so abruptly I bump into his broad back. Shaken from my errant thoughts, I huff and shake my head, but my best friend ignores me and opens his arms, gesturing at his body like he's presenting a damn trophy. "Beck, come on!"

I roll my eyes at the way he not-so-subtly flexes his biceps, eyes shifting between me and Fish with blatant desperation.

"Will you go sit down?" I say, nudging him towards the bleachers. "The meeting's about to start."

"I think the only thing that got bigger is your head," Fish says, smirking back at me as they head to a row of open seats, continuing to bicker.

Cade throws his hands up dramatically. I ignore them both. Especially Cade, who very clearly needs someone—*anyone*—to comment on the extra ten pounds of solid muscle he's packed on since the end of last season. He looks like he swallowed another smaller wrestler whole, but like the good friends we are, Fish and I are both pretending it's not noticeable. We won't give him the satisfaction of feeding his cocky ego.

I give the room another once-over as a handful of unfamiliar faces settle into the bleachers. This year's freshmen, most likely.

Coach McCoy bursts into the room, ready to get the season started, loudly clapping his hands to get everyone's attention. I'm not really paying attention, taking advantage of my vantage point as everyone takes a seat.

I'm still scanning the room for a head of wavy blond hair and broad shoulders when Sean, one of my co-captains, nudges my thigh. I snap my gaze to him, and then to Coach McCoy, who is staring at me like the idiot I am. Everyone else is sitting, waiting expectantly for Coach to start the orientation. But I'm still standing here like an idiot.

I sit quickly, cursing myself for being so ridiculous. I really am perfectly aware of how ridiculous I am. But even as Coach launches into his first pre-season speech, my mind is still preoccupied by the ghost I thought I saw yesterday. And then again this morning.

For my own peace of mind and sanity, I need to know who that actually was. Because if my brain is dragging memories of him up, of that day, that match, those humiliating minutes of my life that changed everything—then something in me is slipping.

Yesterday I thought I was crazy. It was only the briefest glimpse. A familiar stocky build making his way down the hall through the chaos that is move-in day in the athletic dorms. But it wasn't just that. It was the set of his shoulders, wavy hair bouncing with each step. It was familiar enough to jar me, jolting something loose in my chest, my heart rate kicking up so fast I had to catch my breath. The person disappeared before I could recognize the spike of adrenaline for what it was. Fear. I brushed it off, believing my mind was playing tricks on me. The world isn't *that* small, after all.

Even knowing it couldn't possibly be him, I'd dreamed of him last night anyway. My mind twisted the memory into an exaggerated version of events that were even worse than the reality. In the nightmare, I was naked, bare and exposed so there was no way to hide. Everyone could see my shame. They pointed and whispered, their laughter growing louder as he pinned me again and again and again, until I sat up in bed, panicked and sweating.

To make things worse, my already frazzled nerves got a jump start again this morning. While in line for the smoothie bar at the student union, I swear I saw him again, at the far end of the dining hall, in line to pay for the breakfast buffet. Light fell over his eerily familiar frame, catching on wavy golden hair from across the room.

I stepped out of line, heart slamming in my ribcage, walking towards him to get a better look, but Cade and his monstrous head and biceps had blocked my view. By the time I shoved him aside, the phantom was gone. I stood there, dazed and blinking, my brain feeling overloaded and spinning back to a day I've been trying to forget for over two years. I've been on edge ever since.

Walking into my first day as captain obsessing about the worst day of my life is not how I wanted to start the year. But here I am, acting like an idiot instead of focusing on the perfect image I've built for myself, the good life I've been clinging to, worrying that my life is about to crumble around me again over nothing but a memory.

Squeezing my eyes shut, I pinch the bridge of my nose, trying to push back the barrage of memories that threaten my sanity, flinching when Sean nudges me again. He's standing now, looking down at me like he's concerned for my wellbeing. I'm not acting like myself.

For the past two years at Huntston University, I've been a model student and athlete. Always poised, always on my game, never slacking. Perfect. Polished. Controlled.

Despite that, it apparently takes nothing more than a memory to throw my carefully curated façade into a bin and set it on fire. This isn't me. I can't be losing it on my first day as a captain of this team.

Shaking it off, I mutter an excuse about having a headache, and turn around to acknowledge the team.

And immediately lock eyes with my worst nightmare.

This can't be happening.

Everything comes flashing back all at once.

The embarrassment. The shock on the faces of my father and team. The terror of having to face them. The shame of losing in such a spectacular fashion and being unable to explain myself. Even worse, the realization—or confirmation—of an internal struggle I'd always been able to overcome, until that one moment of weakness sent me into a spiral.

I'd walked into the last championship match of my high school career at the top of my game. I'd already been accepted to one of the most prestigious schools on the east coast, my father's alma mater. And while I didn't need the full-ride scholarship monetarily, it helped me win the approval of an extremely difficult to please man. I was number one in the country for my weight class, and my victory that day, in my mind, was all but guaranteed. After fighting so hard to get to where all the pieces of my carefully choreographed life were falling neatly into place, I was ready to bask in my glory and move on to the next phase of my perfect life.

Or so I thought.

I realized something was wrong the moment I stepped up to the mat. The atmosphere in the room felt off. Ignoring the odd fluttering in my stomach, I faced my opponent, looking into a set of unnervingly friendly, warm blue eyes. The ground shifted, like the earth's axis had shifted a degree to the side, and my heart clogged my throat. The first period was a mess, a technical failure of awkward grappling that ended with a near fall and barely avoiding getting pinned. I started the second period in a daze, on my knees with the heat of my opponent at my back. His breath brushed the hairs on the back of my neck, and then my body betrayed me. I couldn't breathe or get my limbs to cooperate. Every muscle in my body locked up, and out of nowhere, I was pinned down, looking up into wide, disbelieving blue eyes.

Eyes that *knew*.

Eyes that are staring back at me now, recognition sparking and then transforming into something terrifying. Something like... happiness. Over my discomfort? Over the reminder of my loss, not just of the championship title but my goddamned dignity? Of remembering exactly how I fell apart under him?

One dark blond eyebrow raises, turning his grin cocky and cruel. And I know.

I know this man is going to ruin me. Again.

He's going to dismantle everything I've built. Take away everything I've earned after clawing my way back from shame.

He's going to rip it all away from me.

Just like he did before.

World ... Cup

CHAPTER 2
BRODY

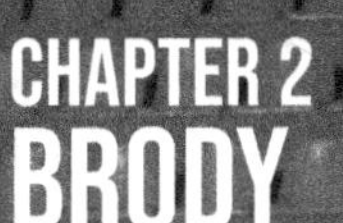

A murmur of appreciation rumbles out of me as I follow my new roommates into the Howlers Wrestling Club for our first team orientation. Stepping inside the state-of-the-art facility has me feeling excited for the year ahead despite how chaotic the summer, and my decision to transfer, have been. I could wallow in the unfairness of needing to move closer to home, but I'm choosing to focus on the opportunity that landed in my lap. I'm extremely lucky that there was a place for me here, and one that my existing scholarships mostly cover.

Huntston University is a great school. It competes with the Ivy League in academic prestige and has an incredible athletics department. I'm transferring from another Division One school in the Midwest, where wrestling is practically a religion, but this place is *fancy*. Standing in the building now, I honestly can't believe my circumstances led me here.

The building is a large rectangular structure on the far side of the main athletic complex. From the outside, it looks like most of the rest of the campus—red brick and pristine white pillars with gabled roofs, surrounded by sprawling lawns and lush greenery. Inside, it's sleek and modern. There are two entrances. One at the front of the building facing the parking areas, where spectators and visitors enter. The team enters through the back entrance that faces the dorms, where there's a small lobby with a desk and sitting area, and two open doorways on either side of the desk. One leads to a large meeting room, study area, and back entrance to the spectator section of the main floor. The other leads to the lockers and athletic training offices. We walk through the locker rooms first, which has my mouth gaping. I knew that Huntston University had money, but this place looks like a locker room I would expect professional sports teams to have.

While I'm sure the team will eventually stink up the place, everything is pristine, shiny and new-looking. A grin spreads across my face at my name on a little engraved nameplate on one of the lockers. Inside, it's packed with a brand-new sports bag, water bottle, several practice and competition uniforms, sweat bands, a hat, and a bunch of other team swag, all emblazoned with the Howlers Wrestling Club brand.

After touring the locker and shower rooms, we walk through a recovery and sports-medicine suite, where there are treatment rooms and offices for various trainers and physical therapists, hydrotherapy and cryo-chambers, and a sauna. Then we walk through a gym with all kinds of strength and conditioning zones, cardio equipment, free-weights and kettlebells, plyometric boxes, and everything else a gym could need. And that's all before we finally spill out to the main floor.

It's a vast space with high ceilings and bright lighting surrounded by acoustic-panels to reduce echo. There's a catwalk above the main floor with a running track that circles the room, and wide staircases leading up to the coaching staff's offices and a large team briefing area. The center of the room is dominated by three competition mats, surrounded by several smaller practice mats, easily enough space for all weight classes to practice.

My new roommates lead me to the spectator stands, where the team and staff are gathered for the orientation. Since I arrived later in the day yesterday, I haven't had much of a chance to meet anyone outside of Aaron and Jay, but they seem like really great guys. I can easily see myself making friends and fitting in here.

We reach the group, and Jay starts the introductions. I shake hands and exchange easy conversation about stats and excitement about the season. Everyone seems decent—loud, and obviously competitive, but welcoming enough.

This is a good thing. A great opportunity!

I have to remind myself of that several times when I come face-to-face with someone from my past. And since I look pretty much the same as I did in high school, with some added height and muscle mass, he doesn't even need an introduction.

"Holy shit, it's Miller Time!" Pierce Jamison crows, bringing back a taunt I'd hoped to never hear again. A couple guys laugh automatically, not knowing the history behind the joke. Why would they? To them, it's probably just a beer brand tagline. A harmless joke. Funny.

Ha. Ha.

I thought I'd left this bullshit behind when I moved halfway across the damn country for school. I knew there was a possibility of seeing people who knew the old me, and you'd think that we'd all matured out of the bullying stage. But seeing Pierce and that smug, amused smirk proves otherwise. It sours the positive spin I was using to take the edge off my situation.

I force a chuckle and bump my old high school rival's shoulder like we're old friends, even though the contact makes my stomach twist. "Good to see you, Pierce. You look well."

"So do you, man. I assumed you would have dropped out or followed in your old man's footsteps by now!" He laughs. "I'm just kidding! Didn't you get a scholarship and move out to Oklahoma or something?"

"Nebraska," I correct with a forced laugh, my stomach twisting into a painful knot.

"Right, right. One of those armpit states." He snickers. "So what the fuck are you doing back here?" His tone is so light, you'd think he was actually being friendly if you didn't pay too much attention to the words he's saying, or understand the malice behind them.

"I thought I might move closer to home," I answer cryptically. The last thing I'd ever want is for this douchebag to know the truth.

"Yeah, but how the hell did *you* end up *here*?" He says pointedly, guffawing at his own joke.

"I got a scholarship," I answer proudly, because I am proud. I might have grown up poorer than Pierce and most of my peers did, but I worked hard and earned a place where people like this twatwaffle don't think I belong. Being poor or having parents with... *issues*... doesn't make me less than anyone else. It didn't then, and it doesn't now. If anything, my placement at this school is proof of that.

"I guess Huntston's standards have dropped this year," Pierce murmurs, chuckling. He thinks he's funny, but no one around him laughs.

Pierce shrugs, like he can't imagine why no one else is finding his lack of wit amusing. "Oh, Miller knows I'm just playing around," he says, nudging me with his elbow.

I chuckle, because I kind of have to. I learned a long time ago that the only way to respond to this shit is to laugh with them. Don't give the bullies the satisfaction of knowing they get under your skin, and eventually they'll get bored and move on. Besides that, if

I take it seriously, then it becomes real. Then it all starts again and will never end. Maybe if I don't take the bait, he'll be mature enough to let it go.

Aaron is watching me a little too closely, brow furrowed. "You two know each other?"

"Yeah man, Miller Time and I go way back."

I make what I hope is a friendly, agreeable facial expression. "We went to the same high school."

Aaron nods, and I get the feeling he's seeing more than I'd like him to. He shoots a look at Jay, who scowls at Pierce. Not that Pierce notices, he's too busy telling a couple of his buddies about some of the stuff my older brother used to get into. Not that any of it has anything to do with me, but I suppose the stories are entertaining. To them.

I just laugh like the good-natured idiot I trained myself to be. And when Pierce asks how my brother is, his tone suggesting he's been up to no good, I don't let the urge to punch him overtake me. Instead, I redirect the conversation, grateful that news of my brother's condition hasn't gotten out. Or at least, it hasn't made it this far.

My chest tightens with the instinct to defend Davis. To defend my dad. But I don't. I never did. Like I am now, all I ever did was laugh along. Until the day I packed up and moved away, abandoning my mom and Davis and ignoring any signs that they might have still needed me. I moved halfway across the country, thinking that making something of myself would be easier without the stigma attached to my name. And it was, for a while. Unfortunately reality, as it so often does, caught up to me.

Jay takes the opportunity to avert my attention elsewhere, which I'm grateful for. He and Aaron introduce me to some more people. I meet a guy named Jeremy Fisher who calls himself Fish.

He's in my same degree program and we have a couple of shared classes. He tells me to message him on the campus message app, Howler, so we can hang out to study.

"It's not just for hooking up," Fish says, when someone makes a joke about Fish coming onto me. "I promise I'm not hitting on you," he says with an oddly serious face.

"Okay," I say with a chuckle. "I wouldn't be offended, though." And I definitely wouldn't. Fish is a good looking guy, with a playful grin and an endearing smatter of freckles across the bridge of his nose.

Just then, an older man with a no-nonsense attitude barrels into the room, clapping his hands and getting our attention with a shockingly loud voice.

"Sit your asses down! Let's get this started!"

Since my transfer was somewhat last minute, I haven't had the pleasure of meeting Coach McCoy face-to-face, but his reputation precedes him. My coach back in Nebraska said he's hard to impress, but fair. Jay and Aaron warned me about some of his quirks. Namely, that he's very loud all the time, is prone to shouting abruptly, and often tosses out off-the-cuff remarks that come across as blunt or even inappropriate. They appear to be amused rather than irritated or frightened at all, which seems like a good sign.

We all take our seats quickly, Aaron startling so hard he almost sits on my lap, as Coach launches into his welcome speech.

"First things first—"

Coach pauses and stares at someone in the front row who is still standing. I'm watching the way Coach McCoy reacts to one of his students disobeying him, not turning my head until someone else stands to pull the other guy down. A few people snicker, and the two guys sit down together. All I see of the guys are their backs and the tops of their heads once they sit down.

Finally, we all turn our attention back to McCoy.

"Anyway," Coach says, as if trying to remember what he was talking about. "Rules!" he shouts loudly and abruptly enough that I would have flinched if not for Jay and Aaron's warnings.

"Listen up, because I don't like to repeat myself." He paces in front of the mats like he's preparing for battle. "Rule number one: show up on time. Early is on time, on time is late, and late means you're conditioning until you're showing the rest of the class what color your breakfast was. Rule number two: shower. With. Soap," he says, enunciating and popping the p. "Actual soap. I shouldn't have to specify that, but here we are."

A few guys snicker. Coach side-eyes them like they already smell bad. "Practice hygiene like you might talk some poor girl into going down on you. It's unlikely, but hope is important." He pauses and quirks a brow like he just remembered something. "Or guy. That's another thing—we don't discriminate here at Huntston. There's a zero-tolerance policy for that kind of shit."

Well, that's certainly good to know. Considering it doesn't seem like Pierce Jamison has grown up at all, I'm better off bracing myself for the inevitable taunts about my sexuality, which I've never felt the desire to hide. It's reassuring to know rumors won't get me in trouble here the way they did back in high school.

"Anyway, I don't care who or what you're into. Just wash your ass. Rule number three: don't be stupid. Half of you are already failing this one, but it's important to set goals. There are rules on this campus for a reason, follow them. Don't party so much you forget you're here for an education. Act like you've got some sense."

"Rule number four," he continues. "You're a goddamn athlete, so act like it. If I find you skipping workouts without a good reason and eating like shit, I'll make you do wind sprints until you hallucinate. We talk about weight a lot in this sport, but it's all about balance. Exercise regularly, and eat real, healthy food. Protein and vegetables. A protein shake is not breakfast, it's a supplement. A handful of almonds or a bowl of iceberg lettuce drenched in Hidden Valley is not lunch. A donut is not... Well, okay, sometimes a donut is a meal, but not every day. Balance, people!"

He pauses like he might have forgotten what else he wanted to talk about, but then looks up sharply. "Last rule—BONERS!"

I snap to attention, confused and slightly amused by how loudly this man, who looks a bit like if Dr. Phil was a short, jacked drill sergeant, wearing too-tight short athletic shorts and a tucked in polo shirt, just yelled the word *boner*. I'm pretty sure it echoed off the ceiling.

"Boners happen. Walk it off. I don't want to hear about it, and I damn well don't want to see it. Walk. It. Off."

He looks around the room, dead serious, and then claps once. "Alright, moving on. Let's meet your captains!"

He gestures towards the bench, and two guys stand up. One of them, Sean Cabot, has a reddish farmer's tan that accentuates his bulging biceps and a Huntston University ball cap pulled low over his forehead, which Coach McCoy promptly smacks off his head. Sean nudges someone in the first row, who stands to join them as Coach introduces the second guy.

Roman Bailey has dark brown skin, close-cropped black hair, and a wide smile. He's laughing as he bends to pick up Sean's hat, tossing it to the third guy when Sean reaches for it. Sean pushes Roman in a way that suggests they're good friends, and Coach's amused scolding tells me that, overall, this is a good-natured group of people. Coach McCoy certainly has an interesting sense of humor.

All my thoughts come to a screeching halt when Coach McCoy gestures to the last captain, drawing my eyes away from the two guys now grappling and towards the third guy. It's the same person that was standing earlier, and I recognize him immediately. I even remember his name before Coach introduces him.

How could I ever forget?

My eyes roam over his tall, lean body. His black shorts show off his perfectly toned thighs that make my mind go south before I avert them to his grey team shirt, but the sight of his biceps isn't much safer. The olive tones of his skin are deeper than I remember, but it's possible he spent the summer somewhere sunny. I can easily imagine him jogging shirtless on a beach somewhere. There isn't a hair out of place, his deep chestnut hair neatly coiffed and combed to the side, giving him a regal look. Like an athletic Disney prince.

Despite recognizing him right away, I don't actually know Lincoln Beckett. I've only met him once and *met* is a stretch. But after our short interaction in the strangest match of my wrestling career to date—certainly the most memorable—I sometimes think of him. I've always wondered what happened to him, if he was okay, or how deep the shock and fear I saw in his eyes had gone. I wondered what would have happened if I'd followed him when he stormed off the floor. I almost did, but I saw a few people follow him, and I figured it was best to let it go.

His dark eyes lock on mine and widen. I think he must recognize me too, which makes me smile. He seems taken aback by it, and scowls at me, which is both concerning and kind of cute. I raise an eyebrow, trying to have a mental conversation with a complete stranger, and his eyes turn stoney.

Something tells me he's not happy to see me, but his reaction is... *something*.

It's a start. I'll take it.

World Wrestling Cup 2016

CHAPTER 3
BECK

My pulse hasn't returned to normal since orientation ended.

I pretend to listen while Coach splits the team into groups. The freshmen are herded off for paperwork and presentations, while the upperclassmen are left to mingle and explore some of the upgrades around the facility. But all I can see is *him*.

Brody Miller. Standing here. In *my* gym. With *my* team.

This isn't real. It can't be real. *How? Why?*

I force my eyes away from him and walk away, angling myself towards whoever happens to be on the opposite side of the room from him. Sean and Roman peel away to help Coach organize the first-years.

Everyone is in high spirits, breaking off into smaller groups to catch up with old friends and discuss the year ahead. Cade and Fish run off to race up the new climbing ropes in the corner of the gym. There's chatter and laughter all around me. I'm considerably less excited, and by the looks that my friends and teammates keep giving me, I'm not hiding it well enough. I'm on edge, trying to mask my nerves with a flat expression and indifference.

I might throw up. My lungs feel like they're on the verge of collapse.

Why is he here?

What does he want?

Is he talking about me right now? Is he going to tell anyone about what really happened that day, why I lost so spectacularly?

Is he going to tell everyone my secret?

Brody's grin looked awfully knowing when he saw me. And his eyes... The spark of recognition left no question that he knew who I was. He remembered every humiliating second of that match.

My stomach drops so violently I almost crumple to the ground.

He knows what happened to me that day. And now he's here, not just in the same building, but on my fucking team.

———

I hover near the edge of the mats, pretending to check my phone just to look busy. Across the room, I hear him being introduced to more of my friends and teammates. His laugh is warm and easy, like he's known everyone for years. He's clearly the friendly, charismatic, never-met-a-stranger type. He doesn't even have to try to get everyone to like him right off the bat.

The tension in my neck and shoulders bleeds up into the back of my head, a headache throbbing to life. I force myself to breathe as I listen to him laugh and joke around while other guys gossip about the new guy. I drink it all in greedily, because I need to know everything about him. More importantly, I need to know everything he's saying without getting close enough to tempt fate.

So far, all I've overheard are discussions about where he moved from and his impressive stats. No one seems to know why he transferred, but they're all excited to have another heavyweight champion on the team. I home in on their conversations while I do an internet search for his name. If he has better stats than I do, I'm going to be pissed.

There's a ripple of laughter, and it feels like a reaction to my thoughts, like everyone here can sense my weakness. *His* laughter is the loudest. It grates on my nerves and makes my head throb harder.

I close my eyes, and instantly I'm *back there*. Flat on my back in the championship match, staring up into those blue eyes as every muscle in my body locked and betrayed me.

The pressure of his weight. The warmth of his breath. The sound I made. God, that sound. That unbelievable, humiliating sound that gave me away more than my body ever could.

A strong shoulder bumps mine. I jolt.

"Beck," Jay Norman says gently. "You good?"

No. I am absolutely not good.

"Fine," I lie, and quickly turn away. "Just a bit of a headache."

He gives me a look suggesting he knows there's more to it, but he leaves it alone. His best friend Aaron calls him away, and I drift towards my roommates, needing a distraction. They're huddled near the lockers with Pierce Jamison, who is being predictably douchey about something.

"I'm surprised they even let him enroll here, much less gave him a scholarship. I thought Huntston had better standards than that," Pierce says loudly. Everything this douche says is loud and pompous. "But I suppose brawn and a few good stats are enough to overlook the stench of cheap beer and stale cigarettes if it gets us another championship."

Cade snorts, but Fish doesn't look amused.

I lean against the lockers, arms crossed. "What are you talking about?"

Pierce puffs up like he has exclusive information. Of course he does. Guys like him live to gossip. "The new guy, Brody Miller. I know him from high school. Grew up on the wrong end of town, if you know what I mean. Total trailer trash."

Cade winces. Fish whispers under his breath, "Really?"

"What?" Pierce shrugs. "You can say it right in front of him, and he just laughs. He knows it's true."

I doubt that, but I keep my mouth shut, saving every scrap of information for the potential threat. I need to know who Brody is. What he wants. Whether he's planning to ruin me. Or how I can ruin him first.

"Get this—There were rumors that he was gay, too…"

"Dude." Fish's voice sounds like he's warning Pierce, which gets my attention. "I don't want to hear that shit."

My shoulders are stiff. I'm not sure what to think about Fish's reaction to that bit of gossip, but I wonder if it's true…

Before I can process Pierce's information, I hear whistling. A low, deliberately cheerful whistle to the tune of *It's A Small World*. My neck aches with how stiffly I'm holding my posture, and a cold chill trickles over my skin as he strolls up behind me.

Brody has his hands tucked behind his back like a child feigning innocence. He smiles too widely when he reaches us.

"Speak of the Devil," Pierce sneers.

Fish elbows him. "Hey Brody, meet our other roommate–"

"Lincoln Beckett," he finishes for him, eyes locked on mine as he reaches out a hand to shake. "Fancy meeting you again."

I bristle immediately and stare at his hand like it's a loaded gun. My skin prickles hot and cold at once.

"Nice to meet you, I guess," I say curtly, ignoring his proffered hand.

Turning away from him and my friends' curious expressions, I make excuses about needing to tend to my captain's duties and walk towards the offices.

When I chance a quick glance over my shoulder, I see Brody studying me with a confused expression, maybe curiosity with a tinge of amusement.

This can't really be happening.

———

Coach McCoy stands over the digital scale with his arms crossed, face blank and stern. He seems unimpressed with the results of the first team weigh-in so far. Hopefully, he'll chill out now that he's made his way through the freshman and sophomore wrestlers and is starting with the veteran athletes who are less likely to have slacked off all summer.

Marcy, our athletic trainer, stands next to Coach McCoy with a clipboard, calling each of us forward to assess our weight class potential. The team stands around half naked, waiting for their turn to either be reamed or teased by Coach. The majority of us left to be weighed aren't nervous the way the freshmen were, although Pierce looks like he might have tried sweating off some pounds this morning considering he showed up huffing and wearing too many layers. Most of us will stay in the same weight class we were last year or move up.

I'm a little jittery, but not because of my weight. I've kept on top of my strict diet and exercise regimen all summer. My father wouldn't have let me slack even if I wanted to, not that I ever do. I didn't sleep well again last night and can't seem to kick the throbbing headache that's been bothering me since yesterday.

Once I've shown the underclassmen where to go for the next stage of our first team physicals, I pull off my t-shirt and step in line.

I'm doing a good job keeping my eyes forward and not worrying about anyone else until the door opens and Brody Miller walks in. Late. Not that Coach says anything about it.

Brody peels off his hoodie and drops his athletic pants right there in the corridor. Someone, probably Cade, whistles, and I roll my eyes to cover the way they automatically drift toward his body. He's thick everywhere. His chest, his back, his fucking thighs that look like they could crush a person to death. The tight compression shorts ride high on his hips, the fabric stretched tight over the firm globes of his ass.

Jesus.

He's a couple inches shorter than me, but he's bigger and broader by far. He's solid. Probably at least one weight class higher than me, if not two. At least we aren't likely to be paired up for training.

Not wanting to be caught staring, I snap my eyes away from Brody's body, but I'm not sure I'm fast enough. In my periphery, I can see his lips quirk.

"Looking good yourself, Lincoln," he says, moving just behind me and dropping his voice low so no one else can hear him.

"Don't call me that," I deadpan, blatantly ignoring his acknowledgement that he did, in fact, catch me looking.

"What? Your name? What else am I supposed to call you, then?"

"Nothing," I say, my voice sharp. "You don't call me anything."

He tsks. "Are you really this butthurt over losing one match to me in high school?"

My gaze darts to his, finding his blue eyes assessing me teasingly. I scoff, because he knows very well what I'm *butthurt* about. He cocks his head, but I turn away, unwilling to give him the satisfaction of talking about it. He just wants to make me say it out loud, but I won't do it.

One by one, guys step up onto the scale, step down, and shuffle away, while we move up in line. The tension thickens the longer we're this close to each other. Close enough that I can feel the heat rolling off him and smell his soapy bodywash. Close enough that I'm acutely aware of every slow inhale he takes, like he's taking up all the oxygen in the room. Brody's breathing and his massive shoulders are taking up too much airspace and pushing the rest of us away to make room.

Finally, it's my turn. I exhale, step on, and wait for the beep.

"One seventy-five point four," Coach reads off. "Not bad for preseason. Well done, as expected. You can go, Mr. Beckett."

I step down quickly, because I don't want to be standing too close when Brody is weighed. I don't want to be tempted to turn around and look at him. I absolutely do not want to look. I don't.

But I do anyway, my morbid curiosity getting the better of me.

Brody steps up with a casual roll of his shoulders that sends a ripple down his arms and over his back as he settles his stance. He's thick and carved in a way that's almost indecent, all the way down to his cut v-line that points to a far too prominent bulge.

I blink rapidly and direct my eyes up to the number on the scale that flashes 179.2.

My mouth is suddenly dry. That's not possible. Sure, he's shorter than me, but with a build like that he should be way heavier.

Coach grunts something approving, muttering something under his breath that I can't hear. Brody jokes casually with him, like they're friends or something, and says some stupid shit about being a corn-fed Nebraskan for the past two years.

Cade appears at my elbow like he's been waiting for the right moment to piss me off. "Oh, well will you look at that? You're going to be sharing a weight class with your new bestie."

"Fuck off, Cade."

"Oh, come on. You have to admit he's a damn good addition to the team. He's a goddamn brick shithouse."

"He's... fine. I guess."

Cade snorts. "Fine? Are you pretending not to notice him, too?" He pushes my shoulder playfully. "Or are you just jealous that you didn't pack on the muscle as well as some of us have?"

"Shut. Up."

"Whatever you say, Captain. Have fun grappling with that monster."

If someone could tell me why the fuck my eyes automatically drop to Brody's crotch, that'd be great. Covering the shake I have to give my head to empty my thoughts, I shove a laughing Cade aside. I'm failing at pretending none of this bothers me.

Brody is looking at me now. Directly at me, like he caught every second of where my eyes, and my thoughts, travelled to. He drags his eyes down my body, neck, chest, and abs. He does it slowly enough that I can feel his gaze on me. My face gets hot. Then he tilts his head, just slightly, like he's sizing me up for real. It's almost like he's saying, "Yeah, I could take you," without saying the words out loud.

Something I can't name but feels like heat settles low in my stomach. I swallow hard and look away.

I briefly entertain the thought of cutting weight to drop to a lower class. But that's stupid. I'm already in peak condition. I'd lose strength and stamina, not to mention I'd be handing him power he doesn't deserve.

No. He needs to leave. Go find another team and another person to torment.

Apparently, I'm not the only one who thinks so.

Pierce Jamison must have caught the snarl I can't wipe off my face, because he suddenly thinks we're buddies. He catches me near the benches during a break. "Hey. Some of us are thinking we should, you know, show the new guy how things work around here. Make sure he understands his place."

I don't respond, but I don't stop him either, which he takes as encouragement.

"Don't worry, Captain," he says with a smirk, smacking my shoulder. "We'll take care of it."

My stomach twists. It's not right, and it's certainly not befitting of my role. It's not who I should be.

But the panic of having him here, someone who knows how to beat me, how to ruin me, makes me selfish. Selfish and stupid.

Maybe a little harmless hazing will keep him quiet and away from me, or even better, get him to rethink his place on this team.

Maybe it's the only option.

———

The rest of the week passes easily enough, aside from being constantly on edge that I'll run into Brody Miller at any moment. The one saving grace is that it seems we don't share any classes. Which is definitely for the best. It's bad enough that my eight a.m.

Corporate Finance class is going to destroy me. The professor's voice is so monotone, it might as well be a lullaby sung by the Sandman himself. Every student in the class looks dazed and dead inside by the end of the first hour, myself included, and I don't need any more struggle to focus.

It's not until Thursday that I see him again, thanks to my efforts to avoid the common areas like the student union and waking up an hour earlier to get my workouts in.

As much as I wish I could, I can't avoid him any longer. Today is our first unofficial practice. It's a tradition for the captains to run the first two weeks of practices to show the underclassmen how things go. So it's on me, Sean, and Roman to show up early and lead drills.

After some basic warmups and explanation of how we do things here, the class pairs off. The underclassmen are paired with an upperclassman in a similar weight class.

Except Brody, since he's new despite being a Junior. He's standing off to the side, stretching his legs, humming some awful pop song under his breath.

Sean thumps me on the shoulder. "You take Miller."

I whip around. "What? Why me?" Despite my attempts to disguise it, my voice is too sharp. Can they see how freaked out I am?

Sean shrugs. "We've got enough upperclassmen to cover the newbies, and he's the only one not paired up. Besides, you're in the same weight class," he says like it's obvious. It is obvious, but I was still hoping to avoid pairing up with him, at least until the coaching staff are breathing down our necks.

But it's not like I can say no. There isn't anyone else for him to pair off with, and the entire team is watching. Refusing to practice with him is only going to draw attention to the issue and make me look even weaker.

I can feel Brody's eyes on me even before I turn. He's completely relaxed and unbothered, like he hasn't been haunting my nightmares. I force myself to walk over, jaw tight, trying not to show the way my pulse spikes with every step I take towards him.

Brody straightens, his grin slow and warm. "Hey, Captain. Ready to get sweaty together?"

My jaw ticks. "Why would you say it like that?" I grouse, playing off the way the comment sends fire sizzling straight through my gut.

We run through basic warm-ups. Drills I could do in my sleep, if not for every brush of his hand against mine, every accidental bump, every shift of muscle under his skin lighting me up in places that do not belong on these practice mats.

And he knows it. I can tell by the way his eyes flick to mine whenever his skin comes in contact with mine. Like he's cataloguing every reaction to the little jolts of electricity that course through me. Like he can feel the deep and uncomfortable awareness I've spent over two years shoving into a locked room inside my chest. It's all starting to seep out, sensing a familiarity that I'm not all that familiar with.

"Alright," Roman calls out. "Let's move on to some light grappling next. Keep it easy."

We circle each other, and I avoid his eyes, not wanting to see his stupid grin, like getting under my skin is a fun game for him.

"Relax, Lincoln," he murmurs.

"I told you not to call me that."

"Fine. Beck then. That's what everyone else calls you, right?"

"Not you."

"Aww, come on, Captain. Why not?"

"Because that's what my friends call me. And you are not my fucking friend."

His grin crooks up on one side. My pulse stutters. I step in, a touch faster than I mean to, trying to muscle him into a standard tie-up. He flows with it too easily, hands sliding across my shoulders, fingers brushing the back of my neck.

It's a stupidly intimate touch for a wrestling drill, and I'm not having it.

"Hands up," I snap. "Pay attention."

"Oh, I'm paying attention." His eyes drop slowly, deliberately, to my hips, then lower.

A cold bolt of humiliation slices through me. "Stop that," I hiss. "Quit looking at me like that!"

His eyebrows lift innocently. "Like what?"

"You know what."

He chuckles. "You think a lot of yourself, huh?"

He grabs my wrist. His grip is confident and warm. He pivots effortlessly, and for one humiliating second, I stumble. I'm off balance and out of control.

He doesn't take me down, though. He lets me recover.

And somehow, that's even worse.

We move again. My heart is pounding too loudly. The gym lights are hot and glaring.

Brody shoots for my leg, not even at full speed, and my body reacts in the wrong way. I overcorrect, shielding my sensitive groin, and he uses the opening to pull me into a loose clinch, bodies pressed chest-to-chest.

His breath brushes my ear. "You alright there, Captain?"

White-hot fury rushes through me. At his audacity. But mostly at myself for being so damn weak.

I shove him hard, using too much force for the light drill. He stumbles, but catches himself easily, looking more amused than offended.

"Damn," he murmurs, voice low. "Didn't know you liked it that rough."

My face flushes hotter than a nuclear explosion. I lunge before I can think better of it. This time I get hold of him and with a twist of my hips, I slam him onto his back harder than I meant to. The thud of his body hitting the mat echoes.

Pinning him with my body heavy across his, my knee against his thigh, forearm braced beside his head, I listen as his breath leaves him in a harsh grunt. Then he looks up at me.

And smiles.

A sly, salacious smile turns up one side of his lips. It's cruel and knowing. Like he's seeing something I didn't mean to expose.

My voice is low and rough, trembling in a way I hope shows my rage but not my fear.

"I'm in charge here, Miller. I'm top dog. And I'll damn well find a way to get you kicked off this team and sent back to whatever shit-hole you came from if you try to screw with me. Do you understand me?"

For the first time all practice, Brody stops smiling. Not because he's upset, I don't think. He looks... interested. Possibly amused, but there's an undercurrent of fierce determination that makes my mouth go dry. I lick my lips, and his gaze flicks to my mouth.

My body goes hot. Then cold. Then hot again.

Brody hums thoughtfully. "I hear you," he says softly. His hips shift under mine, just enough to remind me how he's built. How close we are. How stupid my body is. "Loud and clear."

Awareness blasts through me, rising so fast I feel dizzy, and I stumble back like I've been burned. My heart is a wild, frantic thing inside my chest.

I need this to stop.

I need him gone.

Whatever it takes, I need my life back.

Because if he stays, and if he keeps looking at me like he can see through me, I don't know what's going to happen.

I just know it won't be something I can control.

World Wrestling ... Cup

CHAPTER 4
BRODY

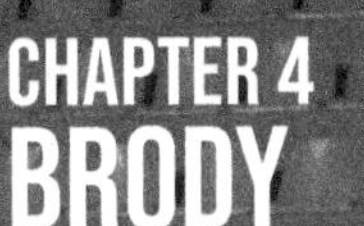

For the second time, Lincoln Beckett pivots on his heel and storms away from me. The doors to the main wrestling floor slam so hard the frame rattles. For a long moment, nobody moves. Everyone looks around and then at me, flat on my ass on the mat, staring after him like an idiot.

They're all probably wondering what it is I did to set him off. What I continue to do, since he's very obviously hated me since the moment I got here.

But does he really hate me that much?

I get that my playful attitude rubs him the wrong way. I admit that I may have pushed it a little too far just to rile him up, but the running away is concerning. He's not fighting with me, cursing, or shoving. He just runs. And people don't run like that unless they're afraid of something. Or hiding something.

I have a theory about what he might be hiding. A thought I've pondered since I pinned him to the mat just over two years ago. A theory he all but just confirmed.

Because the way he reacted? The way he looked at me, back then and again today? The silent panic radiating off him every time our bodies brushed against each other?

I've seen it before. Not often, but enough to recognize it.

It speaks loudly of a guy who is trying very, very hard not to get caught wanting something he's been taught not to want. A guy who thinks his whole life will implode if anyone sees him for what he is.

It would explain the hostility and obvious nerves, the toxic show of masculinity. The intensity of his vitriol for someone he doesn't know. Someone who might know something about him that no one else does.

Not that I'd ever out someone like that. But he doesn't know me, and I don't know him.

What I do know is that calling him out or cornering him won't help him. Threatening his sense of control won't help him.

So I don't go after him. Instead, I exhale slowly and peel myself off the mat, smoothing my shorts down and pretending what just happened is normal, despite the way everyone is staring at me.

If Lincoln is closeted—or scared, or confused, or something else entirely—that's his business. I understand the fear. Being anything other than straight, especially in a sport like this, can be daunting. But that doesn't excuse his behavior. It doesn't give him the right to lord his power as a future leader of the elite class over me and try to make a fool out of me.

I need to figure out how to stop scaring him without backing down. I'm not going anywhere. I'm here to finish my damn degree and take care of my family. Wrestling is what's affording me that ability. It's the only reason I'm here.

Still... I can't help but be intrigued.

My skin prickles remembering the way he shivered when he pinned me.

The way his breath caught.

The way something soft and vulnerable flickered behind his anger.

I don't know exactly what's going on with him, but I'm curious enough to try to find out, and maybe try to help. Quietly, and without blowing up either of our lives.

I don't want to be his enemy. But I'm not going to roll over and show my belly, either.

———

"Alright, spill. What the fuck is up with you and Beck?"

Fish drops his tray on the table and stares at me like he's waiting for some big news that would explain the icy cold shoulder and behavior their captain has shown me since I arrived at Huntston. He's a moody jerk whenever he's around me, and seems to go out of his way to avoid me outside of practice.

I shrug. "He's just intense."

Fish raises an eyebrow. "It's unusual for him to be this hotheaded."

I shrug and dig into my eggs.

"How do you two know each other, exactly?" Aaron asks.

I keep my tone light, feigning indifference. "We wrestled once in high school."

"No, there's got to be more to it than that. I can see him being competitive if you won, but he's acting like your presence here is a personal vendetta against him." Fish cuts his eyes to a nearby table, where Pierce is telling a story—probably about me—to a table of mostly freshmen athletes. His voice is loud and self-satisfied. "Not to mention whatever Pierce's issue is."

I groan. "It's too early for this crap."

"Pierce is just intimidated that someone he deems below his social status might show him up," Aaron mutters. "But he and Beck seem to be getting along better than usual. That's concerning enough."

"Does anyone else get the impression that Pierce is up to something? He's been more annoying than last year," Fish.

Jay nods. "I assumed he's feeling cockier because he's not the youngest anymore. Would explain why he's buddying up to all the freshmen the way he is."

"I heard he's getting them to do stuff for him, like his homework and laundry," Aaron says, lips turning down in a disapproving grimace. "I don't get it."

I'm not surprised. He and his brother always had their own little cult of assholes that followed them around. The smaller a mind is, the easier they are to impress and control. And when you've been born into the kind of privilege most can't comprehend, it comes with the kind of confidence that makes even the weakest person believe you're worth more than their deeds.

"Doesn't explain why Beck is suddenly tolerating him though," Fish says quietly, almost to himself.

My breakfast suddenly isn't very appetizing. "Whatever it is," I say carefully, "I'm not interested in drama."

Fish gestures vaguely. "Too late. This could only be more interesting if you were prettier and had boobs."

Smirking, I lift my arms to pull my hair loose from its top knot and flex my pecs. Fish wolf-whistles, and Aaron bites back a laugh.

Jay nudges my tray. "For real, though. You settling in okay?"

I look around at the chaotic dining hall, at the team scattered between tables, and the guys around me that have been welcoming despite multiple members of their team acting like I'm some kind of pariah.

"Yeah, I am," I say, and mean it. Despite yesterday's mess of a practice and the discomfort of knowing Pierce is up to something, I had a great first week of school. I like all my classes, at least a few of my teammates seem cool, and I feel better knowing that I'm closer to home if my mom and brother need me.

I'll just have to make the best of the rest of it, and hope that everyone else gets used to my presence.

Still, I keep my guard up, especially as I notice more and more of my teammates and classmates watching me with curious and judgmental eyes. I hope I'm just paranoid, but the way some of them watch me reminds me of what it was like in middle and high school.

By the time I get to the wrestling building for afternoon practice, I'm more tense than I want to admit to even myself. I don't know if it's anticipation or instinct, but my body feels braced for impact in a way I can't quite explain.

The locker room is mostly empty when I walk in. I'm early, but I head to my locker to get dressed and do some extra lifting before practice. I almost slip in a puddle of something on the ground. I frown and look down. A dark, foamy puddle spreads from the bottom seam of my locker door.

For a second, my brain doesn't compute what it is. Until the smell hits.

Beer.

The pungent smell of stale beer is strong enough to make me think it could have been here all day, maybe since just after morning lift when I was last at my locker. The stench makes my stomach roll.

I open my locker slowly. A mostly empty can of Miller Lite lies on its side on the top shelf, tipped just enough to let the last of it drain down over my uniform, my shoes, and my towel. The label is facing outward in case I don't get the punchline.

I stare at it for far too long, forgetting to school my features. The room is quiet around me. I can hear the hum of the overhead fans, the distant thud of someone dropping weights outside the locker room doors. My hands go a little numb from the way I'm clenching my fists.

This is stupid. Really, it is. It's completely juvenile. And it's also obvious who's behind this stupid prank, considering it's not the first time Pierce has done this sort of thing. And just like every time before, I resolve not to let them see how much it upsets me.

But sometimes it really sucks being the bigger man. My first instinct is to take the can and crush it in my fist. The second is to breathe. So I do the second.

Then I remove the can, set it on the bench, and start pulling things out. The shoes are thankfully salvageable, and everything else is washable. But of course I'll be late for warm-ups on the first day of real practice with the coaches, considering I'll need to run back to the dorm to get some new workout clothes.

Even when Pierce's voice slithers up behind me, I don't turn around right away. I keep moving, like this is a normal inconvenience.

"What's wrong, Miller?" He asks with an insincerity that wouldn't be funny even if this weren't such a tired script.

I finally look over my shoulder. His grin is casual. He's expecting me to react, to make a fool out of myself so I'm the one who looks bad. But he should know better. I've never given it to him before, and I'm not going to give it to him now. The only difference is that I can't find it in myself to laugh.

"Real funny," I say. "Did you get it out of your system?"

His eyebrows lift. "What? We thought you'd appreciate a free beer."

"Well, I don't drink. So, thanks but no thanks."

For a moment, something flickers on his face. Surprise, maybe? He probably expected me to laugh along like I normally do. I'm not showing how much it got to me, but I'm also not ignoring what he's done here.

"Relax, man. It was just a little team joke." He claps a hand on my shoulder like we're old friends. "Welcome to Huntston."

My smile is more of a gritting of my teeth than anything else. My jaw ticks as I watch him go. As much as I want to wring my wet shorts out over his expensive leather loafers or shove the empty can down his throat, I don't move. I don't follow him. I don't call him out in front of the team. Not yet.

After two years of feeling free to just live my life, I once again find myself in a situation where I'm going to have to keep my guard up. I'm not happy about it, but it could be worse. None of this is anything new. I can handle it.

I can handle it.

I keep repeating those words to myself, as I look down at my ruined clothes to decide if getting to practice on time is worth wearing the smell that's clogging the back of my throat. My nerves might be too raw to pretend.

Fish and Aaron come to my rescue. They save me from having to sprint back to the dorm by lending me gear, which is nice of them. Unfortunately, they're both built very differently than I am. The shorts I borrowed from Aaron ride high on my thighs and cling everywhere they shouldn't. And Fish's tank is tight enough that I'm one deep breath away from ripping a seam. I feel ridiculous the second I step onto the main floor.

Some guys whistle. A couple laugh. I'd rather eat glass than let anyone see that it gets to me, so I throw my shoulders back, do a slow little turn like I'm on a runway, and spread my arms.

"Try not to faint, gentlemen," I announce.

They howl, and I grin like it's all part of the joke. Like I'm not hyper-aware of how much ass is hanging out and how hard I'm working to keep everything—my nerves and my junk—contained.

Only Lincoln Beckett's face makes the humiliation worth it.

He's staring so hard he might actually detach a retina. His jaw is clenched so hard, I worry for his molars. His gaze snaps up the second he realizes I caught him looking, and the scowl he hands me is hot enough to sear through what little fabric is clinging to my skin.

"Staring is only going to make these pants tighter," I say before I can stop myself.

He opens his mouth. Then closes it, coughing like he swallowed a fly.

Then he practically teleports to the far side of the room to correct a freshman's stance with the intensity of a man defusing a bomb. Anything to stay as far from me as possible.

When he finally stalks back, he seems to have gathered himself together. He's calm on the surface in a way that doesn't quite reach his eyes.

I try not to smile but fail.

"Let's just do the drills," he says, clipped.

"Sure thing, Captain."

He flinches almost imperceptibly, and his face grows visibly redder.

"Do you not like that either?" I ask, cocking my head

He seems to think about it for a moment, then shakes his head. "Can you just keep your mouth shut for once so we can get through these drills."

Once we start, we go through the motions jerkily while barely touching one another. He won't look directly at me, but it gives me a moment to examine him. The crisp technical precision of his form and posture. The almost automatic way he moves smoothly through the motions. His practice uniform looks pressed, and there isn't a hair out of place, even though his skin is shiny with a light sheen of sweat. He's perfectly poised in every way.

Except that every time my hand touches his arm, or my chest brushes his shoulder, his breath stutters. He covers it well, the hitch barely noticeable. But I feel it. And every time it happens, heat pools low in my stomach.

I try not to think too hard about it. Seriously, these shorts are dangerous enough without the added pressure of excess blood flow. And I'm not trying to tease him or make him uncomfortable. Not after yesterday.

But something about our bodies moving in sync and the way he's pointedly trying to pretend he isn't affected sends a thrill through me I can't control. It's honestly the perfect distraction, and I barely even think about Pierce's little prank.

"Quit smiling," he snaps when he catches my stupid expression.

"It's practice," I say lightly, brushing him off. "It's supposed to be fun."

"No, it's not. Wrestling isn't supposed to be fun."

"Says who?" I laugh.

"Says me."

"Oh, right. And you're the captain. The top dog," I say in a forced tough-guy impression. Then I wink and nod. "Got it."

"Brody," he warns, and I feel my grin stretch wider at the sound of my name broken down into so many slow syllables.

I lift my hands. "Okay, okay. No jokes. But could you, like, pretend this is enjoyable even once? What's the point if you're not having fun?"

I'm not even trying to get a rise out of him. He looks like he's one wrong move from imploding, and I want to take the edge off. Because before I came in here and started joking around with him like this, it was me who felt like I was going to lose it.

He ignores me, not appreciating my attempt at levity. We move into counter drills, and it's more automatic movements, like an over-rehearsed dance. He shoots, I sprawl. I shoot, he defends. Our bodies collide again and again, sweat slick between us, breaths mixing.

I don't know what sets him off this time, because I feel like I've been half-lulled into a trance, but something between us shifts again. He goes too hard. It's nothing harmful, but it's definitely not light.

It feels like he's trying to prove something. Or punish one of us, maybe both of us.

My ribs ache when his elbow catches me.

"Easy," I say.

"I am being easy."

"You sure?"

"You're just being a little bitch."

I raise an eyebrow. He launches into me again, faster and harder, until I have to ground my weight to keep my balance. Luckily for me, I have a pretty low center of gravity, so I'm not easy to take down. And unlike yesterday, I don't let him have the win so easily.

For whatever reason, he's pissed. At me or himself, I'm not sure. At everything, maybe. Perhaps he's feeling overstimulated in the same ways I am, and there's too much tension bubbling beneath the surface for it to not result in an outburst. His angry little display is kind of cute, despite the really shit afternoon I've had.

So I laugh. Because that's what I do when things go sideways.

He stops dead. "If you're not going to take this seriously," he grits out, "why are you even here?"

Before I can answer or attempt an explanation at how uncomfortable I am, he lunges.

Unlike yesterday, it's a calculated move, probably meant to show he has more control than he displayed yesterday. He catches my thigh, pulls, and takes me down in one motion, driving me into the mat with a thud. Pinning me with a clean, flawless technique that I could respect and appreciate if not for the personal vendetta to show me up.

I make a move to flip him, but then I see it.

There it is again. That flicker of something behind his eyes. The faint tremor that runs through him and causes a chain reaction in me.

Oh, damn.

His eyes widen and his throat works like he's struggling to swallow. His fingers curl as if he's resisting the urge to grip me, either to shake me or pull me closer, there's no telling.

He's trying so hard not to feel it. But I know he does.

I know it because I feel it too. I suck in a sharp breath at the way my entire body reacts to his, blinking up at him to try to focus on the bigger issue here. Not his body, or the way it's pressing into me, or the way we're hardening against each other. Him, and his obvious fear over his reaction to me. Has this never happened to him before? Coach is right, boners do happen. Especially in middle and high school. But even now, too much rubbing against each other is going to stimulate some nerves. Add in whatever this tension is between us, and it's a recipe for a stubborn, hard dick.

Without thinking, I open my mouth. "You don't have to worry," I say, my voice low.

His breath hitches. "W-what?"

He tries to pull back, but I hook his leg like I'm trying to flip him. Really, I'm just trying to keep him close, so he has to hear me out.

"I'm not here to upset your spot on this team," I say. "And I'm not here to out you."

All the color drains from his face. His eyes bug out. And then something inside him snaps.

He makes a choking sound, then shoves off me so he's on his knees, looming over me. He's breathing heavily, bent over me like he's two seconds from wrapping his hands around my throat and squeezing the life out of me. In the moment of stillness, I cut my eyes down to where our dicks are less than six inches apart, both of us straining in our gym shorts. He can't miss that he's not the only one, because Aaron's tiny shorts are doing nothing to help mask my situation.

The whistle blows, calling for the end of practice. I reach down and adjust myself so I'm not in danger of flashing the whole team, hoping that the waistband of these shorts and the stupid tight shirt will at least help disguise the issue. We both stand slowly. He doesn't take his eyes off me, watching me warily until he realizes we're the only ones still standing on our mat. Everyone else is heading towards the locker room, slowing when they pass us to watch the way we're squared up to each other.

Lincoln sneers. "You smell like a goddamn brewery, Miller. Clean yourself up."

There are a few snickers around us as he turns on his heel and heads to the locker room. I don't miss Pierce looking smug and laughing with his little cronies. A hand lands on my shoulder. Jay, looking down at me with concern. I shake him off, flashing one of my signature fake smiles.

"It's all good," I tell him. "Let's just go."

The rest of the team watches me like I did something wrong. I swallow and force my shoulders loose, widening my grin and making a joke about my circulation in these shorts.

Because if I stop smiling now, they'll see what it cost me not to snap. And I refuse to give Pierce Jamison or Lincoln Beckett one more victory today.

World Wrestling Cup 2016

CHAPTER 5
BECK

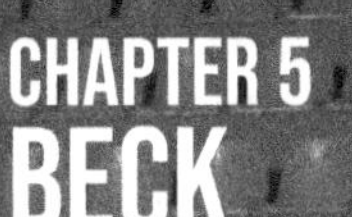

Coach McCoy's backyard is loud with laughter, shitty old country music, and a team full of wrestlers who have no respect for the neighbors. It's the same chaotic energy every year —overloud bravado about which rivals we're going to take down this year, the eager chatter of excited freshmen, and Coach's barking voice as he regales us with tales from his glory days. Normally, this is one of my favorite pre-season events, a familiar event that reminds me I'm among family and gets me excited for the year to come. It's chaotic and loud, yes, but it's also predictable. And I like predictable. Predictable people, predictable routines, predictable nights.

But nothing feels predictable tonight, least of all the way Brody Miller has slotted himself into the team like he's always belonged here, bright and easy and unburdened.

The longer I watch him joke with Fish or listen to him laugh at some story Roman is telling him, the more something acidic spreads under my ribs. I'm not sure if it's jealousy or dread. Both feel equally poisonous. Maybe it's just indigestion from the charred burger I ate.

Everyone is buzzing about going out after this. It's tradition for the upperclassmen to have one last wild night before pre-season kicks our asses. It's never been my favorite part of the night, and one I've skipped out on before, but being captain means putting my team first. It's my job to look like I'm enjoying myself even if I'd rather gouge out my eyeballs than spend the night babysitting a bunch of drunk assholes.

So I straighten my shoulders, step into the center of the yard, and impose order onto the chaos because that's the one thing I'm good at.

"Alright, listen up," I call out, raising my voice over the chatter. "After the barbeque we head straight to the Howl. No wandering off, no getting separated, and if you're drinking, keep track of what you're actually consuming. Pierce, you're responsible for keeping the freshmen from doing anything stupid. Please remember that your behavior reflects on Huntston University, this team as a whole, and Coach McCoy. Cade, you–"

Cade doesn't even wait for me to finish. He throws his head back and goes, "Yes, daddy. Thank you, daddy," in a sugary voice that makes half the team dissolve into laughter. Even Coach barks out a laugh from behind the grill.

My jaw tightens, but Cade just grins wider, licking barbecue sauce off his thumb. Idiot. No matter how many years I've spent cultivating a perfect mask, Cade always seems to be able to either piss me off or make me laugh.

I roll my eyes and turn away before I say something I shouldn't, pretending that the interruption doesn't bother me and letting the whole thing go. Maybe I'll make sure everyone gets to the club, then cut out early. I'll say that Caty wanted me to meet her or something.

A throat clears behind me, and I turn to see Brody approaching with his trademark self-important smirk. He strolls over with that relaxed, loose-hipped confidence of his, the kind of posture that says he's never once worried about how people see him. He stops in front of me, arms crossed, eyes warm but sharp.

"You ever relax and just have fun?" he asks, voice low and conversational like we're normal teammates who don't spend half our time circling each other like predators. "Or is micromanaging everyone else your idea of a good time?"

"Back off," I mutter, because it's the safest thing to say. Anything else would reveal how much he's affecting me.

He doesn't back off. He doesn't even flinch. Instead, he tilts his head and regards me with an unsettling steadiness, like he can read the parts of me I've buried so deeply, even I've forgotten where they're hidden.

"As much as I find your grouchy, uptight thing adorable," Brody says, "the attitude toward me is getting a little old. I'm not your enemy."

Heat flares behind my sternum again. It's not anger exactly, but something close enough that I cling to it.

He steps slightly closer. Close enough that I feel the warmth radiating off him. Close enough that I have to fight not to step back.

"We're teammates," he continues. "And we're going to continue being teammates for this entire year, and the next. Unless you're planning on quitting."

I scoff. "As if you could make me quit."

"Good," he says, sounding like he's actually happy to hear it. "Then get used to me. Because I'm not going anywhere either." He lets his gaze drag over my face like he's cataloguing every twitch.

"And before you get your panties in a twist and start spiraling," he adds softly. "I want to point out that I haven't done a single thing to threaten your ego, your secrets, or your top-dog spot on this team."

My pulse stutters at his mention of secrets, as if mentioning that I have one is akin to threatening to tell everyone.

"So," Brody finishes, stepping in even closer, "either you get over yourself, or I'll show you just how easily I can put you in your place."

He walks away before I find something to fire back. I can't, because I'm too frozen with the humiliating clarity of what the feeling in my chest and abdomen are. The realization that occurred when it flared to life with his words.

It's not jealousy or apprehension or even heartburn. It's far worse than that. It's...

Want.

———

The Howl is a blur of pulsing lights and thumping base that vibrates all the way into my teeth. It's packed in here, the air thick with the humidity of a late August night and sweaty bodies grinding together.

I'm perched on a barstool, trying to pretend that I'm here because I want to be and not because I have an image to maintain.

The guys are scattered across the club. Fish is playing pool with Jay and Aaron. Roman and a few other teammates are doing tequila shots from some girl's cleavage. Sean is laughing with his roommate Carl, talking closely, probably so they can hear each other over the music. I look over at the dance floor where Cade is dancing with two, or maybe three, girls at once.

Which of course leads my eyes right back to Brody, at the center of it all. The gravity that keeps pulling my eyes back unwillingly.

His shirt is off and tucked into the back of his jeans, his hair slicked back with sweat, golden skin glowing under the neon lights.

He's dancing with girls and guys alike without hesitation, laughing when someone pulls him close, throwing his head back like he belongs here more than anyone else in this room. His jeans are unreasonably tight, sitting low on his hips. Every roll of his body sends a ripple down the defined slope of his torso. His abs flex with every shift of his weight, every grind of his hips.

It's obscene. And I can't stop my eyes from wandering in his direction.

Brody's ability to not give a single fuck what anyone thinks of him is easily his most infuriating trait. He has no idea what it's like to live under the weight of expectations and obligations. Meanwhile, everyone expects me to be *that* guy. The perfect, reliable, straight as an arrow, professional man my father raised me to be. Men like us don't falter. We don't slip. And we damn sure don't want things we're not supposed to want.

I force myself to face the bar to keep my eyes anywhere else. The bartender is pretty and slender, almost feminine even. Not exactly the type I'm supposed to want, but close enough to pretend. The type that fits neatly into my life without threatening to unravel it. He gives me flirty smiles every time he catches me looking—smiles I don't return, but he still reads interest in my stillness. Guys like him can always sense it.

If I stood up right now and walked towards that dark hallway behind the bar, I bet he'd follow. I wouldn't even have to speak.

It's predictable. It's the safest kind of risk. It's something I've done a few times, when the pressure builds too tightly inside me. In moments like this, it's easy to remember how much I hate myself after.

I'm weighing my options when the air shifts beside me. A familiar, unsettling presence leans against the bar, far too close for my liking. I can smell his sweat and the underlying soapy scent of his bodywash.

Brody reaches for the water the bartender hands him without even being asked, like he's been waiting for his cue. Brody's smile is easy and warm, making the bartender suddenly forget I exist.

I don't know why I feel embarrassed. It's not as if either of them know where my thoughts had gone. But it still feels like a calculated move on Brody's part to humiliate me, to take something else from me. He pisses me off so fucking much. I turn to glare, ready to say something cutting, but he's not even looking at me.

He tilts his head back and chugs the water, Adam's apple bobbing, throat flexing. A bead of condensation rolls off the bottle and slides over his fingers, then drips onto his chest. It traces a path down his sternum, slips between his pecs, glides over the ridges of his abs. Lower and lower it trickles, gathering speed as it dips into the waistband of his jeans.

And I watch it all the way down. I can't not. I don't want to. I don't mean to. But I can't tear my eyes away.

His jeans cling like they were molded to him. The V of muscle on his hips draws my eyes down and traps them there, where his button-fly strains.

My mouth is dry, and my groin has a pulse.

I have just enough wherewithal to blink back up at him, and my face heats when I see he's watching me take him in. The bastard winks and leans in.

His breath brushes my cheek, warm and humid from dancing. "So are you out or what?" he murmurs. It's so casual. So calm. So devastating.

I jerk back as though he slapped me. "What?" I choke out. "No. What the hell? I'm not into guys."

One eyebrow inches up, slow and deliberate. Then he leans in again, closer this time, his sweat-dampened curls brushing the back of my neck.

"I don't believe you," he whispers, voice dark and smooth. "But don't worry, honey. You give off very macho, straight-boy vibes."

The word *honey* hits somewhere humiliatingly low inside me. I open my mouth to refute him, but I just end up gaping.

"But Lincoln," he adds, his smile tilting dangerously, "if you keep staring at me like that, I'm going to give you exactly what you want."

A rash of chills spreads out over my body, and my breath misfires. All of my blood recirculates to pool in the center of my body, to the point that I can't feel my fingers or my toes.

My tongue feels swollen and too heavy to open my mouth and speak, but I manage to stammer out a weak, "I—D-don't call me that."

I'm mortified.

"What? Lincoln? Or honey?"

"Either!"

He lifts his hands in mock surrender. "Alright, alright. What am I supposed to call you, then? You don't like nicknames. Beck is *just for friends*. Captain gets you all worked up, and you're working so hard to pretend you aren't interested."

"I'm not."

"Uh-huh. So what exactly can I call you without you spiraling? Huh?"

I can't bring myself to tell him that my father is the only one who ever calls me Lincoln. Or that the idea of him calling me anything makes me feel like I'm spiraling.

"What if I just used your last name? Can I call you Beckett?"

"I'd rather you not call me at all."

"You know what they say about protesting too much, right?"

God, he's more argumentative than Caty. Let's hope the two of them never end up in a room together.

I cling to the thought of Caty like a lifeline.

"I have a girlfriend," I blurt.

He looks entirely unimpressed. "Sure you do," he says dryly, then leans forward again. "Do you watch her dance the way you've been watching me, *Beckett*?"

His breath caresses the sensitive skin of my neck and makes me shiver. He leaves me sputtering for breath and returns to the dance floor, swallowed by the music and bodies. Every time he moves, the crowd moves with him, orbiting him like he's the center of their galaxy.

I pull out my phone like it's a lifeline, typing out a text to Caty. Maybe I can get her to come by and show him. It'll be a good reminder to everyone else, too, of what kind of guy I am. Caty's a fucking smoke show. I'll invite her here to dance and leave Brody fucking Miller swallowing his stupid ideas about who I am.

Before I can finish typing out the message, the bartender leans in over the counter, startling me. I'd actually forgotten he was there.

"Jesus, I almost came from the way he was eye fucking you." He fans his face. "Are you alright?"

I roll my eyes and turn away from him. "I'm fine. He's a goddamn clown."

"Well, if you're not going to take him home, you wouldn't mind if I do, right?"

My jaw clenches. "You can do whatever you want. I'm not interested."

"Riiight," he says, one eyebrow arching knowingly. "Is that so?"

He rests his elbows on the bar, his grin turning salacious. "So you're saying that if I disappeared down that hallway," he nods towards the dark corridor I noticed earlier, "and you happened to find me on my knees, you're saying you wouldn't want this mouth?"

He slowly licks his lips, then turns towards the hallway without waiting for an answer.

I stare after him, at the darkness. At the familiar, easy temptation. The predictable script I know I can follow without thinking. The opportunity to escape my headspace for just a short while.

Then, because I'm an idiot, I look back at the dance floor.

Brody is watching me. Not vaguely. He's blatantly watching me, his eyes alight with mischief, smirking because he knows what I'm thinking about.

The fucker winks at me again.

Something inside me fractures, knowing that he's in my head. And that even if I followed the pretty bartender, all I'd see are Brody's bright blue eyes looking up at me.

———

Two weeks pass in a blur of early morning lifts, long days of classes, and practices where I pretend not to feel Brody's presence vibrating against my skin like a second pulse. Ever since that night at the club, I've kept my errant thoughts and feelings tamped down hard and him at a distance. I've been nothing but an iron wall of clipped commands and controlled movements, completely refusing to engage with anything resembling friendliness. As a captain, my attitude spreads through the team like a sickness. No one says it aloud, but the majority of the team follow my lead instinctively. Or at least they try to, until Brody's infectious attitude starts to wear everyone down.

Pierce and his band of minions haven't let up. The pranks have been small, juvenile hazing type shit that Coach pretends he doesn't know about.

An extra-heavy barbell loaded before Brody's bench press. Which, of course, he takes in stride and shows off his impressive strength by pressing out a few reps before even commenting on the weight. A shaker bottle filled with protein powder and salt, which he spits out, but laughs about. His wrestling shoes get tied together and hung from the rafters. He jokes that they needed to be aired out anyway, then finds a member of the maintenance staff to help retrieve them quietly after practice. When his gym bag is "accidentally" thrown into the cold plunge, he asks if anyone has any detergent because laundry day came early.

I should shut it down. It's my job to shut it down. But I don't. I let it happen right in front of me, and I don't even pretend I can't see what's going on. I stand at the center of it all, like I'm not responsible for this team and its members. Hell, I even make the excuse to the other captains that it's bringing the underclassmen together, and Brody doesn't seem to mind. Roman laughs, but I can tell it bothers Sean. He's too quiet of a guy to protest too much, and I notice him checking in on Brody regularly.

To his credit, Brody never snaps or complains. He never sulks or retaliates. Aside from the incessant empty beer cans that get left in and around his locker constantly, which I don't really understand,

Brody just laughs and moves on like it's all background noise. And somehow, that makes it even worse. The team likes him even better for it. It makes them warm to him. It makes him look good and me look...

Jealous. Intimidated.

It makes me look just as weak and sniveling as Pierce Jamison.

Every day, people gravitate towards Brody a little more. He jokes with Aaron on the walk to class. He spots Jay during lifts. He helps freshmen with their stances. His laugh, the one I pretend grates on my nerves, becomes familiar enough that even the guys who used to follow my lead begin drifting towards him.

Everyone likes him. Except Pierce, of course. Pierce hates him for being everything he's not—friendly, warm, naturally gifted, and worst of all, unintimidated by people like us.

Despite all that, I hold the line with my hard indifference. I make sure no one sees or even suspects how hard it's getting to look at Brody without feeling that same unwelcome shiver crawling up my spine. The same one that makes me want to bolt from the room before he can see something on my face I didn't mean to show. Because the more he doesn't falter, the more he takes in stride, the more I become just as impressed with him as everyone else. Except I can't admit that to anyone, not even myself.

Which is exactly why my head is pounding before this stupid alumni mixer even begins.

Coach McCoy's wrestling facility has been transformed into a suffocating maze of collared shirts and old money. Athletic donors, former captains, alumni from the glory years, and a host of other insufferable people all clog the room like a wall of expectation I'm destined to climb.

My father is here, wearing a suit that costs more than the catering company and a disdainful expression that suggests he's been disappointed since the moment I was born. He's been talking to Coach, which I'm grateful for at first, because it buys me a few minutes to gather myself and look for Caty, who has always been the best buffer between me and my father. He might hate me, but he loves my girlfriend.

"It's good to see you, Chuck," McCoy says, grinning far too warmly as he claps my father on the shoulder. "Your boy here is shaping up to be as good as you were back in the day." I roll my eyes at the way Coach calls my dad Chuck, smiling like they're old friends instead of rivals who spent four years trying to destroy each other on the same team I find myself struggling with. The irony leaves a bad taste in my mouth.

My father returns Coach's smile, but his eyes barely shift toward me, like acknowledging me directly is some tedious formality he'd rather skip. When Coach moves off to greet someone else, Dad finally turns fully in my direction, expression faintly critical like I'm a building he's inspecting for structural damage.

"I hear the team's shaping up," he says, smoothing a hand over my lapel to remove some invisible lint. "Dale mentioned some new additions. Said you've got a transfer this year, you didn't tell me *Broderick Miller* found himself on your team."

I force a nod, my heart rate kicking up. "Yes sir, a transfer and quite a few impressive freshmen as well. One guy is a heavyweight that played as a lineman on his high school football team. He's a beast." My head swivels around the room, hoping to point out the freshman and divert my father's attention.

I should know better.

"I recognized that boy the second I walked in here," my father continues, tapping a finger against his drink, a metronome that betrays his frustration.

My dad's gaze travels across the room, and I know he's looking at Brody's messy blond curls and stocky build. I swallow, jaw tight, pulse loud in my ears.

"Imagine my surprise," Dad says lightly, "when I find out you've been paired up with the boy that took the championship from you your senior year. The very one that embarrassed you, and me by extension."

My throat closes, and I refuse to look up where my father is staring at Brody like he's something he stepped in.

"I expect you've shown the little upstart where his place is."

I say the thing I know he wants to hear, because that's what I always do. "Yes. He's not had it easy since arriving here."

My father's approval isn't warm. It never is. But there's a sharp, mean gleam in his eye. "Good," he says. "I raised you to be a winner, Lincoln. Winners don't let humiliations like that go unchecked."

The way he says *humiliations like that* makes my stomach twist. Like that match was a stain on the family name instead of whatever hellish awakening it actually was for me. My father has never given me any indication that he knows exactly why I ran out of that competition, but I'm not naïve enough to assume he doesn't have at least some idea. He was there, after all.

"Yeah," I mutter through my teeth. "He's... he's not a problem."

"Is he not?" My father glances across the room.

This time, I follow his gaze. Brody is laughing, loud and bright, head thrown back, something warm blooming in his eyes as he talks to Fish and Sean. One of my best friends and one of my co-captains, who happens to be one of the top Division One wrestlers in the country. Someone my father has compared me to for most of my time here at Huntston, despite us being in completely different weight classes.

Brody's smile lights up his whole face. It lights up the people around him too. Something inside me knots.

Dad gives a low, displeased noise. "Clearly you're doing a good job keeping him in line." His tone is edged with dry amusement. "Look at him. Carrying on like an idiot. Doesn't look like he takes anything seriously," he says, eying Brody's black slacks and faded tuxedo t-shirt with disdain.

The words slip out before I can stop them. "He doesn't. It's infuriating."

I can feel my shoulders drawing up to my ears, tension crawling up my neck until my temples start to throb. Watching Brody laugh so easily with everyone, watching his arms draped over friends and teammates who used to follow me unquestioningly, makes something sharp and stupid flare inside me.

Dad steps past me, already scanning the room for someone more important to talk to. "Work on it," he says over his shoulder. "Knock him down properly. He needs it."

Then he's gone. And I'm left standing there, seething so hard I can barely breathe, every muscle tight enough to snap.

I look at Brody again and scowl so hard I'm surprised lasers don't shoot out of my eyes and cut him clean in half. He doesn't see me watching. He's too busy being liked. Being natural and effortless as always.

That ugly, tight feeling claws its way up my chest. Something that feels like panic and want and shame all tangled together.

I clamp it down like I'm swallowing down nausea and bury it deep.

Because if anyone—my father, my teammates, Brody—ever saw what was actually happening inside me, it would ruin everything.

And Lincoln Beckett does not get ruined. He ruins whatever threatens him. Because he is his father's son and that's who he's been raised to be.

Or so I tell myself.

CHAPTER 6

BRODY

Two more weeks blur by, and for the first time since transferring here, I feel every single moment of them in my bones. I like staying busy. I always have, but there's a difference between busy and 'I will collapse if one more professor assigns a practice exam'. The combination of midterms, early morning lifts, afternoon practices, and late-night study sessions has turned my brain to oatmeal. The mushy instant kind, not the hearty steel-cut kind.

Fall break couldn't have come at a better time. I'm looking forward to three whole days without classes, practices, coaches, or stupid pranks. And no teammates like Lincoln Beckett glowering at me like my existence is a personal insult to his family lineage. Which, consequently, is exactly how I noticed his dad staring at me during the alumni event a couple weeks back.

All I want is to go home. To hug Mom and make sure she's taking care of herself and sleeping more than four hours a night. To see Davis and check with my own eyes that he's eating, healing, getting out of bed. Anything besides the silence and Mom's assurances that he's doing great. As if I don't know better.

My brother has been out of rehab for barely two weeks, and he went through a lot between the hospital and rehab. The doctors told us it was going to be hard. Mom pretending that everything's just fine only makes me worry about them more. And honestly, I miss them. As upset as I was to move home, I hate being this close to home and still feeling like I'm a thousand miles away.

Plus, I need clean underwear.

Seriously. If this hazing shit keeps up, I'm going to have to take out a loan specifically for boxer briefs and socks. At first, the pranksters would steal whole outfits—shorts, shirts, even my towel. That stopped the day I proved I wasn't ashamed to walk across campus with nothing but an empty gym bag held strategically in front of me so I didn't get arrested. Students stared. A few laughed. Even more cat-called and whistled. Of the pranks that have been pulled on me this year so far, that one honestly didn't bother me all that much. I've never had anything to hide when it comes to my body.

But now it's only underwear that goes missing. Always the under-wear, and usually just one sock. And unlike everything else, *those* never seem to make it to the lost-and-found basket Aaron leaves outside our dorm room for whatever pranked items magically reappear over time, or hanging up in a strategic display meant to embarrass me, which never works so it's been happening less and less. But the underwear hasn't slowed down, so now I've been walking around commando with mismatched socks.

I don't want to think too hard about what they're doing with them.

The only joke I can't seem to laugh off are the beer cans. But even though I never react, they keep popping up everywhere. My book bag, my gym bag, my locker. Sometimes I'll turn around and one will appear at whatever desk or table I'm at. The laughter and the sound of empty cans clinking together haunts me everywhere I go.

My last name has been an easy target my whole life. "Miller Time." "Crack open a cold one." "No wonder your dad was a drunk."

Kids in grade school thought it was hilarious. Middle schoolers thought they were clever. High schoolers weaponized it, even going so far as to get my mother fired from one of her jobs because her boss noticed her back seat filled with beer cans. But grown adults should know better. Pierce sure as hell should, considering he knows what happened to my father.

But he's either too cruel or too stupid to realize he's going too far.

The other day he walked right up to me, handed me a cold, unopened can still sweating from someone's fridge, and said, "Figured you might want a fresh one. It's been a stressful few months for you."

I forced a smile that tasted like blood in my mouth. "Thanks, man."

I didn't drink it. I don't drink at all, actually. I've never even taken one drink. Not after what happened to Dad. Not after what it did to Davis. Not after watching what addiction has done to my life.

All I could do was carry the can back to the dorm, where Aaron and Jay both looked up from their midterm prep with matching concerned expressions. I offered them the beer like it was funny, but they saw through the mask that day.

Aaron told me about getting harassed in middle school for being small. Jay said I'm on the right track, that every bully grows bored eventually if you don't give them a reaction. They encouraged me to ignore it, to keep doing my thing. So far it's been working for me, aside from Pierce's persistent bullshit.

I told them that the hazing doesn't bother me. Not really. I've dealt with worse. I can handle a few weeks of their immaturity. Once the season starts and I prove I belong here, it'll stop. Probably. I hope.

But what *does* bother me, what gnaws at me more than I'll ever admit, isn't the beer and alcoholic jabs. It's the way Lincoln Beckett treats me. His aloof, purposeful mistreatment of me both annoys the hell out of me and kind of gets my motor revved.

The rest of them are annoying, sure, but predictable. The freshman-level pranks, the chest-thumping posturing, the macho jokes, they all play by the same tired rulebook. But Beckett is in a league of his own. Cold one minute, hostile the next, and then acting like I kicked his dog simply by breathing in his direction. It's like he crafted his personality from a manual titled *How to Make Brody Miller's Dick Hard and Life Difficult, Vol. 1.*

And yeah, maybe I'm not helping. Full disclosure, I know I'm not. I could leave him alone completely, pretend he doesn't exist, but I don't. Maybe I would if he wasn't being a shitty captain, encouraging the stupid pranks by pretending he doesn't notice it happening.

Instead, I keep slipping into the things that get under his skin. Like cycling through the stupidest pet names I can come up with just to see the vein in his neck throb or using his full name with exaggerated politeness because it makes him tick.

He hates it. I know he hates it. Which only makes it harder not to do.

I don't know how else to be. I'm not wired for silent misery. My whole life, the only way I've survived bullshit was by laughing through it, shrugging it off, finding some stupid way to make everything lighter so it wouldn't crush me. The alternative is turning into someone like *him*. Someone who walks around like the weight of the entire universe is resting between his shoulder blades.

And honestly, why *is* he so miserable?

He's got friends everywhere. Guys who practically orbit him like he's the campus sun. Coaches who trust and compliment him constantly, even if he and I both know I could take him in any match if I actually tried to. Professors who seem to like him. Hell, he even has a girlfriend. I didn't believe that at first, but I've seen her with him more than once, hanging off his arm, all smiles and sweetness, looking at him like he invented oxygen. They seem happy enough, so what the hell is he so pissed off about?

Then again, one glimpse of his dad at the alumni event put some things into perspective.

The man looked like someone carved resentment out of granite and dressed it in a business suit. If addiction can run in families, I guess being an asshole can too. Maybe Lincoln Beckett never stood a chance.

Whether or not Beckett's dad likes me, or whether or not his dick does, doesn't excuse him for taking it out on me. It's not my fault I got his dick hard. And it's not even like I've taunted him that much about it or told anyone else. Nor would I ever.

I've tried to lay off the teasing. Really, I have. But every time he gets that sharp, superior tone, like he thinks he's teaching me a lesson or like he knows more or is better than me, something in me snaps right back. Then he gets that wounded, furious look, like *how dare you talk to me,* and suddenly I'm in the middle of the world's stupidest pissing match.

You'd think I'd stop letting him win at practice. But I keep letting him. I give him just enough push back to make him think he's working for it, and then I let go just to see the change in him when he gets the upper hand.

There's something in his eyes when he's fighting to stay on top. Something scared, like he's fraying at the edges, and I get this stupid urge to let him have it. Like maybe he needs the win more than I do.

But I'm only human. And patient as I am, there's a limit.

One of these days, he's going to push me too far, and when he does, I'm going to stop holding back. I'm going to show him exactly how easily I could take that "top dog" crown off his pretty little head.

And maybe, just maybe, that'll finally wipe that tortured look out of his eyes and replace it with the lust I know is hiding beneath it.

———

By Thursday afternoon, my brain is mush, and my bag is packed for the trip home. I'm tired, but excited. I'm thinking about the list of things I know still need to be done at home, whether or not Davis will talk to me, how good it's going to feel to sleep in my old bed for a night or two. Not to mention the underwear. I'm literally down to my last two pairs, and they're both dirty. My dick is starting to chafe in my jeans.

The sky is cloudy and the air is sharp with the bite of a cold front moving in. I pull my hands into my hoodie as I walk across the student parking lot to get to my car. My beat-up old Nissan is in the exact place she was the last time I drove her weeks ago, but as I get closer, I realize there's a problem.

The front driver-side tire is flat.

"Great," I mutter, running a hand through my hair. "Fantastic. Perfect timing."

It's annoying, but not catastrophic. Tires blow. They get punctured. They go bald. Mine were probably overdue for replacement anyway.

With a cleansing huff, I throw my bag in the back seat, roll up my sleeves, and get to work. It's annoying, but I handle it with my usual level-headed drive to move past the stress and get it done.

I get the old tire off, put the spare on, and tighten the bolts. It doesn't take me more than ten minutes, and I'm ready to go. But when I lift the ruined tire to put it in the trunk, the whole car shifts too far to one side.

Odd.

I walk around the back of the car, then freeze. The back passenger-side tire is also flat. But it's more than that. There's a slash in the tire, at least two inches long.

That's not an accident.

My breath leaves in a long, heavy exhale, fogging up the cold air. My fingers dig into my scalp as I tug at my hair in frustration.

"Fuck."

I only have one spare. Which means I'm stranded unless I call someone. Which means blowing a huge chunk of the rapidly dwindling savings I've been living on, especially considering I'll either need an after-hours mobile service or a tow. But if I don't call, I won't make it home, and I can't do that to my family. I need to see them with my own eyes, to check in to make sure things are okay. Not just for them, for me.

I grab my phone and dial roadside assistance, pacing in slow, tight circles. When the automated hold music clicks on, I lean back against the trunk and try to breathe through the frustration rising like a tide in my throat.

I want to blame the tires themselves. They're definitely old and worn and have needed replacing for longer than I'm willing to admit. But no amount of wishful thinking covers up a clean slit across the rubber.

My jaw clenches until it aches. Someone did this on purpose. But why?

Why the hell would someone do something like this? A prank is one thing, but this is a fucking crime. And it's hateful. Who would do that?

Something moves between the trees on the far side of the parking lot. A tall silhouette. Broad shoulders. Narrow waist tapering down into long legs. The kind of build that might as well be carved into my memory at this point.

Lincoln Beckett.

He disappears into the dorm building like he doesn't notice me. Like he isn't the most obvious suspect in the world. He doesn't look back. Doesn't flinch. He just walks away as if he didn't just leave me stranded on campus with two flat tires and a head full of fire.

My fists curl so tight my nails bite into my palms.

I've taken everything this team has thrown at me. I've laughed off every prank. I've ignored every sideways comment. I've given him his space, respected his boundaries, let him keep winning even when he's treated me like some kind of plague.

But this...This is too far.

I'm done pretending none of it bothers me. I'm done letting him act like he can push me around until I snap. I'm done giving him the benefit of the doubt.

If he thinks I'm going to be the kind of man who rolls over and takes it forever, he's got another thing coming.

And if he thinks cutting me down will make me walk away?

Beckett doesn't know a damn thing about who he's dealing with.

CHAPTER 7
BECK

The second I slip back into the athletic dorms, I'm grinning like a self-satisfied idiot.

I didn't flatten Brody's tires myself. Hell, it wasn't even my idea. But I definitely didn't stop it from happening. It was Pierce and his little band of cronies that are so desperate for my approval they keep coming up with new ways to torture Brody while I sit back and watch the show.

Thus far, nothing seems to get to that bastard. Not the locker room pranks, not seeing his underwear hung from the rafters of the student union like a goddamn victory flag, not even having to traipse across campus butt-ass naked—hell, he almost seemed to enjoy that.

The only thing that's gotten to him in the slightest has been Pierce and his irritatingly persistent antics with the beer cans. I still don't understand what's up with that, but it's the only thing that seems to get under Brody's skin. Not that he shows it.

He tries to hide how much the beer jokes bother him, but I see it. The way his smile cracks for just a second before he glues it back in place. I hate myself for the pang of sympathy I get when I see it. How maybe *that* one actually hurt him.

Which is stupid. It's none of my business. I don't know why it keeps bothering me. I barely notice it, and it's only because I'm watching so closely.

So I can watch him crack, obviously. Not for any other reason.

Watching him finally lose his shit, dragging his hands through his messy hair, pacing the parking lot like a caged animal? Now that's a reaction.

I finally saw him break.

That was satisfying. Or... it should've been.

But on the walk down the hallway to the elevators, the satisfaction curdles. It settles weirdly in my stomach, sharp and acidic, like guilt pretending not to be something other than what it is.

He deserved it. Right?

It's not like he hasn't been pushing my buttons nonstop since the day he got here. The smirking. The stupid jokes. The way he says my name like he's licking the inside of my skull—*Lincoln*—over-pronounced every time. And the pet names. God, the fucking pet names. Always whispered in my ear like some kind of filthy taunt when we're on the mats. *He's* the one that's been trying to get a reaction out of *me*, just as much as the other way around.

So I should be able to enjoy this victory, whether or not I'm the one that messed with his tires.

I reach the elevators, thinking about watching him from the window of my floor, just to see if he's still pacing around the parking lot like an angry wet cat.

Before I can push the button for my floor, a sudden weight slams into my back. My chest hits the wall so hard the breath punches out of me. A heavy arm bars across the back of my neck, pinning me in place. The pressure is firm, unyielding, terrifying. It sends a shock straight through my body in a way I absolutely do not want to acknowledge.

A voice growls in my ear. Low, rough, and spine tinglingly familiar.

"You think that shit was funny?"

My breath shorts out. Brody isn't just upset. He's furious. I can feel it radiating off him, hot and crackling and so dangerous it makes my knees weak.

"I didn't—" My voice comes out cracked, pathetic. I try to steel myself. "Get off me."

He presses harder. Not enough to hurt, just enough that I can't move. Enough that my entire traitorous body goes stiff. My *entire* body.

He notices, because of course he does. He's the harbinger of my personal doom. Of course he has to notice my weakness.

A dark scoff huffs out of him. "You've gotta be kidding me."

Before I can tell him to shut up or push him off, the elevator dings behind us, signaling that someone is coming this way. I consider calling out, but something keeps me quiet while Brody curses under his breath and drags me sideways, gripping the back of my neck like it's a handle. He yanks me into the stairwell, slamming the door shut behind us and manhandling me against the wall.

I stumble, breath hitching, spine pressed to the cinderblock wall. He doesn't let me go. His arm comes up again, pinning me in place with a force that shouldn't ignite every nerve ending I have—

But it does. God help me, it does.

He leans in close. So close I can feel his breath stir the hair at my temple.

"I'm not done with you," he murmurs.

A shiver rips down my spine.

I try to speak, try to snarl something back. Try to regain even a fraction of control. But my throat is tight, and my jaw won't work, and I can't get air into my lungs.

Every inch of my skin prickles, oversensitive like the pain of a limb waking up when it hasn't gotten enough circulation. Probably because all the blood in my body has rushed straight to my dick. Why the fuck is my dick so hard?

His blue eyes are burning holes through me. Seeing everything. Knowing everything. The same way he looked at me that day on the mat, two years ago, only less surprised and more like he's blaming me for it. Like he could see the exact moment my body betrayed me and he thinks I'm pathetic.

His gaze drags downward, so slowly.

His lips part.

"...Lincoln," he says, voice dropping to something dark and disbelieving. "You're shaking."

I am. Goddamn it, I am. So much so that I can't even correct him for using my first name.

My knees feel loose. My pulse is pounding—in my throat, my wrists, then lower, and lower... Heat rolls through me, humiliating and impossible to hide.

Brody's jaw ticks.

"You like this," he says softly.

"No," I rasp.

His eyes flick up, sharp as a blade. "Say it again. Look me in the eye and say it."

My mouth opens, but nothing comes out.

Because I can lie with my voice. But my body won't let me. My body is pulsing with adrenaline and panic and something far, far more dangerous. Something I definitely don't want Brody Miller to see. Something I have spent years burying so deep I hoped it would die.

But it's not dead. It's alive, clawing its way out of me from the inside, hissing and starving.

Brody's lips curl—not in amusement, but something darker.

"Oh, Lincoln," he murmurs. "You really are screwed up."

Humiliation floods through me so hard my vision blurs. My fingers twitch helplessly at my sides. Shame burns through me like acid, but my first thought is somehow that I don't like him calling me Lincoln.

"Don't call me that," I whisper hoarsely.

He leans in closer. His forehead nearly touches mine. His voice goes low enough to gut me from the inside.

"You think you're the biggest, meanest fucker at Huntston," he says. "The captain. Top dog. Golden boy. Untouchable." His breath brushes my jaw. "But look at you. Look at what a little pressure does to you."

"S-stop," I choke out. He ignores me.

"You've been trying so hard to tear me down," he says. "To prove you're better. Stronger. Straighter." He lets out a rough, humorless laugh. "But you can't even pretend right now. You're so fucking hard for me."

"I said stop—"

"Say you don't want this."

I open my mouth to speak, but I can't. I physically can't force the words out. All that comes out is a pathetic, breathy sound. A cross between a moan and a whine. A plea.

Brody's expression shifts into something terrifying. Something predatory and hungry. He rakes his eyes down my body, and I have no doubt he sees me for what I am—a pathetic, simpering, weakling. And the humiliation of it all is only making my situation worse.

I'm not just hard. I'm aching. Leaking. And seconds away from begging—for what? I don't know. For escape. For release. For a goddamn moment of peace.

"Drop your pants."

My eyes flash open wide, staring into his blue eyes that are darker than I've ever seen them before. Like he's another person. No longer the happy-go-lucky, charismatic charmer with the energy of a labrador. That Brody isn't here. The man who stands in front of me is a cold, hard, demanding, dominant beast of a man I've never seen the likes of before.

And I'm powerless, a slave to his whims.

I try shaking my head. I try choking out a protest. But I don't actually move or say a word. I only part my lips, and untie the drawstring on my athletic pants.

They drop to the ground in a soft swish of fabric that settles around my ankles.

"These, too," he says, snapping the waistband of my boxers. "And hold up your shirt."

Brody steps back, not far, just enough that the air between us is suddenly cold and empty.

"Thought so," he says quietly, and smirks as he looks down at my exposed erection. He sweeps his gaze up from my leaking dick to my watery eyes. "I thought big, bad Lincoln Beckett would have a bigger dick. I should have known better, considering you try to rub it on me every day at practice."

"I don't—" His hand closes around my throat, keeping me pinned to the wall while he puts a few more inches of space between us so he can get a better view of my shame. My face is burning so hot, the flush is bleeding down my chest. My dick is already so flushed and engorged it's purple, so the rest of me might as well turn the same color.

"There's something wrong with you, Lincoln."

"Don't—"

"Don't what? Don't tell you how pathetic you are? Don't tell you that I don't give a damn what you like to be called, not when you've been set on making my life miserable since the day I walked through those doors? And why? Because I make your pathetic little dick hard?"

It's not little. I want to say, but I don't. He laughs in my face because he can read me too well.

"Smaller than mine," he laughs. My eyes fall to the considerable bulge in the front of his jeans and I swallow dryly. He's hard, too. Is he going to do something with it? Make me... touch it? Put my mouth on it?

My cock jerks and dribbles pre-cum.

Brody chuckles darkly.

"You're so weak for me, I bet it wouldn't take more than one word to make you lose your shit and make a mess all over yourself like the pathetic little man you are."

A whimper escapes me. A fucking whimper.

"That's right. I bet you want to come for me. And I bet it wouldn't take more than a word to make you do it."

I'm really shaking now, all my veins trembling, limbs weak and wobbly. A tear falls down my cheek. My mind screams with the need to hide, to vanish, to claw out of my own skin. But my body rebels. My abs tighten. My ass clenches. And my cock jerks and weeps and waits for my damnation.

I blink open teary eyes and find myself locked in Brody's dark glare.

"Come."

One word. One simple, clipped command given in a low, gravelly voice. And I am undone.

My skin burns with humiliation, but I cry out, hips thrusting into empty air as my cock erupts. Tears splash against my cheeks and my cum splashes on the floor, on my legs, on my underwear and pants piled around my feet. Brody steps aside so it doesn't land on him, and observes blankly as he watches me fall apart in real time.

He releases me and takes a slow step backwards, eyes never leaving me. I sag against the wall, trembling, skin burning, heart pounding in my throat.

"The next time you or your boys fuck with me, I'll make you sorry," he says, his voice low and sharp enough to saw through bone.

Then he turns away without waiting for a response. Without giving me a chance to breathe, or recover, or gather up the pieces of my shredded dignity.

The stairwell door closes behind him.

And I slide down the wall onto my ass, shaking so hard I can barely keep myself upright.

I should hate him. I should be furious. I should want revenge.

But all I can feel is the raging fire in my veins and the horrible, unavoidable truth that I have never in my life felt so fucking calm. Like nothing that was troubling me before Brody Miller pinned me in a stairwell exists. I can't even bring myself to freak out over what I just let happen.

I just feel... free.

CHAPTER 8
BRODY

I'm a bad person. A bad, terrible, awful human being.

The whole hour-and-a-half drive home is torture. Not because of the traffic, or the fact that I'm exhausted, or because my gas tank is hovering closer to empty than I'd like.

But because of what I did. Because of how I reacted. Because the image of Lincoln Beckett—cornered, flushed, trembling under my hold—keeps replaying in my mind until my grip on the steering wheel goes numb.

I don't know what possessed me. Honestly, I don't know where that version of myself even came from. That wasn't usual behavior for me. I'm really not like that. I'm not violent, I don't manhandle people, and I certainly don't hold them down, make them strip, and degrade them in the off chance they might get off on it. That's not my thing.

Or at least, I didn't think it was. But the second I touched him, the moment I felt him react like that, something primal and ugly and hungry lit up inside me. A fuse I didn't know existed sparked and burned straight down a line I never intended on crossing.

I shift in my seat, grimacing, once again cursing the rub of denim over my bare dick. Thank you, Lincoln Beckett, for your very creative hazing traditions.

Maybe there's a chance the pranks will quiet down now that I've put Beckett in his place? I run a hand over my face, exhaling hard.

I can't even think that way.

I need to apologize. No way around it. He crossed lines with me, sure. But what I did back there was... not okay.

I'll talk to him when I get back. After fall break.

Definitely before I hand him the bill for the tires. Because holy hell—almost five hundred dollars when you add the extra fees they charge for someone to come out and change two tires in a parking lot, plus the cost of two brand new tires to replace the ones that were both definitely slashed.

I should have just filed a report to get my revenge, not... whatever I just did.

Should I apologize before or after demanding compensation?

Probably before. Definitely before. Maybe. I don't know.

What if he won't talk to me about it? What if I actually made the whole thing worse and he punishes me for showing his weakness to that extent, because I'm sure that's how he sees it.

I really don't know what I think of it all, other than I'm twisted up about it.

By the time I roll into my mom's driveway, it's dark and quiet. The wind swishes leaves all over the un-raked yard and rattles the fence someone left open. The house sits quiet and a little lopsided in the glow of the porch light, exactly the same and somehow worse than I left it.

The place needs help. A lot of it. The siding I patched over the summer is peeling again. The porch railing's loose. A few shingles are missing from the roofline.

I make a list in my head, even though I don't have the time, money, or bandwidth to actually accomplish half of it this weekend. Especially now that I'm a day late and five hundred dollars short.

Inside, the house smells like the lemon cleaner Mom uses at work and the vanilla plug-ins she uses to cover the musty smell of old carpet. The house is falling apart, but Mom does her best with what she has, and it's always clean and homey inside.

The kitchen shows evidence of a meal cooked that no one was around to enjoy. There's a plate wrapped in foil waiting in the fridge with a note stuck to the top that Mom got tired and will see me in the morning. My chest tightens.

I shove the plate in the microwave thankfully, not having eaten since breakfast this morning. I'd originally planned to grab something on the road, but by the time I left campus, I was late, several hundred dollars poorer, and too jittery about what I'd done to eat anything.

I shovel Mom's tuna noodle casserole in my mouth, listening to the silence settle around me. Mom is sleeping. Davis probably is too. As tired as I am, I'm not sure I'll be able to get to sleep anytime soon. I can't get my brain to stop working overtime. And I want to see Davis with my own two eyes.

I clean up my plate and wash the few dishes in the sink while I'm at it before padding quietly down the hall. I pause when I get to Davis' door, thinking I heard something.

I knock softly and a muffled sound answers me. I push the door open a sliver and peek inside, seeing Davis awake. Sort of. He looks like he might be only half conscious, or like he's close to falling asleep. He's sweaty and his eyes are sunken in. He's lost weight since I last saw him, and he didn't have much to lose as it was.

He's lying on his side, controller in hand, TV glow flickering across a face that looks years older than me instead of a mere eighteen months.

"Hey," he rasps, eyes barely tracking me.

"Hey." I toe off my shoes and ease myself onto the bed beside him. The mattress dips under my weight. He hands me the second controller without looking away from the screen.

We play silently. It feels like being twelve again. Except this time, neither of us is really putting forth any effort to win or taunting the other.

After a long while, he mumbles, "How's school? That fancy place treating you alright?"

"Good," I say automatically. Then, quieter, "Mostly."

His eyes flick towards me, dull and unfocused, but still edged with the concern of a caring older sibling. If nothing else, at least I can say I saw proof that my brother is still in there somewhere. "Mostly?"

I let out a breath that sinks deep in my chest. "Yeah. Mostly."

Davis raises an eyebrow and gives me a look that reminds me of our dad. It's heavy-lidded and exhausted but still present enough to be big-brotherly. "What happened?"

I scrub a hand over my face. I really, really shouldn't say this out loud. Not to him. Not to *anyone*. But I'm tired and confused and on edge in a way that weeks of torment, guilt, two slashed tires, and whatever the hell happened in that stairwell all mix into one big *fuck it*.

"I, uh… might've accidentally sexually assaulted my team captain who hates me."

Davis' eyes sharpen for the first time all night. "I'm sorry—what?"

"Not like that," I hiss. Then wince. "Okay. Kind of like that. But not… like *that*."

He turns fully towards me, brows lifting. "Brody."

I flop back against the headboard with a groan. "He hates me. Like, actually, really hates me. For no good reason other than I beat him once when we were in high school and maybe, possibly felt him get hard. I never told anyone. But he's been such a dick to me and there's all this bullshit with Pierce Jamison, and I just—snapped. I shoved him and he shoved me and then…" I cover my face with my hands. "I don't even know. It escalated. I held him against a wall, and said some things. And then he… reacted. And I reacted to him reacting, and now my brain is a fucking pretzel."

Davis stares. Then, unexpectedly, he huffs a laugh. A small, broken one, but real. "Jesus Christ. So, what exactly did you do to him? Because my brain isn't exactly firing on all cylinders and I'm pretty sure this is the most I've tried to process since before rehab."

I sigh. "I… sort of… um… Overpowered him and said some weird, humiliating type stuff about him being hard. And then I made him come. But in a mean way."

There's a long beat of silence where I stare at the ceiling and pretend I can rewind time and never open my mouth. Or maybe never do that to Beckett in the first place? But if I'm being honest with myself I didn't hate it, but only because he seemed to like it.

He arches a brow. "You need a drink?"

"Not funny."

"Too soon?"

"Fuck you, Davis."

My brother chuckles, which, considering I haven't heard him talk this much or laugh at all in a very long time, means that maybe there's a silver lining to this awkwardness.

"So, he liked it?"

My face burns. "I... don't know. Maybe. Yes? I mean, he came. But does that really mean anything? And he also might have been crying? I don't know. No? Fuck, I shouldn't be talking to you about this."

"Probably not," he says, grimacing, "but here we are." He nudges my shoulder with the controller. "Have you checked on the guy?"

"What?"

"You know, if you think he liked it but you're feeling guilty, maybe you should call him or send him a text or something. Check in on him."

I bark out a humorless laugh. "What would I even say? 'Hey man, sorry I humiliated you into coming all over yourself'?"

Davis snorts. "Why not?"

"Well for one, I don't have his number," I say. "And I don't think he'd appreciate me asking anyone else for it. He's the worst kind of closet case."

He smirks faintly, the closest thing to his old self I've seen since he got out of the hospital. "Fine. But Brody? Guys like that don't just... take it like that. I'm sure if he hated it, he would've swung. Hard."

I huff out a heavy breath. "Maybe."

The knot in my stomach doesn't loosen. Not even a little.

"Did I hear you mention Pierce Jamison?"

"Yeah. I think his older brother Levi was in your grade. Pierce is a year under me."

Davis nods unhappily. "I hated that guy. He's giving you shit?"

I sigh. "Just more of the same crap from grade school. Leaving empty cans around, calling me Miller Time, making stupid jokes. Annoying, but nothing I can't handle."

"That's bullshit," he mutters, voice slurring around the edges with exhaustion. He goes quiet again. Too quiet. I wish I hadn't said anything.

Davis struggled with the bullying a lot more than I did. Whereas I was able to find a way and laugh things off to redirect the attention, Davis sank into it. He was sensitive and would lash out. He's always felt things so much bigger than I did.

His hands are shaking.

"You okay?" I ask gently.

He flinches like I slapped him. "I wish everybody would stop asking me that." He sounds sharp, but the strength behind it is threadbare.

The doctors warned us this would happen. Withdrawal combined with Davis' mental health struggles would make it harder for him to cope. Mood swings and depressive episodes are to be expected, but expecting it doesn't make it any easier to watch.

I wish I could make it all better for him. He's drowning, wasting away right in front of me.

"Sorry," I say. "I just—miss talking to you like this, even if I had to humiliate myself to make it happen. You haven't called or texted me back at all since you got out of the center."

"It's fine," he grits out. But I know our moment is over. He's shut himself off again.

"I just worry about you, and—"

"Yeah," he grits out, "well, don't." He pauses the game, shoves the controller aside, and turns away from me. "Get out."

"Davis—"

"I said get out," he snaps. Then his shoulders sag, and he lets out a breath. "I'm sorry. I'm just tired."

I swallow the sting in my throat and back out of the room quietly.

The door clicks shut behind me, and the silence of the hallway feels hollow and loud. I stand outside his bedroom, wanting to go back in, wanting to say something, anything, to make it better, but I know I can't.

Instead, I head straight to my old bedroom. While none of the house has changed that much over the years, my childhood bedroom looks like time never moved forward at all. If you ignore the dust that only gets wiped up whenever I visit, you'd never know much time had passed.

It's still the same room I've slept in since I was a toddler. Over the years, the décor got upgraded a few times, as I grew out of Sesame Street and found a love for comic books.

My old wrestling trophies line the dresser, some shiny, others showing their age and dusty. Old movie posters on the wall are sun-faded at the corners. There's a shelf full of old comic books and graphic novels.

Above my full-sized bed, covered in a faded navy blue comforter, is the framed set of DC Pride issues I was gifted for my birthday one year. I remember how excited I was to have them, to display them on the wall. To me, they were proof that I could be something extraordinary, despite what the kids at school, my teachers, and my coaches thought. They were proof that maybe one day I wouldn't feel so out-of-place everywhere I went.

At the end of the bed is a desk, still covered in notebooks and pencils from my last high school exams, plus some of the books I still have from The University of Nebraska. On the wall above the desk is a collage of family photos. It's mostly pictures of Davis and me over the years. Sporting events, Davis' art shows, a science fair, wrestling meets, and birthday parties. The older we get in the pictures, the more the differences between us are apparent. As time went on, Davis turned in on himself, got paler and more sullen. And the less he smiled, the more I felt the need to. From this perspective it looks like I was sapping the life from him, growing while he wilted.

In the very center is the last family photo we took before Dad died. We're all smiling. Dad's arm is around Mom. Davis and I look like complete opposites. I was always short and stocky, with blond hair like our mom, although I got dad's curly hair. Davis is tall and willowy like our father, with straight, dark hair and haunted eyes. Or at least, that's how they look now. We look happy in those pictures, even though the teasing had already started by then.

I sit down on the edge of the bed and hold my head in my hands. I knew being here wouldn't be easy, but I didn't expect to feel so beaten down. It's not like me to not be able to find a silver lining naturally, to sit here and force myself to remember that Mom is okay, she's working and living her life while taking care of Davis. Davis, who is struggling, but sober for the first time in a very long time. Everyone might not be doing great, but they're okay.

We're okay.

We're going to be okay.

———

The next morning, I wake to the smell of coffee and the sound of my mom singing along to whatever song is playing in her head. It's kind of hard to tell what it is at first, since she's not the greatest singer, but the sound is comforting nonetheless.

After cleaning up in the bathroom, I pad out in my pajama pants and a t-shirt from my high school wrestling club.

"Hey, Mama," I say, wrapping an arm around her shoulders and giving her a hug while she attempts to scramble eggs.

"Hey, baby. You're up early."

"It's almost nine." I'm usually up before six for morning lift and conditioning.

She pauses for a moment. "Yeah, but you got in late last night, didn't you?"

"Not too late, but it was after ten. Sorry I didn't make it for dinner."

"That's alright, not like you could help it. What are the chances that you'd have two flat tires?" She throws up her hands, like *what're you gonna do about it*?

I didn't tell her about the tires being slashed. The last thing my mom needs is more stress on her plate. And honestly, I'm still processing what to do about that. Or what to do about what I did about it.

But that's not something I want to think about right now.

I notice there are only two plates out, so I pull out two coffee mugs and toast two English muffins. Mom brings the pan over and divvies out the eggs, putting enough for three people on my plate. I sprinkle some pepper on mine before we carry our plates to the table and sit across from one another.

It's quiet while we eat, neither of us knowing exactly what to say. Mom is smiling, but it's tired. The dark spots beneath her eyes are sunken. She looks like she's aged ten years just in the past few months.

"I talked to Davis last night."

"Oh, really?"

"Yeah. We hung out for a while before he kicked me out. Had a pretty good time until I made the mistake of asking him if he's okay."

Mom cringes. "He's going through a rough patch, but he'll get better. The doctor said he might experience lows like this for a few weeks or even months while his body and brain are getting used to the withdrawals." Her voice is strained, eyes filling with tears as she speaks. I don't miss the way her shoulders shake with the effort of holding it all back.

I move over next to her and pull her in for a hug. She doesn't sink into me and let me comfort her, instead patting my back and wiping her eyes before sitting up straight again like she didn't almost break down. I'm not sure how I feel about that. On one hand, I want to be here for her and take some of the pressure off. On the other, I've seen her break once before and it still haunts me. Even though I'm an adult now, I'm not sure I can stand to see her like that. It's selfish, I know.

Mom has to go to work for a few hours, so I clean up after breakfast and then head outside to check the patch job on the roof again and tighten a few screws on the loose porch railing. I do as much as I can to help around the house, but I know it's just little things. Things that make me feel like I'm helping even if I'm not solving anything real.

Davis doesn't leave his room all day, or at least not when I'm around to see it. The breakfast Mom left him goes untouched, but I notice the crackers from the plate I leave him at lunch disappear. He doesn't even come out when Mom arrives home with groceries. I help her carry them in and make a show out of turning up some music and singing and dancing while we cook dinner together, the way we used to when we were little.

He finally emerges for dinner, but barely picks at his food and doesn't contribute much to the conversation. It's clear he's trying though, so I try to appreciate that for what it is. Mom and I try to convince him to watch a movie with us, but he says he's tired and goes back to his room.

Later that night, I wake to a sound that scares the hell out of me.

From down the hall, I can hear gagging. Or choking. A desperate, helpless sound that I can't decide is due to illness or despair, or both.

I bolt down the hall and push Davis' door open. He's in bed, curled on his side, sweaty hair plastered to his face, trembling like he's freezing. His breath comes in short, panicked bursts. I'm not even sure if he's fully awake.

I sit on the edge of the bed and gather him against me, lifting him halfway onto my chest. He shivers, a violent tremor that I feel in my own bones.

"It's okay," I murmur, brushing his hair back. "I'm here."

His whole body jerks, and a groan tears out of him—low, raw, and so painful it breaks something inside me. I hold him tighter, noticing how small he feels in my arms.

My big brother. The man who sat on the sidelines of every one of my high school wrestling meets and practices, who took more than his fair brunt of the bullying in school. Whose wild antics used to both worry and amuse me. The man who hid his pain under so many layers, we never knew how bad his drinking had gotten. We had no idea he'd resorted to harder things when weed and alcohol didn't help numb the hurt he'd been covering for so long.

Now I'm holding him like he's made of glass while he sobs and dry heaves.

Once the worst of it has passed, I'm afraid he's going to kick me out again, but he doesn't. Instead, he lets me curl up next to him like we did when we were kids after Dad died.

I stay awake for hours after he finally drifts off, just listening to his breathing. Trying not to cry every time he groans or whimpers in his sleep. Trying not to cling harder, knowing he's drowning inside his own skin, and all I can do is keep him afloat for another night.

I should have stayed. It wasn't enough to transfer to a closer school. I should be here for him. For both of them.

Eventually I fall into a restless sleep, waking several times throughout the night. When I wake up again to daylight peeking around the edges of the blackout curtains, Davis isn't next to me. I'm pleasantly surprised to hear the shower running, and since Mom is in the living room, it must be him.

"Mom, we need to talk—"

"Don't," she says, stopping me in my tracks. "I know what you're going to say. And don't. Don't do it. He won't forgive himself if you do it. It'll just make things worse."

"I can take a semester off, help take care of things here, and go back when things are better."

She's not having any of it. "Absolutely not. I forbid it. And before you say that you're a grown adult and can do what you want, think it through. You'll lose your scholarship, your place on the team. And take it from someone who knows, it's harder to go back than you realize. All the hard work you've done to get this far will all be for nothing."

"I hate that I've left you both here alone to deal with everything," I say, eyes growing hot. "I should be here helping."

"You do help, Brody. So much more than you know. More than you should, when what you should be doing is experiencing the world and enjoying your college years, not taking care of us." She sighs. "I really mean it though, don't let him hear you talk about coming back. He's already messed up about you moving to Huntston."

"He is?"

"He was up early this morning. He told me about the Jamison boy."

I curse under my breath. "I'm sorry, I shouldn't have said anything."

"No, I'm glad you did. I think it might have given him some perspective."

By the time I have my things packed and I'm ready to head back to Huntston, I still haven't had a chance to really talk to Davis. He doesn't answer when I knock on his door, and I worry that the last time I see him will be the episode last night.

But as I'm walking out to my car, I'm surprised to find him sitting on the ratty old rocking chair on the porch.

"You gonna be alright?" He asks me.

"Are you?" I reply, returning his crooked smile.

"I'm gonna try." I hear what he doesn't say, that right now, trying is going to have to be enough.

I nod. It's something. I'll take it.

"And hey Brody—check in on your guy, yeah? Whatever it was, make it right."

"Yeah, okay. He's not my guy, though."

I pull out of the driveway, leaving a smiling Davis behind me.

World Wrestling Cup 2016

CHAPTER 9
BECK

For a guy who absolutely does *not* want to see Brody Miller, I'm spending an alarming amount of time trying to keep tabs on him.

Not in a weird way. Or an interested way, even. It's a strategic way.

A *know your enemy's movements* kind of way.

A *make sure he doesn't sneak up behind you and reenact the worst moment of your life but worse* kind of way.

Totally normal captain stuff.

That's what I tell myself as I sit next to the window on the third-floor common room, pretending to scroll my phone while actually staring at the parking lot like I'm waiting for an important package. Freshmen play pool behind me, yelling and laughing and living their carefree lives while I sit here marinating in dread and lust and shame and whatever the hell else this is that I'm feeling.

I haven't been sleeping well this weekend. Not since... Okay, that first night I slept like a goddamn baby. I'm not even sure how I got back to my room, all I know is I woke up pantsless with my dick in my hand. But as soon as the morning fog cleared from my mind and I realized what I had done, and what I had dreamt about all night, I couldn't deal. Every time I close my eyes, I'm back in the stairwell. Back under his control.

You like this.

I bet you want to come for me.

Come.

Lust crawls down my spine. I pinch the inside of my arm until it stings and the feeling eases.

I'm a mess. A complete catastrophe of emotions full of rage and humiliation and an overwhelming urge to jerk off constantly.

And the worst part is, I don't even know which of those feelings is the loudest.

Sometimes I'm furious. Livid. I'm pissed and embarrassed and pissed at just how embarrassed I am, and I want to beat the shit out of him.

I live on the edge of ready to fight him the second he walks back through the door and prove I'm not the weak, pathetic, shuddering mess he saw last week.

Brody caught me by surprise and I acted out of character, but it damn sure won't happen again. In fact, if Brody even looks at me funny, I'll make him sorry he ever glanced in my direction.

Then again, there are moments when I remember—no matter how much I try very, very hard *not* to remember—the absolute burning euphoria that coursed through my veins. Because of the way he looked at me. The way he took control of my mind and my body. It was like everything else just melted away, and—

Nope. No. Absolutely not.

I pinch my arm harder. I shouldn't get enjoyment out of the terrible, degrading things he said to me. Or the way he looked at me like I was nothing, just a sorry piece of meat that he found wanting.

And I didn't. I *didn't* like it.

I don't like that sort of thing. I don't want it to happen again.

Ever.

Not even a little.

God. I need help.

Just when I convince myself Brody might have come to his senses and decided to drop out of school or transfer back to the Midwest, headlights swing into the lot. My breath hitches as Brody's shitty blue hatchback pulls in.

Brody climbs out and rolls his shoulders back like he might be sore. His posture suggests that he's tired, as if the weekend drained him as much as it did me. He grabs his duffel and starts towards the dorm.

I definitely do not scramble down the stairs to the main lobby and casually sit on one of the couches near the door. That would be ridiculous.

When our eyes meet, it shouldn't come as a surprise. But I startle. He holds my gaze for three seconds, maybe four. Long enough that something tightens low in my gut.

Then he takes a step forward and opens his mouth like he might want to say something. And nope.

Nope. Nope. Nope.

I'm out of my seat before the thought finishes forming, knocking into his shoulder as I push past him and out of the building to sprint down the walkway that leads to Caty's campus apartment.

I practically break her door down with the force of my knocking.

She opens it mid-sip of a Diet Coke, blinking at me as I fidget nervously in her doorway. "Jesus, Beck. Did you kill someone? Do I need to help you hide a body? You know there are people that you can pay to do that, right?"

"I need to talk," I choke out.

She widens her eyes and steps aside. "Well, this should be good."

I drop onto her sofa and bury my face in my hands. It takes a few deep breaths to get started, but once I do, the words pour out of me. I tell her everything. And I do mean everything—The stairwell, how he held me against the wall with his hand on my throat, the way I froze and didn't fight back. The way my body reacted, the way *he* reacted, and the way I've been spiraling ever since.

By the time I finish, Caty has tears streaming down her cheeks.

From laughing.

"Caty, this isn't funny."

"Oh, honey." She wheezes, clutching her stomach. "It's *hilarious.*"

"Catyyyy," I moan, burying my face in a throw pillow.

"Big, scary, uptight Captain Lincoln Beckett got manhandled by the guy you've been treating like shit for weeks, and you *liked it.*"

"I didn't like it," I snap.

"I do believe you just said, and I quote, *I came so hard I nearly passed out and he didn't even touch me.* Babe, that means you liked it. You liked it a lot."

I groan. "Why are you like this?"

She wipes a tear. "Well, we know why you're like this."

I glare.

"What? Beck, I've been your beard for two years. I could give a TED Talk about how your brain works and your fucked up family dynamics."

"I don't want to hear this."

"Shush. Yes, you do." She sits back, crossing one leg over the other. "Let me tell you exactly why you reacted the way you did."

"I didn't react—"

"Oh my God, shut up. You *reacted* so hard you nearly blacked out," she says. "Literally *and* figuratively."

I bury my face in the pillow again. She rips it away. I never could hide from her.

"Listen," she says, all fake-serious. "You've been under pressure your entire life. You're the golden son of a demanding man, captain of a team that worships you, a straight-A student. You're the worst kind of perfectionist and judge yourself for every perceived slip, even things beyond your control. You can never falter, never have a single crease or crack in your perfect little façade."

"Caty."

"This is relevant," she insists. "Because of what that kind of pressure does to a person. Especially someone wired like you. All that self-control? All that rigidity? All that need to be in charge of every little thing around you?"

She taps her fist lightly against my forehead. I reflexively run my fingers through my hair to smooth it down.

"You're a rubber band stretched so tight you squeak when you breathe."

"That's not—"

"And when someone finally out-muscles you," she continues, her voice softening just a fraction, "when someone *takes* the control out of your hands, even for a second? Your brain interprets that as relief. A release valve. A break from the constant strain you put on yourself."

I go very still. Because as much as I don't appreciate being read, what she says definitely checks with how I felt in that moment.

She nudges me with her foot. "It's not the degrading that gets you hot, babe. It's the surrender. The letting go. The feeling of not being the one responsible for once."

My cheeks burn, and Caty looks entirely too pleased with herself.

"It's why you've always had issues getting it up during finals week or whenever your dad breathes too close to you. I've told you for years that you need therapy, a weighted blanket, and better lube."

I glare harder. "Shut up."

"And it's why this thing with Brody hit you so hard," she finishes, voice turning gentle in the exact way that makes it worse. "Because in that moment, even though you were mortified, over-whelmed, and terrified he'd see too much... your body interpreted the loss of control as the first actual breath of relief it's been given in who knows how long."

My chest feels tight. I feel embarrassed and exposed. Not so much because Caty recognizes all of this. But because Brody obviously did, too. Who else can see through me well enough to tell that I'm really just a tightly wound freak?

"And that," she says, grabbing her Diet Coke, "is why you came like a porn star on fast-forward."

"Caty."

She pats my knee. "Congratulations, sweetheart. You're not a freak. You're just emotionally constipated."

"Fuck you."

"Um, no thanks. Ew. Not my thing. Although I am a top, and you are clearly a bottom."

"The fuck I am!" My cheeks flame with indignant anger. I love the girl, but how dare she?

"And who said that's a bad thing, honey? Do I need to delve into all the reasons you consider bottoming negative? Because they're almost all the same reasons why you're going to *loooove* getting fucked."

"No one is fucking me. And I hate you."

"No you don't. Because I will always tell you the truth." She smiles sweetly, the same smile that fools my dad and all the other socialite parents. "And because I always tell you the truth, I'm going to be honest about one more thing. You fucked up, Beck. Messing with his car was a low blow, and you're lucky he didn't actually beat the shit out of you."

"First of all, *I* didn't mess with his car—"

"You knew it was happening and didn't stop it. Same thing."

"And second, he wouldn't beat the shit out of me. I could take him."

Her grin is slow and savage. "You're right. I bet you would."

My entire face, chest, ears, and brain feel like they might burst into flame.

Caty pats my knee. "You should probably apologize and pay him back for the tires. We all know he isn't as well off as the rest of the students here, those probably set him back more than however much time he lost since he was clearly on his way out."

"Not going to happen." After this conversation, I'm giving serious consideration to dropping out and moving myself out to the Midwest. If there's even a small part of Brody that recognizes what my best friend just enlightened me with, I'll never look him in the eye again.

"Right. Because you don't want to be in his good graces." She smirks. "You want to be under his—"

I throw a pillow at her head. She cackles.

———

I avoid Brody for the rest of the week. Or at least, I try to. But he's everywhere. Always at a table nearby in the dining hall or library. Lifting in the gym every morning. And at practice every afternoon.

It's infuriating.

What's worse is that he won't fight me like a normal teammate. Not really.

He thinks I don't know what he's doing, but he lets me dominate every drill. Lets me take the lead. Lets me pin him when I know— deep down, humiliatingly—that he could break out of my hold anytime he wanted to. He knows it. I know it. And it's maddening. *He* is maddening. And by the time Thursday rolls around, almost a full week after our stairwell incident, my nerves are frayed.

"What the hell is your deal?" I snap after practice.

Brody blinks at me like I'm asking him to solve a difficult math equation. "*My* deal?" Maybe he isn't as clever as I've been giving him credit for.

"You're not even trying."

His head tilts. A slow realization dawns in his eyes.

"Ah," he says, like he's solved it. "You're mad I've been letting you win."

Blood drains from my face. "You haven't been *letting*—"

"Lin—*Beckett*," he amends, stepping closer and closing the distance between us. He lowers his voice. "Look, I feel bad about what happened. In the, uh, stairwell. I shouldn't have gone there like that. I've been trying to ease off and give you space."

"You're not giving me space, you're trying to turn me into a joke."

"What? No. I just... You care a whole lot about how you look to other people. And I didn't want you to feel challenged or intimidated."

I scoff. "As if you could intimidate me."

Brody's jaw ticks. "I'm trying to be *nice*. Trying to make sure you know I'm not going to go spreading your little secret around. And I wanted you to feel comfortable, so I've been holding back so you can feel like you're in control."

My jaw clenches. "I *am* in control," I grit out.

"Right. Because you're the captain. The top dog." His tone makes it obvious how much he believes those words.

My arms cross, and a wave of humiliation runs the length of me. Because I'm fucking broken, my body interprets it in a way I absolutely do not agree with. *I don't like it.*

"I've been trying to be a nice guy, but if you're dead set on pushing my buttons," he continues, voice low enough no one else hears, "I'll show you just how easy I've been on you."

My breath stutters, but I can't give him the upper hand. I just can't. Because not only do I not want him to win this little standoff that's starting to get the attention of the rest of the team, but there's a fucked up part of me that *does* want to push his buttons.

I step closer, squaring off. A wordless challenge to answer his.

"Fine. You want to act like a little bitch," he murmurs, "then no more nice Brody. No more letting you flip and pin me. Tomorrow I'll show you who's in charge."

Wait. *Tomorrow?*

"Tomorrow?"

He grins. "I hope you're ready to put on a good show in front of the student body and all our friends and family members."

My stomach lurches. Tomorrow night is the intra-squad showcase where the team shows off our skills by pairing up against each other. And of course, Brody and I are the only ones in our weight class. So we have no choice but to match against each other.

"Oh, and hey Captain?" he adds, leaning in close enough that his breath grazes my cheek. "Try not to get hard in front of your dad."

I shove him away so fast I almost fall over.

He only laughs.

———

The second Coach calls our names, something low in my stomach tightens so sharply I almost pitch forward. It's ridiculous—I'm not nervous. I'm not. I know I can beat him. I've beaten bigger, stronger, tougher guys. I've crushed athletes he couldn't handle on their best day. That's what I'm telling myself, at least.

Realistically, I know well enough that Brody is an exceptional athlete. He wouldn't have the stats he does if he weren't, and he wouldn't have earned a scholarship to one of the best Division

One schools in the region. But I'm a damn good athlete, too. And really, when I think hard about it, we've never truly faced off against each other. Because the first time I was too shocked and horrified by what happened, and every time since I've been too scared.

I need to stop being scared.

But the moment my eyes land on him across the mats—hair damp, shoulders loose, expression annoyingly relaxed—a hot, traitorous twitch sparks in my gut.

Not now. Not here. Christ, please not here.

I force my lungs to stay even, force my jaw to lock, force my brain to behave. In a room full of parents, siblings, alumni, and my own goddamn father, I will *not* let my body give away anything.

I pinch the skin on the inside of my arm hard enough that I know it's going to add another odd bruise, but it's better than the alternative. Pain helps. Pain focuses. Pain redirects.

The twitch subsides. And once I've gotten my bearings, I look up at the stands to where my father is watching me with a stone-faced expression. Next to him, Caty is grinning and waving with a knowing look on her face that I both love and hate her for. She places a small hand on my father's shoulders and bats her eyes up at him innocently as she says who knows what, and he actually laughs.

That girl is some kind of witch, I swear it.

The ref calls us up to the mat. Brody steps up first, rolling his shoulders like he's warming up for a dance floor instead of a wrestling match. He looks like he's having fun—as always, like this is a game, not something that matters.

He shakes my hand with a smile that borders on wicked. I grip harder than I should.

Then we crouch into position.

"Set."

My stance tightens automatically. Weight forward, hips low, elbows tucked. I talk myself through it. I have the height advantage and a longer reach. If I focus, I should be able to easily control the pace.

The whistle blows.

We circle each other. He reaches with his left hand, and I dodge it and swat it away. He chuckles. That bastard actually chuckles. But his cockiness gives me an opening. I throw myself at him, taking him down with my shoulder in his hip and my hands wrapped around the back of his thighs.

He's sturdy, and the moment of resistance lasts long enough that I mentally start recalculating, but I keep my feet driving, head up, my chest to his thigh. His balance shifts, and I get the takedown as we crash down to the mat. Brody is already building up on his base, trying to peel my hands away. I hook his ankle with my leg and press my weight forward.

God, he's strong. He keeps turning his hips, forcing me to slide my chest higher across his shoulders.

"Ride him out!" one of my teammates encourages.

Brody makes a sound, halfway between a groan and a chuckle. "Yeah, Beckett. Ride me out. You can take it."

He shifts his hips, pressing up into me like he's thrusting, no longer trying to escape but pulling me down on him harder. I falter, and he snaps his hips out from under me. My grip slips, and he catches my right arm, hooks it tight, and rolls. His back brushes the mat for an instant before he's behind me.

I hit the mat with my palms, scrambling to turn, but he drives forward, chest against my back. Coach calls the points for the reversal. *Fuck.*

I try to shift my weight to get leverage, but he presses hard into my back. His hands reach under my arms to lock my wrist. No matter how much I try to bridge and roll, he's got me pinned down.

Coach is counting. The more I wriggle and fight, the harder he presses into me, and I can feel... it. I fight harder, managing to roll a little, but he forces me flat again, breathing into my ear.

"Is this how you want it? Want me to hold you down and ride your ass while you writhe beneath me?"

The period ends with my mind reeling, my gut churning, and my cock stirring but thankfully not too noticeably awake.

The coin toss for the second period lands in Brody's favor.

"Top," he says immediately, voice steady and unbothered. He gives me a smirk only I can see as I drop to the mat. I try to ignore it. I try to ignore the way his hands glide confidently, strategically, over my hips as he sets position.

"This feels familiar," he murmurs near my ear. His breath pools warm against my cheek. "You're shaking."

I suck in a sharp breath. "Shut up."

He chuckles. "Careful, Captain. You don't want them all to know, do you?"

"Know what?" I grind out.

"That you want me to fuck you just like this."

My vision goes electric-white for a moment.

The whistle blows, and he moves fast, quicker than I anticipate. His grip is ruthless, bearing down on me in a way that feels like he's mocking me. I try to drive upward, but he anticipates each shift, tightening his hold until I'm pinned on my back.

Coach counts.

Brody's face hovers above mine, breath ragged, cheeks flushed. His eyes flick downward—towards where our bodies are pressed indecently close—and a thoughtful expression crosses his face.

"Like this would be okay too," he says softly. "I'd get to see your face when you take my big—"

I buck, and he leans forward, trying to secure control, but I catch a gap at his side and twist hard, grabbing his arm and pulling just enough to break his grip. My momentum carries me forward and I spring up, practically tackling him. My chest slams against his, and before he can react, I'm on top, hooking my legs around his to control the movement of his hips, pinning him flat against the mat.

With our chests pressed together, arms tight and legs entwined, I can feel every inch of him. His heart beats frantically against mine. For the first moment he doesn't move, but as soon as Coach starts the count, he struggles, elbows scraping, but I've got leverage and a good hold.

Not daring to chance looking down at him, I huff out a raspy, "You're the one that's going to take it."

He fucking laughs, the fight giving out of him as Coach finishes the count and blows the whistle.

I push off Brody and get ready to go again, keeping my eyes focused on him and how out of control he makes me feel. How angry that makes me. How desperate.

I'm definitely getting hard, but I bend at the waist and ignore it, hoping it's not too noticeable. The thought has me flashing back to the comments he made about my dick size—which was bullshit, by the way. I might not be as big as him, but I'm still on the larger side of average. I've measured from several angles just to be sure.

His massive cock-having self is the one that should be worried about getting hard.

Yes.

He should be the one who's worried.

Suddenly, I know what I need to do. I need to turn the tables on him. I need him to be the one to lose the match and walk away with an erection, especially because I know everyone in the room would be able to see it. He'd be lucky if it stayed in the stupidly tiny shorts.

It's my choice now, and I know the right move is to choose a neutral or bottom position, but there's no part of my pride that will allow me to say the word *bottom* around Brody Miller and I don't give a fuck what Caty and her judgmental psychoanalyzing bullshit has to say about that.

"Top," I say firmly. Let's see how he handles me behind him.

His eyebrows lift, amused. My pulse stutters.

We set up, and when the whistle blows I press my chest harder into Brody's back, hands gripping his hips to control their movement. I try to quickly get control of his arms, but Brody shifts his elbows inside, posts his hands, and rolls, closing the gap. I drop forward to try and press him onto his back.

We're chest to chest again, bodies intertwined, legs braced for balance, hands grappling for control of each other's arms. Every time I press forward, he rolls slightly, elbow inside, trying to free himself, but we're locked in a stalemate, sweaty and breathing hard as we continue to grapple.

My lips part to let out a short puff of air, and Brody's eyes lock on my mouth. I lick my lips in response, almost forgetting that I'm supposed to be the one teasing him this time. I roll my hips slightly, and Brody's answering chuckle is dark and dangerous, sending a rash of chill bumps down my spine.

"I'll make you a deal," Brody rasps. "If you win this match, I'll let you fuck me in whatever position you like."

He huffs as our arms thread, hips shifting, each of us trying to tilt the other. We're rubbing against each other in a way that feels dangerous, but I can feel him getting harder, too. I lean into it, but I can't really say if it's to fuck with him or feel him. I forget for a moment that we have an audience.

"But if I win..." He locks my wrist and shifts his hips against me. "You're mine to use as I please."

I switch my angle, trying to focus on getting out rather than getting away. If my cock keeps rubbing against him like that...

He sprawls when I shift, and I roll, but it gets me nowhere. It's just a back-and-forth struggle.

"Come on, Captain. What's it going to be? You afraid of losing?"

"You. Wish. Asshole."

"That feels like a yes to me," he groans. The sound stuns me for half a second, but it's enough for him to make a subtle move, turning his hips and taking advantage of the slight shift in my balance. He pops up, chest heavy into my shoulder, hooks the arm closest to him, and drives me onto my back. The whistle blows, and he groans in a way that sounds filthy and pained at the same time.

The whistle blows again, and Coach makes some notes on his clipboard.

Brody wins—by one point.

The crowd claps politely. Teammates slap Brody on the back. My father stares down at me with a look that could peel skin off bone.

Brody turns, breathing hard, a half-smile tugging at his mouth.

"Good match," he says softly. There's no mockery in it, but I can't register it for anything other than the loss it is. And the fact that I know I didn't lose because he's better than me. I lost because some part of me—some twisted, shameful part—is more afraid of what I want than of failing.

And that terrifies me more than anything he has planned for me when he collects his *winnings*.

World Wrestling Clubs Cup 2016

CHAPTER 10
BRODY

I spend a solid thirty seconds after the match trying to catch my breath and pretend I'm fine. I'm not. I'm not fine at all.

My dick is staging a full rebellion in my singlet. Coach walks by, clapping a hand on my shoulder and chuckling to himself.

"Jesus Christ, Miller," he mutters with a wheezy laugh. "Hit the showers. Walk it off, kid."

I choke on nothing and duck my head, pushing past him and straight for the showers.

Cold water. I need cold water. Or a lobotomy.

The locker room is blessedly empty. I strip out of my uniform so fast I almost tear the strap and stand under water cold enough it could legally classify as torture.

It doesn't help.

Not with the way Beckett looked tonight. All pissed and determined and... *Fuck.*

I think I might actually want Lincoln Beckett. I thought I was just playing with him, but that little display back there fucking did things to me.

When I can finally stand up straight without embarrassing myself, I towel off and pull on a pair of sweats. I'm about to head back to the gym to watch the end of the showcase and mingle when I hear voices.

I freeze on instinct, back hitting the wall. I'm not sure why until I register the familiar biting tone. It's low, controlled, and venomous.

"...one point? One point? That's what you bring me? This is unacceptable, Lincoln. I expect better from you."

Lincoln?

I almost step out, because surely someone isn't talking to *the* Lincoln Beckett that way. But then Beckett's voice replies, small and defeated and unlike anything I've ever heard from him.

"I'm sorry I disappointed you. It was a close—"

"Close? Close is for losers. I didn't raise a son to settle for close. I raised you to win. To dominate."

Damn. Mr. Beckett is just as cold as he seemed sitting in the stands. I kind of feel bad for taunting my surly captain with his dad now.

I inch closer, not enough to be seen, but enough to feel the barbs in his voice when he starts talking about me.

"You embarrassed yourself. And me. You had every advantage, and you still managed to fail. You choked and handed what should have been an easy victory to some bottom-feeding charity case like the Miller boy?"

Ah, there it is. I was wondering when my social status would enter the conversation. It's good to know exactly where I stand with people before I ever even meet them. Not that it's surprising at all. Most of these people are all the same.

But Mr. Beckett isn't done. His voice cuts through the air, hitting his son like a lash from a belt would.

"Do you know what people saw out there? They saw a future CEO getting pushed around by a low-class scholarship nobody. You don't let trash like that take anything from you. Not points. Not ground. And certainly not your goddamn dignity."

My jaw cracks from clenching.

"What do you think happens to Beckett Holdings if its heir apparent gets manhandled by someone whose greatest accomplishment is likely to be a minimum wage job as a factory worker? You think shareholders want a weak link at the top?"

Jesus Christ. What an asshole.

He lowers his voice, crueler than anything I've ever heard.

"You've gone soft, Lincoln. Weak. Hesitant. I didn't spend years grooming you for leadership just for you to fold the second someone with calloused hands grabs you."

Calloused hands? Obviously he means me, but does that mean he's picturing me touching his son? Overpowering him?

Does he have any idea how close he is to the truth?

Meanwhile, Beckett stands there, taking it, because this is normal to him. And this was only an intra-squad matchup. A friendly showcase for friends and family. It wasn't even a real competition.

"You are not here to *try*," Mr. Beckett finishes. "You are here to crush anyone beneath you. Do you understand?"

Beckett's answer is barely a whisper. "Yes, sir."

My chest aches for the boy that had to grow up with a parent like that. No wonder he takes everything too seriously, can't enjoy anything.

Before I can move, the team floods the locker room. Noise explodes everywhere. Mr. Beckett snaps into his polite-parent persona like flipping a light switch.

He walks out, and Beckett moves to follow him. Instinctively, I follow Beckett. He stops in the hallway, shoulders still rigid. I take a step toward him without thinking.

His entire body snaps upright. He slams the side of his fist against the locker room door like he's been caught doing something he shouldn't. Then he turns to me with a perfect, hard-edged mask.

"Here to gloat?"

My eyebrows shoot up. Does he know I saw the whole interaction with his father?

He steps closer. Not touching, but crowding, trying to reclaim some of the dominance his father just ripped out of him. Trying to act like the version of himself he thinks he's supposed to be.

"You did win, after all," he says, jaw tight. "One point. Maybe that's something to brag about where you're from."

There it is. A sharp little jab, a direct imitation of his father's cruelty.

His posture and tone don't give me the impression he's acting out for the sake of insulting me. No, I think he wants me mad. He wants me to fight back, because fighting me is familiar and safe. It's a distraction from everything clouding his mind right now.

He wants the heat, not the hurt.

I step into his space, slow and intentionally. "You offering excuses now?"

He bristles. "I'm not offering anything."

"Funny," I say softly, "You already offered yourself."

His breath catches, and I see it. A spark. There's some trepidation there, sure. Definitely some unresolved rage. But more than anything, what I see is interest. Need. *Want.*

Before I can press further, a girl calls his name. Then his father barks his name sharply.

"Lincoln. It's rude to make people wait for you."

I watch Beckett's spine straighten. Watch him plaster on a too-bright smile. Watch him transform.

He walks out of the hallway with purpose, and I slink around the corner to watch, keeping myself out of view from his father.

A tiny girl in a frilly top launches herself at Lin—*No.* Just Beckett. I think I understand now why he doesn't like people to use his first name. After hearing all of that, I'll never call him Lincoln again. Beckett picks her up like she weighs nothing and spins her around once. When he places her back on her feet, Mr. Beckett gives him a curt handshake before bending to give the girl a double-cheek kiss. She giggles.

As Mr. Beckett walks away, *my* Beckett bends down to whisper something against her lips.

The burn in my stomach turns molten, but I don't look away. I pay attention. And I notice that he's not actually kissing her. He's using her as armor. He wants people to see him kiss her—wants his father to see it.

And when he cuts his eyes in my direction, I know it's also for me. He wants me to see it. He wants me to react. Because he wants to get under my skin, rile me up for what he really wants.

A distraction. Something intense to wipe out the echo of his father's voice and all that heavy anxiety he carries around.

When he finally says goodbye to the girl and walks back towards the hallway, I speak before I can stop myself.

"Who was that?"

"My girlfriend," he says.

I snort. "No shit?"

"No shit."

My eye twitches, even knowing he's doing this on purpose.

"Does she know you're going to be choking on my cock later?"

He chokes, eyes huge. "What... the fuck?"

"I won, didn't I?"

"By one point."

"Still sounds like I won."

"You think one point is worth—"

"Did I or did I not win?"

"Technically, yes, but—"

"And wasn't the deal that I get you any way I want you?"

He doesn't answer, gaping at me without anything left to say. "Well then, technically," I say, lowering my voice so only he hears, "you're going to get down on your knees and suck me."

I watch the exact moment his breath picks up. His pupils darken. And his dick presses against his shorts like it's trying to escape.

"That's interesting," I murmur, cutting my eyes to the front of his uniform..

"It's—because I'm angry," he blurts. "It's... angry. An angry boner."

I grin so hard it hurts. "Can't wait to see how angry it gets later. Midnight. Outside the rec room."

"You can't be serious."

"As serious as your angry boner," I say, adjusting myself just to watch him turn red before I walk away.

———

I get to the rec room early. Not because I'm eager. Okay, maybe because I'm eager.

Mostly it's so I can hide in the shadows near the stairwell and see him come down the hall, but I almost miss him because the bastard shows up at eleven forty-fucking-five.

"Eager, are we?" I say, turning my own eagerness on him.

He jumps, then scowls at me. "Says the guy who got here even earlier to lurk like some kind of creeper."

"Well, at least we know it's dark enough." I smirk. "And duh, of course I'm eager. I'm about to get my dick sucked."

He hesitates. "About that..."

"Going back on a challenge so easily?" I tease, although obviously I'd never force him to do something he doesn't actually want to do. The thing is, I truly believe he does want it. He just needs the excuse as a cover. He needs the direction and dominance to get him out of his head.

"N-no!" he says way too fast. "I just... I'm not into men. So I've never done... *that*... before."

"Ah," I say, nodding in a way that makes him think I believe him. I don't. "I understand."

"You do?" he asks, hopeful.

"You're scared," I say simply. "But don't worry. I won't hurt you unless you want me to."

His whole damn body reacts. Even in the dark, I can see him fold forward a fraction, like he's trying to hide the way his hips jerk. Oh yeah, he wants this. He wants it bad.

I step closer.

"Is it the dirty talk?" I ask quietly. "Or the humiliation?"

He shakes his head. "I don't know what you're talking about."

"That's okay," I say, letting my mouth drop low enough to brush along his neck. "I'll figure it out myself."

I lean in, lips almost touching his ear.

"Get on your knees."

CHAPTER 11
BECK

"Is it the dirty talk or the humiliation?"

The question echoes in my mind, bouncing around my skull and lighting up neuro-pathways that didn't exist before. His voice, curious and taunting, makes me think he already knows the answer. It's the same way Caty dissected my psyche like a puzzle that was meant to be solved. It's almost as if Brody can already see what I am beneath the layers of exterior polish I've cultivated.

I am a perfectionist, a master of control in myself and everything around me. I'm a champion, a leader, an influence to others.

"You're a rubber band stretched so tight you squeak when you breathe."

Can I be all of those things and still crave the surrender of someone else taking charge? Someone who doesn't put the same expectations on my shoulders that everyone else does?

My father demands perfection. My team demands leadership. Even my relationship with Caty demands a façade when we aren't behind locked doors.

Every facet of my life demands control. But Brody demands nothing. Nothing except the soft underbelly of the hardened shell I show to the world. Nothing but the truth of who I am at my basest level.

And my surrender.

This asshole wants me to service him, and I don't want to. I don't want to.

I don't!

But if I'm honest with myself, there's a part of me—a small, ugly, shameful part of me—that is quite literally twitching with anticipation. Vibrating like my veins are live wires sending pulses of electricity to and from those secret pathways in my brain and body I can't seem to turn off ever since that day in the stairwell. The day that awakened the part of me that came alive when he stripped me of my control and told me exactly what to do.

I clamp my teeth together like I can bite off the urge to answer instead of insisting I don't know what he's talking about.

Maybe he can see me. Or maybe this is just a game to him. A game he won. A game I didn't have to agree to, but did, because deep down part of me craves the downward spiral into oblivion.

His breath brushes over the sensitive skin of my neck and sends a shiver down my spine. He's talking to me, but the feel of the words spoken over the shell of my ear is louder than his voice.

It takes too long to process the words that made my knees so weak. I had to lock them up to avoid buckling to the floor.

"Get on your knees."

"W-wha– *already*?" My mind scrambles to make sense of things, to stall the inevitability of the moment. "But it's not midnight yet," I say dumbly.

Brody smirks. "No time like the present. We might as well get it over with. Unless you want to talk about your feelings or something first." His words are delivered in a biting, sarcastic tone, but underneath it, I get the odd feeling that he's serious.

The idea of talking about what's happening here, admitting to any part of it out loud, is far scarier than the idea of putting his dick in my mouth. And he knows it.

I swallow thickly, then flinch when Brody places a firm hand on my shoulders. "I won't repeat myself again, Beckett. Get on your knees, or I'll make you."

There's something wrong with my legs. Some kind of muscle malfunction or stroke-like activity that shuts down how they're supposed to function. They buckle and fold so easily, it's like Brody's voice has more control over them than my own brain does.

"Good boy," Brody croons, combing his fingers through my hair. My eyes flutter, the gentle scratch of his fingernails on my scalp lulling me into a peaceful, docile moment where I forget what we're here to do and just sink into a blissful state.

I'm barely able to keep myself rooted in reality, but I cling to an edge of sanity just long enough to dart my eyes around the dark room. "What if someone comes down here?" I ask, my voice a rough whisper. It's a Saturday, and although most of the dorm is either out partying or hanging out in the rec room, there's always a chance someone might decide to take the back stairwell. Most people use the elevator or the larger set of stairs at the front of the building, but plenty of people who live towards the back of the dorms use this stairwell regularly.

Brody shrugs, like getting caught with his dick out wouldn't be a big deal. Of course, he'd be the one getting his dick sucked, not caught on his knees submitting to someone he hates, so it'd be way less embarrassing. Does he not care if anyone knows he's hooking up with a guy?

No, not hooking up. This isn't a hookup. It's a bet. A power exchange. A way to humiliate and embarrass me. My punishment for being a weak asshole.

"You didn't see me when you came down here," Brody says, giving me a sliver of peace of mind.

"But what if–"

"You need to think less," Brody says. "Think less and pay attention to me more. Because right now, I'm in charge. You might get to be top dog everywhere else, but right now, I'm your fucking captain. Understand?"

I don't answer. I can't. My vocal cords basically collapse. It takes so much mental fortitude to keep myself from nodding that I start to sweat. My mouth is dry.

"What's wrong, puppy? Don't want to call me captain?"

Brody combs his hand through my hair one more time, then brings it around the back of my head and around to cup my face. His thumb presses against my lips, caresses back and forth, before applying pressure. My lips and teeth part, letting him push into my mouth. It tastes faintly of salt and soap, the skin smooth as it glides over the tip of my tongue. Suddenly my mouth is no longer dry. Instead, there's an abundance of saliva that I don't know what to do with. I can't get my throat to work to swallow, but the movement of my neck to attempt it seems to encourage him to push his thumb in farther to stroke over my tongue.

"That's it," he croons. "Turn off your brain and open that pretty mouth for me."

His thumb disappears only to be replaced by two long, thick fingers. They push into my mouth, filling my senses with more of the vague reminder of salt and soap. They rub back and forth over my tongue, pushing farther back, testing my gag reflex.

He hooks my bottom teeth and pulls me towards him as he bends down to put his face in mine. His breath is soft, warm, and smells sweet, brushing over my spit-covered open lips in a husky whisper. "If at any point you want to back down, all you have to do is tap me twice on the hip, and when I pull out, call me captain. Got it?"

I don't respond fast enough, because he yanks my head up and down, then side to side. "Do you understand me? You do what I say and choke on my cock, or you call me your captain. That's your safe word."

Finally, I give in and nod my agreement. He pushes practically his whole hand deeper into my mouth, my jaw forced to widen, purposefully pressing the back of my throat to make me gag. My gaze lifts to glance at him, curious to see how he's reacting to me like this, and let out a breath through my nose, not realizing that I'd been holding it. Drool leaks from the corners of my mouth and down my chin, and a tear falls from the water gathering in my eyes.

This seems to encourage him. He bites his lip as a low, almost silent pleased sounding groan escapes from his full, parted lips.

"Unzip me," he orders, in a gentle yet still commanding tone.

I blink a few times in hesitation, but Brody presses harder on the back of my tongue, tickling that reflex to cough.

As if on autopilot, my hands reach out and unfasten the button of his faded blue jeans, slowly lowering the zipper. The sound of it echoes in the space, making me realize how loud our breathing is.

With his free hand, Brody reaches into his pants and pulls his cock out. I'm vaguely aware of him stroking himself, but I don't dare look away from the intense eye contact that has me locked on stormy blue eyes that almost look black in the dim lighting. The way the red glow of the exit sign is shadowing and highlighting his normally soft features makes him look otherworldly. Demonic, maybe.

My mouth is empty for just long enough for me to swallow the excessive spit that's built up. God, how long have we been here already? It feels like forever and yet no time at all. Normally, I'd be counting the seconds and minutes, mentally calculating the time the way I subconsciously do during every moment of the day, especially during conversations. But I've let go of every other thought other than what's happening here and now.

The moment the blunt head of Brody's cock replaces his fingers, I stop thinking about anything at all other than the command to lick the results of my teasing from his leaking head, and the feel of him pushing inside and over my tongue.

I expect him to hold my head and use my face like a cock sleeve, taking my mouth as harshly as his words fucked my brain. It's what I would have done. Instead, he's slow and gentle, letting me ease into the act of letting another man slide his truly massive cock into my mouth while I attempt to unhinge my tight jaw to accommodate him. I'm only taking half of him in, simply holding my mouth open to let him feed me his dick.

"There we go. That's not so bad, is it? You're taking me so good. I know you like the taste of my cock on your tongue." He says soothingly, wiping a stray drop of spit from my cheek. It makes me realize that going slow isn't something he's doing for my benefit—it's a tactic. He's not going to let me just get this over and done with quickly. He's going to make me categorize and remember every insufferable moment.

He's making me feel the weight of his flesh. Coating my tongue with the flavor of his salty cum. Making me taste and feel him so neither of us can walk away from tonight without processing exactly what occurred here tonight.

Brody gives a few experimental thrusts, still cupping my jaw like I'm something precious while he violates my face. Because that's what this is. Consensual or not, it's a violation. A ruining. Not just because I've been forced to my knees to submit to him, to suffer the indignity of him using my mouth for his pleasure. And not because of the potential of someone opening the door not even two feet away from us and seeing me on my knees for him. But because my cock is harder than it's ever been, pressing against my pants in the most painfully obvious way, leaking enough pre-cum that I wouldn't be surprised if I look like I've pissed myself by the end of this.

Brody gives a satisfied growl and tells me to "suck". My lips close around him, my tongue curling up to feel the smooth, silky skin of his wet cock pushing in and out of my mouth. Brody's hand moves to cup the back of my head, gently guiding me to bob up and down the length of him.

He wasn't kidding when he said he was bigger than me. In fact, no matter how far on the large side of average I am, my cock would look pathetically small next to his. The realization sends a confusing surge of humiliation and excited pleasure through my body, and I squeeze my thighs together. My fingers dig into the fabric of his jeans to prevent myself from using them to get myself off while he uses my mouth.

"That's right, baby, suck me harder. Make your captain come like the good little cock slut you are."

A shiver wracks my body, and I push forward, impaling my throat on him and making me gag.

"Oh, fuck yes. Like that. Choke on it."

A whimper tears out of me when Brody's fingers grip into the back of my hair and he starts thrusting to meet my mouth. My hand flies up, instinctively wrapping around the base of his cock to keep him from going too far back. He bucks and moans out a curse when my hand tightens around him.

My eyes are so watery I can't make out his expression, but I get flashes of the fire behind his eyes whenever I blink my tears away. My nose is running, making my deep inhales and attempts to breathe through my nose sound wet and ragged. The suction of my mouth and the obscene sounds of me trying not to gag reverberate in the echo chamber that is the concrete stairwell, amplifying the sounds of heavy breathing and moans spilling out of Brody.

No, not just Brody. My body gets caught up in the illicit surrender that takes over me, and I'm moaning just as much as he is. Maybe more. My hips thrust on their own accord, humping the air, the friction of tight fabric over my cock just enough to drive me wild with need.

God, that's embarrassing. But I can't stop. I'm on the edge of coming in my pants, my body tight with tension, both anticipating and apprehensive about the end game.

This isn't over until he comes. I need to rush to the finish line to get this over with so I can leave and never speak to him or look him in the eye ever again.

That's what I tell myself, but there's also a part of me that craves his release. Maybe not the physical manifestation of it, but the satisfaction of knowing that I accomplished it. That I didn't chicken out and I followed through.

"Fuck, Beckett. I'm going to come. Are you going to take it like a good little cum slut?"

My eyes widen in trepidation, suddenly worried I won't be able to handle it. The obscene sound of it echoes in my ears, and I start to shake. I feel Brody's thighs tighten, and I dart a hand to my cock to put pressure on the pulse of pleasure throbbing in my dick. But it's too late. By the time he's calling out a warning, I'm choking on my own orgasm before his even hits me. His cock pounds into the back of my throat a few times, and I gag, hard.

Broady grunts loudly and pulls my hair, pulling his cock from my mouth with a wet pop. I cough harshly and sputter, then gasp hard enough to choke on my own spit when the first rope of hot, wet cum splashes over my face. The first spurt hits me across one cheek, all the way to the opposite eye, some of it getting up my nose. The second and third spurts paint my lips and land in my open mouth. I sputter and spit, spraying some of it back at the gun that shot it and across Brody's thighs.

While I sputter indignantly, Brody's ragged breaths and grunts of pleasure fill the air until he's squeezed the last drop from himself and painted it across my bottom lip.

"Fuck. Look at you. So pretty painted in my cum. Marked. You're fucking mine now, Beckett."

Something about those words shocks me so hard I almost white out and fall back on my heels. I wipe my hand over my face to clear my eyes and mouth of the filth he just painted me with and look down at it coating my hand. My mind is too blank to process what I'm feeling.

Filthy. Degraded. Humiliated. Used.

And so fucking keyed up I don't even balk when Brody keeps calling me filthy things through his comedown, twitching and writhing through my own. Nor do I argue when he tells me to take my shirt off and use it to mop up the mess *I* made.

Brody grabs my arm to help me up, a soft look in his eyes that jars me back to my right mind. I brush him off, straightening what's left of my clothes and trying to hide the evidence of what happened to me while getting him off.

"Beckett–"

I scowl. What is this bastard doing to me? It has to be some kind of mind control tactic or something, but to stop using it as soon as he gets his rocks off is just rude. Let me come back to earth before you force me to process this shit. *Damn.*

His eyebrow raises and he straightens, the demonic look returning to his face. I look away, still lost in the headspace I was swimming in only a moment ago. His hand comes up to grip my jaw.

"Next time you're going to swallow what I give you and thank me for it, Beckett. No wasting a single drop."

Next time?

Oh.

CHAPTER 12
BRODY

Sunday mornings on campus are dead. The sun is barely up, the air chilly and damp. The only idiots awake are me and Beckett. Of course he's up. He's probably been here since well before dawn.

I'm halfway through my warmup when the feeling of eyes on me becomes unbearable. All morning I've had that feeling, like a hand crawling up the length of my spine.

I glance up, and Beck jerks his gaze away so hard he almost falls off the rowing machine.

I smirk. Last night really did a number on him.

He tries to hide it, but there's a little bounce in his step, a tiny hitch in his breath whenever I move. He refuses to smile at or even acknowledge me, but he's got a glow about him that is unmistakable. A post-orgasm looseness that can't be denied. He's trying desperately to hide it, like he keeps catching himself looking happy and has to put a stop to it immediately. It's adorable, honestly.

By the time we're in the dining hall, it's almost painful not to poke the bear. This early, there's just fresh fruit, cereal, oatmeal and baked goods, and a help-yourself offering of coffee and tea. Beckett has a hot cup of tea in his hand and is choosing from the fresh fruit display.

"You're awfully peppy this morning," I say as I slide up next to him and pick a banana.

He startles, almost dropping his tea. It takes him a few seconds to pull himself together.

"I—um—*what*?"

"You seem like you're in a good mood."

"Oh. Um, yeah, I guess. Nice day."

It takes real effort to keep myself from smirking or looking at all smug.

"Couldn't have anything to do with last night," I say, peeling the banana slowly and making a show of opening my mouth to slide the banana in.

Beckett looks around as though we aren't in a nearly empty dining hall. There's only one other student in here, a swimmer based on the hoodie he's wearing, and two cafeteria employees in the back.

Then he eyes me warily as I push the banana farther in my mouth. I don't gag, and I don't look away, keeping direct eye contact. He cuts his gaze away from me when the banana touches the back of my throat.

Trying not to snort, I pull the banana out and take a reasonable bite, winking when Beckett chances another glance at me. He moves farther down the line, giving a bowl of apples a thorough inspection.

"How many times have you jerked off today already?" I ask when I've swallowed down half of my banana.

His eyes widen into saucers, and he quickly glances around us again. Which just confirms it for me. My smug smirk can't help but make an appearance, and I grin like a wolf that's been handed someone's pet rabbit.

"Come on, Becky… tell me."

I didn't actually mean to call him Becky. Beck was about to slip out, and I waited too long to add on the "ett" and got tongue-tied. But my guy freezes. His lips part, and a full-body shudder runs over him at the accidental name slip.

Oh, shit. He liked that. I felt that shudder in my gut. And lower.

"Y-you can call me Beck," he whispers. But I'm not letting him ignore my question.

"H-how many times?" I coax softly, leaning forward just enough that he feels the heat of my breath.

He swallows. Hard. "Two."

I bite my lip and look up at the ceiling like I need strength from above. God. Damn.

"And how many times did you come thinking about gagging on my cock?"

His breath stutters, and the cup in his hand trembles. Red spreads across his cheeks, his neck, and the tips of his ears. He's sweating.

He's trying to hold himself together and failing spectacularly.

"T-two," he whispers.

I hum low and approving. "Good girl, Becky."

He shivers again, and I have to turn away before I pounce on him right here.

I'm barely out the side door of the dining hall when I hear Beckett call my name

"Wait!"

I school my face into something neutral before turning to face him.

Beck jogs up, breathless and still holding his cup and an armful of food. "What are you doing today?"

"It's Sunday," I say blandly. "I'm going to go do some gay shit like the Lord intended."

He barks out a surprised laugh, the sound echoing off the courtyard. It reverberates through me and settles in my chest, warm and happy.

"Can I walk with you?" he asks, looking down at his fruit haul like he forgot it was there. He drops everything but an apple, a protein bar, and his tea on a picnic table and looks back up at me a little shyly.

I shrug. "Sure."

We head down one of the quieter paths. Campus is still nearly empty, the sun warming the leaves that haven't quite given in to October yet. It's gotten significantly warmer since our morning workout. It feels too warm for the season—climate crisis, *hooray!* —but it's peaceful.

I take the long way without making it too obvious that I'm trying to drag this out.

After a while, when Beckett has finished his snack and discarded his cup in a recycling bin, I sit down under a tree, leaning back against the rough trunk. The shade hides us from the path above. Beck hovers like he's afraid the ground might swallow him.

"Relax," I say, patting the grass beside me. "It's just a tree. And we're outside. I'm not going to jump you in public." Not that there's anyone around to see even if I did.

He snorts, glancing around again before sitting closer than I expected, close enough that the heat of his thigh kisses mine whenever either of us shifts.

"Are you really…" he starts, then seems to think better of what he was about to ask and leaves it hanging.

"Gay?" I supply.

He blinks as though he wasn't expecting me to say it out loud. "Uh. Yeah."

I nod. "It's not a bad word, you know. Say it."

"What?"

"Say it. Say gay."

He hesitates. "Gay."

"Again."

"Gay."

"Good. Now repeat after me: Brody Miller is gay."

"Brody Miller is gay," he parrots.

"And I am too."

"And I—Wait, no. I'm not."

"Bi then?"

His shoulders fall, breath deflating. "I'm straight. It's the only thing I can be."

"Because of your dad?"

Beckett nods but barely, like the motion alone is too much of an admission.

"He seems like a real douche canoe," I say.

Beckett snorts. "I'd pay good money to hear someone call him that. From behind a two-way mirror. Because I do not want to be there for the aftermath."

"Is your dad in the mob or something?"

He laughs again. Wow, twice in one morning. At this rate, I'm going to start thinking he likes me.

"No. He's an investment banker. But I've seen him tell people off so thoroughly they cowered in fear of him ruining them."

"Sounds like an adult tantrum. Maybe he needs a nap. Or a spanking."

Beckett goes still. Color drains from his face, then floods back thick and bright.

Interesting.

"Then again," I add casually, "he might like that too much."

He scoffs. "I sincerely doubt that."

"You don't know. He might."

"He wouldn't. He's not—Anyway, who would like something like that? That's ridiculous."

"Don't kink-shame, Becky." I say, pointing at him accusingly. "Different strokes. Everyone's got a thing. Or two. Or ten. There's nothing wrong with liking what you like."

He turns his face away, pulls a dandelion free, and twirls it between his fingers. "Like what kinds of things?" he mumbles.

Oh, buddy.

"Like spanking, for one. Foot fetishes. Nipple play. Breeding kink. Pain. *Degradation...*" I cut my eyes sideways. "Being told you're a nasty little slut who takes what he's given and thanks me for it."

The dandelion falls from his fingers.

He swallows. Hard.

"Well, I don't like that stuff," he insists. "Feet are gross, and I'm a dude, so…"

"So what?" I laugh.

"So, I mean, nipples and breeding wouldn't be a thing."

I stare at him. "Oh, you poor, ignorant, repressed thing."

"Excuse you? I'm not ignorant. Or repressed."

"Sure, baby. And I bet you're a pro at eating pussy."

He makes a face before he catches himself.

I point. "Ha!"

"What? What's ha? There's no ha."

"You looked horrified."

He bristles. "I just didn't like it, okay? If people are allowed to like things, then I'm allowed not to."

"Calm down," I say, patting his shoulder. "You can like or not like anything you want. Including nipple play, being licked, sucked, bitten, spanked."

Another priceless expression spreads over his face. I think I could sit here and teasingly educate him forever. I want to teach him everything in graphic detail and then give him a hands-on tutorial. I want to watch him fall apart and put him back together.

"And getting your ass filled with cum," I add casually. "You might not be able to get pregnant, but that doesn't mean your ass can't be bred like a prize–"

"Please stop," he whispers, voice cracking.

I look at him for a long second. His whole face is red, and it's bled down his neck down past the neckline of his crewneck sweater.

I lean in conspiratorially. "I'll stop when you admit you like one thing. Just one."

"Why?" he begs weakly.

My voice drops low. "Because I have a feeling you're so flustered because you *like* the idea of me holding you down. Of toying with all the parts of you that you think are shameful."

Beckett's throat clicks dryly.

"I bet you even like the idea of taking my big cock inside you. Just imagine it—begging me for more while I stretch you and fill you over and over, harder and faster, until you don't know which way is up. You'd take it like a good girl until I'm done with you, until I'm pumping a load so deep you'd feel it in your—"

His hand slams over my mouth.

And holy shit. He's right there, inches away, flushed and sweating like he's still lifting weights, pupils blown so wide his eyes are basically black. Pain mixes with need in his expression, but the need...

The need is winning.

I lick his palm, causing him to yank it back as though I bit him. He stares at his hand. Then at me.

Curious about his reaction, I lean forward and flick my tongue along the edge of his jaw. Quickly, pulling back to watch his expression again.

His mouth drops open.

I do it again, this time darting my tongue out at the spot just below his plump bottom lip. Then I do it again, slower. I don't back away before lashing my tongue out one more time.

This time he lunges forward, catching my tongue and sucking it into his mouth.

I moan loudly and kiss him back, hungry and reckless and dizzy with how good he tastes. I press him into the tree trunk, run a hand up his thigh.

He buckles like he's been shot. And then he *moans* into my mouth like he's dying.

No. Like he's coming.

He's coming.

In his pants.

Because of a kiss.

Fuck. Me.

I rub him through his shorts, feeling the wet warmth spread, tasting the way he pants against my lips as he trembles through his climax. If he was confused and embarrassed before, I know this is going to cause him to have some kind of existential crisis. But I want him to know just how sexy it was that he lost control like that.

I bend down, press my mouth to the soaked fabric of his thin gym shorts, and suck. Tasting him like this makes me want to rub myself through my pants, to take his hand and show him just what it does to me.

He cries out, cock jerking beneath my lips. Lifting my head, I kiss my way up his neck to his lips, panting into his mouth.

"Oh, baby," I whisper. "I knew you wanted it. But I didn't know how bad."

Beckett flinches as if the words burned him. His breathing turns sharp, and his eyes widen in panic.

"Oh, hey. *Shh*, it's okay." I murmur, reaching up to smooth his hair back.

He slaps my hand away, scrambling back, and gets to his feet. He's still half-hard and looks wrecked. He stares at me for barely a heartbeat, breath ragged, then turns and bolts across the lawn and back towards the dorms.

I sit under the tree a second longer, giving my body a chance to calm down. My heart is pounding, and my lips are bruised.

I can still taste him.

And while I feel bad that Beckett is freaking out, all I can think is that I can take control and show him what I know he wants. What he needs.

I'll give him space, but I'll be right there the moment he shows any signs of being ready to explore this new side of him.

He's gone right now, but he's not going far.

CHAPTER 13
BECK

My lungs burn, my heartbeat is a frantic mess, and my legs feel like they're going to collapse. And none of it has anything to do with the sprint I just made around campus to get back to the dorm. The sticky mess in my shorts is an acute reminder of how completely fucked my head and body are.

As expected, Cade and Fish are in the kitchenette, looking like they rose from the dead barely five minutes ago. Cade's hair is smooshed on one side. Fish is blinking like the sun is a personal attack on his retinas.

Except they both seem to be awake enough to notice that something is off, if the way they're staring at me is any indication.

"Dude," Fish says. "Did you go for a run?"

"Yeah," I gasp out. "Morning run."

It's technically not a lie. There was a lot of running involved. It just wasn't a casual, planned jog like it normally would be.

Cade leans his elbows on the counter, smirking. "We saw you and Brody walking around the courtyard," he says, nodding his head towards the one window in the living area. "What was he saying? You looked... I don't know. Weird."

My stomach free-falls. I shrug hard enough to seem annoyed. "Just talking shit. He's always talking shit."

"Yeah, but you don't usually look like you're about to pass out when he bothers you," Cade says, ripping open a protein bar with his teeth. "Are you sick or something?"

"I let my dad get in my head last night," I mutter. It's an excuse that's easier to believe. "I don't really want to talk about it, though."

They exchange an understanding look, then change the subject. They launch into a recap of the intra-squad showcase, which also happens to be high on the list of things I don't want to touch with a thick, nine-inch pole.

I last maybe ninety seconds.

"I'm going to take a shower," I announce abruptly. "And then meet Caty at the library."

Cade blinks. "On a Sunday morning?"

"Yes," I snap, unfairly annoyed. "Some of us have grades to worry about."

My two best friends exchange another worried look as I slam the door behind me.

———

I don't go to the library, but I do head straight to Caty. She's the only person I have to talk all this mess out with. I have the decency to text her on my way this time, so she's ready for me. She greets me at the door with an iced coffee and a look she reserves just for my particular brand of bullshit.

She hands me the coffee and gestures for me to come inside, plopping down in the middle of what looks like the makings of a conspiracy theorist's manifesto, but I know are her study notes. She's a visual learner, so she tends to write out her notes on cards and stick them to the wall. "Alright, spill it. What did you do?"

I drop into the chair that faces her small sofa. "Okay, so, don't laugh."

"I will absolutely take your request into consideration and give it the level of effort it deserves. Go on."

I tell her everything, starting with last night's meet up and ending with my embarrassing reaction to his words in the courtyard. I don't give her all the filthy details, much to her dismay. I don't think I could stomach it. Instead, I give her enough detail that she has a basic understanding of my pain.

She listens thoughtfully. Her eyes widen and then soften, then widen again at various parts of my sordid tale. By the time I'm done with my embarrassing ramble, she's fixed a flat, neutral expression on her face. I think of it as the face an older sibling might give their errant younger brother when they're beyond exasperated but trying not to show it.

"First," she says, pointing a green highlighter at me like it's a dagger, "you do need to open your mind a little. He's right about that."

"I'm open-minded," I grumble.

"Maybe when it comes to other people, but even then I think you're a little naïve. Being into one thing or another says nothing about the type of person they are. There are plenty of big, strong, manly leaders of the world that like to crawl around on all fours and get their dick squished by a dominant half their size and pay grade."

My eyes blink several times. "What?" I can't even tell if she's serious.

"The people that give into their kinks and comforts are probably stronger for it," she says matter-of-factly. "As long as your kinks don't involve hurting someone against their will, there's nothing wrong with it and it doesn't change who or what you are."

"I don't have kinks," I say too quickly, then amend my statement. "At least I don't think I do." *Also a lie and you know it, Beck.*

"You're allowed to be curious, Beck," she says, because she knows I'm a liar. "And if you're curious about Brody and his list of fun things to try, maybe you should give in a little and experiment."

Am I curious about Brody, or is it what Brody has to offer?

"I'm not sure what I'm feeling is curiosity," I mutter. "Not exactly. It's just—I don't know. Easier."

"What is?"

I swallow. Hard.

"All of it. It's the way he talks to me. Like he's compelling me, making me do stuff." My face heats. This is humiliating, even to myself. "Because then... whether I'm curious or not, it's like the choice is taken out of my hands."

She softens. "Oh, honey. It *is* your choice. Always. If he does anything you don't want, you tell him to stop, and if he doesn't—"

"You'll fuck him up?"

"Don't underestimate me because I'm smaller than you," she says, pointing the sharp end of a talon-like nail at me. "I'll absolutely fuck someone up. But if you *like* it, then go with it. Tell yourself whatever story you need to make it all fit into your square narrative. Just don't lie to yourself about it being your choice. I don't think that's healthy."

"He gave me a safe word," I assure her. "And I'm not square," I say defensively.

She bursts into laughter. "You are the squarest person alive."

"I've done stuff with guys," I blurt.

She scoffs. "Because being anything other than straight is promiscuous?"

"I didn't say that."

"It was heavily implied. Being gay or bi or anything else isn't a kink, Beck. It's just who you are. I'll concede that getting a blowy somewhere you shouldn't have could qualify as promiscuous. But the identity of the-other person involved isn't a factor unless you're specifically seeking them out because of some concept of it being forbidden. Which is an entirely different conversation."

My lips turn down in a frown.

"Am I an asshole?" I ask Caty, my voice low enough to let her know I'm being serious.

"Sometimes, but I think you're redeemable." She smirks, but I know her well enough to know she'll always tell me the truth. "I think you have some very backwards ideas that you need to unlearn. But I also think that maybe you're on your way."

"Your parents aren't any better than mine. How did you become so wise?" I'm grinning, but it's an honest question.

"Lots of people struggle with identifying or coming to terms with their sexuality or identity. For whatever reason, I didn't. I knew from a young age, and I'm stubborn, so my parent's attempts at redirecting my crush on my third-grade teacher Ms. Colleen did nothing to deter me."

"Stubborn or spoiled and used to getting your way?"

"You know what? I hope Brody puts you in your place one day. You're the biggest brat I've ever met."

"Takes one to know one."

She glares at me. I glare back. She grins. I hate her. I love her. And I definitely need her in my life forever.

I roll my eyes and grin back, pulling my phone out of my pocket when it buzzes. There's a text from Fish.

"Fish and Cade and some others are heading to the Wolf Cafe for dinner later, you want to go? I'm not sure I'm in the right mind for a group outing without a leash."

"Wanna help me organize my sociology notes?"

"Only if you promise to give me very long, boring descriptions of each and every concept you're learning about."

Caty cackles. "This is why I love you."

———

I should have texted Fish back and told him I wasn't coming after all when Caty got too involved in the concept of eliminating social bias in data collection. I also should have turned my ass around the second I saw the table, where my traitor roommate is sitting next to Brody of all people, animatedly chatting like they're best friends.

Calm down Beck, there are plenty of other guys here to buffer any interactions.

I sit as far away as the table allows, eyes fixed on the menu like I haven't been eating here regularly since freshman year and don't get the same thing almost every time I come.

It takes exactly thirty seconds before I feel Brody looking at me.

I glance up when his gaze starts to burn, planning to get him to cut it out and quit staring.

If he notices my glare, he doesn't acknowledge it. His face looks entirely earnest when he mouths, *You okay?*

Heat crawls up my neck, spreading over my face too rapidly to talk myself down before it's too obvious that there's something very, very wrong with me. I shove back my chair and head straight for the bathroom.

Cold water. Cold water. Cold water.

I splash my face and bend over the sink, gripping porcelain like it's an anchor and only straightening when the door opens.

Of course it's Brody.

"You good?" he asks softly.

He looks apologetic. Which is disarming. I don't know what to do with soft Brody. Frustrated Brody I can deal with. Angry Brody. Even teasing and smug Brody is easier to deal with than this.

Soft, apologetic Brody? I can't handle it. Nope. I need to get out of here.

"I'm fine," I snap. "You can go about your business," I say, gesturing to the stalls.

The bastard walks right over to the urinals and unzips, hips angled just enough for me to see everything in the reflection I'm trying so hard not to notice.

"Watching people pee is not on the list of things I'm curious about, so you can quit trying to get me to look."

Brody cocks his head at me, a slow grin playing over his lips. "No? I'll mark it off then." He finishes, zips himself up, and walks over to the sink next to me to wash his hands. "So what is on the list?"

I gape. I wanted to diffuse the tension and redirect us back to more comfortable territory, but it's just as dangerous here. Maybe more so.

"Nothing," I mutter. "I mean, I don't have a list."

Brody's eyes narrow like he's already caught me in a lie. "You seemed pretty curious to me."

"I'm not," I snap, too fast. "I just... *react* when you say things. Sometimes. It's stupid, and I don't like it, and it needs to stop."

Brody drags a thumb across his bottom lip, thoughtful in a way that makes my stomach plummet. "See, the thing is..." He pauses, evaluating me, deciding something. "I don't believe you, but I'm also not trying to be a creep. So here's what we're going to do."

He takes one slow step forward.

I instinctively take one back, only to feel the cold edge of the sink behind me. There's nowhere for me to run. Nowhere to hide. His presence fills the room, pours in through my lungs and chokes me.

"Remember our safe word?" he asks quietly.

My throat bobs. I nod once.

"Say it."

The heat in the room is stifling. Part of me doesn't want to, because I know if I say it, it shuts the whole thing down. The other part of me doesn't want to acknowledge the existence of a safe word because then I can't pretend this is out of my control.

Don't lie to yourself about it being your choice.

Caty's voice buzzes in my skull like a warning and a dare.

"Becky?" Brody prompts, soft but commanding, a dangerous blend that makes my knees tremble. "What is the safe word?"

I squeeze my eyes shut, hating and loving everything about this at the same time. "C-call you c-captain," I stammer.

Brody hums, low and pleased, like he's savoring the vibration of it in his own throat. Then he steps into my space, so close our chests almost brush.

"That's a good girl..."

I push off the sink ledge and skirt around him to get some more space. He's not really going to test my boundaries here, is he?

By the looks of the devilish grin on his face and the way he licks his lip, he is most certainly thinking about it.

My stomach flips. I hate him.

Okay, I don't. Not entirely. But I hate that I don't hate him the way I wish I did. The way I should.

He steps closer, and I can tell he likes the chase. What I can't tell is if *I* like it or not. I might, sort of, very deep down, like that *he* likes it. He backs me up until my shoulder blades are pressed against the row of stalls.

"Brody," I warn.

He arches a brow. "Say it like that again."

"I'm not doing this here."

"You sure?" He nudges the stall door behind me. "Because I think you are."

"I'm not—"

He pushes me gently inside the first stall, crowding me inside. His voice is gravelly, eyes flaring with lust. "Why don't you take me out and see how hard your bullshit makes me."

My insides squirm. The inside of my pants squirms more.

I flick a nervous glance at the door. There are enough gaps around the edges that someone could easily see that two people are in here, not to mention the twelve inch gap at the floor where our feet can clearly be seen. "Someone could come in."

He shoves the stall door closed with a sharp slap that makes me jump.

"You better be quick then," he says, murmuring against the side of my neck. A violent shiver races down my spine. His voice drops dangerously. "Take. Me. Out."

That hot, electric fire floods my veins, and I obey instantly.

I push down the front of his athletic pants with one hand, my other wrapping around his cock. My breath catches. It's hot and smooth, veiny, and heavy in my hand.

He doesn't need to tell me what to do.

I stroke him, rough and eager, not bothering to be gentle even though there's nothing but the sweat of my palm to ease the glide of my hand. He quickly starts to leak, thrusting into my hand, making my palm slicker.

He purrs filth against my ear to encourage me. "Good girl... just like that... such a good girl for me..."

The praise reverberates through my bones. My knees almost buckle as if I were the one being jacked off.

Instinctively, I stroke him the way I like to stroke myself, tightening on the upstroke and rounding over the tip.

Brody groans so deep in his throat it could be mistaken for a growl. He even bares his teeth before his mouth drops open. His hips jerk, and he drops a hand to cover mine, guiding me to squeeze harder, pump faster until he gasps and comes.

Cum fountains out of him, the first spurt shooting up my arm. The rest I manage to catch in my hand, thanks to him holding it in place while he pumps his last small bursts of release into it.

For whatever reason, I'm panting harder than he is. Both of us lean back against opposite walls of the stall, my handful of cum and his dick still lolling out of his pants. Brody is smiling like the devil himself, no doubt pleased to have ruined me some more.

He reaches a hand out and grips my shirt, pulling me against him. I hold my hand out to the side, unsure of what to do with it. My eyes widen with shock when my chest lands against his. I can feel his softening cock along the hard ridge of mine, straining through my pants.

He tries to pull me in for a kiss, but I flinch. I don't even mean to. It just happens. It's not like I didn't kiss him earlier today, but it was too much. Like sucking his tongue was more erotic than sucking his dick. I felt too much and came in my pants for absolutely no reason. It was the single most mortifying moment of my life. Worse than the stairwell even, because he was being so damn nice to me.

Brody's eyebrow raises. Before I can apologize, his eyes drop to my hand and my palm full of his cum.

I stare at it too, wide-eyed and horrified that I'm still just holding it like this. But what am I supposed to do? I'm half frozen with fear and far too hard to leave this stall. It's his mess, he should be the one to clean it up.

"Lick it," he says.

My head snaps up. "What?"

"You heard me." His voice is low, controlled. "I told you I wouldn't let you waste a drop next time, didn't I?"

I hesitate. I'd be lying if I said I wasn't curious. The little bit I got last night was surprisingly not terrible. It was like the first sip of a milkshake, that little burst of flavor that makes you want more. At the same time, the idea of it kind of grosses me out. I'm definitely not supposed to like stuff like that. What if I put it in my mouth and gag?

Or worse... what if I like it?

"You're not ignoring your captain, are you?"

He tilts his head, curious how I'll respond. He's given me an out with that simple question. But I chickened out earlier and flat out ran away from him like a coward. And it's not the first time I've done it. If I keep it up, will he get bored of me? Will he stop this ridiculous, dangerous game we've been playing?

Whether I want to admit it to myself or not, I don't want it to stop. Not like this. First of all, I can't let him win.

Slowly, I bring my hand to my mouth. And without breaking eye contact, I run my tongue over my palm, licking up most of the cooling load. I let it coat my tongue before holding my mouth open, tongue out, so he can see it dripping off my tongue.

A soft, approving rumble escapes him. I swallow reflexively, acutely aware that a part of him is inside me now.

"That's right, kitten," he murmurs. "Lick it all up. Tastes good, doesn't it?"

Heat floods me, shame and want tangled in my gut and ramping me up even more. It's not gross. The fact that it's cold is a little off-putting, but I don't hate it. I don't hate it at all. It's salty and sweet and just slightly bitter, but the flavor isn't strong enough to overwhelm. Honestly, it smells stronger than it tastes.

"So good for me," he adds, leaning in to lick the corner of my mouth. Close but not kissing.

I shouldn't want more. But I do.

Fuck me, I do.

Brody licks what I can only assume is some of his own release from my lip and hums. "You like being good for me, don't you?"

No.

Yes.

Fucking hell.

"Do you want me to reward you, Becky?"

Goddamn it all to hell, I fucking nod like an eager little bobblehead.

He must see the torment in my eyes, because he chuckles and says, "It's okay, baby. I know you want it."

My traitor cock twitches almost painfully.

"All you have to do is tell me you're my good girl."

I choke and pull back incredulously. He'd better be kidding, because he knows that's not happening.

Nope. Not happening.

He leans against the wall casually, smirk firmly in place. I fucking hate that smirk more than anything in this fucked up pornographic *Twilight Zone* episode I've been calling my life. Please tell me I'm going to wake up soon.

My chest caves. "Brody—"

"If you want me to make you come," he says calmly, "you have to be good for me. And I want to hear it."

I scoff, trying to claw back my dignity. He crosses his arms.

"If you want to play my game, you have to play by my rules. And only good girls get to come. So, are you a good girl or aren't you, Becky?"

My cock throbs. My throat works. But nothing comes out.

I can't do it.

He grins.

"You know where to find me."

And then he fucking leaves me there. Standing in a bathroom stall at the most popular campus café. Harder than I think I've ever been before and shaking like a leaf in fall.

Just fucking leaves.

———

I'm dying.

Or I've already died or may as well have, because I'm walking around campus like a ghost. I don't talk to anyone or barely acknowledge when I'm spoken to with more than a dazed nod.

Every time I see Brody, I look away. I can't bear to look at him. If he walks near me, I tense like a struck nerve. And every time I see that evil, self-satisfied, knowing smirk, I consider murder.

I want to hit him. Hurt him. Strangle him.

But I can't get close to him because any time I do, I consider...

No. Nope. Not going to happen.

Even though I'm so fucking hard just thinking about it. Even though I can't get off to save my life.

It's impossible.

I've tried. I've tried so hard. I haven't come in over a week. All I've accomplished is edging myself into insanity.

Brody fucking broke me.

Naturally, I take it out on him the only way my broken brain can think of—I pair him with the biggest wrestlers for practice, shoulder check him every time he dares pass me, or trip him when the moment calls for it.

And I've stolen every pair of underwear he leaves in his locker or gym bag. Don't ask me how I know the combination code to the new lock he bought for his gym locker. I have no boundaries anymore.

None of it fazes him.

Not. One. Bit.

Smirk. Smirk. Smirk.

The only time he reacts in even the smallest way is when Pierce makes those stupid comments about Brody's dad and beer—whatever that's about—and he gets a little quiet.

It's barely noticeable. But I notice. And I hate that I notice. And I hate even more that I feel a tiny bit bad about it, because even though I don't understand it, it clearly hurts him. And he deserves to be in as much pain as I am!

By Thursday, I swear my balls are blue and the slightest breeze makes me so hard I've doubled over in the middle of practice, walking across the quad, or even just sitting in the library. By Friday, I'm in so much pain I think I might need an actual doctor. The ache is second only to the mental anguish I feel over not being able to make myself come because some dickbag told me not to.

But I can't make it through another day, another weekend, or, fucking hell, even another hour like this.

Finally, I go looking for him after practice. This needs to be dealt with. I've got to find a way to put an end to this without giving in to his ridiculous demand.

I hang back a little in the hopes I'll be able to catch him alone for a moment, but I end up getting dragged into Coach's office to discuss our first dual that's still weeks away.

He goes over the roster, opponents, and techniques the under-classmen need to work on. I try to focus. Sort of. I'm really not capable of much cognitive effort. I can't think past my throbbing dick, which I've spent most of the week hiding with baggy clothes and strategically held hoodies and bags.

To shut him up, I let out a long and overly specific rundown of every wrestler's stats and potential weaknesses we could exploit. Coach stares at me, maybe because it sounds like I'm badly reciting a memorized essay, or maybe because my voice is choppy and wavering.

"I've had some extra time in the past two weeks," I say when he doesn't seem to know how to respond.

It's true. To get my mind off my boner and try to lull myself to sleep, I've been staring at wrestling stats and reviewing the opposing team's footage for hours at a time.

It's either that or spend too much time trying to make myself come, which I've figured out is futile, or imagine myself falling to my knees and begging Brody to touch me.

Finally, Coach lets me go.

I trudge to the locker room, intent on a brisk shower before I try to track Brody down at dinner. *Ugh.* What if I have to suffer the embarrassment of knocking on his dorm room?

He's not really going to make me say it, is he?

I'm still overthinking it, barely holding back very real tears when I get to the locker room. I expected it to be empty, but there's a shower running. And I can...

Goddamn it, I can *feel* that he's here. My dick is basically one of those well-detector sticks now, leading me right towards the only cure for my thirst.

With heavy feet and a heavier brain, I make my way towards the sound of running water. I don't even have the wherewithal to pretend I don't want it to be him.

The sight of Brody's broad, muscular back and firm, round ass has me blinking an actual tear away. Water sluices over every inch of his body, carved like a marble statue of pure sin.

His head is tipped back, eyes closed as he basks in the pressure of the shower spray.

He doesn't know I'm here yet. I could back away. Pretend I didn't come running to him the way he knew I would.

What's it going to be Beck, your pride or your ruin?

My throat is dry despite the steam. It's overly hot, and I can't seem to take a full breath in.

I take one shaky step closer.

World Wrestling Clubs Cup

CHAPTER 14
BRODY

I can tell he's there before I see him.

The prickly awareness between my shoulder blades is a familiar sensation. His eyes are on me, tracing every drop of water trickling down my body. Along my shoulders, down my spine and locking on my ass. It takes every ounce of my self-control not to flex.

Instead, I let the water beat down my neck and pretend I don't notice him watching me.

I rinse shampoo from my hair and soap the last of the chalk and sweat from my skin. My body is loose from practice and the extra reps I took to draw it out, but there's a tight, insistent pulse between my legs that has nothing to do with wrestling, exercise, or the hot water beating down on me.

I rinse, drag my hands over my face, and only then do I turn.

Beck is standing at the edge of the tile, just inside the entrance to the shower room. Still in his practice uniform with a hoodie wrapped around his waist, hair damp with sweat, and staring at me like I'm something to be feared.

Or like he hasn't slept in four days. Which, knowing how long I've been teasing him, might be true. He's been more on edge than usual. I'm surprised our last interaction stuck with him as much as it has. He was so incensed when I wouldn't get him off without hearing him say those simple words, I almost thought I'd actually pissed him off and pushed him away. I thought I'd have to go to him and change the rules so we could keep playing.

I turn off the water, and the sudden quiet rings in my ears. My lips tilt up in an easy grin.

"Need something?" I ask, reaching for my towel like I don't already know.

He swallows. His eyes flick down my body, then away so fast I can't help but chuckle. Just to fuck with him, I dry my body with the edge of the towel and focus most of my energy on my hair, leaving my body bare.

My cock is hard and pointing right at him. I know he's interested because he's not just cutting his eyes at it in fear or dismay. No, there's lust there, too. Thick, powerful lust that makes me want to take him and ruin him so thoroughly, he'll drop all his silly straight-boy scripts and beg me to make him come every single day for the rest of his life.

He already knows I'll make it so good for him. That no one else can play him the way I can, because I've latched on to every nuanced facial expression, every sharp intake of breath and flash of fiery lust in his eyes. He doesn't want to admit it, but he wants me. He wants me to make him come because he knows his own hand can't make him free fall into oblivion like I can.

He wants to say it. I can tell. It's right there, clogging his throat—want and pride, strangling each other.

I'm going to burn his privileged pride to ash, strip away every half-truth and excuse and leave him with nothing but the part of him that belongs to me. The part of him that's blushing and shaking and begging for more.

"Hey," I say, trying to sound as nonchalant as possible. My voice comes out low, roughened by the steam and the way my pulse jumps when I look at him. He looks rough and desperate, but doesn't seem to notice any weakness on my part. "What's up?"

Beckett's jaw works. His hands curl into fists at his sides. He looks like he'd rather chew glass than admit he wants anything from me, but he still takes a step closer.

"I—" He licks his lips. "We need to talk."

"Do we?" I tilt my head, maybe a little cruel. "About what?"

"About what you said in the bathroom."

"Darlin', that was almost two weeks ago. Care to refresh my memory?"

His face flushes darker. I witness his battle of internal conflict, rage and pride competing with desperation and devastation. His pride is killing him, but the need is killing him more.

Oh. My. God.

"Becky," I breathe, astonished. Has he been... holding off entirely? I told him I wouldn't make him come, but did he interpret that as not being allowed to come at all?

And he fucking obeyed?

He stands there, eyes huge and begging, even though he can't bring his mouth to say the words. Even though he's clearly in actual physical pain.

No fucking wonder he's been such an asshole lately.

I toss the towel over the wall and consider turning the shower back on to cold to calm myself down.

"Get on your knees."

He drops. Just like that, without hesitation. No fight. Immediate obedience, like his body has been waiting for the command.

Because he *has* been waiting for it.

A slow, satisfied heat uncurls in my chest.

"So," I murmur, looking down at him. "You'll get on your knees, suck my cock, and lap up everything I give you like a cat, but you have too much pride to say a few simple words?"

His throat bobs.

"Crawl to me," I growl.

He stiffens for just a second. Then he does it. On the cold, wet tile, his muscles flexing under his clothes, hands squelching through puddles of water, he crawls forward, all the way until he's barely a foot away from me.

My breath punches a little shorter. I have half a mind to give him what he wants and give him a break. I cannot believe he hasn't made himself come in twelve days, all the while punishing himself for following a command he thinks I gave him.

When he stops at my feet, I rest my fingers lightly in his hair, softly combing the front back from his sweat-dampened forehead.

"Do you want me to touch you?" I ask, keeping my voice steady. "You say no, I back off and we forget this whole thing."

He squeezes his eyes shut.

"I..." His voice is a strained whisper. "I want to come."

It's not all he wants, but it's a start. His determination is impressive, but I see an opportunity to burn a little more of that bullshit pride away. And I'm damn well going to take it.

I curl my fingers, tug his head back so he has to look up at me. "Then say it."

He shakes his head, panic flaring in his eyes. "Don't make me."

"I'm not *making* you do anything," I say calmly, my voice purposefully low and melodic. "I'm offering. *You're* choosing. You want my help? You say the words. If you don't want to play anymore, you can get up and walk away. Or use your safe word and I'll walk away."

His jaw clenches. His gaze drops. He's breathing like he just finished running sprints for an hour. His silence is so loud it's deafening.

"Strip," I say.

There's a moment of hesitation, the briefest second of time between my giving the order and his brain processing it. He's on his feet in the next second, cheeks burning as he peels off his hoodie, which was doing a truly poor job of hiding the monster erection he's packing. He kicks off his wet shoes and socks as he pulls his snug team tank top over his head. The shorts are next, and then he's down to nothing but his tight white compression shorts. Those last inches of fabric are straining over him, front soaked, clinging to every ridge of his cock so tightly, I can see the thick vein that runs up the length of his shaft.

"I said strip," I remind him softly.

He swallows and pushes the compression shorts down, baring himself completely. His cock is flushed, heavy, and glistening at the tip. He's already leaking so much, it drips to the floor.

I walk slowly around him, letting him feel me circling him like he's prey. Letting the air and the waiting sink their teeth into his already frayed nerves.

"Looks painful," I murmur. "How long has it been, Becky?"

He squeezes his eyes shut. "Don't—"

"Days?" I continue as if he didn't speak. "Weeks?"

Beckett lets out a small, breathy whimper.

"Were you waiting for me? Or have you been touching yourself?"

I leave a long enough pause that he knows I expect an answer. "I tried," he admits, keeping his eyes clenched tight. "I couldn't—"

He cuts himself off before he can admit just how much of a hold I've had over him these past weeks.

"Couldn't what, Becky? Couldn't make yourself come? Or didn't want to?" I want him to admit the truth to me. I'll force him if I have to.

"I didn't want—"

I tsk and pet his hair. "You didn't want what? Didn't want to make yourself come? Didn't want to admit how much you wanted me to make you? Is that why you waited for me?"

"I didn't want to wait!" he rasps. "You got in my head, and I couldn't—I couldn't make myself come, okay?"

Holy fuck, that's... hot. And kind of amazing. To have that kind of power over someone else. It's heady and intense.

I reach out and touch him lightly with just the tips of my fingers. With a barely there touch, I brush over the dark, swollen head of his cock, gather a slick bead and pull back.

He hisses like I burned him, and his knees buckle a little.

"Easy," I say, and because I can't resist, I lift my fingers to my mouth and lick them clean.

The sound that escapes him is low and wrecked—half pain, half reverence. All desperate.

It's intoxicating.

I step back to give us both a second, turning on some of the nearby showerheads to muffle the sounds I know I'm going to draw out of him. My own cock is heavy and aching at the mere sight of the great Lincoln Beckett brought to such dire straits because of *me*. I wrap my hand loosely around myself, pumping in slow, firm strokes as I watch his visibly throbbing cock strain and leak, dripping onto the floor.

"Kneel."

He sinks without protest this time.

Water patters on his shoulders from the showerhead over. His hair is damp, his cheeks are pink, and there's a brightness in his eyes I haven't seen before. It's something more desperate and raw than he was even in the stairwell the first time I made him come.

"You want my cum?" I ask, voice low.

His lashes tremble. "Yes."

"Where?"

He swallows. "Anywhere. I don't care. Just—please. Please let me come too."

I hum, lazily working my fist, watching every twitch in his face. "You know what I want to hear."

His jaw flexes. He shakes his head again, stubborn to the end. He can deny it all he wants, but he came here for a reason. He listened and obeyed for a reason.

I walk around his body and get to my knees next to him so he can feel the heat of my body, smell the soap and mutual need on my skin. My hand moves a little faster on myself, breath hitching as my fist bumps against his hip with each stroke.

"Say it," I murmur.

"No," he rasps, though his hips jerk at the word like defying me turns him on.

"Say it," I repeat, firmer.

He blinks his eyes furiously, shoulders hunched, like the syllables themselves might kill him. "Please, Brody—"

My hand moves faster, the slick sounds of my fist working my cock audible over the hum of excitement and splash of water on the tile. "Say it," I snap, raising my voice over the sound of the shower, letting it crack like a whip.

He flinches. Tears shimmer in the corners of his eyes, falling when he clenches them shut, frustration and humiliation and need all tangled together.

"Say it," I demand again, moving behind him and bending closer so he can feel my breath on his shoulder blade. "You want me to give you what you've been begging your fist for all this time?"

His breathing turns ragged, borderline sobbing. "Please," he chokes. "Please, I can't—I can't—"

"Yes, you can." My tone softens just a fraction. My free hand slides around his hip, gently caressing the rash of goosebumps that erupt, pressing my thumb into a dimple at the top of his ass. "I've got you," I say against his skin. "Just say it, and I'll take care of you."

His lips tremble, and for a second I think he's going to bolt again. But then he shatters so beautifully, it nearly brings tears to my eyes.

"I'm a good girl," he wails, the words tearing out of him on a sob. "I'm *your* good girl—"

That's it.

The sound of it, the way he says *your good girl* snaps something inside me. I groan, hips jerking as release hits me hard, hot and sharp. I spill across the small of his back, streaking his skin, his spine, his hips while he kneels there shaking and confessing everything he's been fighting.

"That's fucking right you are," I pant, squeezing the last of it from myself.

For a moment, all I hear is water and his breathing. He's still on his knees, shoulders heaving, hands fisted on his thighs. The muscles in his back twitch under my gaze, adding to the quaking of his trembling body.

I slowly drag my hand through the mess on his skin, spreading it in lazy circles over the small of his back, the curve of his hips. He shudders under my touch, but he doesn't pull away.

"Hey," I murmur, softer now. "Breathe. You're okay."

I keep my palm broad, steady, massaging it in like lotion, like I'm grounding him instead of just marking him. His breathing gradually evens out, the wild edge smoothing.

"That's it," I soothe. "Good. You did so good for me."

He makes a broken sound, head hanging.

"You want to come?" I ask.

His answer is desperate and immediate. "Yes. Please—"

I smile against his shoulder, then reach around and wrap my hand around him at last.

He jerks like he's been shocked, knees sliding a little on the slick tile.

"Shh. I've got you."

I barely squeeze his cock and give him one firm pull before he erupts.

He spills with a shout, his body bowing forward, hands slapping against the wet tile to catch himself. My name is garbled out on an anguished wail, the sound echoing off the empty walls, raw and unguarded.

I slow my hand, easing him through it, then let go.

He sags, breathing hard.

I shift around to face him and gently tip his chin up with my fingertips, leaving a streak of our combined release on his jaw that I don't bother wiping away. His eyes are glassy and unfocused, lips parted and panting, cheeks flushed.

He looks wrecked. Beautifully, gloriously wrecked.

"That wasn't so bad, was it?" I ask softly, dropping a soft kiss to his forehead.

He swallows and makes a sound, maybe trying for some snarky comeback, but nothing comes out. Just a small, bewildered sound.

I smile and press a kiss to the corner of his mouth this time. He goes still, reminding me that even now, in this broken state, he's still fighting this.

"Next time you want to come," I murmur against his skin, "you won't wait so long to find me, will you?"

His breath catches. He doesn't answer, but the way his body stiffens and the way his eyes flick up to mine then away lets me know he heard me.

I don't think I'll need to wait as long for him to break on the next round.

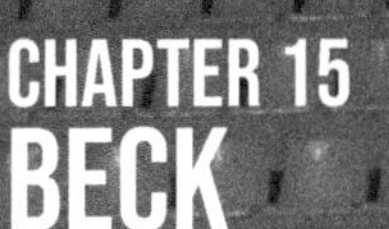

CHAPTER 15
BECK

I walk out of that shower like I've been hit by a bus. A sexy, terrifying, orgasm-withholding bus, but a bus, nonetheless.

My legs feel heavy and unsteady. My head feels hollow. And my heart is yet to resume a normal beat. But the worst part...

I'm still hard.

Painfully, humiliatingly hard. Even after an orgasm so intense I swear I felt my soul leave me. My spine could have detached from the rest of my body, and I wouldn't have been surprised. It took me apart so entirely, I feel like every joint and muscle has been stitched together with yarn, like a rag doll.

What the hell is wrong with me?

I grab a towel from the shelf and wipe myself off in frantic, sloppy motions. All I want to do is get dressed and pretend my life isn't spiraling completely off the rails. I need food, probably some electrolytes, and to sleep for a week.

Brody is thankfully missing when I shove into the locker room with a towel wrapped around my waist, and another held in front of me like a shield. As if I can get anything past the evil soul sucker himself.

I glance around in case he's hiding behind a row of lockers and waiting to pounce, but he's really gone. I'm alone in the locker room. Even knowing that, I can't seem to relax. Especially when I see my bag out of my locker. It's sitting on the bench, wide open and messy, like it's been rummaged through. My body tenses, and I have to remind myself that I've been breaking into his locker for weeks. If anything, this is confirmation that he knows it was me, but he's only just now confirming it was yet another win he let me have.

A blinking light gets my attention. My phone, sitting on top of my rifled-through bag, has a notification.

One new message.

I tap the icon to open the message and find a text chain started by me, or rather my phone. Brody must have used my phone to send himself a text, then updated the contacts.

> Captain: You don't have to pretend you don't like it, you know. I'll give you everything you need.

Captain? He put his name in my phone as CAPTAIN? And of course he changed my name to *Becky*. I want to throw the phone across the room, but also my chest feels all fluttery and my cock twitches and I want to throw *myself* into moving traffic.

I type before giving it much thought.

> Becky: Stalk much?

Three dots appear instantly.

> Captain: I think you like it.

I groan aloud. Even alone in the locker room, my face goes up in flames.

> Becky: Captain? Really?

Captain: That's what I am to you.

> Becky: I'm not calling you that.

Captain: Mmm. I hope not.

> Becky: Fuck off.

Captain: If you want to come again, all you have to do is ask me nicely.

My body jolts so hard I almost drop the phone. I can't do that again. I just can't.

Is it the waiting for as long as I did that I can't fathom? Or the giving in to his demands?

It doesn't matter. This is absolutely not happening. No chance.

> Becky: I'm blocking your number.

Captain: Sure you are.

I snap the phone shut just so I don't have to look at it.

———

I make it until Wednesday.

Barely.

By morning conditioning, I'm a wound-up disaster pretending to be a functional human being. My dick hurts. My brain hurts. My pride hurts most of all. If anything, I should be able to hold out longer than I did last time, at the very least. Shouldn't I?

Brody saunters into the gym wearing shorts that should be illegal on someone with thighs that thick and muscular. With no compression shorts under them. And then the bastard starts squatting.

Fucking squats.

Deep, slow squats that make his thighs flex obscenely, his ass tightening with each press.

I swear to God I might actually combust. It's so hot in here. Why is it so hot? You'd think with the cost of tuition in this place, we'd have decent air conditioning.

My head swings around the room, looking anywhere but at Brody's indecent shorts.

"Yo, Beck," Fish calls. "You alright?."

"Huh? What? Oh. Yeah. Just, um, looking for my water bottle."

"It's in your hand," he says blankly, pointing at my silver and red Huntston Howler's water bottle.

Shit. "Ha! Duh. I knew that," I say, putting all of my attention on sucking down as much water as I possibly can.

"You coming tonight, Captain?."

I choke on my water so hard some of it sprays out of my nose.

"What? I'm not—"

"The dorm Halloween party," Fish clarifies, eyebrows raised so high on his forehead they nearly disappear into his hairline. "You seem tense, Beck. Maybe you should visit the massage therapist before you leave. Or actually relax and have a drink tonight."

I nod weakly, still sputtering.

Across the gym, Brody grins back at me through his reflection and chuckles lightly. I flip him the middle finger, and he winks.

Obviously, I have no choice other than to push harder through my workout. Because I hate myself, and I need the distraction.

This, of course, becomes a challenge. A competition breaks out, which turns into me and Brody shoving each other to fight to get to the next piece of equipment first, which turns into a playful bout of sparring like we're flirting teenagers.

It takes too long to realize that it's only me and Brody acting this way. No one else is competing or playing like we are. In fact, everyone else is watching us curiously. Jay Norman is staring like we're a puzzle to solve. Fish has an amused, but equally confused, expression frozen on his face.

What the fuck am I doing?

I break apart from Brody so fast I nearly trip over my own feet.

"I, uh—I'm going to go ask about that massage. Or maybe an ice bath," I tack on, because the bite of plunging myself into freezing water might help shock me back to my senses. At the very least, it should help with the boner that seems to get worse the more I embarrass myself.

———

I sink into the ice bath after practice, shivering violently as the cold seeps into my bones. It barely dulls the ache, and my head is still exactly where it's been since the semester began. Worse.

Apparently determined to make sure he's the only thing I can think about, Brody slips into the room like a shadow and perches on the edge of the tub. He's still wearing those stupid shorts.

"Is it helping?"

It's obvious what he's asking about.

I sigh. "Not really."

"I'm curious…"

I'm worried.

"…do you enjoy denying yourself? Get off on the withholding?"

"No," I say incredulously. Why the fuck would anyone like feeling like this?

"Then why do you torture yourself?" he asks quietly, dipping one finger into the frigid water and swirling it around. "You know exactly what you need. And it would only take a few words."

His eyes raise to mine, the blue of his irises practically glowing in the dimly lit room. I look away, stomach tightening.

He sighs, softer. "I'm not trying to upset you. I'm trying to figure you out."

You know enough, thank you very much.

I blink hard, staring at my legs under the water. "It's hard to explain."

"Try," he says, his voice low, warm.

I swallow. "It's easier when you just tell me what to do."

He nods like he knew that already. "Because you want to pretend you don't want it."

Immediately, I open my mouth to argue, but I stop. My throat works as I give an almost imperceptible hint of a nod.

His voice drops lower. "So if I told you that you could come, but only with my cock in your throat, that would be easier than saying please?"

My breath stutters. I stare at him for probably too long before I nod again. He frowns thoughtfully.

A long, heavy silence settles between us. I feel exposed, cornered, and too damn cold, minus any of the benefits I thought this dip would give me. So I stand from the ice bath and climb out. Brody hands me my towel, still studying me intently.

He's just going to say something like that without actually offering? Was it another taunt? A tease meant to break me down and make me beg again?

Wordlessly, Brody opens the door for me, following me into the hallway on the way back to the locker room. It's quiet now, which means most if not everyone has headed out already. There's a distant sound of voices getting farther away, the echo of a locker slamming, then a thump as the main doors swing shut. Water drips in the shower room. Faint music can be heard coming from the main gym, but it's an older, calmer sound than what most of the team listens to. It could be maintenance getting started on the facility. The night crews typically take care of the bathrooms and locker rooms, but it's good to be aware someone could come in.

When we step into the locker room, Brody close on my heels, I stop short. Brody runs into my back but doesn't pull away. He leans in slightly instead.

"You alright?"

My mouth is dry, pulse throbbing loudly in my ears.

"Can I?" I whisper.

"Can you what?" His voice is barely a rumble, something I can feel more clearly than I can hear.

I swallow. My whole body is buzzing, terrified and wanting, confused and somehow safe. It takes some mental coaxing to force the words out.

"Can I suck you?"

Saying it feels like shoving myself off a cliff. My heart leaps into my throat. My blood runs hot enough to warm my chilled skin.

Brody inhales slowly, sharply, like the words hit him somewhere deep. A hand touches my waist, and he shifts closer. I can feel his breath and his warmth and the hard proof that he wants me pressing into my ass.

"I'm so fucking proud of you using your words like that," he murmurs.

Warmth floods through me so fast I almost sway on my feet.

His hand brushes over the skin just above my towel, low on my hips, feather-light. "You're going to be rewarded for this. Good girls get to come, remember?"

He presses his lips to my shoulder, not so much kissing as rubbing his lips back and forth. "Not here," he says. The words make my skin react before I can process them.

Then he's backing away from me. I hear the rustle of a bag, and the door opening and swinging shut.

Meanwhile, I'm destroyed by the effort it took to so much as utter those words, dizzy from his praise, and hanging on the edge of something I don't have a name for.

But he's gone.

Confusion spikes through me, then anger. I lower myself to a bench and curl inward on myself, resting my elbows on my thighs and breathing deeply.

Part of me wants to scream or hit something. Or cry like a kid who lost his favorite new toy. But under all the frustration, beneath the humiliation and the ache and the need, something else sits warm and steady.

Trust?

Do I trust Brody Miller?

It doesn't make sense. I don't understand it, other than Brody has never lied to me. Some deep part of me knows he'll take care of me like he says he will.

The only question is how hard I'll have to work for it, what else I'll have to prove, and how badly it's going to hurt.

That's if the anticipation doesn't kill me first.

———

The Halloween party is loud enough to rattle my bones. I'm so on edge, I consider having a drink. Just one to numb the frayed edges of my nerves. I've thought about it several times tonight already, even contemplated taking a shot when Fish, Cade, and a few others were pre-gaming.

Instead, I'm stone cold sober and examining every masked guy who vaguely matches Brody's height and build. It feels pathetic, as though I'm chasing after him like some kind of pathetic needy girlfriend.

Caty would call you out for thinking like that.

I don't want to be chasing anyone. Maybe if I think of it as hunting him, it'll give me the confidence to let him come to me instead of trudging through a sea of slutty zombies, fairies, vampires, and firefighters. There's more leg, tit, ass, and man chest on display than a swimsuit catalogue.

My phone burns a hole in my pocket, but I refuse to take it out again. It's bad enough that I've sent him so many desperate messages, only for them to go unseen and unanswered.

Becky: You going to the party tonight?

> Becky: I'm on my way.
>
> Becky: You here yet??

I check one more time. No reply. Nothing.

I resist the urge to change his contact name to Captain Douchebag and type out a fourth message demanding that he answer me for fuck's sake. Keeping me on edge like this is cruel.

"Stop scowling," Caty says, elbowing me as she adjusts her blonde wig. "You're supposed to be a brooding southern vampire, not an annoyed frat boy."

"I am a brooding southern vampire," I mutter through my incredibly realistic retractable canines.

She rolls her eyes. "Brooding vampires don't check their phones every eight seconds, *Bill*."

I roll my eyes and shove my phone back in my pocket. "Fine, *Sookie*," I say, over emphasizing the ridiculous way the character from her favorite show *True Blood* pronounces the name. She giggles, and I let her drag me to the dance floor. She's such a dork, doing the corniest possible dance moves in the middle of a crush of grinding, scantily clad bodies, that for a while I forget myself.

A few songs in, Caty stops trying to hook random people on an invisible fishing reel and pauses, looking over my shoulder. I start to turn towards whatever she's looking at, but she puts a hand to my face and grins.

"Don't look now, but we've got an audience."

I look, because of course I do. I turn my head and glance over my shoulder. Sure enough, a dark figure stands just outside the dance floor, facing us. His face is hidden by a terrifying Purge-style mask, and he's wearing a nondescript black hoodie and dark jeans. And he's watching us.

He doesn't move, doesn't wave or gesture towards me. He just watches. Even without being able to see his eyes, I know he's watching me, specifically. His head tilts slightly, studying me, expressionless and creepy, but the movement is familiar all the same.

I feel his slow, deliberate stare in every vein and nerve ending. I'm frozen under his gaze, until he turns and walks away, slipping into the crowd.

I'm rooted to the spot, confused and disappointed to be left behind again.

Caty wakes me up with a swift swat to my arm. "Go, you idiot!" she hisses, then smacks my ass so hard I jump and lurch forward.

"Fuck it," I say, and walk towards the crowd that Brody—or who I think (hope) is Brody—disappeared into.

I push through sweaty bodies, trying not to be too obvious. I try to act like I'm on my way to the bathroom, hoping I won't be stopped by anyone when my pulse is hammering like my life is in danger. Or about to do something I shouldn't.

People shout greetings as I push by, but no one tries to stop me. I barely register the chaos of a college Halloween party, counting on most of my teammates, classmates, and other athletes to be drunk enough not to notice I'm on a mission and follow me. I keep my eyes scanning the crowd, catching glimpses of a black hoodie and broad shoulders weaving through the party. His sure-footed, purposeful posture and gait give him away more than anything else.

He disappears around a corner, out of sight. My breath catches and my legs move faster to catch up. Behind the corner is a small stairwell, which makes my lips quirk up, expecting that this would be the place he'd most want to harass me. But it's empty.

The echo of a door clicking shut comes from the basement, and I quickly follow. I burst into a corridor that leads to the laundry rooms, and the lights go out. I'm swallowed by darkness, broken only by the glowing exit sign that leads to an outside courtyard and the glow of several vending machines.

The music of the party is much quieter down here, but the bass can still be felt. It seems to sync with my heartbeat, ramping up my nervous energy as I move through the dark space. I half expect Brody to jump out at me any second. It has my senses on high alert and the hairs on the back of my neck standing on end.

"Brody?" I whisper, feeling stupid and reckless. How would I explain looking for him when everyone thinks I hate him? Because I do, obviously. So what excuse could I give for following some rando down a dark hallway on the off-chance that it's him?

There's nothing but silence.

Hands seize my shoulders from behind, making me gasp loudly. My back hits the wall hard enough to knock some of the breath from my lungs.

Fear sparks through me momentarily, then the masked man is in my space, pressing a hand to my shoulder to pin me against the wall. His scent and the heat of his body are familiar and comforting. Which, really, should freak me out. But all the fear, fight, and critical thinking drain out of me like air from a balloon., and I sag in his grip.

He doesn't speak. He just stares silently for a long moment, as if considering what he might want to do to me now that he has me here.

He must decide quickly, because I'm suddenly flipped around, chest pressing against the wall. His hands grip mine and guide them up against the wall, spreading my fingers wide. His grip rearranges me like I'm nothing more than pliant clay for him to play with. He nudges my hips, and I tilt them automatically, curving my spine to push my ass out like I have any business doing so.

The position feels obscene and humiliating but somehow also so natural. Like his hands and my body know what I need and how to move to accomplish it.

His breath brushes the back of my neck as his hands move around my hips and undo my belt. He unzips my pants and pulls them down over my ass with clinical precision.

Cold air hits my skin, reminding me just how exposed I am. I try to straighten, to turn towards him and say something—anything —but he presses me forward until my cheek is flat against the cold cinderblock wall.

SMACK

Fire streaks across my right ass cheek, the sound reverberating down the corridor, sharp and loud. My knees almost buckle, breath leaving me in a state of confused paralysis.

I don't fight him. I can't. My body stops pretending it's in charge and lets go. Lets him take over.

A warm hand smooths over the throbbing flesh of my ass before he's suddenly not behind me anymore. He's not at my back.

He's gotten to his knees behind me.

I can feel his breath on my cheeks as he brushes a light kiss over the spot where he smacked me. Then his hands are on me, caressing and kneading my ass cheeks like they're modeling clay.

Brody spreads me open, his fingers firm on my skin. I'd be embarrassed if I had any dignity left, but I'm pretty sure my last bit of dignity was drowned in that ice bath yesterday.

I flinch as his tongue swipes through the cleft of my ass and over my hole.

What the actual fuck was that?

I choke on a moan, high and desperate, not knowing what this is or how to react to it. It feels weird. Weird and foreign, and wet and soft, and so fucking delicious.

His tongue slides over me again, and my body bows forward, hips twitching involuntarily. The sensation is slippery but so damn good, setting off forbidden nerve endings that tingle and shoot sparks of pleasure from my asshole to my spine. He taps his tongue against my hole, and I feel it in my balls. They draw up against my body, and I pant to hold myself back, not wanting to come from nothing but Brody's tongue on my asshole.

I can't compute how out of this world it feels. It's filthy and intimate and so far beyond anything I've ever let someone do that my brain can't compute which way is up. I mean to ask him to wait, to hold on, to give me a moment to breathe, but all that comes out is a desperate moan.

Before I can form a thought, he drags me around by the hips, turning me to face him again. Not that I can see his face. When I look down, all I can see is that blank, eerie mask that he's pulled up on his forehead to free his mouth.

His mouth that wraps around my cock, engulfing me entirely in one go.

Oh sweet Jesus.

I can't breathe. My hands claw at the wall behind me. I throw my head back so hard I almost knock some sense into myself. Then the tight, wet pull of his mouth lures me into that blank space where I'm nothing but need and nerve endings again.

Holy fuck he's good at this. I'm no stranger to blow jobs, but he has me reeling. The hot, perfect suction of his mouth makes my vision spark at the edges. My legs shake.

His tongue slides under the head, circles, and sucks before he takes me all the way to the back of his throat.

"B–Brody—" I gasp, not even sure he can hear me.

One arm pushes on the inside of my thigh, and he hooks my knee over his shoulder. At first, I'm rocked by the motion, trying to keep my balance while my shoe keeps the end of my pant leg attached to my foot. But the motion drives my cock deeper into his mouth where I can feel his throat swallowing around me. I nearly collapse. My body curves and my hands steady themselves on his shoulders.

When his hand moves between my legs and a slick finger presses against my hole, I tense. It feels weird and I'm not sure I like it, but I don't tell him to stop. He pushes it inside, slow and deep and intrusive, and curling it in a way that forces a sound out of me I've never heard myself make. I'm stunned for a moment, confused about the shift from weird to holy fuck.

He does it again, repeating the same motion and pressing against that raw spot inside me. An electric pulse of sensation that's somewhere between intense pleasure and the need to pee rips through me. I come so hard and fast my vision whites out.

My hips jerk uncontrollably. I scramble for something to hold on to, pushing his mask off in the process. He looks up and locks hungry eyes on mine. My mouth falls open around a wordless cry, and the hallway spins.

He holds me steady, watching me as his mouth and sneaky finger milk me for every last drop of cum, dignity, and clear thought left in me.

When I can't take anymore, he releases me with a wet pop, dropping a soft kiss to the tip of my cock, then the inside of my thigh. And then, as if he didn't just destroy me, he stands and fits his mask back on top of his head.

I'm boneless and shaking, slumped against the wall, pants around my ankles with one leg inside out, breathing like I've run five miles uphill.

"W–what..." I manage. "What did you just do to me?"

Brody steps into my space, his mask inches from my face, breath hot against my lips.

His voice is low and steady. It's devastating.

"I made it easier for you to know what to beg for."

CHAPTER 16

BRODY

I slowly step back from Beck, giving us both a breath of space, but I don't take my eyes off him for a second. He looks wrecked. He's flushed and trembling, his pupils blown so wide they swallow the brown of his eyes and turn them into black oil.

He's still leaning against the wall, chest rising and falling like he just ran a mile. He's watching me warily, as if I just performed some kind of suspicious sorcery rather than gave him a simple blow job. Although the finger seemed to be a shock, so maybe that was his first time having his prostate stimulated.

He probably thinks straight boys don't play with their butts.

I drag my thumb across my bottom lip, collecting the last faint trace of him on my skin. Then I pop it in my mouth and suck, licking it once to be sure I got it all.

His gaze locks onto the movement like he's hypnotized. His jaw slackens. His breath stutters.

"Do you want to know what you taste like?"

Pink lips part, and his tongue peeks out like he wants to get a taste, too.

"You taste like sin and sweet desperation," I say, surprised when he doesn't argue about being desperate. "You taste like mine."

Beck doesn't move, he just stares at me like he's trying to solve a problem he doesn't have the math skills for. Then something in him wavers. He leans forward, barely, but enough.

He's going to kiss me.

A hot jolt of something I don't want to inspect too closely pumps through my bloodstream. I lean in to close the distance, hoping he'll be able to taste the sweetness of his release on my tongue still.

Then voices spill down the hallway, loud, drunken, stupid laughter, and Beck jerks like someone tugged on his puppet strings. His face goes sheet-white, even paler than the makeup he used to make his skin look undead.

He scrambles to pull up his pants, hands shaking as he struggles to untangle his foot from one of his pant legs. He's breathing so hard he's practically wheezing, no longer lost in the aftermath of a moment I wish we could have kept for so much longer.

He looks at me, and I can see the dam about to break behind his eyes. He's right on the edge of saying something important. But he doesn't.

He turns and bolts just as a group of rowdy partygoers lurch around the corner, cackling about something to do with the batboy being too pretty for his own good. Baseball players, then.

I pick up my mask and lean casually against the wall. One of the guys notices me and stops.

He steps away from his group as they continue towards the exit door, someone already lighting up a cigarette. He approaches me with that slow, loose swagger of someone who's drunk but still in control of it. His costume is a mess of ripped flannel, fake blood, and dirt. He looks like an extra for *The Walking Dead*.

"Hey," he says, voice pitched low enough to be intentional. "I've seen you around but haven't had a chance to introduce myself."

He has?

He sticks out his hand. "I'm Tripp."

I accept the handshake, noticing how his grip lingers. Definitely longer than necessary. Damn, he's bold.

And cute, if I'm being honest. Lean, athletic build, rich brown hair, and what looks to be a smattering of freckles under the smeared gore. He's a good mix of jock hotness and boy-next-door charm that probably gets him into plenty of trouble.

"Brody," I say, matching his low tone.

He smiles, and if the slow perusal of my body means anything, he's definitely flirting. "Good to finally meet you."

There's a small part of me that considers taking Tripp up on the unspoken offer, whether it's just for the night, or maybe something more. He's good-looking, open, and direct without having to spell it out. I'm sure we'd have a good time, no games or repressed aggression. No waiting for a bomb threat in the form of a panic attack.

I bet he wouldn't run away from me like he's been caught at a crime scene. A guy with his charm and confidence would probably stick around to endure the heat. Hell, he might even enjoy it.

It'd be easy. Simple. A hell of a lot less effort than chasing a closeted, uptight, over-privileged control freak who alternates between choking on my cock and choking on his denial.

A huff of laughter escapes me at the warm, syrupy feeling that trickles down my chest and into my stomach at the mere thought of Lincoln Beckett.

My body knows better than my brain does. Because the truth is, I get a hit, a visceral jolt of lightning through my whole self, every time I'm around Beck. Something inside me recognizes him, like I've been waiting my entire life for someone with his exact combination of arrogance, panic, and submissive need hiding under a perfectly starched collar.

And Beck wants me. He just doesn't know how to *let* himself want me.

It's why he pretends nothing is happening the second the moment is over and his lust haze breaks. It's why he pretends he hates me. It's why he denies me until he's so desperate he's out of his mind, shaking and begging me in dark hallways.

Beck knows he isn't straight, but he won't say it out loud, and not just because he isn't ready to come out. He might never be ready, but I don't care about that. What I care about, what I want him to do, is accept himself for who he is. Every last part of him, down to his submissive need and very sensitive prostate.

I'm okay if he wants to use his submission as an excuse to experiment—for now. But I won't let him hide behind it forever. Because there is a difference between helping someone explore and letting them lie to themselves until it twists them into knots.

Beck is on a journey. A long-overdue, messy, very necessary, sexy journey. And I'm happy to be the one to guide him through it, even if I have to whisper commands in his ear or drag him by his hair.

By the time I'm done with him, he'll accept who he is. And there will be no more running away.

I give Tripp a friendly nod. "It was nice meeting you," I say, polite but a touch dismissive. "I'll see you around, yeah?"

His eyes flicker with disappointment and maybe curiosity, but he nods back and returns to his friends.

I pull my mask back on and trudge back to the party, hoping to find the one I really want and reel him into another sexy trap. This time, though, I'll steer him to somewhere less public.

Because I want him all to myself.

———

Beck avoids me all weekend.

He dodges me at the Halloween party after running off, dodges me in the dining hall, dodges me at the gym, and at Monday morning lift he manages the Olympic-level feat of not looking in my direction once.

It's almost impressive. Really, I have to hand it to him for being so determined to pretend I don't exist, but I'd be lying if I didn't admit I'm growing tired of this back and forth, especially when it's not as obvious that he's tormented by either my presence or my absence.

He can avoid me all he wants, but I want it to hurt, dammit.

Luckily for me, Coach McCoy announces that Beck will be running the pre-practice film review Monday night. I make sure to get there early so I can settle into a seat with the perfect vantage point. I sit back with my arms folded behind my head, watching him fumble with the remote and straighten his notes twice before it starts.

He's cute when he's trying too hard.

Once he gets started, he remembers that he's comfortable taking control when it comes to this team and the rest of his life. He just doesn't want to be in control when it comes to me. Something warm and fuzzy unfurls in my chest, growing twice as large when Beck notices me smiling and forgets what he's doing. He probably thinks I'm up to something, planning a way to humiliate him, when really, he's the only one who's ever made himself feel inferior in public.

We've gone over most of the intra-squad showcase footage, talking through probable opponents for next Sunday's duals, and breaking down what we did well and what we didn't. Most of the team offers basic comments.

Coach seems to feel that Beck's presentation is missing something, and I have to agree. Taking the remote from Beck, he pulls up *our* match, freezing it just before the first period. On the screen, there we are, faced off and getting ready to take things to another level that he definitely didn't see coming. Neither did I, but I just couldn't help matching his energy with some of my own.

"Let's talk about this one," he says. "Best match of the night. Beckett and Miller had the closest score. It was the match of the night to call, but ultimately it went to Miller. Let's find out why."

Beck stiffens beside the projector, and I feel a giddiness perk me up like a shot of espresso. I lean forward, elbows on my knees, feigning interest in the video when really I'm more focused on him.

Coach runs a clip from the third period, and the team watches. On the screen, we're in tight, shifting weight. Beck tries to roll out of my trap but can't quite get the momentum.

"There," I say, pointing. Coach pauses the tape, rolling back to the moment I stopped him, and waits for me to explain. I smirk at Beck. "Your hips are too high. If you'd backed it up another inch, you could have flipped me."

I throw him a wink, and he scowls so hard I can feel the heat moving up his neck. A few guys whistle, and a couple laugh. Beck does his best to ignore everyone and moves on too quickly, voice higher than normal and his face darkening.

Ooh, I'm going to pay for that. A delicious ache pulses between my legs at the thought.

When we finally get to the end of practice, we line up to spar. Beck is on his A-game, maybe a little too aggressive. Snappy and irritated for sure. It's fun.

At one point, we end up in almost the same position we were on that screen. Only this time, I make him stop by pulling his hip up and into me. His ass presses into my crotch.

"See? Like this," I murmur, splaying my hand over his stomach and feeling his abs clench. My cock fills with blood, and I know he can feel me growing against him.

This time, I'm the one too distracted by my boner to react fast enough. Beck flips me just how he should have during that match, laying me flat out on my back and pinning me down.

"You're too cocky for your own good," he snaps.

I smirk. "I'm cocky because I can back it up." I thrust my hips a little for good measure.

His face does that flustered pretty thing again. He shoves me harder, but that's just foreplay at this point.

———

Jay and Aaron flank me on the sidewalk after practice.

Jay elbows me. "Dude, is everything okay between you and Beckett?"

"Yeah. Why?"

"He seemed a little more murderous today than he usually does," Jay laughs.

"Oh," I say deadpan. "That just means he loves me."

They both choke on air.

"He what?" Aaron asks.

"He loves me," I repeat. "He's just not ready to admit it yet."

Jay snorts. "Pretty sure he can't stand you."

"Same thing," I shrug.

They stare at me like I'm insane. Which is fair.

I'm not sure what to call whatever it is we're doing. I know Beck, even if he doesn't know himself yet. And I know I need to work on being less obvious, because the last thing I want to do is force him out of the closet.

I tell myself I'm going to do the right thing and cool it when we're in public, but the very next time I see him, I'm already being tested.

Most of the team has crowded into the dining hall for dinner, taking up several large tables filled with athletes more often than not, since the student center building is the closest dining hall to the athletic dorms.

Beck, of course, chooses whatever seat is farthest away from me, but the table fills on both sides, pushing us towards the center of the table until we end up directly across from each other. The glare he gives me—no doubt in response to my obvious glee—would level a sane person. But I am living my best life getting to play brat to his grumpy act.

"Stop it," he mouths.

I mouth back, "What?" and don't even try to hold back my smirk. I know he loves to hate it.

He cuts his eyes down to my mouth. So I lick my lips slowly, nearly laughing out loud when he snaps upright, spine as straight as the stick up his ass, and darts his eyes around frantically. He settles his attention on Cade and a sophomore football player, who are arguing over which women's team has the hottest girls. Football bro says the volleyball team, and most of the guys around us nod emphatically. Then Cade clears his throat and gestures across the dining hall to where a truly stunningly gorgeous woman with golden skin and vivid blue hair is standing talking to a cute little twink in a pair of baggy jeans and a crop top.

"Gentlemen, I present to you Ivy Quinn from women's tennis singles."

Even the football bro nods like, yeah, you've got me there. "She's only one chick, though."

"Quality over quantity, my man. She's got it all."

Pierce, sitting three seats down, snorts. "I guess if you're into that sort of thing. She's a little *alternative* for my tastes."

"Is that code for she looks like she has opinions?" Fish asks. Aaron snorts.

"She is a bit mouthy actually, since you brought it up. Always waving her flags around like everyone needs to know her business. And look at the way she dresses. Talk about full of herself."

Brody looks over. She's wearing athletic leggings and a white t-shirt with orange, red, and pink letters that says, "I have a nut allergy."

"You have a popped collar and a sweater tied around your shoulders," Aaron points out. My mouth drops open in shocked amusement. Since when does sweet, quiet Aaron throw out sick burns like that?!

The table erupts. Watching Pierce get his bullshit flipped on him might be just as satisfying as getting Beck all flustered earlier.

"I don't understand the shirt," Cade stage whispers to Fish.

"Dude, she's a lesbian."

Cade perks up. "Really?"

Fish rolls his eyes. "Cade, a smart, sophisticated woman like that wouldn't give you the time of day even if you did have the right equipment."

"I don't care. That just makes her hotter."

"You're a walking red flag," Fish says and rolls his eyes.

They continue bickering, giving me time to slide my foot across the floor under the table and nudge Beck's ankle. He jerks like he's been shocked. His eyes widen comically, giving me a look that suggests where I should go with my audacity before he looks away so dramatically it might qualify as theater. I fucking love it.

So, I slide my foot up his calf. Slowly. Deliberately.

A blotchy red flush creeps up his neck.

Mmmph. Beautiful.

"Yo, Brody. Where'd you go the other night? Did you hook up with that Amanda chick?"

"Amanda the swimmer?" Jay asks, eyebrow raised.

I'd talked to her for a while at the Halloween party before I saw Beck dancing with Caty. I catch Jay's eye and shrug.

"Nah, girls aren't my thing."

Beck freezes, as do several of the guys around us. It goes over Cade's head. Pretty sure his muscle mass ate his brain. Poor thing.

"But there were girls all over you at the Halloween party. You had to have hooked up with someone."

"He's a homo, you idiot," Pierce yells across the table, getting the attention of several other tables. "He takes it up the ass."

I notice the heavyweight captain, Sean Cabot, stand and give Pierce a very pointed warning glare as he walks to dispose of his tray. Pierce deflates a little.

Cade's mouth opens and closes while he processes. "So you like dick?"

I give him a bored look. "Yep."

Fish holds out a fist. "My favorite sister is gay. Respect."

I roll my eyes but give him the bump. In the meantime, I do my best not to give Pierce the satisfaction of my attention or a reaction to his clear attempt to start shit with me.

Cade slaps the table, causing several people to jump, and then points at me with a very serious expression on his face. "I like you so much more now that you're not competition."

Everyone laughs. Except Beck.

He stands so abruptly his chair screeches, mutters some excuse, and leaves. I move to follow him.

"Yo, Brody," Cade says. "You should join the Pride Alliance. Buddy up to Ivy for me."

That earns another roar of laughter from the table.

If I leave now, it'll look suspicious. And Beck wouldn't want me to draw attention to his abrupt exit. So I sit back and try to act normal even though I really want to be chasing after him. He seemed upset, and I don't really know why.

Eventually, my phone buzzes.

Becky: Why did you do that?

Captain: Do what?

Becky: You can't just tell everyone that shit.

Captain: Would you rather I be ashamed of who I am?

Becky: I'd rather you have some discretion.

Captain: Worried people are going to figure out your secret by association? Insecurity isn't sexy, Becky.

Becky: Fuck you. I'm not insecure.

Captain: Is that why you haven't been able to look me in the eye since I milked your prostate on Saturday?

Becky: Shut up. I didn't like that.

Captain: The geyser you shot into the back of my throat says otherwise.

Becky: That was just because of the blowjob. Not that.

Becky: Also, delete these messages immediately.

I grin wide.

Captain: Nah. I think I'll keep them. Save them for later when I need something to jerk off to.

Becky: Seriously, Brody. Delete them. And leave me alone.

Captain: I'll delete them if you can prove me wrong.

Becky: What does that even mean?

Captain: Meet me outside and I'll show you.

> Becky: …

The three little dots that show me he's typing out a response pop up and disappear four times, but no message comes through.

> Captain: Come on, Becky. Be a good girl and let me play with your ass. If you don't come on my fingers in ten minutes or less, I'll delete all the messages and leave you alone forever. That's what you say you want, right?

He knows I'm right. His response takes even longer this time, but he finally texts back.

> Becky: That is what I want, yes. But I don't need to prove anything.

Sure it is.

> Captain: Then put your ass where your mouth is, Becky. Meet me at your car. Five minutes.

I stand, toss my tray, and slip out the back doors. He's already waiting for me outside. He looks nervous. And angry as fuck. But I can tell he's turned on and more than a little curious. It's his default state of being at this point.

"Why my car?" he mutters, looking back and forth to see if there's anyone else around who might witness him being cordial with me.

"I want to see your car," I say, strolling past him towards the lot. "I bet it's really nice and roomy."

I've seen his car, and I know it's nice as hell. It's a brand new gunmetal grey Range Rover Sport that reeks of privilege and, according to the internet, is rated the highest for cargo space in luxury midsize SUVs.

And isn't that convenient?

It's also convenient that I happen to know he parks as far away from other cars as possible to protect it from getting scratched. It's practically in a private corner of the lot, perfectly hidden from view.

Cold air nips at our skin, fogs our breath. Beck wraps his arms around himself, shoulders hunched, jaw tight and pointedly not speaking to me.

When we reach the car, I push him gently against the back bumper.

He gasps. Then whispers, "No."

His voice breaks on the word, and his pupils are blown wide. He wants so badly to say yes.

So I step closer, breath brushing his cheek.

"I didn't ask," I say softly. "You know what to say to make me stop."

His knees tremble.

"Why don't we crawl in the back, and you can bend over somewhere no one can see you?"

I ghost my fingers down his hip, stopping just above the waistband of his pants.

"Or, if you'd rather, I can bend you over right here," I murmur, "and put on a show."

He chokes out a sound—half shock, half arousal—then fumbles to open the liftgate.

That's my desperate boy.

The trunk opens and I step behind him, lowering my voice into that tone I know liquefies him.

"Take your pants off and climb in."

He hesitates for a single breath and drops his pants but doesn't kick them off or crawl into the back. I give him a moment to decide if this is really what he wants, or if he's going to run again, but he doesn't move.

His posture is straight and stiff again, nose slightly in the air. I see what he's doing. He's trying to take control of small details to assert himself. Interesting.

Well, if he wants to expose his ass to forty-degree temperatures to make himself feel stronger, more power to him. We're blocked by trees, the SUV, and shrouded in darkness. The moon and a nearby streetlight give me just enough light to see.

I step up behind Beck and put pressure on his back, guiding him to bend for me. He does, placing his hands on the edge of the trunk. My palm caresses the spot on his ass that just days ago was pink with my handprint. I drag the tips of my fingers through his crack, a barely there tease to remind him to relax.

Shifting to the side, I bring two fingers to his face. "Suck, Becky. Get them nice and wet for me."

He whimpers and opens his lips, letting me slide them into his mouth. I pump them between his lips, a preview of what's to come.

"I can't wait to hear you beg again," I say, gripping one cheek and spreading his ass so I can look down at his perfect, tight hole. "And I can't wait to feel this tight ass squeezing my fingers while I milk you."

He shudders and releases a shaky breath when I spread his spit over his hole and rub circles around it, watching it pulse and wink at me.

"Just fucking get it over with," he hisses, but his voice is weak and raw.

"You want it?" I ask him. "Want my fingers inside you, stretching you, filling you?" I tease his hole with the tip of my middle finger, putting pressure on it but not pushing.

"I guess we're going to find out," he chokes out. His voice is surprisingly resolute.

I step closer until his back brushes my chest. He's bent over the lifted trunk, hands braced on the floor of the cargo space, pants pooled around his knees. His breath clouds the cold air in sharp, uneven bursts.

God, he looks perfect like this.

"Someday I'm going to fuck you like this," I murmur against his ear. "So pay close attention and do exactly what I tell you to."

A shiver rolls through him.

I drag my fingers down the mounds of his ass, watching the way his body tenses and melts in the same second. His skin is heated, and when I pull his cheeks wider and spread him with my thumb, the sound he makes is already a half-plea.

"You ready for my fingers?" I ask.

He nods so hard he's almost rocking the vehicle.

Words, baby. Come on.

"Use your words," I say, letting my tone dip to that register that turns his bones to jelly. "Tell me."

"I... I want your fingers." He swallows. "Please."

Oh, holy night.

Not *I'm ready for your fingers*. Not *get on with it*. He *wants* them.

And he said please.

I bend low and spit directly onto his hole, adding to his mostly dried saliva that I used to soften and tease him. The sound is loud in the cold, quiet lot. I spit again and tease my finger just inside, slickening the tight, trembling ring of muscle.

The first finger presses in slow. He gasps, his spine arching like a cat. I pump my finger in and out, letting him get used to it while I push more spit inside his hole. I go a little deeper with each pulse, until I'm sinking in to the second knuckle.

His thighs shake with the first light stroke over his prostate, and I know I could probably prove my point with just the one finger, but I'm desperate to see his ass gape.

Beck bites down on the inside of his arm to muffle the sound in his throat, but he can't hide the way his back arches, pushing his ass into my hand.

"Relax, Becky," I hum. "You know you love this."

His breath sputters out in a shaky moan. "I... I don't."

I curl my finger.

He chokes on a cry. It's muffled, but sharp and desperate. His knees buckle so hard I have to grip his hip to hold him up.

"Baby, you can't lie to me," I rasp. "Your body tells the truth even when your mouth doesn't. Now bear down for me."

I add a second finger.

His body jolts forward, forehead dropping to the carpeted trunk floor. His hands fist in the fabric of his hoodie, now pushed up his torso to expose his muscular back to me. His thighs tremble so violently I can feel it through my wrist.

Jesus Christ and all his disciples, I beg you, for all that is holy in this world, please don't let me come before he does. And thank you, Lord, for making this perfect specimen of a man and placing him in my path. In Jesus' name, I pray.

Ah-fucking-men.

"Brody—Oh—*Fuck*—"

"That's it," I say. "Let me open you up."

I work my two fingers steadily, scissoring, stretching him just enough to make him gasp but not enough to overwhelm him. His breath is ragged, broken on every exhale.

Then I angle my hand just slightly, a tiny shift and a beckoning motion, and goddamn. When my fingers drag over his spot, his entire body locks up. He makes a sound I've never heard before. Something wild and untouched and terrified of how good it feels.

"Right there," I say, dragging over it again.

He moans. Loudly. He can't even pretend he's not getting his world rocked.

"That's the spot," I murmur, my breath fogging in the night air. It no longer feels cold, though. I'm burning up. "This is how you fall apart for me."

"Brody—Brody, please—*Please*—"

I curl my fingers again.

He cries out and pushes up, gripping the edges of the trunk like he's trying not to fly apart.

"You want to come?" I ask.

He nods frantically, eyes clenched, teeth between his lips, and hips rocking back onto my hand without shame now.

"Tell me what I want to hear."

His voice comes out shredded. "I want to come… On your fingers…"

"Say it right."

He shudders and forces the words out.

"I want to come on your fingers like a… a *good girl.*"

My cock throbs painfully at that.

"You're *my* good girl?" I ask, my voice quiet, dangerous.

His head drops, shoulders heaving. "Yes. Yes—*Please*—"

"You beg so prettily."

He whimpers.

I focus my efforts, picking up the pace. Not rough, just precise. Deep strokes, curling over that perfect spot each time. His body shakes uncontrollably, and he pushes up on his toes, fucking himself on my fingers.

His body is strung as tight as a wire, every muscle trembling. He's so close he can't even breathe right.

"Come for me," I command softly. "Come, Becky."

Like he was waiting for permission, he doesn't last a second longer. His orgasm detonates. His entire body snapping tight, then bowing beautifully. I hold him steady with one hand as the other stays buried inside him, curling and coaxing every last shudder out of him.

Hot pulses of cum shoot out onto the bumper, onto the carpeted trunk floor, and all over my hand where it slipped under him to brace his hip.

I lift that hand instinctively, letting his warm spill coat my palm.

"God," I murmur, low and hungry. "Look at you."

Beck collapses forward, trembling, breath coming in broken gasps. He's so wrecked he can't even form a word, just a soft whining sound that shoots straight to my dick.

I slide my fingers out of him slowly. He makes a helpless little noise, like he doesn't want to lose the contact.

"Shh," I whisper. "I'm not done with you yet."

Before he can lift his head, I bring my cum-slicked hand down between his cheeks. I spread him open gently, dragging the slick of his own release across the seam of his ass, smearing it up and down the crack.

He gasps a sharp inhale that edges into a moan.

"Brody—"

I hum softly, rubbing the warm, slippery mess right over the spot that makes him twitch. "You feel how hot you are? How sloppy?"

His hips jerk helplessly backwards.

"Yeah," I breathe, letting my voice drop. "That's all you. You did that."

I smear a slow circle over the entrance I just opened with my fingers, letting the cum coat him. He whimpers, pushing back without even realizing he's doing it.

"Such a slutty little hole."

He shudders so violently the car creaks.

My cock aches against the fabric of my pants. The sight of him like this, bent over, open, shining with his own release, is too much.

I step in behind him, pulling my cock from the confines of my pants and positioning myself between his shaking thighs. I grip his hips, guiding him just where I want him, pushing his chest down and tilting his ass back.

"Don't be afraid. I'm not going to fuck you. I just want to feel you."

To his credit, he stays still, or tries to, but his legs are trembling so hard his ass pushes back into me in tiny involuntary movements.

I line myself up between his cheeks and drag the length of my cock through the slick mess I milked out of him, pushing his cheeks together. My breath punches out of me at the heat of him, and the tight slide of his body embracing the ridge of me without taking me inside.

He gasps. Loudly.

"That's it," I groan, rutting slowly between his cheeks, letting the head of my cock glide up and down the slippery crack. "Feel that? That's what you do to me. Such a good girl for me. Such a filthy, slutty, good girl."

He moans into his arms, hips rocking back to match every stroke like he can't stop himself.

"You're perfect like this," I pant. "So fucking perfect."

His body flexes, muscles clenching with every drag of my cock. His spit and cum-shined ass create a slick, hot path I glide through again and again until the pleasure coils sharp and deep in my gut.

Beck tries to lift his head to look back at me, but his neck gives out and he collapses forward again, shaking. He's hard again, jerking himself while I use his ass to get myself off.

I growl, thrusting faster now, pushing his cheeks together and sliding through him with smooth, obscene friction. "Fuck, baby, I'm going to come all over this perfect ass."

His answering moan is so fucked-out and needy it nearly finishes me on the spot.

I brace one hand on the small of his back, pressing him down, angling him just right. My other hand grips his hip, holding him still as my hips snap forward again and again, grinding between his cheeks, over his hole, smearing his cum everywhere.

"There," I gasp. "Fuck—Right there."

Sensation coils in the base of my spine, a tight, thick ball of pressure that expands, pushing out until there's nothing but spine-tingling pleasure wracking through my body.

"Such a good fucking girl." I come hard, spilling between his ass cheeks. Hot stripes paint his skin, mixing with his own release. Beck shouts his release, and I groan, riding out the aftershocks of my orgasm, hips rocking through the last pulses.

When the aftershocks fade and I can see straight again, I still and rest my forehead between his shoulder blades for a second, catching my breath.

I feel limp and destroyed and more fucking satisfied than I ever have.

Beck is quiet except for the small rasps of breath. I drag my fingers through the mess coating his ass, both of our cum combined, and gently rub it into his skin in slow, soothing strokes.

"Good girl," I murmur, kissing the top of his spine. "You did so fucking good for me."

His breath catches again, softer this time. Fragile. I can sense the oncoming panic, but I'm determined to be with him through it all, so I don't let him pull away.

World Wrestling Cup

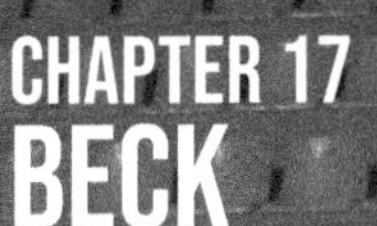

CHAPTER 17
BECK

The cold hits me first, the bite of November air on my previously overheated skin, now pebbled with the chill of cooling wetness splashed over me and rubbed into my skin.

Then the embarrassment hits.

Brody stands behind me, his breathing steady and calm. Too calm for what he just did to me. I'm bent over the back of my car with my pants around my ankles like the world's dumbest porn cliché. Again.

I try to pull away, my face burning. "I think I might have an extra t-shirt or something in the back seat.

"Be still."

His voice, low and commanding, slices through me. Impossible to disobey.

I freeze.

He reaches into his pocket and pulls out a wad of napkins from the dining hall. He came prepared to turn me into a sloppy wrecked mess.

"Seriously? You brought napkins?" I mutter, my stomach flipping.

"Mm-hm." He kneels behind me as if it's the most casual thing in the world, grabbing my hips roughly when I try to move away from him. "Stay."

"I said I can—"

"Beckett."

It's one word. Only my name, but said in that tone, I shut up instantly.

He wipes me gently. Too gently, like I'm fragile. Like I'm something that needs tending, like a toddler who needs help wiping its ass.

"This is humiliating."

"No. This is called taking care of you." Another swipe. "Hold still."

My legs feel weak and trembly. Every nerve feels raw.

When Brody is satisfied that I'm cleaned well enough, he tucks the napkin away and reaches for my underwear. He slides them up my thighs, careful not to jostle me, then my pants. Button by button, he fastens me back into myself.

The intimacy of it makes me dizzy.

He stands in front of me, and despite being shorter than me by a few inches, it feels like he towers above me. He looks into my eyes as he smooths the fabric of my waistband.

I swallow hard.

He grips my waist, his warm hands firm, and nudges me backwards until I sit on the liftgate. The trunk frame cradles me, and he steps between my knees like he belongs there.

He doesn't say anything, just rests his hands on my hips before lifting one to stroke my hair.

I flinch at first, but his touch is calming. Grounding. It settles the wobbly, aching wildness deep inside that makes me want to bolt.

His praise still echoes in my head. The filthy, tender, overwhelming praise he'd whispered against my skin. My chest feels warm, like someone poured a shot of whiskey straight into my bloodstream.

He keeps stroking my hair, and after a minute I melt, slumping sideways against the interior wall of the liftgate. Brody fits himself closer, between my knees, thighs brushing mine. The smell of cold air, sweat, and sex clings to us like a cloud.

Finally, he murmurs, "Do you need me to keep talking dirty, or can we move to real talk?"

My heart seizes.

Real talk?

I'm not ready for that. Not even close.

My mouth opens and closes, pondering what to say. Something dumb falls out.

"You came on my ass."

He chuckles, low and warm. "Hell yeah, I did." He squeezes my hip. "I couldn't help it. You're so fucking sexy, baby."

I wince, but heat floods my cheeks traitorously. God, why do I like that? Why does it feel so damn good to hear him say shit like that?

Whether I've said it out loud to anyone other than Caty before, I've always known I like guys. Or at least had a strong suspicion before the day I came face to face with Brody Miller. There was no denying it after.

I've never considered being anything but the top. Letting someone take me like that? Hell no. I've never imagined it. Never dared. Never even entertained the idea. It's bad enough that my father might find out that I'm gay. I've always known there was a high chance he wouldn't accept me. But I can only imagine what kind of hell he'd shame me with if he knew I was the one taking it.

There was a second, a single breath in time, when I really, truly thought Brody was going to put it in me.

And I wouldn't have stopped him.

I might have wanted it. And I know that he knows.

He leans in, nose running up the side of my throat, and whispers, "Your hole was gaping open, winking at me to take it. Then it was all shiny with cum, and all I could think about was seeing it shiny with *my* cum, too. Marking you. Fucking you. Making you mine in all the ways that count."

My eyes cross. *Holy shit.*

He says it like it's dirty, but underneath there's something almost reverent in his voice. Something real. Something soft that scares me more than anything he could do with his hands.

"Make me yours?" I huff out a laugh.

His face shifts, playful but serious underneath. "You got a problem with that?"

He pulls back enough to look me dead in the eyes, and I swear it feels like he sees every version of me at once.

I panic.

"I have a girlfriend," I blurt.

His eyebrow lifts. Slowly. Very unimpressed.

"You mean the girlfriend who pushed you to follow me at the Halloween party? The girlfriend you pretend to kiss? The girlfriend I never see you with unless your father is breathing down your neck?"

I open my mouth. Nothing comes out.

How is it that this man, who has known me for all of three months, can see through me so well? Like I'm transparent.

"My dad would disown me," I whisper. "And I know it's dumb, but I've lived…" I swallow. "I wouldn't know how to survive."

Brody's face softens slightly. Enough to make something ache deep inside my ribs.

"You don't have to come out," he says quietly. "You don't have to tell the team. Or your dad. Or anyone you don't want to tell."

He presses his forehead to mine.

"Except yourself." His thumb brushes my hipbone. "You have to be honest with yourself."

My voice is barely a whisper. "And you?"

A grin flickers over his mouth, though it doesn't quite reach his eyes.

"I already know your truth, Becky." His lips graze my jaw. "I'm just waiting for you to come around."

———

As gross as it sounds, the wrestling floor on a competition day is one of my favorite smells. It smells like victory. Like sweaty bodies, rubber, and the sanitizing spray they use to disinfect the mats every night. It brings me good feelings the same way the smell of the ocean does, or the popovers my childhood nanny Ms. Delia used to make on holidays. And now Brody. He smells good. Comforting. Like heat and soap.

Huntston is destroying this dual way easier than we thought. We've won almost every match so far, and the gym is vibrating with applause and stomping from the student section.

I walk off the mat after my win, breath still heavy, hair sticking to my forehead. My muscles are screaming from how hard I've been pushing myself lately—earlier than usual lifts, extra runs, late-night study sessions and an obsessive need to check my phone for texts from a certain not-captain who gets on my nerves and takes up way too much brain space. I'll do just about anything to keep my brain too busy to think about all the ways he makes me feel.

My eight a.m. Corporate Finance class is killing me. I desperately wish I could drop it. I can barely stay awake in class, and I never have that problem, but the professor drones on in this monotonous low timber that has half the class nodding off. It's only adding to the constant pressure on my shoulders, because I *have* to get an A. My dad will lose his mind if I don't, especially considering it's my degree concentration.

It's all starting to pile up on me, and now that I've succeeded at this one thing, I'm starting to think too hard about what's next, what's left to do, how to do it all one notch better than everyone else. Otherwise, I'm a failure.

Before I can spiral too far, Brody's voice cuts through the noise.

"LET'S GO, JAY! GET HIM ON HIS BACK!"

I look over to see what's happening. Brody's roommate Jay Norman has his opponent in a tight hold. Brody is on the sidelines, yelling encouragement like he's coaching the Olympics. And it works. The period ends with Jay up thirteen points, a record margin for him.

Brody's match is up next. Before he heads to the mat, I find myself beside him.

"Good luck," I say under my breath.

He flashes me a grin that feels like a punch. "Aww, thanks, *Becky*. You gonna come congratulate me later if I win?"

I roll my eyes. "I won my match. Are you going to congratulate me?"

He winks as he pulls on his headgear. "Of course."

He jogs towards the mat, and I can't look away. His red Huntston singlet clings to him like it's painted on. He looks like a sculpture come to life. His shoulders, his thighs, his stupidly perfect muscular ass—he's perfection.

If only he didn't know exactly what he does to me. As evidenced by the cocky little wink he gives me before shaking his opponent's hand and getting set.

The whistle blows.

I blink, and he's already got the other guy pinned. Straight to the mat. Over in seconds flat.

What the actual hell?

He stands up, brushes imaginary dust off his thigh, and shakes the other guy's hand like he didn't just completely embarrass him. He walks off the mat like it's any other day.

The whole time, his eyes are on mine. He crosses the gym, holding my gaze and telling me without words exactly what he's thinking about right now.

My groin tightens, and my lungs struggle to get a deep enough breath.

Why can't I look away?

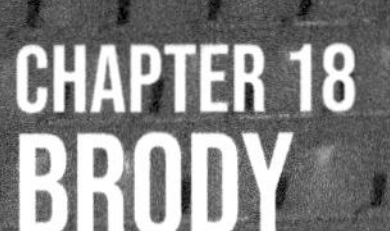

CHAPTER 18
BRODY

I hold Beck's stare, unable to look away from him, even to properly shake hands with my opponent. His eyes on me before the match set a fire in my veins that is quickly becoming a potential hazard for this entire gym. I'm not even sure what happened with my wrestling partner. All I know is I looked down and saw the dude pinned beneath me, looking stunned. I scrambled to get off him quickly before he noticed what kind of impossible situation I'm holding back.

Across the gym, Beck's eyes are fixed on me, like I've got a hand around his throat pulling him closer. The hungry, intense, desperate way he watches me sends a slow, dangerous tingle up my spine. The kind that makes my thighs tighten and my pulse go haywire.

We have a silent, private conversation. You. Me. *Now.*

He takes a few steps towards me, and I start inching towards the nearest exit. I'm pretty sure there's a utility room back here somewhere. Literally any place with enough privacy to get my hands on him would suffice.

Beck's eyes are torn away from mine, jarring me out of my trance-like state. I blink, confused, seeing Beck's back to me all of a sudden. He's walking the other way?

The scope of my vision widens, and I see Mr. Beckett with his hand gripping Beck's arm tightly, dragging him off to the side-lines. Their heads bend low, and by the look of Mr. Beckett's scowl and the rapid-fire movements of his vicious lips, he's likely spitting more of the poison he's perfected.

I watch the fire drain from Beck's eyes. His posture straightens and somehow deflates at the same time. His gaze is trained on the polished concrete under his feet, giving short, clipped nods at whatever bullshit is being spewed at him.

My stomach twists, and I ball my fists so hard my nails dig into my palms. It takes every bit of self-control I have not to march over there and put the esteemed Mr. Charles Beckett on the ground.

I stare so hard that Mr. Beckett must feel it. He cuts his eyes towards me and gives me a dismissive once-over, sneers, and turns back to his son. Beck chances a glance, hollow-eyed and apologetic. When I'm sure I have his attention, I tilt my chin towards the locker rooms with a wordless command.

Come.

Then I turn to my right and walk along the edge of the gym towards the locker rooms. If he doesn't follow... No. He will. I don't let myself consider otherwise. Not until I'm alone for long enough that I start to question it.

The shouts and clapping from the crowd grows louder as the door swings open, then muffles again when it closes. My heartbeat hammers, and I turn around to face Beck as he walks in.

His shoulders are tight, body language guarded. His eyes have shadows that weren't there ten minutes ago. He looks exhausted.

But when those dark eyes flick up to meet mine, something sparks. Something I can read.

Something I can work with.

Without saying a word, I turn and walk through the entrance to the showers. I can hear his footsteps behind me.

He follows me all the way to the back, where there are a few single stalls that rarely get used. I reach deep into the stall to turn the water on so there's sound to drown out our voices and turn around just as Beck steps inside and pulls the curtain closed.

"Are you alright?" I ask finally. I'm not sure if that's what he wants to hear right now, but I need to ask. I want him to know I care about more than getting off.

"I'm fine," he snaps. Then he shakes his head and takes a breath, actively releasing the tension from his shoulders. "I'm fine," he says more softly.

"You don't have to lie to me. Or downplay anything."

He swallows deeply, looks down at his feet, then back up at me. He rakes a hand through his hair, and shrugs.

I cock my head thoughtfully. "What can I do?" Please say it. I need you to say it, Becky. *Tell me you need me.*

There's a long beat of silence, but his eyes say everything. Make me forget. Get me out of my head. Take control before I lose myself.

I nod my understanding and start peeling out of my singlet while I kick my shoes to the far corner. He does the same.

Our uniforms hit the tile in a tangle, and then his hands are on me, mine are on him, and we're desperately pawing at each other, rolling along the shower wall until we're under the water.

His skin is warm from the match, the steam of the room, and the mess of feelings he's drowning in that he doesn't know how to name. I lick up his neck, and he tilts his head back instinctively, exposing his throat, offering it to me. My mouth works its way to the spot just under his jaw that makes him moan.

"Brody..." he breathes, barely audible.

I kiss along his neck, across his collarbone, down the slope of his shoulder, tasting salt and heat and him. He grips my waist, fingers digging in, and lets me drink from his skin. Fleetingly, I remember how much of himself he's willing to give me.

I press him back against the wall, water streaming over us. His chest rises with each hitched breath.

I reach for the wall dispenser and pump soap into my palm, sliding my hand down between us. He gasps when I take him in hand and drops his forehead to my shoulder. His hips rock forward, pushing his cock through my slick fist, and groans.

"Look at me," I murmur, wanting to see the moment the pleasure cuts through everything else.

He obeys, eyes blown wide, mouth parted, breathless. He's so damn beautiful.

I lean in, eyes locked on his mouth, and he turns his head, my lips landing on his jaw instead. I grunt and try to capture his mouth again, but he turns at the last second. He isn't smiling, if anything there's a touch of sadness behind the lust again. It's a plea for me to understand.

He's not ready for this, but he doesn't want to make it a thing. He wants the game. He needs it.

"You don't want to give me your mouth?" I ask, trying to keep my tone dark and teasing, even though his avoidance pisses me off a little. At least I'll be able to take it out on him in a way that satisfies us both. "I don't need to look at your pretty face to get off," I say, and grab his shoulders to spin him around.

I turn him towards the wall and tell him to hold on while guiding his hands to the metal bar. His muscles flex under my palms, water carving lines down his back. I consider what I want to do to him. Not wanting to use soap to lube an attempt to see how many fingers I can stretch him around before he comes, I settle my gaze on his thick, muscular thighs.

"I don't like it when you don't give me what I want, Becky," I warn. "Now you're going to have to do some significant begging if you want me to let you come." I lick up his spine, and he arches so beautifully I want to praise him, but that's not what he needs right now. "I'm going to use you like a toy, mark you in my cum, and leave you wanting if you don't convince me you're a good girl before I'm finished with you."

I pull his body back against me, our skin slapping together with a wet smack, and Beck lets out a sound I don't think he meant to make out loud. "I'll take that as a yes," I say, biting his earlobe.

How's that for getting out of your head, Becky?

I reach for another handful of soap and coat my dick before pushing my hand between Beck's thighs. I tease his taint and his balls until his hips are twitching back against me and he moans, pulling away just as he's starting to melt into the pleasure of me playing with him. I push his shoulder blades down, pull his hips out, and make a show out of rearranging his body like he's a life-sized doll.

Guiding my cock between his thighs, I tap on his hip lightly. "Squeeze your legs together, sweetheart. I'm going to fuck this slit like it's my own personal pocket pussy."

He chokes out some kind of garbled reply, but I ignore him and start thrusting, not bothering to go slow, adjusting his position until he's just right. Not just to maximize my pleasure or because we don't have long before we aren't alone in the locker rooms, but to enhance the sensory experience for him. I want him to smell nothing but the basic bitch sports brand body wash I'm using to lube my assault on his thighs. I want him see nothing but the tile wall in front of him and his cock bouncing as mine juts out beneath it. Hear nothing but the water running, the wet squelch of my cock moving between his flesh, and the smacking of our bodies as they collide.

He's a writhing, moaning mess. He's tried to let go of the stability bar several times to jerk his cock, but every time I fucked into him harder and faster, until bubbles start to run down the inside of our legs.

"Brody—" he whispers, voice barely holding together.

"Are you going to be a good girl and let me come all over you?"

He nods and moans, pushing back against me and arching his spine. Fuck, that little move has me riding a razor-thin edge. I grunt, the first burst of my release rocketing out of me as my thrusts slow just in time for our teammates to start filtering into the locker room. Luckily, they're all loud fucks, so we know when they enter and it usually takes a few minutes for the showers to start.

Brody stiffens and tries to move away like I'm going to stop, but hold his hips tighter and keep pounding, my hips making loud, wet smacks with each thrust. The whole time, I'm holding my breath to keep from moaning and shouting how fucking perfect he is. I wrap my arms around his waist from behind and keep him there until I'm spent, and then longer because I'm not ready to let go.

"Best pocket pussy I ever used," I murmur quietly.

He laughs, but nervously, pulling himself from my arms and flicking his eyes towards the curtain and the sounds on the other side of the locker room.

"I guess you'll have to beg for me later," I say, making an exaggerated pouty face and looking down at his straining dick while I rinse myself off. There's a mess of cum and foam from the soap I used between his legs all over his thighs and down his legs, and his knees are shaking.

"You're a mess, baby girl. You should probably clean yourself up."

Leaving him in the shower stall looking dazed and terrified, I walk out naked and into the locker room, loudly greeting my teammates with congratulations and compliments about some of their various matches.

Fish asks why I'm wet and naked already, and I wink jokingly before making up a bullshit excuse about having to pee and deciding to get a jump on the line for showers.

"I'm fucking starving," I say, drying my hair while walking to my locker. "What are we doing for lunch?"

"I dunno man, but I'm going to need you to put that thing away before it eats me," Cade says, pointing at my dick with his entire arm outstretched.

"Aw, this little guy?" I say, giving my flaccid dick an affectionate pat. "Don't worry, he's not aggressive."

Our friends around us laugh, but as I'm pulling on my boxer briefs, fucking Pierce Jamison has to throw his two cents in.

"That's no surprise. I hear whiskey dick can become a permanent issue. But I guess if you're the one getting pounded, you don't need to be able to get it up."

"You're the least equipped person here to know anything about that, Jamison," I say as sweetly as possible, deliberately cutting my eyes down towards his crotch with emphasized faux sympathy.

"Quit looking at my dick, fucking perv."

"There's nothing to look at from where I'm standing."

Pierce looks like a cartoon bomb about to go off, smoke practically coming out of his ears. His face is almost purple, and the way he's holding his breath makes him look constipated.

"Now feels like a good time for you to pick a fight with someone bigger than you. Or maybe say something obnoxious and homophobic again, if you're looking to make a bigger ass of yourself," I say casually, giving him my back to pull some clothes from my locker.

"Fuck you, Miller. We all know you're one bad week away from drinking yourself into an early grave just like your old man."

"Pierce!" Sean barks, his voice bigger than his usually quiet demeanor would suggest. It's enough to get everyone's attention.

Of all people, Beck steps between the guys who have crowded around to watch the spectacle. He must have slipped in when everyone was paying attention to the showdown.

"That's enough, Jamison. That was out of line, and you know it." He stares him down. "Sit your ass down before you embarrass this team any further."

Then he turns those deep brown eyes on me, just as stern and with every bit of anger and animosity he's held for me all year. "For fuck's sake, Miller, put some goddamn pants on."

Cade snorts, and several others burst out laughing. Beck turns back to his locker, and the rest of the room settles into their normal after-dual routines.

Not an hour later, I bombard Beck on his way back from lunch with his roommates, pushing him into our favorite stairwell, and dropping to my knees.

I miss a day of classes, and I know I'll pay for it later, but when the care home calls to say Ms. Delia is having a reasonably lucid day, I don't even think twice. I drop everything and make the forty-minute drive to spend as much time with my true family as I can.

Visiting with Ms. Delia, even when she can't remember my name or isn't quite sure where or when she is, is no hardship. She's always pleasant, even when it's clear that she's confused or when she randomly realizes I'm not my father. That's usually the only time I have to break her reality. I never correct her unless she's distressed, but I can't stand seeing her look at me with thinly veiled disappointment while she tells me I ought to spend more time with my son or asks if Mrs. Beckett plans to come in and hold the baby today. Most of the time, she's asking me if I want her to make me some mashed potatoes and peas or asking about my friends from middle school. At her worst, she's quiet and tired a lot. Those days we listen to music or I read to her from her stack of Jane Austen and Bronte novels.

But the days when I walk through the doors and see her eyes light up with recognition, pride, and surprised tears in her eyes over seeing how much I've grown since the last time she can remember, every hug and minute spent chatting with her means so much more.

We're sitting in the sunroom attached to her suite, a tiny room with big windows and daffodil-yellow painted walls. It's just big enough for a tiny round tea table, two chairs, and a row of plant holders below the windows. There are hanging plants, plus a small terrarium of succulents we made together over a year ago on the small table. It's as warm as a greenhouse in this little alcove of her bedroom, and I'm sitting back, watching her fuss over her plants like they're babies, humming under her breath as she spritzes the leaves.

She glances over her shoulder. "You're quiet today, Linc," she says. "Is everything alright with school? I can't believe you're a junior in college already. It's like I blinked and you grew up." She pauses thoughtfully. "Then again, most of the time I don't know what year it is, so who knows? Tomorrow you might walk in here a married man with two-point-five kids and a potbelly."

It'd be sad if she weren't snickering at her own joke. This is how I know she's fully here with me. As much as it hurts to know she's lost time and missed things, she always falls back into her old self, joking and making light of things that feel too heavy. It's a personality trait of hers that greatly benefitted me growing up. I always took everything so seriously, even more so than I do now.

"I'm not sure that's in the cards for me," I laugh.

She makes a 'pish-posh' sound that always made me giggle as a kid. "You're still quite young to worry about things like that. You'll meet someone someday, and all kinds of possibilities will open up for you. Maybe not the potbelly, and maybe not kids if you don't want them. Hell, not even marriage. Lord knows I wasn't interested in that. But you'll find love and build your own kind of family." She reaches out and lays her hand on mine, soft and warm. "I found one kind of love when I was young, and I let it get away from me. But I found a family and a new kind of love when your parents brought you home."

However cold my parents were, whatever pressure I felt to be and act a certain way, Ms. Delia was always my safe space. The one person I knew I could go to, who sheltered and truly cared for me.

My eyes fill with tears. "I love you, Ms. Delia."

Her hand squeezes mine, a tear falling from her watery grey eyes. She rarely cries, even when her disease has taken her through her worst days. "I love you, child. And I hope you know that I mean that unconditionally."

I swallow a lump that threatens to suffocate me.

Looking away to swipe a tear away and clear my throat. "I'm still dating Caty. I don't know if you remember meeting her?"

Ms. Delia narrows her eyes. "Yes, I remember. Nice girl. Tiny thing, right?"

I grin. "That'd be her."

"She's certainly gorgeous. And smart as a whip."

"Yes ma'am. I'm lucky to have her."

"Does she know that you're only dating her to distract your father?"

I choke. "Ms. Delia!"

"What?" She asks incredulously. "I thought we had an understanding that our love is unconditional. So we can be honest with each other, right?"

"Well, of course, but—"

"Linc, honey. Who knows how long I'll be... Well, *me*? Sometimes when you're here, there are things I want to tell you and talk about, but I can't seem to move the words from my brain to my mouth. So while I have the chance, I want to make sure you know you have someone on your side. Someone who knows and loves and supports you no matter what. Even if I am a walking advertisement for dementia."

"I know that..."

"Well, I need to know that you aren't leading that lovely young woman astray. Because if you're stringing her along, making her think—"

"She knows," I blurt out. "She knows, and she's doing the same thing, for the same reasons." My voice tapers off, and I stare at a yellow spot on a pothos for so long, I worry Ms. Delia has left the room.

But she's sitting in the other chair, her cardigan rumpled and glasses hanging off a chain around her neck, watching me. When I turn back to her, a slow grin spreads across her face.

Diabolical woman.

"I thought that might be the case," she says haughtily. "She had a vibe about her."

My eyebrows press up my hairline.

"What?" she says, shrugging. "It's called gaydar."

I sputter and laugh when Ms. Delia throws back her head and cackles like she just told the funniest joke, and I'm the punchline. This old woman is something else.

When our laughter calms down, she gives me a gentle smile, and her voice softens. "Come here," she says.

I get up from my seat and walk over to her. I try perching on the arm of the chair, but I'm worried I might break it, so instead I sink down onto the floor next to her and set my chin on the arm instead. She smiles and brushes some hair back from my forehead, gently combing my hair with her fingers. It's so comforting that my eyes flutter shut, causing a tear to fall from each eye.

"I've never been a particularly religious woman, but since the day your parents brought you home, I've felt called to pull you in close and love you like you were my own. I sometimes wonder if there might have been forces in the universe that brought us together, because what we both needed at those times in our lives happened to coincide. That's why you're my *Linc.* And maybe that same force, God, or whatever you want to call it, brought me clarity today to tell you something very important."

My eyes sting. I swallow hard and force myself to give her the respect of my full attention, eye contact and all, even though I seem to be hard-wired to turn away when I feel too much.

She sniffs. "Your father is an idiot."

A bubble of laughter escapes me. It's something she's said a handful of times since I reached my teenage years and she wasn't my full-time caregiver anymore. By then, I think she didn't worry too much about whether she might get fired, or maybe she'd just gotten old enough to be fed up. She didn't agree with the way my father spoke to me, or his high expectations that I follow the exact path he laid out for me under the penalty of losing all his support. It was Ms. Delia who had me open separate savings and investment accounts with any allowances or gifts I was given over the years, in case he made good on his threats.

"I never liked that man. You couldn't have paid me enough to stick around if it hadn't been for your mother dropping you in my lap after the first nanny they hired quit three days in. Not because you weren't the sweetest, most perfect cherub, but because she caught your father sniffing around the poor young thing, as if that was her fault. Luckily for me, I was already too old to be of any interest, and I happened to have some talent for settling you." She smiles dreamily, her eyes bright with whatever memories are playing behind them.

She huffs. "Charles Xavior Beckett thought intimidation was a tenet of child rearing. He treated you like an employee, punished you for accomplishments any other parent would have praised you for, and made you feel inferior, so you'd never consider rising above him. I like to think I counteracted some of the damage that man could have done to an impressionable child, but there was only so much I could do and shield you from. Between wanting to keep you safe and losing my mind somewhere along the way, I never got to tell you one thing."

A tear slips down my cheek before I can stop it, and she brushes it away with her thumb.

"You are perfect exactly as you are. And I'm not talking about all the trophies and straight-A's and the bright, successful future you have ahead of you. I'm talking about who you are, and every part of you that makes you whole and happy."

I cover my face with my hands, too raw to hold back the overwhelming emotions coursing through me.

She pries them gently away. "To hell with your father or anyone else who can't accept you for the amazing man you are."

I huff. "If only it were that easy."

"Well, I'm here to tell you that it gets easier to not give a damn as you get older. But I don't recommend waiting too long, because I am also here to tell you that holding back who you are and not allowing yourself the freedom and comfort of living and loving the way you were meant to, will only lead to regrets down the road."

Her pale grey eyes are intense, the meaning behind her words clear in their intentions.

Ms. Delia has regrets and has held onto something painful. If I'm reading the heartbreak behind her eyes correctly, it's because she held back an integral part of herself.

I know your truth, Becky.

"Can I tell you about this guy I met?"

———

Life is strange. Or rather, it's different.

There's been a significant shift in, well, everything. I've noticed that I am both more at ease and on edge than usual. Bouncing between settled and anxious like there's no state of being between the two extremes.

My classes are the same, as are the regular interactions with my father. The closer we get to a wrestling event, the more I get the pleasure of hearing from him. He calls often and asks if I've been working on my form and endurance, or he wants to break down defense techniques because he feels my hand-fighting and shot defense still need work. This, of course, is on top of the regular inquiries about my schedule, because he doesn't think I'm disciplined enough. He wants detailed breakdowns of how I've been spending my days, and how I'm staying on top of my diet and conditioning program, whether I'm doing my lifts on schedule, if I'm getting enough reps in, and how my classes are going. In case I need more reminders that anything less than perfection isn't good enough, and that a 3.85 grade point average means there's "room for improvement."

What's changed, I think, is me. Since my visit with Ms. Delia, I've felt less reactive to my father's overbearing nature. Maybe I needed the reminder that he isn't perfect, and that his standards are near impossible. Whether or not that's by design, I don't know, it's too much to consider.

The energy between Brody and me has also shifted. There's less animosity during practice and when we run into each other on campus. I wouldn't say we're friends, but there's no outright fighting. Morning lift has become almost companionable. This morning we found ourselves side-by-side on the treadmills for some light cardio and didn't try to compete with each other. Brody even passed me one of his earbuds to share his music with me. It was ... Well, it was weird. But not unwelcome.

And that might have something to do with my visit with Ms. Delia too. Because for the first time in my life, I said the words I've never said out loud before, not even to myself. Not because I didn't know, but because I didn't want to acknowledge it. Even when discussing the details of my toxic relationship with sex and self-acceptance with Caty, I never actually came out and said *I'm gay.*

Part of me hoped that if I didn't acknowledge it, it would go away. Before meeting Caty, I thought that maybe if I dated enough women, tried acting the way I was *supposed* to, or did everything I could to *prove* my straightness, that I could discipline it out of me, but I hated everything. Meeting Caty was perfect because I didn't have to pretend with her. She recognized me from the start as someone who shared something in common with her—the necessity to put on a show for their parents.

It was at a mixer during our freshman year. I'd gone to the poorly disguised meat market with the intention of finding a girl my father would approve of who wouldn't require me to actually *do* anything. Someone with low expectations of the kind of attention they'd receive from me. On the outside, Caty seemed sweet and innocent, she had a kind of *saving myself for marriage* vibe I thought I might be able to work with. Until she opened her mouth. And her eyes, because she kept staring longingly at the tables that were reserved for the campus Pride Alliance, where a gorgeous girl with golden skin and blue hair was chatting with a tall, willowy black man wearing shimmery eye shadow. I asked if she knew the blue-haired girl, and Caty had sighed and muttered, "I wish," before she could stop herself. When she narrowed her eyes at me and said, "You didn't hear that," I mimed zipping my lips.

Later that night, Caty informed me that she's a raging lesbian, but her parents had threatened to cut her off if she didn't prove to them that she's a *good girl* which meant straight-A's, a degree from a prestigious university that her mother is on the board of directors for, and being on the arm of a dashing young man from a good family—rich, conservative, and powerful—whether that was what she wanted or not. She was playing along so she could get a good degree, make her own fortune, then someday publicly donate every cent of their blood money to the most offensive queer charities she could find. Her words.

I think I started planning our lavender marriage on the spot.

Without realizing it, my relationship with Caty gave me the space I needed to stop pretending and pushing myself to change. And it was Caty's 'try it, you might like it' mentality that led me down my first dark hallway to let a man put his mouth on me for the first time.

It was Brody, of course, who gave me the opportunity to try so much more. So, so much more.

But the acceptance of the only person who's ever loved me is what gave me the confidence to admit to her, and myself, that this is part of who I am.

So maybe that's why I've so easily fallen into an unspoken routine with Brody. Where a look is shared between us, and we both show up at our spot on the stairwell without ever making the plan to meet. Or randomly following each other into empty rooms around campus. There's less fight there, but I'm not sure how to feel about that. He gives me what I need by telling me what to do, and taking control of not only his pleasure, but mine too. He used to make me orgasm as a point, as if to prove to me that he saw through my lies and denial.

Now that I'm not denying it, it's not much of a game anymore. And that alone is freaking me out. It's making me antsy in a way that only seems to be soothed by spending *more* time in his presence. Which, of course, fucks with my head even more.

So I decide to do what any mature adult would do in a situation like this.

I make a plan to fuck with his head as much as he's fucking with mine.

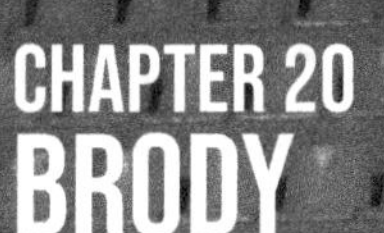

CHAPTER 20
BRODY

I don't know which one of us made the first move. It could have been him. It might have been me.

Or maybe it was both of us. Maybe the second our eyes locked across the dining hall, he felt the same hot, electric jolt ignite him into movement that I did. A flash of something primal and desperate that let him know I was going to bend him over and own him in front of everyone if we didn't get to somewhere private as soon as possible.

All I know is I'm on my knees, face buried in his ass, sucking and tonguing his hole like I might extract the last drop of lifesaving ambrosia. I've got a proprietary grip on his thighs, pulling him back against me while my mouth makes him squirm and push back on my face.

We're in a stupid position, in the middle of the stairwell where he tripped and I caught his hips to tear off his pants and underwear. His boxer briefs are torn and hanging off his ankle, pants strewn haphazardly on the stairs somewhere behind us. Beck has one hand gripping the handrail, the other braced against a stair, one knee pushed up higher than the other, body bent forward in a way that makes every moan, gasp, and whimper echo off the concrete. My knees feel like they're bleeding from when I fell onto them so heavily when I tackled him. But the way he's falling apart, breaths heavy, and raspy voice breaking as he tries to keep his sounds inside him, is so needy and wrecked that I don't give a single thought to the likelihood of us getting caught. All I care about is making him say my name and marking my territory however I can.

Beck struggles to hold the railing as he rocks his hips, whimpering when his silent demands for more only result in me releasing him. I lean back, just enough to look at his glistening wet hole. One hand palms the curve of his ass, the other cups my aching dick.

I rest my thumb lightly against the center of him, not breaching, not giving him what he's begging for, just circling lazily, admiring the way he trembles at the slightest touch. Leaning forward, I blow a soft stream of air along his crack and press a kiss to his hole.

"How did we end up here?" I murmur against his skin, breath warm.

He answers with a desperate sound that isn't a word, pushing back towards my hand like he can't stop himself.

"That's right. You were being a brat. Isn't that right?"

Beck groans. "It's not like you weren't doing the same thing, and you know it!"

"You started it. I was just proving a point."

"Okay, well you did it. Point made. Now just... *Nyghh*—Please, Brody," he growls, pushing back against me.

I let the tip of my thumb barely penetrate the tight rim of his hole, but don't allow him to push back any farther. The frustrated little cry he lets out is delicious.

"You really think you deserve to come after that stunt?" I ask, using my other hand to reach into my pants and stroke myself. "Because I think what you deserve is to go back to your room soaked in my cum and go to bed dirty. Maybe then it'll sink in who you belong to."

Beck gasps, and his ass tightens around the tip of my thumb. Goddamn his desperation is fucking me up. It's so hard not to give in and give him what he wants, what we both want because the only thing better than making him beg for me is making him come for me. Hearing my name on his lips as he shatters to pieces.

But he did that shit on purpose. He was asking for me to punish him when his little girlfriend, with her perfectly polished nails and big-eyed innocent smile, sat next to him at dinner, and he pulled her right into his lap. Her pert little ass perched right on his big, strong thighs.

The very same thighs that I'd shoved myself between on the floor of a library study room so I could dry hump him to completion. *My* thighs. *My* lap.

That was *my* man she was sitting on, even if he won't say it. Even if deep down I know she's just his beard, a really fucking pretty beard at that, and they're both pretending. They're still pretending that he's not mine, and I don't like that.

He's mine.

Mine. Mine.

Fucking *mine*.

I felt myself getting hot even though I knew he was doing it on purpose. It was obvious by the way he cut his eyes to me while he was whispering in her ear, checking my reactions every time she giggled. Or smirked like he'd won something when my eyes tracked his hand on the outside of her thigh as he played like he was teasing her.

Fuck that. I wasn't about to give him the satisfaction of letting him know he'd gotten to me. I might let Lincoln Beckett pin me on the wrestling mats here and there, but I'll be damned if I let him win this game between us.

So I looked away. Tried to paint a cool, calm, aloof version of myself that Beck could be proud of. And as I did, I accidentally locked eyes with the baseball player I'd talked to the night of the Halloween party. Tripp Landon, who I now know is the shortstop for the Howlers baseball team.

Tripp is cute, and an unapologetic flirt. So when he sauntered by to chat with me, I stood up and gave him the attention Beck was so obviously fighting for. If I'm being really honest, I don't even remember what he was talking about. He was telling me something about talking up their team's batboy in a bathroom the night before, and getting shut down by their catcher, who he thinks is far too involved in the other guy's business. I think I might have joked about the catcher and batboy possibly having something going on, which made him bark out a laugh that had Beck suddenly on his feet.

I could feel his stare drilling into the side of my face. Hell, I could almost hear the damage he was doing to his molars from clenching his jaw so tightly.

Very quietly, I told Tripp that I would see him around. Quietly enough that he had to lean in a little too close to hear me. And there was that flirtatious little grin he had no idea was putting him in danger of spontaneously combusting from the lasers in Beck's eyes.

Then all of a sudden, Beck's little girlfriend walked between us and pushed Tripp playfully as she admonished him. "What's this I hear about you harassing sweet, innocent Ellis Hope?" But as she passed me, she gave me her own saucy smirk and whispered, "Well played."

I chuckled, then cut my eyes at Beck.

We both stood there for a moment that felt long and weighted by the tense energy between us, while the rest of the dining hall seemed to go about their business around us.

Then Beck swallowed, and I tracked the motion of his Adam's apple and realized I needed to get away from the general population before I ended up knocking everyone out of my way with the huge boner growing behind my shorts. I suppose Beck realized the same, because he started moving at the same time.

One second we were staring at each other from opposite sides of a table, the next I had him tackled in a stairwell. And now I'm hovering over him, looking into his soul through his asshole, trying to decide which one of us needs to be taught a lesson the most.

He's bent in front of me, breaths echoing off the cold concrete, whimpering that he's sorry. His body is trembling, and there's a puddle forming on the step his cock is bobbing over, dripping because his reaction to me in a state like this is always so helpless.

Oh, fucking hell. He really did do this on purpose.

"Tell me, baby. What kind of reaction did you think you were going to get out of me, huh?" I ask, pulling my thumb from him and caressing my hand over the roundness of his muscular cheek.

He opens his mouth to answer, or possibly to mouth off, I don't know. Whatever he was about to say quickly morphs into a high-pitched shriek that adds to the reverberation of my palm smacking against his skin.

His whole body stiffens, then shudders, and melts in one fluid movement.

Again. *SMACK.*

SMACK.

SMACK!

With the last crash of my palm against his ass, Beck moans out unintelligible gibberish that includes words that sound like, "Oh my God, I'm going to come."

I reach around his body to take his cock in my hand, and Beck pushes against me, murmuring, "Yes. God. Yes. Please."

I pinch the head of his dick hard enough to make him yelp again. Enough pre-cum slicks my hand that I'm almost worried it was too late, but the way he's cursing me lets me know I was able to stop his orgasm.

I know, I'm awful.

But he asked for this. He wanted this.

Because getting each other off nearly every day isn't enough. It isn't enough and it's too much at the same time.

I curve my body over Beck's back and speak against the shell of his ear. "I'm sorry," I whisper. "I thought we were done with these kinds of games, but I see now that you still want to play."

Wrapping my now slick hand around my cock, I jerk myself hard and fast. I'm so on edge after this whole ordeal, that it doesn't take much before I'm shooting all over Beck's ass. It drips down his crack onto his balls, and I smear the rest of it around with my hand.

Massaging my cum into the hot, red handprints I left on his ass.

"Tell me who you belong to, Becky."

"Y-you," he whimpers immediately.

I'm floored. I was expecting him to keep playing the game, to make me force it out of him. But he doesn't.

"I'm *your* good girl," he whispers.

I'm your good girl.

I shake myself out of my shock long enough to get my bearings. But I manage to get myself together enough to wrap my hand back around his cock, shove two cum-slicked fingers inside him, and growl as I make him come all over the concrete stairs.

"That's fucking right you are."

———

Competition days are my favorite. There's something more in the air than just the smell of sweaty bodies and antiseptic cleaner. It's more than Coach's voice echoing off the rafters of the Huntston wrestling facility, calling us to order with a pep talk that wavers between awkward and violent. There's an electricity that hums beneath my skin and gets passed between teammates.

Today is even better, because it's our first quad meet. Huntston is hosting three other teams for an all-day competition. As an upperclassman and one of two people in my weight class on my team, I'll have three matches ahead of me before the day is through. Some of the guys are understandably intimidated or exhausted by the idea, especially the newer guys who haven't competed in a quad meet before. But to me, it's invigorating.

Getting ready for this meet has been more fun than usual. The one thing that sucks about wrestling is cutting weight, but when it involves getting sweaty with a certain grouchy submissive asshole, I don't mind it so much.

I'm feeling energized. I've been buzzing all morning. Although it feels like I'm always buzzing lately, whenever he's in my orbit. Since the other night in the stairwell, things have been intense, to say the least. I'm not sure what this is exactly, and I can tell he's still trying to play with me as if it puts more space between us, but I don't mind the games when the prize is so fucking sexy.

Like finding creative ways to make Beck desperate for my cum before he even thinks to beg me for his own orgasm, like he did less than an hour ago when I helped him with his refueling after getting weighed in this morning.

"Jesus, Miller. What the fuck?!" Cade screeches, shielding his eyes. "Put that thing away, you're scaring my ancestors!"

I shake my head and laugh as I finish pulling on my uniform. "My dick isn't even out, Cade. And I told you not to worry about it, it doesn't want to hurt you."

"Well thank fuck for that, but why you gotta be swinging it around like that, man? Did you forget to feed it or something?"

I laugh into my sports drink and finish the bottle. "Can't help it. I was just thinking about this real pretty girl I know."

Cade starts to nod, but stops. I chuckle, winking at Beck as I walk past him and out of the locker room. I hear Cade's confused questions as I'm pushing through the door. "Wait. What did he say?"

I'm almost expecting the sharp push that comes from behind me.

"What the hell is wrong with you?!"

Beck tries to look stern, but I can tell from the twitching at the corner of his mouth and the pink flush of his cheeks that he doesn't hate it.

"What? Should I have told him about how that pretty girl got down on her knees for me and—"

Beck smacks a hand over my mouth and whisper-shouts, trying to hold back a laugh. "Shut it! Shut up!"

"Okay, okay! Geesh, Becky. Who knew you were such a prude?"

Beck rolls his eyes, and I snicker as we make our way to the main gym floor. The other teams are each set up in opposite corners of the gym. Today we're hosting three teams, UNC, Greensboro, and Davidson College. The wrestlers from Davidson College are set up closest to us.

I hear the snide laughter before I register who it's from. And in the few seconds it takes to look over my shoulder, my good mood plummets.

Pierce is halfway across the divide between us and the Davidson team, chatting and laughing with yet another familiar face from my past. Gregg Thompson was another rich douche who followed Pierce and his brother around like they were holding court. And if I remember correctly, he was one of the jesters. Gregg loved to play stupid pranks, trip me in the halls, and insult my family as loudly, and publicly, as possible. The more people around to hear his bullshit, the more he got off on his own sick humor.

There's some more laughter, and a few of the underclassmen who still follow Pierce around join them. I don't miss the way they're jeering at me as they snicker and whisper.

Beck snaps at Pierce to knock it off and take the meet seriously, and Sean calls the underclassmen over to him to discuss some last-minute strategy before the first matches begin. Pierce shoots a look back to Gregg that I don't like at all. It's like I can feel things going sideways before it even starts.

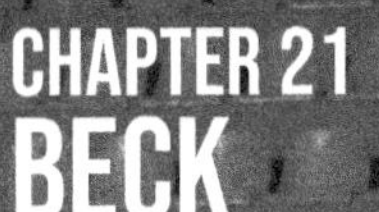

CHAPTER 21
BECK

I don't know who this douchebag is, but I'm glad I'm the one paired with him instead of Brody. There was something about the tension in his shoulders the moment he looked over and saw this guy palling around with Pierce Jamison that concerned me. I know he doesn't like Pierce, and for good fucking reason, so this guy probably deserves the beatdown I'm giving him so far this match.

The start of the third period was an aggressive grapple, but we've found ourselves on our feet. I'm locked in, confident and controlled, knowing that I only need to keep him from closing the gap in points to take this as my third win for today.

My opponent flicks his eyes up over my shoulder. I take advantage of his momentary distraction and get him in a near-fall, but he recovers before I can get him down. He's pissed that he can't get control of me, and despite being a decent opponent because I haven't been able to pin him down yet, I'm running this match.

Gregg leans in. I'm anticipating the shit talk. This is how it always happens. They have to lean in close enough so the refs and coaches can't hear it, but that's not what he does. This bastard pitches his voice loud enough to be heard.

"So, Beckett," Gregg says, mouth curling in a cruel smirk. "I heard you're Miller's new butt buddy. Which one of you bends over and takes it. I bet it's you. You look like you'd spread real easy for him."

For a moment, the gym falls into a strange hush. A breath of silence long enough for everyone nearby to register what he said. There are some gasps. A few choked laughs.

The loudest sound, though, is a buzzing that starts in the back of my head and gets louder until I can't hear anything else. I freeze.

In slow motion, I stumble back and lose my footing. Gregg doesn't come after me to take advantage because the ref steps between us immediately. There's a whistle, I think, but it's muffled. He signals, and with one hand in the middle of Gregg's chest, gestures to the Davidson coach. The Davidson coach steps forward to grab Gregg by the arm, but movement to my left has me turning towards the bench. My teammates look pissed, their mouths open and yelling something, or shaking their heads, but my attention is directed behind them.

At my father.

My father, who stands up, locks his eyes on me long enough to show his disappointment. No, his disgust.

Coach McCoy takes my arm and directs me off the mats, his face red as his booming voice yells something at Gregg and the Davidson coach. A few of my teammates come forward. Brody comes forward.

I back away and shrug everyone off, lifting my chin.

I'm fine. That guy was an idiot. Doesn't know what he's talking about. I'm fine.

I'm fine.

The team buys it. Coach McCoy buys it. I don't look at Brody at all.

I chance a glance up at my father again, but he's not there. My head swivels, and I see him halfway to the front door.

He didn't buy it.

World Wrestling Cup 2016

CHAPTER 22
BRODY

I haven't seen Beck since Friday's match.

After watching his father stare at him so coldly, then stand up and leave without a word, I saw him shut down completely. He'd already shut me out, having been called out by one of my old teammates the way he did. I understood he needed to put physical distance between us.

He did well brushing off everyone's concerns and pretending like he didn't care what Gregg Thompson had said. Everyone was shocked enough that Thompson had the balls or the complete lack of brains necessary to shout that out. He had to know that would get him disqualified. Then again, he probably knew he couldn't win anyway.

Beck might not have faltered at all if not for his father's reaction. I saw the look in his eyes when he'd stood and stared Beck down, that he saw the truth of what Thompson had said. Or at least that there was some truth to it. Maybe he knows his son well enough to read his body language, or the look of fear I saw in his eyes before he was able to cover it up.

Until that moment, I thought he'd be able to recover from this, but after the match, he disappeared. And now for the first time since this push-and-pull thing between us started, I don't know how to reach him. And every fierce and protective instinct I have screams that Beck is drifting somewhere I can't let him go.

I don't want to push him too much, but I'm worried about him. It's been days since I've seen him, and I don't know what to do about it. I don't know if I've earned the right to be this concerned or do anything about it. What if this is more one sided than it felt just days ago?

Beck didn't show up to any workouts over the weekend, nor did I see him once in the dining hall or dorm rec room. I checked the library and stalked his hall in the dorms for a while. So many times I was tempted to knock on the door to his room, but I knew it would put him more on edge if someone saw me show up to check on him. We haven't been outright fighting, and have even been cordial to each other lately, but suddenly showing up to see if he's okay after someone from my past made a comment like that? It'd be suspicious, and I know he wouldn't appreciate it. Not now.

I've texted him, but there's been no reply. The messages aren't being marked as read, so I don't even know if he's seeing them. I gave him space all weekend, checking my phone more often than I want to admit.

He's not at Monday morning lift, and when he's not present for practice or the film review session this afternoon, I'm annoyed. I stop pretending I'm giving him space. He's avoiding me. On purpose. With an almost impressive level of commitment. I text him way too many times, expecting him to get annoyed and text me back with some kind of denial or even for him to get angry with me. But I get nothing.

When Beck misses another team lift and isn't at the library for his normal Tuesday afternoon Finance Club meeting, my frustration shifts into worry. Avoidance is one thing, total disappearance is another. Fish and I are in an Exercise Science class together on Tuesday afternoons, our last class before the holiday break begins. I run after him once the class is dismissed, pretending to be casual.

"Hey," I say. "You heading home for break after today?"

Fish nods. "Yeah, I'm actually headed straight out now so I can hopefully avoid traffic around Atlanta, otherwise my drive home goes from eleven hours to fourteen."

"Dude, that sucks."

"You leaving tomorrow?"

"Yeah, but my drive is only an hour and a half."

"Lucky bastard."

I laugh and shrug, listening to him drone on about one of his uncles setting their shed on fire while trying to deep fry a turkey last year, until eventually I steer the conversation where I need it to go.

"You seen Beck?" I ask as casually as I can manage.

Fish makes a face. "Yeah. He's sick as a dog."

"What?"

"Yeah, flu or something maybe, I don't know. Cade and I have been keeping our distance."

So he's sick and alone? A cold, heavy weight drops into my gut. Why didn't he tell me?

"Cade left already," Fish adds, shifting his backpack. "And I'm heading out now. Beck will probably sleep all day. I'm sure he'll be back to practice after Thanksgiving."

He thinks I'm worried about him missing practice? Maybe because he's my sparring partner. Whatever, he can believe what he wants. I have what I need now.

I walk out to the parking lot with Fish and wave him off, getting into my car to head to the nearest pharmacy. I load up on sports drinks, cough drops, tissues, an overpriced humidifier, and about five different cold meds that they probably think I'm making meth with, but I don't know what symptoms he has. After explaining why I'm buying so much random shit, the clerk helps me narrow it down to three, and directs me to a deli. On my way back to campus, I stop and get two large containers of soup.

By the time I reach his dorm, arms heavy with several bags of wellness supplies and way too much soup, I'm half expecting him to not answer the door at all. But after the second knock, the door cracks open, and there he is. His hair is mussed, his eyes are dull, and his face is pale except for the feverish pink blotches on his cheeks. There's a damp line of sweat on his collarbone and his white t-shirt has seen better days but even wrinkled, his plaid pajama pants make him look preppy.

"Well, you look like shit," I say.

Beck blinks rapidly, looking startled as hell to see me. "What are you doing here?" he asks, his voice rough.

"Move," I tell him, not unkindly but with the tone that always makes him straighten up without thinking.

His eyes widen and he steps back almost on instinct. It's different from his usual reaction, but then I realize by the way he's looking over my shoulders that he doesn't want anyone in the hall hearing me. Even sick and miserable, he doesn't want anyone picking up on what we are. Or whatever this is.

I don't like that.

The second I'm inside, I set the bags down on the small kitch-enette counter and begin unpacking them like I own the place.

"What are you doing?" he asks again.

"I came to be your sexy nurse," I say, setting out the meds and unboxing the humidifier. "Duh."

"I'm fine," he lies, swaying slightly as he follows me to the only bedroom door that's open. I can tell it's his before I even step in. It smells like him. Well, him plus body sweat. "You don't need to—"

"Sit," I interrupt, using the same voice as before.

He sits.

He scowls angrily, but sits and watches me move around his room, clearing off his nightstand to plug in the humidifier. I point at him to tell him to stay before walking back to the kitchenette to grab more items.

I don't bother with bowls, just open the soup container and hand him a spoon. He takes it reluctantly, but the moment he tastes the broth, his shoulders drop just a little. The pharmacy clerk told me that this deli's hot and sour soup could cure just about anything. I suppose we'll see.

"Have you taken anything?"

"I don't need—"

"Shut up and answer the question."

He shakes his head, and I grab some of the nighttime cold tablets. It's early evening, but I know from experience that this stuff works great and will help him sleep off the worst of his aches and pains. Beck swallows them with some of the sports drink I got, and settles back, apparently done with eating for now.

I see his laptop on his desk, so I pick it up and search for a streaming app, then climb onto the bed next to him once he's propped up against the wall. He's acting annoyed, like he doesn't want me to be here. But I know it's really because he doesn't want me to see him sick and vulnerable and wearing wrinkled pajamas. He doesn't push me away, though. He doesn't have the energy to.

At some point, his head tilts and lands against my shoulder. He mumbles something incoherent about the episode of *Ted Lasso* we're watching. I pretend I don't notice how close he is or how much warmth rolls off his skin. That could just be the fever.

He shifts slightly, looking at me with eyes that are clearer but softer too.

"You didn't have to come," he murmurs.

"Yeah," I say quietly, brushing my fingers through his hair. "I did."

He stares at me like he's unsure what to think about that. Then he leans forward, and before I can think or second-guess, his lips press against mine in a soft, tentative kiss. It's not heated, or desperate, or even all that sexy.

It's slow. Warm. Almost unbearably gentle.

It tastes like cherry cough drops and exhaustion and involuntary trust.

When he falls asleep half on top of me, hand fisted against my side as if to stop me from going anywhere, I pull the blanket over both of us and let him rest.

I don't fall asleep until much later, but when I do, it's with my arm curled around him and the quiet realization that I'm screwed.

Without really realizing it, I kind of fell in deep, and I'm falling deeper by the second.

I wake up to sunlight hitting my face and the sound of Beck shifting beside me, his forehead pressed against my collarbone, his breath warm and a little congested against my skin. For a moment, I just lie there, letting myself enjoy the weight of him draped half across my torso. It feels illicit and domestic at the same time. Like something I was never supposed to experience.

Eventually, I maneuver him off me and slip out of bed. I use the restroom and start some hot water brewing in the tiny coffee maker. I have some tea back in my room that I'll bring back with some clothes and toiletries. I've decided I'm staying, whether he likes it or not.

Sending Beck a text in case he wakes up, I steal his room key and head down one floor to my room to grab a few things. I call my mom while I'm there and tell her I've been exposed to the flu and woke up feeling off. It's not a complete lie. I've definitely been exposed to something, and I do feel off. I just don't feel off as in *sick*.

Beck is in the shower when I get back to his room. When I hear the water cut off, I make him a cup of tea with lots of honey and lemon juice, and some toast. It's on the counter waiting for him when he steps out in a clean pair of sweats and a hoodie.

"You aren't cold?" he asks, his voice weaker than yesterday. I shake my head and press my hand to his forehead, which he lets me do with only a slight flinch.

"You still have a fever," I say, and hand over some more meds.

"These knocked me out," he complains, but takes them anyway. He sighs into his cup of tea.

Beck tries to argue with me when I ask him where he keeps his clean sheets, but I give him my best unimpressed look. "You might as well just let me do what I want," I tell him. "We both know I'm going to win."

———

I'm heating up more soup and considering when I should head out to get more when I sneeze so hard I end up splashing myself in scalding chicken broth.

Beck's head lifts from the couch and gives me a concerned look. "Oh, no," he says.

"I'm fine," I say, but the scratchy throat I woke up with this morning tells me I probably got whatever Beck has. Not to mention the backache, which I'm secretly glad isn't because of sleeping half under a certain someone.

"You shouldn't have come here," he says, bleary and adorably annoyed. "Now look at what you've done."

I sneeze again. Well, fuck.

"What do you mean, what I've done? You're the one who keeps getting high on cold meds and kissing me."

Beck squints at me, and his already pink cheeks get dark. "Says the guy who keeps feeding me the cold meds."

"Don't pretend you don't like the excuse."

He rolls his eyes and makes a disgruntled noise that's half smug, half apology. "You didn't have to stay."

"Yeah," I say again, softer now, "I did."

Later, my mom calls me, and I don't even have to pretend to be sick. I inform her that Beck did, in fact, give me the plague. He scoffs and ends up in a coughing fit.

"Neither of you sounds good. Do you need a doctor or anything?" Mom asks, not questioning who I'm with or why I'm in his bed. She makes me put her on video chat so we can stick out our tongues and answer a bunch of questions about our symptoms, then tells us to stay hydrated and to check in with her tomorrow.

When I hang up, I get up to plug my phone in and grab us some water. Beck is watching me from his pillow with an unreadable expression. He opens his mouth like he wants to comment on something, then he closes it again and settles deeper under the covers, as if retreating is the safer choice.

I crawl back into bed beside him, fighting the urge to reach for him, only for him to beat me to it in the most reluctant, stubborn way possible. He hooks his foot around my ankle under the blankets, like he's pretending it's accidental even though it definitely isn't.

We stay like that for most of the evening, drifting in and out of sleep. Every time one of us coughs or shifts, the other adjusts instinctively. At some point, Beck's head ends up tucked under my chin, and my hand settles in his hair without a conscious decision on my part.

For the next three days, we stay suspended in our own little world. We watch bad movies on his laptop, half of which Beck complains about loudly until he falls asleep twenty minutes in. We argue about whether *The Panthers* are going to win the *Super Bowl*. Beck orders more soup and supplies to be delivered, and I decide not to make fun of him for being privileged because it's actually really nice to not have to leave our bubble. We take turns forcing each other to hydrate. And we talk a lot, although we fall asleep mid-conversation more times than I can count.

Sometimes we talk about nothing—the weather, the awful paint color of the dorm walls, whether the dining hall has better food than a mall food court. Sometimes it gets deeper without warning. He tells me about his childhood nanny, Ms. Delia, and it's nice to hear him talk about someone who might not be blood, but certainly counts as family, with affection. I want to ask about his father and whether they talked after the last meet, but I decide not to bring it up. I tell him that my brother is sick, which isn't a lie, but I don't tell him the whole story. I tell him my dad died when I was a kid, but no deeper details, especially considering how pissed off he gets about Pierce on my behalf.

And sometimes when the medicine makes us loopy and the world feels soft and blurry, we kiss. Slow, drugged with warmth that burns through me. We learn each other's mouths in a different way. These kisses aren't frantic or desperate, they don't hurt, and they aren't driven by a need to dominate or consume him. They're cautious kisses, learning how to fit together like puzzles that were missing pieces.

Every time Beck pulls back, his eyelashes flutter like he's overwhelmed.

"This is different," he breathes.

It's different because he's not fighting me. It's different because he's letting himself feel.

For three days, we exist in this suspended space. Two sick idiots wrapped in blankets and each other, pushing pause on reality. No wrestling. No teammates. No stairwells. No games.

By the time the fever has broken, and the worst of the body aches and congestion have faded, I almost wish we could stay like this a little longer. I've fallen so deep into this quiet, this softness, this fragile peace where he doesn't run and I don't have to chase him, that I really don't want to have to leave again.

What's going to happen when his roommates come back tomorrow? When we have to step back into the world and start acknowledging that whatever this is between us has changed irrevocably.

What are we? What are we doing? What happens next?

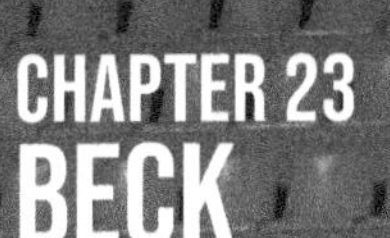

CHAPTER 23
BECK

The morning I finally break us out of the sick bubble we've been in, I feel... wrong. Out of sorts. Confused and lost.

After spending almost five days together, three of those days wrapped up in each other the way we were, I feel like I've blinked and stepped out of some alternate universe, one where Brody Miller slept beside me, pressed warm and solid at my back, and kissed me softly while half-delirious on cold medicine.

Which is why I tell him he has to go back to his own room well before anyone gets back. Both Fish and Cade have texted me, and I know when they're both due to arrive, but I don't want to take any chances.

Not because I want him to leave. But because I don't. I'm not so deluded that I can't admit that to myself now.

But because the more this time with him sinks into my chest, the more terrified I get of what happens when Brody starts wanting more from me. Things I can't give him. Things like open affection and honesty. Or like letting myself want him without conditions or excuses.

So I stand up out of bed Sunday morning and tell him it's time to go. We're both well enough to take care of ourselves, and we don't need to play doctor anymore. Or house. Or whatever the fuck it is that we've been doing.

Before he leaves, he leans in like he's going to kiss me. Like he has —like we both have—far too many times in the last few days. We've gotten far too comfortable.

I turn my head and cough into my elbow. It starts as a fake cough, but don't worry, I get properly reprimanded by a real coughing fit that both hurts and leaves me almost as breathless as the kiss would have.

For the next few days, I do my best to pretend everything is normal. Finals are next week, so if my stress is obvious, no one notices. Everyone on campus is stressed and tired and wired as they gear up for the end of the semester. Well, everyone except Brody. As usual, he walks around with the grace of someone who doesn't have a worry in the world, like he has all the answers to life's problems and the final exams that everyone else is dreading. I try to tune him out, to pretend that nothing has changed in our dynamic other than not having time to hook up like we had been before the holiday break.

But Brody doesn't let me.

He inserts himself into my space with the subtlety of a bulldozer. First by staying by my side and insisting on commiserating about how weak his muscles still feel while we work through morning lift and conditioning. Then by plopping down next to me in the dining hall without an invitation.

Then there's the library. Caty and I are lucky enough to have a standing booking for one of the private study rooms on the third floor. I'm midway through a practice test about corporate valua-tion models when someone pushes the door open without knocking, and Brody strolls in like he was invited. By the way Caty's eyes light up instantly, I'm assuming he was.

The traitorous bitch.

"Brody," she says brightly, lifting one brow in a way that makes my stomach flip because I know she's up to something. "So nice of you to join us."

I don't bother pretending to be happy to see him and stare her down. "What is this?"

"What?" she asks innocently. "I saw Brody in the dining hall, and he mentioned needing to study, and this is such a nice, quiet, private space."

She's doing this on purpose. She's doing this because I told her that he and I spent the holiday together involuntarily because we were both sick, which she didn't buy. So she interrogated me until I admitted that, in a drug-induced haze, we spent what felt like meaningful time together, and I'm all fucked up about it. Caty suggested I not ignore him and talk about my feelings or some absolutely ludicrous business like that, and I am having none of it. So, of course, she's meddling.

"You don't even know each other."

"Nonsense. We both know you, and that's enough."

Brody nods. "We're basically besties now."

The glare I shoot them would wither even my father. Except both of them grin back at me with equally snarky, knowing expressions that are far too similar to be a coincidence.

I've done this to myself, haven't I? I've managed to attract a best friend and a boy... *situation* that share the ability to see right through me.

"I hate you both."

"Uh-huh, I know you do, honey," Caty says while patting my hand placatingly.

Caty spends the next twenty minutes or so making faces at me whenever Brody isn't looking. Which should be more often considering Brody is really bad at studying or isn't even trying to fake it. He glances at me every three minutes like he's waiting for me to meet his eyes. I don't.

Except when I flick my eyes over to him to make sure he's studying, not for any other reason, and catch him watching me. Our eyes lock like magnets, and my face heats when I can't seem to look away.

Caty snorts and closes her laptop. "I think I'm done for today. I need some caffeine, or I'm not going to make it through my biology lecture this afternoon. You two have fun."

That drags my gaze away. My eyes widen at her, pleading for her not to leave me alone in this small, private room. Not with him. Please save me.

Her lips crook into a knowing smirk that rivals one of Brody's, further proving that I attract sadists.

"You two get lots of studying done," she sing-songs as she lets herself out, closing the door behind her.

Suddenly the workspace feels overwhelmingly tight. I'm choking on Brody's energy, on the tension between us. All I can think about is the last time we were alone together in one of these study rooms. How he'd made me crawl under the table and read my Communications notes at his feet until I finally broke because I couldn't concentrate.

Brody scooted his chair all the way back so I could straighten up and looked at me for so long I was worried he wasn't going to do anything to alleviate my situation, making it impossible to get up and walk out of here comfortably. It's one of the first times I initiated contact, where I touched him first. I'd practically climbed into his lap to rub myself on him, but we were in danger of breaking the chair, and the table creaked when he sat me on it.

We ended up on the floor, with Brody on top of me, rolling his hips against me the way I've seen men fuck women in movies or porn. As much as I told myself that I shouldn't like it, his hard bulge rubbed me just the right way, and I wrapped my legs around him tighter, flexing into him as he thrusted against me. When I came, he swallowed my cries and breathed in every whimper, telling me how sexy I was and how much he liked making me break for him.

Because that's what he does. He breaks me.

I'm afraid that he's broken me beyond repair this time. That I can't pretend this is a game ever again. Because it means something now. There are feelings involved. I can see it in the way he's watching me right now.

"I know what you're thinking about," he says, his tone light and teasing.

"I sincerely doubt that."

"Tell me then."

"It's none of your goddamn business. Now, are we here to study or what?"

"Or what," he answers pointedly.

"That was rhetorical."

"I'm aware." He grins and I hate the twitch at the corners of my mouth that make my mouth want to copy his.

I turn my attention back to my practice test, but the question about enterprise versus equity value and calculating implied share price might as well be written in ancient Greek. The letters and words merge and blur on the page.

Finally, I give up and look up to find him still watching me.

"Why are you here?" I snap. "How did you even get Caty to invite you?"

"I saw her in line at the student union and asked her if I could join your study group. She didn't even hesitate. Say what you will about that girl, but she knows a good thing when she sees it."

I ignore his indirect jab at Caty and scoff. "Let me guess, you think you're the good thing?"

"I think *we're* a good thing."

"*We* aren't anything."

He sticks out his bottom lip in an exaggerated pout. "Come on, Becky. You know that's not true."

"Stop calling me that."

"You love it."

"I do not."

He's right. I do love it. But I don't want to. I don't want to like him looking at me like I'm a cute, fluffy rabbit and he's a big bad wolf about to devour me whole. I don't like that the idea of being devoured by him is so enticing. And I absolutely do not, under any circumstances, enjoy feeling like a soft, delicate thing in his grasp. I hate being petted and cooed at like a weak little pet. Even more, I hate turning and presenting myself when he so much as blinks at me the right way, because some primal instinct gets triggered in his presence.

I've come to terms with the fact that all these things are true. But I don't want them to be true.

"Come here, Becky."

"Brody. Not here. I'm studying. If I fail this finance class, I'll be fucked."

Brody leans forward and snaps my laptop shut. "What was the last question about? Get it right and I'll leave you alone."

I huff indignantly. Brody doesn't even bother to smirk like he normally does. He just watches me intently.

"Was any of it sinking in before I arrived, or are you just using my presence as an excuse?"

"It's not an excuse. And no, it wasn't sinking in before you got here, but that was your fault too."

"And why is that, Becky?"

"Because you're in my head!" I whisper-shout, probably still too loudly. Maybe I'll get lucky and one of the library attendants will come in and I can tell her that Brody is intruding on my study time. Maybe he'll be banned from the library, and I'll have one place on this fucking campus that is safe.

"So let me help you."

I scoff, and yes, as I'm doing it, I realize how much I find myself scoffing at Brody Miller. Probably as much as he fucking smirks. But he's infuriating, and sometimes there just aren't words that can better intimate the overwhelming, all-encompassing frustration I feel when he's being impossible. Which is always.

"You're suddenly a finance major, then?"

"Hell no. That sounds boring as fuck, actually. But I bet I can make it fun. Maybe incentivize the study process a little?" He pumps his eyebrows.

I almost forget to be difficult and perk up. Finance is boring as fuck. And incentives do sound promising...

But no. I'm not letting him steadily turn everything in my life into yet another reminder of him. It's bad enough that wrestling has been affected. Someday, years from now, I don't want to be standing in a boardroom getting hard in front of shareholders because discussing terminal value unlocks some kind of subconscious Pavlovian kink.

"Stock analysis."

Brody raises an eyebrow. "Sorry, what?"

"Stock analysis. The last question on the practice exam I was working on was about stock analysis."

His eyes narrow as he comes around the table and sits on the chair next to me, dragging my laptop closer and opening it. He gestures at the screen for me to input my password to bypass the screensaver, then reads the question.

"Wrong."

"What? No, it isn't."

"The question asks what the implied share price of a firm that has an enterprise value of $850 million dollars, with $120 million in cash, $300 million in debt, and 50 million shares outstanding."

"It's calculating equity value, which is used for stock analysis, to calculate the market value of what shareholders own."

Brody hums thoughtfully, ignoring my reasoning for my answer being correct. "So what's the answer to the actual question?"

I bend forward to scratch out some basic math to calculate the answer.

"$11 per share," I answer.

He types in an answer on the screen and bites his lip. "Wrong," he says, the word coming out like a low growl.

"No it's not, it's—" I look over my math and go over the question in my head, silently cursing myself. "I forgot to add the cash back. Equity value is the enterprise value, minus the debt plus cash. So the share price is six hundred and seventy million divided by fifty million, not five hundred fifty million divided by…"

My voice trails off, realizing that Brody is studying me the way he should be studying how to do jumping jacks or whatever Exercise Science majors learn.

"Good girl," he says slowly. "But you still got it wrong the first time, so we'll compromise on your reward."

"Compromise?"

"Yeah, compromise. Like a shareholder accepting a moderate dividend rather than a full payout."

I gape. "You're equating corporate finance to getting off now?"

"Wasn't that the point?" Brody lifts an eyebrow like it should be obvious. "You didn't earn the full payout, but I'll give you a little something to make you happy."

I'd rather eat lead than admit that this is working. But it's working. *Goddamn*, it's working. I am hard and regretting my decision to wear khakis instead of athletic pants like Brody is wearing.

"Come here."

This time, I obey. He's barely two feet away from me, so there isn't far to go. I make my best guess and figure he wants me on my knees in front of him. He spreads his legs and pushes his foot between my thighs.

"Sit."

Brow furrowed, I sit, basically straddling this foot. Then he starts to move his foot, rubbing it between my legs in a way that I don't want to admit is working for me. But before I know it, I'm meeting the movement of his foot, rocking against him.

"That's a good girl. Keep rubbing yourself off on my leg and tell me why shareholders would accept a moderate dividend instead of a full payout."

I straighten and stare at his leg in horror. "I'm not a dog."

"Do it or I'll make you howl like a dog in heat," he says calmly.

Reluctantly, I press into his shin and slide down to sit on his black and white off-brand sneaker. I fidget uncomfortably, trying to find a position that doesn't make me look or feel ridiculous.

Then Brody palms himself over his grey athletic pants, readjusting his thick erection so it's supported and held against his stomach by the elastic of his waistband. My mouth waters as Brody's hand slides up and down the hard ridge of his cock through his pants, and I groan. My hips have started rocking on their own accord, grinding my swelling cock against the top of Brody's shoe.

"What is the benefit of accepting the lesser payout, Becky?"

"I, uh—the company could be sacrificing some earnings to make investments?"

"Good. How does that benefit the shareholders, though?"

"They could—" I swallow the abundance of saliva building up in my mouth and grip Brody's calf in one hand, my other grasping onto his other thigh so I can get better leverage. "Th- the profits from reinvesting could benefit shareholders."

"Yes," he says, aggravatingly calmly. "So they're accepting short-term profits with the goal of receiving a bigger payout over time. How might this compromise cost them, though?"

"Cost them?"

He nods, his bored gaze on the hand that has crept farther up his thigh. It seems unintentional, but I desperately want to touch him. Taste him. Feel something other than the friction of my groin rubbing against his shoe. The hand that's been stroking his cock thumbs the waistband of his pants, pulling it down just enough to let the swollen red tip barely peek out. Oh God, please take it out. Maybe I say it out loud. Or mouth the words. I don't know. Brody always seems to know what I want. He gestures with his hand to indicate that I should keep going if I want him to keep going.

I spread my thighs wider to get more friction where I'm grinding against him.

"Risk versus return," I say breathlessly. "The company could choose to invest the money in ways that don't benefit the shareholders as much."

"Such as?" Brody asks, pushing his waistband down to expose more of his thick shaft.

"Risky projects could mean a higher return but could also tank. Stable projects would mean lower returns but could contribute to sustainable growth and longer-term profits."

"Good girl," he purrs, and uses both hands to push his pants down below his ass. The movement makes his leg flex, foot pressing up into my groin so deliciously I let out an audible shudder.

Brody holds his hand out to me, and I know by now that he's not asking for my hand or anything I'm holding. I lean in and spit in his palm. He spits as well, then uses our combined saliva to slick his hand down his rigid length.

From this angle, I have the perfect view of the thick vein that runs up the bottom of his shaft. My tongue darts out to lick my lips, wanting to drag it along the path and lick the pre-cum from his tip when I get there. I swallow and whimper as Brody's foot shifts again, and I fall forward a bit.

"So how can shareholders guarantee their interests and get their maximum payout?"

"They can negotiate agreements for a mutually beneficial balance."

"Like?" His hand moves steadily up and down his cock, rounding over the head each time he reaches the tip, spreading his pre-cum down his shaft while mine soaks through my underwear.

The words rush out of me, breathy and barely holding on to the brain cells needed to answer the question. "The company can choose a moderate payout ratio, giving shareholders some cash now, while keeping enough retained earnings to fund operations, growth, and higher-risk projects. If the business profits rise, the shareholders get a bigger payout over time. If they don't, they aren't losing all the money that would be going to the shareholders, because only the agreed upon funds would be earmarked for investment."

"So how does this entire scenario relate to you right now?" Brody asks me, his voice finally starting to show signs of his own arousal.

What happens if I get the answer wrong? Does this stop? Or does it keep going? Which is better or worse? Either way, this is torture. I want to come, but not like this, although the closer he gets to his orgasm, the more I realize it doesn't matter as long as I can have *his* cum.

"To me?" I repeat, almost trancelike, attention focused solely on Brody's hand and how close I know he is. I know it because I feel it. My hips grind harder and faster with each stroke, building and building in tandem. I'm right on the edge.

"Yes, you. If you're the shareholder in this scenario, and I am the company, what do you stand to gain or lose?"

"Mmmph. I don't know… I, um… Fuck."

I can't fucking think. I barely understand the question. I'm burning up from the mortification of being so close to blowing my load in my pants while rubbing myself off on his foot, from the heat and tension in the room, from the sound of his voice, from my impending orgasm and the promise of his.

"No contract was made, Becky. No agreements on what your payout was going to be or who would get what in this exchange."

My eyes widen and flick up to meet his. Still pumping himself with one hand, he reaches out and grips the back of my head with his other. The pain of his fingers gripping my hair so tightly makes my eyes roll back, and I gasp into his mouth, his face suddenly in mine dizzyingly fast.

"I'll tell you what we're both going to get out of it," he growls. "I'm going to give you my cum, but I'm holding something back to use for future earnings."

"What's that?" I breathe heavily.

"I'm going to walk away with the memory of you coming all over yourself from humping my cheap knockoff sneaker."

I want to argue that it's not going to happen. To push him back and scream at him that he's wrong. That I would never allow myself to be debased in such a way.

But there's no point.

When the first rope of Brody's cum hits my cheek, I bow as if cramping up. My mouth falls open, more cum painting my lips and tongue. My hips don't stop grinding, frantically gyrating against Brody's shoe as I ride out my own orgasm, spilling inside my pants. I cry out pathetically, loving the hot splash of Brody marking me, losing myself in the ecstasy of the pleasure ripping through my body, and slumping over his knee when I'm completely spent.

Brody leans back in the chair, chest heaving. His softening cock lays against his thigh, a drop of cum still leaking from the slit. I eye it and move forward, flicking my tongue out to lap up the salty drop before sucking him into my mouth. For a second, I don't do more than suckle him, wishing he'd wake up and fill my mouth and throat, but he's too spent.

After a few minutes, Brody shifts to sit up and removes his hoodie and t-shirt. He wipes my face with it first, then gestures at my lap. I take the shirt, unbuttoning my pants and pushing the soft, worn fabric into the front of my pants when Brody's eyes are covered by pulling his hoodie back over his head.

I clean up the worst of the mess as best as I can, but there's nothing I can do about the dark wet stain that's soaked through the khaki fabric. These were the absolute worst pants for this to happen in. I check the clock. Fortunately, I have time to run back to the dorm and change if I skip lunch.

Brody offers to walk with me, but I decline. I need some space. Every time I try to force space between us, I only end up in this type of situation. So I try using my words this time.

"Thanks for the, um... study session. But I need to do this in a way that's less distracting. This final is really important."

Brody reaches for his now soiled t-shirt, rolls it up, and shoves it in his hoodie pocket.

"Alright," he agrees. "But no more avoiding me. You can't run from this, Beck."

"Run from what?" I ask, busying myself with packing my backpack.

Brody stops me with a hand on my chin, directing my face toward his.

"My future profitability," he murmurs, before kissing me so deeply I lose track of what I'm doing.

———

By the end of the week, my nerves are fried. Between purposefully not avoiding Brody and questioning the space he's giving me, and knocking out my finals one by one, I'm basically sagging with relief that it's over. I might as well be a limp, wet noodle by the time I walk out of my last exam. I'm relieved, exhausted, and feeling strong about my Corporate Finance final. There were some questions about shareholder dividends that made me feel strangely confident. And, yeah, maybe a little aroused.

The moment I step out of the business building and switch my phone back on, it buzzes. When I see *Dad* on the screen, my stomach drops.

I haven't spoken to him since the quad meet. Before the quad meet, to be more specific. He didn't even call to berate me on my performance, or to question what Gregg Thompson had loudly implied to the entire gym or to tell me that a win by disqualification doesn't count.

I stare at the phone long enough that it stops ringing but it picks right back up again. There's no point in not answering, he'll just call Coach McCoy or the dean or hell, take his private helicopter and come here himself.

The moment I click accept, he starts in on his usual bullshit. He doesn't say hello, or ask me how I am. He doesn't even ask why I missed his annual Thanksgiving dinner party. He launches straight into grilling me about my finals, reminding me that exams at this level separate the serious students from future failures.

He doesn't pause for breath between letting me know his expectations for my grades before moving on to questioning me about our next dual.

Like he didn't walk out of the last match without saying a word. Like he didn't leave me standing there, watching after him, humiliated in front of my entire team. A team that he has stressed time and time again the importance of maintaining respect as a leader.

Like he didn't even notice I missed an entire holiday that most people spend with their families. Never mind that I spent that week sick in bed. I bet he'd have something to say about the one person who cared enough to stay with me.

"Finals were fine," I say numbly, ignoring most of what he's said already.

He's already moved on. He continues, unbothered.

"And you'll be in shape for the match Friday? West Virginia has a competitive lineup. This James Parker kid cuts a ridiculous amount of weight and still comes out looking like a heavyweight. The steroid rumors are probably exaggerated, but either way, he's the kind of opponent you don't want to underestimate."

I stop walking. My dad keeps rambling, and I realize he hasn't asked me a single question about me. About my life. About how I'm actually doing. He didn't call after the meet, didn't check on me when I was sick, didn't even acknowledge I didn't come home for Thanksgiving. And now here he is, talking to me like I'm a product he's invested in and not a living, breathing person. A person who's only ever wanted him to look at them with something other than contempt and see them for the person they are and not the investment they represent.

"Dad," I interrupt, surprising even myself. "I haven't spoken to you in almost three weeks. Do you realize you didn't even greet me? Or ask how I am?"

There's a beat of silence before he huffs, annoyed. "I asked about your finals."

"That's not asking how *I* am," I say, my voice shaking even though I'm trying to keep it steady. "That's asking about my performance. My output. That's not the same thing."

There's another pause. This one is cold. I can hear his exasperation.

"I don't have time for this," he says, clipped. "I have more important things on my agenda than to listen to you whine like a child. Even your mother isn't this sensitive."

I breathe through the sting. "For your information, yeah, I feel fine about finals. Even Finance. And I'm feeling better after being sick, since you don't seem to have noticed I missed Thanksgiving. And yes, I'll still be ready for Friday despite dropping muscle mass during the week I was sick. Thanks for asking. Please don't worry about coming to the dual against West Virginia, I do understand that you're a very busy man. I sincerely hope you stay home and get updates from Coach instead of coming just to stare me down from the sidelines and berate me for not winning hard enough, no matter what I achieve."

I'm not sure what my father is thinking about my uncharacteristic outburst, because I hang up on him before he has the chance to reply.

I hung up. On my father.

I stare at my phone like it might explode. Like Charles Beckett might suddenly teleport through the screen and throttle me right here and now. My pulse is hammering, my hands shaking, and the quad feels both too open and too empty.

I blink furiously at my phone screen as it goes black, then look up when I notice a shadow blocking some of the sunlight on the pathway.

Brody is standing right in front of me, hands shoved in his jacket pockets, eyes narrowed and thoughtful in that way he gets sometimes. Like I'm something to be studied and understood, a subject in experimental psychology and abnormal human behavior.

"Was that your dad?" he asks quietly. His voice is stiff, like he might be angry about me talking to my father of all people.

"Yes."

He lets out a low whistle. "Wish I had recorded that for you to show Ms. Delia."

Brody Miller mentioning my Ms. Delia does something funny to my stomach that crawls up my chest and settles there. Like heartburn or something. Before I can help it, a smile spreads across my face.

"You know what, so do I."

Brody's eyes widen comically. "Beck?"

"Yeah?"

He swallows once, slowly, and looks back and forth at the people milling about around the quad. "Either we need to get somewhere private, or I'm going to kiss you right here in front of everyone."

Oh.

Silence stretches between us, the air around us concentrating to a filtered bubble of time and space. My pulse races. Brody's gaze drops to my throat like he can see it.

"My room," he says suddenly, stepping forward and grabbing my wrist with a firm, sure grip. "Now."

"What about your roommates?" I manage, stumbling after him.

"They're in exams."

We run across the quad and into his dorm, bumping shoulders as we sprint up two flights of stairs. The second the door to his dorm shuts behind us, Brody pushes me back against it, breath warm against my cheek.

"I am going to lick every inch of your body," he says, voice husky with want and something deeper. "I am so proud of you. I've never seen you do anything as hot as it was watching you stand up to your father like that."

The words hit me so hard I feel it all the way to my toes.

We stumble around his dorm, kissing like we've been holding this tension under our skin for weeks—because we have. Our hands get clumsy, sliding over fabric, fumbling buttons, greedy for skin. Shoes, coats, hoodies and everything but shirts and pants are dropped directly on the floor and forgotten.

When Brody lifts his mouth from my neck, I hear myself whisper something I've never said out loud before.

"Brody... I want you to fuck me."

CHAPTER 24
BRODY

"I want you to fuck me."

Everything stops, like a full-on cartoon worthy, vintage record scratching stop. I stare at Lincoln Beckett biting his lip and looking at me so earnestly, I don't know how to react. I'm not sure I heard him correctly.

"What did you say?"

"I want you to fuck me..." he says, voice trailing off as if he's unsure of what he said and might want to take it back. But then he lifts his chin and pulls his shoulders back. "You heard me, Brody. And I mean it."

"You want me to—"

"—Fuck me, yes. Do I need to repeat myself again or try another language? I speak some French, but I'm not sure this is in my conversational wheelhouse."

I let out a chuckle, but it's a bit humorless considering I'm still struggling to figure out if this is real.

"Brody," he snaps, raising his arms and getting me out of my head. I blink up at him, trying to clear some cobwebs or something from my mind. "Are you hearing me?"

"Yeah. You want me to fuck you."

"Yes," he says, dropping his arms as if the journey was exhausting.

"What I'm confused about is how we got here."

Beck puts his hands on his hips and stares at me like I'm the biggest idiot he's ever met.

"Don't look at me like that. I need to know that you're in your right mind and know what you're asking for."

"We're here because you looked at me like that in the courtyard."

"Like what?"

"Like I'm something special or some shit. Not because of my academic or athletic achievements, or because you want some-thing from me. Not because I have something to prove. It's because you looked at me like *that*, then kissed me like you just did, and it was hot and I fucking want to. Are you saying you don't want to?"

"To fuck you…"

"Yes! Brody, what the fuck?!" Normally his exasperation would amuse or even arouse me, but I'm genuinely blown away.

Beck has begged me for a lot of things. He's begged me for more, more fingers, more tongue, more intensity. But he's never come out and fully acknowledged that we were doing anything or building up to anything more than the games we've played. In fact, he's purposefully put us back in that place over and over again. Every time we take a step forward and I think he's accepting this thing between us, he drags me, kicking and screaming, as he takes two steps back. And I just keep shuffling along with him, because as much as I like to play the big strong dominant, I think we both know who's in charge here.

I step forward and take his mouth again, deeper and slower than before. He lets me control the pace, slowly guiding us to my bedroom. Once we're shut inside, Beck starts working to open the front of my pants, but I bring his arms back around me instead.

I just want to kiss him like this for a little while longer. Balancing on the edge of something that feels monumental. Something that will change everything.

What if we do this and he changes his mind? What if he gets scared and runs away for real this time? What if he hates me after?

But at the same time, what if this is Lincoln Beckett truly coming around? What if this is him accepting me? Accepting *us*.

"Beck, we need to slow down, okay? I'm not saying no, but I want to talk first."

His voice is smooth and calm and flirtatious. Nothing like I've ever heard it before. "What is there to talk about?" he says against my lips, then trails kisses down my neck and throat. He nips at my Adam's apple, and I shiver. "I'm okay, Brody. And I'm serious. I want this. I've thought about it. And I..."

He trails off and presses his forehead to mine. A deep sigh brushes against my mouth. "I just want to feel something good. Something that's mine and doesn't come with so much pressure attached, you know?"

I do know, but I wouldn't be me if I didn't... "I mean, there's going to be a lot of pressure."

Beck laughs exasperatedly. "You're an ass, you know that."

"You like it."

"Nope. Not even a little. In fact, I've changed my mind. I have somewhere I suddenly need to be."

He tries to walk away from me, but I grab him by the arm and fling him back. He falls back against the mattress, and I straddle him, so I've got him pinned down beneath me. We're laughing, but I'm looking down into his eyes, deep brown drowning into pools of black. There's only one other time he's looked back at me like this.

"Promise you haven't been hitting the cold medicine?"

Beck laughs again and shakes his head. "No meds, but I might have caught some kind of bug from you this time."

My stomach flips and my heart beats outside my chest, because that sounded like a declaration of some sort.

"A stupidity bug. So maybe take advantage before I change my mind."

I kiss my way down his neck, fingertips tickling the bottom hem of his shirt.

"I'd rather you change your mind than have any regrets," I tell him honestly. "So you have to promise to be a good girl and be honest with me. If at any point you want to stop, we stop. Okay?"

"Okay," he agrees softly. "I know my safe word, Captain."

"No."

"What?"

"No safe word, baby. You don't need it. We aren't pretending. It's you and me, for real this time."

"For real?"

"That's right, baby," I murmur against his lips, pushing his shirt up his chest, his abs flexing as he sits up. I'm straddling his lap, so I can pull his shirt over his head. He removes mine as well, and we press ourselves together, skin to skin, as we work each other's pants and underwear off.

There's a bottle of lube and condoms in a storage basket under my bed. I reach down for it and bring them to rest next to Beck's head. I'm not trying to freak him out, but I want him to have every chance to realize what we're doing here. That after this, there's no going back.

He looks at them and grins. "Think there's enough?"

"Maybe for round one," I smirk. "But I'll probably need to start buying them in bulk because I have a feeling I'm not going to be able to get enough of you."

"Or you could, you know…"

My balls contract as if they're being summoned to empty inside him at this very moment.

"It's not like we aren't both regularly tested, and I'm not doing this with anyone else."

"I'm not either, but let's think about it some more, okay? I'm not lying to you when I say that the very moment you let me come inside you, I will become an entirely different kind of problem. One you won't be able to get rid of without setting me on fire or staking me in the chest or something."

I lean down and take his mouth hard, plastering my body to his. Our cocks slide against each other like long-lost lovers, and I almost lose myself in the feel of his bare skin against mine. "When I mark you from the inside, baby girl, you're going to know you belong to me."

"I already said I'm yours."

"You'll belong to me in all the ways. Not just your bratty little attitude and your mouth and ass. Down to your marrow, Becky."

I trail my mouth down his body, peppering the skin of his sternum, abs, and happy trail with kisses and pointed words. "You." —*kiss*—"Will."—*kiss*—"Be."—*lick*—"Mine."

Beck gasps when I take his cock to the back of my throat while I lift his legs, pushing his thighs to his chest. He holds them there without instruction, and I kiss and lick down his balls and past his taint.

I work him open with my tongue and one finger, then two. The most he's ever taken from me is three, but I want to stretch him around four before I let him take my cock. Not because my cock is the width of my fist by any means, but because I don't want to hurt him. I want every part of this to feel so good, he couldn't possibly have any regrets other than not giving himself to me sooner.

I want him writhing and begging for my cock. Only once I've worked him up to the point of no return, where he couldn't care less who he is or who I am or what we're supposed to be other than this, do I finally sheathe myself in latex and give my cock a few strokes with my lubed hand.

Hovering above him, I hook an arm under one of his legs and let the other wrap around my waist. I look down between us just long enough to line myself up, then focus on his face.

"Ready for me, baby?"

"I'm ready," he pants, eyes blacked out with lust. "So ready."

When I press into him, there's no resistance. It's not until I'm maybe halfway in that he struggles at all.

"Fuck, baby girl, you're taking me even better than I thought you would. Look at all that cock inside you already, Becky. Look at your ass stretched around my dick."

Beck pushes up to his elbows and looks down, hissing when I push his hard cock against his stomach so he can see past it. I know he can't see anywhere near as much as I can, but he sees enough to clench around me.

"Fuck, that's tight," I groan, pulling out and pushing back in so slowly it almost hurts. I want so badly just to thrust into him, burying myself to the root. I have no doubt he can take it, but that's not what I want for his first time. It has to be perfect.

"Breathe and bear down, baby girl. *Unngh* yes, like that. Oh, fuck, baby. Almost... *there*."

By the time I'm fully sheathed inside him, we're both panting. Me from the exertion of not pumping this load into him immediately, and him from taking me so damn perfectly. I've never been more thankful for all the times I've threatened to fist him.

If I thought Beck was going to be a sweet, tender bottom, I should have known better. Within seconds he's pushing up off the mattress, trying to work himself on me.

"Move. Please move. Please move," he chants as he writhes.

I give him what he wants, pulling out and slowly thrusting back to my new home, pressing him into the mattress so I can get as deep inside him as possible. I roll my hips, each thrust at a different angle, while Beck gets more and more vocal. In between garbled words and moans, he begs for more, deeper, faster, harder. All the things I'm not ready to give him yet because I'm trying to draw this out and make it last. Make it memorable.

Finally, I get just the right angle to light him the fuck up. His moan turns into a shout that I almost interpret as pain, but his ass clenches around me and his nails dig into my flesh, one hand on my ass and the other on my waist, pulling me against him.

"There! Oh, *fuck*. Brody...there. Right there. Oh my God..."

I start babbling incoherently. Praising him, praising deities I don't believe in. Praising him some more, because I do believe in him.

"Fuck. Me. Harder. Brody!"

Hiking his leg higher up, and wrapping my other arm around his lower back, I prop him up on the pillows just high enough to hold him at just the right angle. Beck cries out with each thrust, each pump of my hips driving the air and sound out of him as I speed up my thrusts. The whole time, I can't stop muttering an endless list of praise, about how perfect he is, how I want to live inside him, how he's such a good girl for me.

Beck clenches hard before he registers what's about to happen. The headboard thuds against the wall, beating out a rhythm that syncs with my heart. The sounds of skin and grunting and Beck's sharp cries get louder and louder until we reach a fevered peak. I lean forward and press my forehead to his, cupping the back of his head in my hand.

"Brody—" Beck wails. "Oh my God, Brody, I—"

"Touch yourself, baby girl. Jerk yourself until you—"

My mouth drops open in a silent scream as Beck's ass clenches down on my cock so hard it's unreal. It's so good it's almost painful, and I can't breathe. His ring pulses around me, ripping my orgasm straight out of my soul. The sound barrier catches up, and I roar out my release as I pump the condom so full I imagine it bursting and painting his insides the way I really want to. I shudder at the mental image, rolling my hips and riding out the aftershocks as, thank fuck, Beck comes too, painting our stomachs and chests with hot ropes of his cum.

I don't stop moving inside him until I'm in danger of getting hard again. Then I hold myself there, cradling his face and devouring his mouth, never wanting to pull out and sever this connection.

I have been with other men. I've topped and bottomed and once even got my cock sucked by a woman while her husband's dick was inside me. That was intense, but even that had nothing on Lincoln Beckett.

Nothing has ever felt this good. This intense. This impossibly, mind-blowingly perfect.

When I finally pull out of him, I'm shaking. I reach down with my fingers and rub his hole gently, rubbing his own cum into his ass to massage his ring and wishing it were my own.

"You were so good for me. So perfect," I whisper, and give him one last gentle kiss on the lips before I pull away.

On my knees, still between his legs, I remove the condom, tie it off, and throw it in the trash bin.

"How do you feel?" I ask him, scooting myself lower on the bed.

"I'm fine. Hey, what are you doing?"

"I'm looking at my dick's new home," I say simply. Then I smile gently and take the teasing tone out of my voice. "I just want to see that you're okay."

"Oh hell no," Beck says, scrambling back and sitting up. I don't miss the way he winces and put a hand on his ankle to settle him.

"Well, let's at least get you a warm washcloth and clean you up. It'll feel nice, and—"

"Brody! Fuck. Off. Alright? I said I'm fine."

My eyes lock on his again, and I sense the change in him. This is what I was worried about.

"Do you... I mean, are you regretting it already?"

"I wasn't until you started being a sappy girl about it, Brody. *Damn.*"

I roll my eyes. "Listen, *Becky*. Taking care of yourself or letting your partner do it for you is a normal, healthy thing to do after sex."

"You're not my partner, Brody. We just had sex, that's all. I'd rather take care of myself, thank you."

That's all?

Ouch.

"Yeah. Okay. I hear ya. I'll go get you a washcloth and I'll back off." I don't give him a chance to retort or argue, I need a moment to get my shit together because I'm caught between wanting to scream and rage or cry like the sappy girl he accused me of being.

I'm all mixed up.

I'm even more mixed up when I step outside my door, thankfully having pulled my underwear back on.

Jay and Aaron are standing in the kitchenette, both holding random groceries and staring back at me with wide eyes.

I stare. They stare. No one seems to know what to do or say, but I know that seeing them isn't going to help me get through to Beck.

I point at the two of them, and then at the other bedrooms and gesture for them to get the fuck out while mouthing, "Get. Out. Now." I double down with my best death glare and shake my head when Jay looks like he wants to say something. The two of them pick up the groceries and backtrack to the front door, keeping their eyes on me like I might attack. It'd be funny if I wasn't so terrified of Beck seeing them and knowing we'd been caught. Considering Beck's letterman jacket with his name embroidered below the letter "C" for captain is on the ground, there's no chance they don't know who I was just having the best sex of my life with. They also were likely privy to the fact that I just got rejected after the best sex of my life, and I don't particularly want to deal with that either.

They silently leave the dorm, and the door clicks shut behind them. Turning on my heel, I march to the bathroom and quickly wet a washcloth with hot water. When I come out of the bathroom to give it to him, and suggest we talk, Beck is gone.

CHAPTER 25
BECK

I'm losing my mind.

Rephrase—I have lost my damn mind.

Not metaphorically. Not exaggerating for dramatic effect like Caty always accuses me of. I mean it in the very real, very existential sense that my entire world feels like it's shifted six inches to the left, and my body hasn't caught up yet.

Maybe it's because I had sex for the first time in my life. Or maybe it's because it was with Brody Miller. Or maybe it's because somewhere between his dick in my ass and the way he held my face afterward, something inside me cracked open in a way that feels irreversible.

Whatever the reason, I'm freaking out.

More than a little.

Caty sits cross-legged on my dorm bed, eating pretzels and watching me pace like she's observing a wildlife documentary on the mating habits of closeted jocks. When I finally admit what happened, not in explicit detail, but enough, she chokes on her pretzel.

"You had sex for the first time," she wheezes, hitting her chest. "With Brody. And you're both still alive to talk about it? This is huge."

"I don't want to talk about it," I mutter, rubbing my hands over my face.

Which is, of course, a green light for Caty to talk about nothing else.

"Sweetheart," she says, leaning back against my pillows like she's settling in to stay awhile. "Please don't tell me you're freaking out that you lost your v card to a guy. I thought we were past this. You sucked his dick. He sucked yours. You had his big sausage fingers—"

"Caty!"

"My point is that all of that was pretty fucking gay, Beck. I don't see what there is to panic about now. Let's move on to acceptance and telling your best friend all the dirty details."

"It's not that," I groan. "I've accepted it, or whatever. I'm not about to come out and join a parade or anything, but it's whatever. I just... I didn't expect it to feel like *that*."

"Like what? Did it hurt?"

"No, that's the thing. I thought it would. I didn't think it would be awful—"

"—because of the aforementioned fingers..."

I narrow my eyes in warning. "I can't talk to you about this if you're going to make fun of me. I don't even know how to say the words, I'm not going to be able to handle any kind of humiliation."

Caty drops her bag of pretzels and scoots to the end of the bed to wrap her arms around me from behind. "I'm sorry. I use humor to make heavy things easier to talk about, but I promise you there is nothing but support and acceptance in my heart. I am here to talk about anything and everything you want. And while I'll always be honest, I'll never ever judge you or think less of you as a person. I love you, Lincoln Beckett."

"I love you, Catherine Hunt."

"I promise to keep my comments about Brody's weirdly thick, meaty fingers to myself even though I couldn't think of anything else when we were locked in that study room together. It's why I had to flee. I was going to start making inappropriate comments at any moment and knew I wouldn't be able to control myself once I got going."

I can't help but laugh at my best friend's antics. "You don't even want to know about what happened after you left," I mutter.

"Oh, I absolutely do. In detail," she says, pointing a sharply mani-cured finger at me. "But let's not get distracted. I want to know why you have such big feelings about finally getting dicked down."

At this point, I'm surprised my eyes haven't gotten stuck in my head, because between Caty and Brody, it seems I'm constantly rolling them so far back I can see brain matter.

"I liked it. Um. A lot."

"Yes, and…"

"That's what I'm having a hard time with."

"I don't understand."

"Me either, really. And yeah, I totally get that all that other stuff we did was pretty gay or whatever, but this… The fact that I liked it as much as I did… I mean, Caty—I saw fucking colors I didn't know existed, okay? I felt it in my hair follicles, all the way down past my toes. And then he was looking in my eyes and kissing me and saying things…"

"That's amazing though. That your first time could be that beautiful."

"I just didn't think I was like that."

"Like what?"

I don't have the words to explain what I'm trying to say without sounding as disgusting as the voice in my head. It's not that I don't know that my brain is twisted—I'm very aware. But I can't help putting myself in a new category, one my father would absolutely abhor and describe in the worst ways. A category of men he finds distasteful, weak, emasculated and unworthy to be called real men.

I sigh deeply. "It's one thing to enjoy the occasional blow job from a pretty guy that looks like a girl. It's another thing entirely to like being called a good girl by a brick shithouse of a man whose giant dick makes me feel like I'm on another planet."

"Ohh, I see," Caty says, pursing her lips. "So you're hung up on the bottom-shaming, heteronormative bullshit that big, strong jocks like to throw around in locker rooms."

"It's complicated, okay?"

"It's really not though, *Becky*. You like men. You've always known that. You just convinced yourself it didn't count because you weren't the one on your knees. And now you're having a meltdown because you took it up the ass and think that makes you extra gay or something, or a worse version of gay, or some other absolute ridiculous nonsense."

"Don't call me that. And that's not it. Or at least not all of it. Besides, those guys didn't count."

"How did it not count? Please explain it to me."

"It just wasn't the same," I say weakly.

She rolls her eyes. "Obviously, it wasn't the same. Because you didn't care about them. But this isn't some experiment you can shrug off. The way you two look at each other..." She fans herself with her hand. "It's intense, babe."

I bury my face in my hands. "Caty."

She softens, then asks gently, "Did he hurt you?"

I look up sharply. "No."

"Did you come?"

"Caty—"

"Well, I heard sometimes people don't their first time."

My ears burn. "It was good."

Inside, the truth rolls through me with dizzying clarity. It was more than good. It was incredible. Mind-altering. I loved the way he held me, the way he told me exactly what to do and how to breathe, how careful he was when he was in control. I loved how it hurt for just a moment and then felt better than anything in my entire life. I loved how out of my head I got, how I couldn't stop moaning or clinging to him, how he whispered praise in my ear like he meant every word.

What I'm most embarrassed about, and what I'll never admit to Caty or anyone else, is that afterward, when the adrenaline dropped out from under me and I felt soft and open and ruined in the best possible way, I couldn't look him in the eyes.

Not because I was ashamed.

But because I knew one glance at those stupid sky-blue eyes would make me cry.

And that's the last thing I need right now.

———

I watch Brody constantly, my gaze snapping toward him every time he moves, but I manage to avoid being alone with him. Or being close enough to smell his shampoo. Or making prolonged eye contact, which was hard at first, but he seems to have stopped trying so hard.

He seems down, and I know it's my fault. There's just nothing I can do about it. All I'd do is make it worse, because I'm not ready to admit how he made me feel.

I'm glad he seems to have found good friends in Jay and Aaron. They've been sticking close to him at practices, conditioning, and in the dining hall. Hell, even if I wanted to be alone with Brody, I'm not sure those two would let me. I wonder what he's told them. Why they've suddenly turned into overbearing bodyguards.

At practices, I keep things professional. I pair Brody with Matt Young for drills, claiming that wrestling someone a weight class up will prep them both for West Virginia's lineup. It's not a total lie. Matt is a strong grappler with explosive moves and tough-to-break holds. Brody doesn't balk at the switch. He doesn't blink or argue or have any reaction at all.

Meanwhile, I focus on the underclassmen, barking corrections and forcing my attention anywhere but on the way Brody moves. If I look too long, the memories punch back with brutal clarity. The way he kissed me afterward, slow and deep, and the way he whispered that I was good, so good, as if he'd been waiting forever to be with me like that and I'd surpassed all of his expectations.

And I can't handle that right now.

Not when everything inside me feels so raw.

———

Our first dual away from home is in Lincoln, Nebraska. It also happens to be against the school that Brody transferred from. I can tell he's nervous, but I can't bring myself to say anything about it.

Just before we get on the flight, Coach McCoy hands us each a packet with information about our prospective opponents, which I already know by heart, as well as a list of room assignments.

Naturally, as the only two in our weight class, Brody and I are roomed together.

I spend the entire charter flight pointedly staring out the window or at Coach McCoy's bald spot, refusing to risk eye contact with Brody. Every time I consider asking Coach for a room reassignment, my brain conjures the question he'll inevitably ask, and I can't come up with a solid reason why my apparent dislike of Brody Miller is enough to make Coach change the entire room assignment. So, I say nothing and dread every mile that slips by.

It's the shortest flight of my life, and before I know it we're dragging our bags down a long hotel hallway, branching off as we find our rooms. I feel like I'm being marched to my death, or worse, to give a speech on accepting your sexuality to a group of millions of disapproving parents who all have my father's judgmental eyes.

Coach gave us strict instructions to take quick showers and lights out. We have an early morning tomorrow, and it's been a long, tiring day. I flee to the bathroom, shower fast, and change into pajamas.

When I emerge from the bathroom, Brody is sitting on the edge of his bed with his elbows on his knees and his head cradled in his hands. He looks up and watches me nervously fold my dirty clothes before putting them in my laundry bag.

"Are you okay?" he asks softly.

"Yeah," I lie.

He studies me. "Did I hurt you?"

"No."

"Are you sore?"

"I said I'm fine," I snap. I can't do this right now.

I drop to the edge of my bed and run a hand through my damp hair.

He sighs. "I don't like that you didn't let me take care of you afterward. It made me worry that you were hurt and didn't want to tell me."

My head snaps up. "I said I wasn't hurt. And I don't need you to treat me like a girl."

He rolls his eyes so hard I hear the muscles strain. "It's called after-care, and it's a fully gender-neutral process. And that was your first time. It's normal to have... You know, *feelings* about it."

"I did not—"

"You clearly did," he says gently, infuriatingly certain that he knows me better than he knows himself. "But you didn't have to hide that from me."

I hate how he sees through me. I hate it almost as much as I love it.

"You didn't hurt me," I repeat, in case he has any remaining concerns about that. Clearly, I was the one that hurt him. "I'm sorry that I didn't make that clear. I just feel kind of confused. And the pressure to talk about it or have feelings about it is making it harder to process."

"I'm sorry," he says.

"I am too. I was kind of a dick after you were so good to me."

Brody raises his eyebrow.

"Get over yourself, Miller. I just meant that you were kind, or whatever. You were just trying to take care of me, and I got in my head about it. I'm not used to anyone taking care of me."

"I figured as much." He clears his throat. "I'm sorry I pressured you."

"I don't know that you did. It just... felt too big."

His lips quirk, and I throw a pillow at him.

Desperate to change the subject before I combust, I ask, "How do you feel about tomorrow? Going against your old team?"

He exhales, leaning back on his palms. "Honestly? I kind of have mixed feelings about it. I liked it here. I miss some of the guys. Some of my friends who I've still kept in contact with will be coming tomorrow. It'll be good to see them. But I feel like I've got something to prove, too."

I always feel that way. I nod understandingly. "I can relate."

"I know," he says quietly. He moves to sit beside me on my bed, our knees brushing. He smells warm and comforting, like bar soap and laundry detergent and his cheap, spicy deodorant. How can he smell so good when he hasn't even showered yet?

"I meant what I said about there being no pressure, Beckett," he murmurs. "About *any* of this. You know that, right?"

And I do. It's the one thing I'm completely certain of. Brody pushes me, yes. He takes control, yes, but only because he knows I want him to—need him to. He's never truly forceful and would never cross that line. Somewhere, deep down, I trust him in a way that terrifies me.

Wanting to change the subject again, I bump my shoulder against his and ask him why he moved if he liked it here so much.

Brody sighs, and it's like I can hear torment in that simple exhale.

"You know how Pierce is always cracking jokes about my family? The beer cans everywhere, stuff like that?"

"Yeah, I don't really get the joke about your last name. Because his last name is Jamison, but you don't see anyone making fun of him for that."

"That my last name is Miller is really just fuel for the fire. My, uh—My dad was an alcoholic."

"You said he died when you were little, right?"

Brody nods and looks down at the floor. "He died in a car accident."

Oh. No. Does that mean he died because he...

"He died in surgery because his liver was so damaged, his blood wouldn't clot and they couldn't keep up with his blood loss." He clears his throat. "My dad was a good man. He wasn't drunk when the accident happened. No one else was hurt. As far as we know, he swerved to avoid hitting an animal, but when he ran off the road, he hit a tree directly in front of the Jamison's property." Brody takes another deep breath. "During their insurance company's investigation, they learned that his death was alcohol related, so they tried to claim more money in the insurance settlement. They weren't successful in getting more money, because the accident wasn't alcohol related at all, but the whole mess started a lot of harmful rumors that caused a lot of problems. My brother Davis and I got bullied, my mom lost her job, and everything just got really, really hard."

And that was on top of losing their father.

I notice a tear fall down Brody's cheek and scoot closer, slipping my hand into his to offer him any kind of small comfort. I don't even know what to say, other than to be disgusted that the Jamison family, who as far as I know are just as rich as my family is, would stoop that low over some minor property damage. And to make fun of someone for having an alcoholic father is gross. More than that, it's outright abhorrent.

Before I can say anything to comfort him, Brody keeps going. "My brother and I had very different reactions to what happened to our dad, and to the bullying. I found it easier to laugh things off, even though it hurt. But Davis got really depressed for a long time. Until he started drinking. And then somewhere along the way he started doing drugs."

My heart clenches, and I let out a breath. "I can't imagine how hard that must be."

"At first it was just small stuff, like weed and getting really drunk here and there. Then he was taking something. I still don't know what. It was scary, but also kind of a relief sometimes, because he started smiling again. So I was really mixed up about it."

I know there's more, so I stay silent, letting his fingers play with mine while he stares at the carpet and blinks back more tears.

"Davis started getting into trouble, but we still didn't know how bad the problem had gotten. My dad had a dependency problem, but he never got belligerent or caused any trouble. He mostly drank because he had trouble sleeping, or at least I think that's how it started. And he never did drugs other than taking over-the-counter sleeping pills. But Davis got wild, which didn't make the rumor mill any kinder by the time I hit high school."

He clears his throat again, his voice getting weaker as he goes on. "This past summer, Davis OD'd."

My breath catches, and my hand tightens around his.

"When he was in the hospital... It was like reliving the night my dad died."

"But he's okay?"

"Yeah. I mean, he's alive, at least. And sober. He went through a pretty intense rehab and moved back home in early October. He's struggling, but so far he's been managing well enough. That's why I moved home. I just… I didn't want to be this far away and not be able to help if anything else happens."

"Makes sense. I wouldn't want to be far from them either."

Brody swallows. "I really don't care what anyone thinks about me," he says. "But it's really hard to keep myself in check when people talk about my family. If anyone found out that Davis—"

He doesn't need to finish that sentence. I wouldn't allow it to happen. Never again will I be able to stomach one of Pierce's stupid jokes that turned out to be crueler than I could ever imagine.

The long, painful silence that permeates the space is unbearable. It's suddenly more important for me to fill it than it is to take my next breath.

"I liked it."

He freezes.

"I liked it," I repeat, quieter this time. "But it scares me how much I liked it."

His surprise melts into a slow, bright smile that spreads across his face almost menacingly. There's the Brody I know and enjoy being around the most.

The pride, and possibly smugness, that radiates off him is so overwhelming I can't bear for him to look at me, so I lean in and kiss him.

Brody takes the kiss eagerly, letting me take the lead. He opens his mouth to let me deepen it, but when I don't make any moves to escalate, he seems to understand I'm not ready to take control to that extent.

He twists his body, placing a hand on my waist and pushing me back onto the mattress. One thick thigh pushes between mine and, in a move that nearly takes me out, spreads my legs apart to push in between them. I wrap my legs around him as his torso presses mine into the mattress.

He lifts my shirt from the bottom and pulls it up my body. I raise my arms above my head so he can remove it, but he only wraps the shirt around my wrists and hands, pressing on them lightly to indicate I should keep them there. Then he licks, nips, and kisses a slow, deliberate path down my jaw and neck, then down to my chest. He laves over each nipple, bringing them to hard, sensitive peaks before moving down to swipe his tongue into my belly button and tug on the short hair of my happy trail as he makes his way to the waistband of my boxers and sleep pants.

I never knew my hip bones were erogenous zones before this moment. Then again, I'm pretty sure there isn't a spot on my body that wouldn't respond to his touch. I'm pretty sure the top of my head is an erogenous zone right now.

Brody makes quick work of my pants and underwear, kissing and running his tongue over every crevice of my lower body except where I need him most. I whine and almost move my hands, fisting the fabric of the t-shirt to keep from following the instinct.

When Brody finally takes me in his mouth, I groan so loudly it reverberates off the walls. I clamp my lips shut hard, worried that the guys in the rooms around us might hear me. Brody smiles around my cock, taking me far into the back of his throat and pulling more breathy gasps from me. He brings me to the edge and backs off again, redirecting my pleasure with a sharp bite to the inside of my thigh that makes me yelp. I glare at him, and he laughs.

I hate him. I'm glad he's feeling better, but mostly, I just hate him.

"Are you going to fuck me or not?" I hiss. My moment of tenderness and patience has passed in a haze of edging and barely maintained restraint.

Chuckling, Brody pulls away for a moment to retrieve lube and a condom from his duffle, stripping his clothes on his way back to me. He settles between my thighs again and pushes my knees to my chest. When I don't automatically hold them, he looks up, rolling his eyes at my snarky wordless reminder that he told me to keep my hands up.

"Hold your knees, baby girl. I've got to loosen up this pretty pussy."

I wrap my bound wrists around my knees, sputtering and reeling over what he just said. Not just what he said, but the way it sent a jolt through me, like I might come on the electric impulses of his words alone. *Again.*

Brody opens me up slowly and gently, taking his time but not wasting it. He works with purpose, keeping me pliable with words that stroke my brain the same way his fingers stroke my prostate. And then finally, finally, he's wrapping my hands around the back of his neck, hiking one thigh up to wrap my leg around him, and pushing inside me.

I take him even easier than last time, understanding how to bear down and breathe to relax my body.

"Just like that," Brody moans against my mouth. "That's my good girl."

He fucks me slowly, and so sweetly it feels like something far more intense. So intense I don't have the capacity to worry or freak out over how much I'm feeling, not just physically, but mentally, emotionally.

I come on a breathy, open-mouthed silent cry that has Brody cursing and following me over the edge. We fall, breathless and sweaty, into an exhausted pile of satiated limbs. Eventually, Brody gets up to dispose of the condom and bring me a warm washcloth to clean up with, then pulls me into his clean bed.

I fall asleep in his arms, wondering if I've ever felt this content before in my life.

———

The next day at the meet, Brody greets his old teammates with easy familiarity. He shakes hands and bro-hugs nearly everyone he comes in contact with, laughing and prattling on like he wasn't super nervous just before we left the hotel room this morning. I watch from the side, half warmed by it, half saddened now that I know why he had to come home.

Then someone else approaches, and I forget to be anything other than morbidly curious and more than a little seethingly jealous.

I don't think this guy is another wrestler, considering he's not wearing a uniform or even University of Nebraska team colors. He's wearing dark blue skinny jeans and a soft cream-colored sweater that matches his canvas shoes. He comes forward with a wide smile and watery eyes. When he hugs Brody, it isn't anything like the friendly bro-hugs he gave the others. It lingers. Long enough to make me uncomfortable.

When I see Brody's fingers brush through the nape of the guy's sandy-colored hair, I tense. My jaw clenches when I see how he looks up at Brody almost adoringly, his light brown eyes hiding obvious sadness and longing behind his smile.

Is that guy... Were they...

Is this the kind of guy Brody is normally into? When he isn't stuck at a hostile school with a closed-off guy who has made it his personal mission to make his life miserable? I mean, I'm done with all that, but it hasn't been long enough for Brody to trust that I'm not going to stay on my bullshit.

This guy is nothing like me. He's almost the complete opposite of me. He's small, several inches shorter than Brody and slim. He's not athletic-looking at all. He's soft and pretty, with a stylish haircut that has his longer-in-front hair swept back casually. There are freckles dusted across his nose.

He's... *cute.*

I am not cute. I'm tall, taller than Brody, and broad although not as muscular. I have dark hair and features, and not one freckle can be found on my skin anywhere that I'm aware of.

On top of all that, he carries himself with the confidence of someone who isn't worried that anyone in this gym could be watching and judging him for openly looking at Brody with reverence and longing. I can't even admit I like it when Brody touches me unless I'm under duress.

I hate how my stomach drops when Brody *boops* the pretty boy on the nose and grins.

He doesn't grin at me that way.

"Holy shit," Pierce Jamison says loudly behind me.

I jolt and immediately pretend to study the match-up sheet in my hands.

"Knowing a thing and seeing it are two different animals, am I right? Thank fuck he's not this obvious back at home, right. It's embarrassing for the team."

He nudges me, expecting me to laugh along or talk shit, like I might have weeks ago, if only to throw him off my trail. But ever since Thanksgiving break, everything has changed. I can't bring myself to hate Brody. I can't even fake it. Not when he's the one person who has seen me vulnerable and stuck around anyway.

Still, fear spikes in my chest. Fear that if I defend Brody too strongly, Pierce will notice something. Notice *me*.

I mostly try to ignore him, but when Pierce hints at more of his bullshit about Brody's family, I just can't keep my mouth shut. Not after knowing the truth.

"You need to keep your mouth shut, Jamison. Everyone is sick of your shit, and you should honestly be ashamed of yourself after what his family has been through."

Pierce gapes at me, eyebrows raised in surprise. I roll mine.

"Look, I let you get away with some shit because Brody's an annoying, cocky asshole. But I'm still captain of this team, and enough is enough."

Hands up in surrender, Pierce backs away from me with a cocky, disturbingly knowing grin. But he doesn't relent. Several times throughout the match, Jamison approaches me to make stupid comments or talk shit. I have a bad feeling he's caught on to something, or at least he thinks he has, and he pursues it like a hunting dog.

"I think Brody's got a hard-on for you, man. I know it's fucked up, but if you keep looking at him like that, he's going to think you're jealous or something."

"Shut the fuck up, Jamison. Don't make me tell you again."

"Damn. Did I hit a nerve, *Captain*?" The way he stresses the title disturbs me, even though there's no way he knows about the safe word. What if he saw my texts somehow? My mind reels with the possibilities.

"Why don't you pay attention to your own bullshit for once and maybe try winning a match this year?" I say, looking up to make sure he can see the bored expression on my face. "And put your phone away. You're not supposed to have it out during the competition."

He huffs indignantly. "Maybe the rumors are true then," he sneers.

The hairs on the back of my neck rise. Part of me wants to challenge him, find out what he's talking about or if there are any rumors. But I don't want to feed into his games, and I know he's a vindictive bastard. Luckily, Pierce's phone chimes again. He walks backwards, eyes challenging me as he pulls the phone from his pocket. Turning his attention away from me, he types something into his phone and looks over at Brody with a wicked grin that makes my stomach twist. I can feel that Pierce is up to no good, but I have no way of knowing what bullshit he might pull.

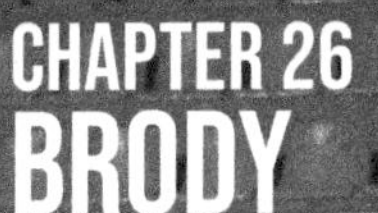

CHAPTER 26

BRODY

I spot Eric as he's crossing the gym, cutting through the Nebraska crowd like he's on a mission. He's exactly the same as he was when I left. Same soft smile, same wide hazel eyes, same nervous energy he always carried around me.

When our eyes meet, his grin widens, lighting up his face. Then he's moving, practically running straight at me. I catch him in a bear hug, muscle memory pulling him tight to my chest and lifting him off the ground. He's shaking. Hell, maybe I am too.

"Brody," he breathes, the way you might say someone's name if they came back from the dead rather than moved to another state.

"Hey, bud. It's good to see you," I murmur, smoothing a hand over the back of his head.

Eric tears up and buries his face in my neck.

"Hey, it's okay."

"It's not," he mumbles into my neck. "It sucks here without you. I can't believe you just left me like that."

My gut clenches.

"Let's go somewhere and talk."

I pull him gently towards the corridor that leads to the athletic offices, where it's quiet. A conversation like this needs a place away from the noise and curious eyes. He follows me without question, like he always did.

In the empty hallway, I lean against the wall, and he leans against me, collapsing right into me, chest to chest, resting his head against my shoulder. It reminds me of the times he'd fall asleep on our couch and end up slumped against my chest. Back then he was just Leo's wide-eyed, optimistic, naïve little brother. He was so sweet it made something in me ache whenever he was sad.

"Why'd you leave?" he asks, voice wobbly.

I swallow hard. For someone who hadn't told a soul about everything that's going on with my family, I sure am getting more comfortable with sharing. Telling Beck was one thing. I'd rather not have to share all the details with Eric, but seeing him this raw and hurt, I can't not tell him something. I always had a soft spot for my roommate's younger brother.

"My brother," I say quietly. "He got sick. And it's pretty bad. Worse than I told anyone. My family needs me closer to home. I want to be closer to home, so I don't have to fly halfway across the country in case—" I swallow. "I just need to be there."

Eric sucks in a shaky breath. "Broderick Miller, you asshole. Why didn't you tell us? Why didn't you tell me?"

Because I was too raw. Because I didn't want to answer questions. Because I was worried you and Leo would think less of me for whatever reason, because I have a long history of people not being kind to my family because of things beyond our control.

Because you would have begged me to stay, and it would have been harder to leave.

But all I say is, "I didn't want you worrying."

He lifts his head then, eyes shining with tears. His lips part, and he leans in. I gently stop him with a soft kiss to his forehead. It's not a rejection. I've never been able to reject him outright. But it's not an invitation either. Back then, it was because he was too young and innocent.

Now I've got a tall, grouchy, uptight mess of a man who I'm pretty sure has it bad for me. Maybe almost as bad as I have it for him.

"I miss you," he whispers.

"I miss you too."

I'm about to tell him he should get back before the dual starts when something catches my eye at the end of the hall.

Pierce Jamison leans against the far side of the wall, casually scrolling or reading something on his phone. He's not doing anything. He hasn't even acknowledged that he noticed us here, but I have a feeling he was listening, and I find myself backtracking over our conversation, making sure I didn't say anything too obvious or inflammatory.

"Come on," I say quickly, guiding Eric back. "We should go."

———

The meet is brutal, in all the best ways.

Both teams fight hard. Nebraska puts on a show for the visiting opponents. And Huntston pushes right back.

Beck is a fucking animal out there. I don't know what's gotten into him, but he's had his fierce game face on all day, and he isn't pulling any punches. He steamrolls Leo, my old roommate, so efficiently that Leo gives me a helpless, breathless laugh afterward.

I can't wait to introduce them later after the competition is over. Coach McCoy already gave me permission to take a few hours to myself after the meet is over, and I'm going to try to convince Beck to come with me to hang out with my old friends.

I'm concerned that Beck doesn't look proud of his victory, nor does he cheer much for the rest of our teammates as we make it through the weight classes.

He looks tense. More high-strung than usual, and considering just how good he was feeling when we left the hotel this morning, his frustration feels out of character.

Later, just after the meet is over, I think I've figured him out. I'm standing at the edge of the gym, laughing and chatting with Leo. Eric says something funny about Leo's epic loss, and I wrap my arms around Eric's shoulders like I'm going to take him down to the mats.

I catch Beck's scowl across the mats. The lasers he's shooting across the gym could set fires if it was dry in here. I feel the friction of it against my skin, and actually squeeze Eric's shoulders protectively.

He's my college best friend's little brother. He's so tiny and innocent, don't hurt him!

I can't help but chuckle. His jealousy should annoy me or piss me off. But rather than be irritated by it, I feel oddly warm and fuzzy inside.

Relax, baby girl. He's just a friend.

Whatever message I'm trying to send with my eyes must not be transmitted or received as intended, because when I press a chaste kiss to the top of Eric's head—an affectionate, but innocent gesture to tease Beck—he looks like an angry cat with his back up.

It's kind of cute. And I kind of love it, even if it makes me a bad person to be teasing him when he's not getting the joke. I'll make it up to him, and rile him up all over again, when I point out what his jealousy really means.

You like me, Lincoln Beckett.

———

Most of our team is already in the locker room by the time I get there. I head straight to the temporary lockers, grabbing my things quickly and looking around for Beck so I can clear the air with him before I head off with my friends, but something feels wrong.

It occurs to me that it's too quiet in here. The locker room is never this quiet after a meet. There's nothing more than a low murmur coming from the far side of the room. When I turn around to see what's happening, I notice too many eyes on me.

Teammates and friends I've made in the last few months cut their eyes at me and dart their gazes away quickly. People look at me with pity, and what looks like morbid curiosity.

Then I notice where the only chatter in the room is coming from. Pierce, holding court in the far corner of the room like the cowardly piece of shit he is. I didn't miss the disgusted and judgmental looks I saw him throwing my friends during and after the dual.

Then I hear fragments of what he's saying. Words that burn me to my core. Slurs, either directed to me or my friend Eric, or both of us since I'm clearly close to him. Something about my father being lucky he doesn't have to witness his sons' downward spiral.

I hear my brother's name. And my vision narrows until he's the only thing in the room.

"What did you just say?" I ask, my voice gravelly with warning.

"What? I wasn't talking to you. Mind your business."

"You've got my name in your mouth, Jamison. Spit it out."

"Maybe your family name, but you're used to being in the news by now, aren't you, Miller? I mean, after your dad made such a mess of things. And now to hear that your brother is following in his footsteps? What a fucking shame." He scoffs, and I hate that it reminds me of the sound Beck makes when he's sick of my bullshit or trying to pretend he is and can't come up with anything to say. Unfortunately, Pierce still has plenty more to say. "It's honestly not even surprising. Davis was a joke in high school, always embarrassing himself. How many times was he arrested? Anyway," Pierce looks smugly at the people listening to him, "everyone knows the whole Miller family is a disaster. Dad drank himself to death and nearly killed people by running his car into a tree in someone's front yard. Mom can't keep a job to save her life. Big brother overdosed and got sent to mandatory rehab and is now living with mommy in a falling-down hovel. And little brother walks around pretending he's above it all while he sticks his dick in trashy redneck twinks and drools over the captain of the wrestling team." Pierce laughs. "You're fucking pathetic, Miller. Why don't you go home and stop pretending you're better than the trash you've always been. Maybe spend some time getting arrested with your brother before it's too late, ya know?"

I've said it before, and I'll say it a hundred times more—I could not give a shit less what Pierce Jamison and his evil, money-grubbing family think of me. I don't give a shit what anyone thinks of me.

But hearing my brother's name in his mouth. Hearing the details of my personal family troubles spewed for everyone to hear.

It fucking guts me.

How does he know about Davis? He shouldn't know any of it. No one should know.

And before last night, no one did know.

I spin around, heart jackhammering, and find Beck in the showers. He's just stepping out of the spray, wrapping a towel around his waist. His wet hair drips down his neck and shoulders and chest. The same neck and shoulders and chest that I kissed last night. After I told him the most painful truth I've ever uttered out loud. Something I didn't even tell a close friend that I've known for years.

Beck looks up and notices me standing, still in my uniform, sweater, and shoes, in the middle of the showers. He has the fucking audacity to look angry. At me.

"What the hell is wrong with you?" I say, my voice choked.

He stalks toward me, looking around us before muttering angrily under his breath. "What do you mean what's wrong with *me*? What's wrong with *you*? Why the hell would you do something like that? You were so fucking obvious, Pierce started asking questions."

I'm seeing red right now. I don't know what the fuck he's talking about. And I can't be bothered to care. He betrayed me, to my worst fucking enemy.

"So you were jealous, is that it? Or was it that you were afraid of being outed by association?" My voice is so low I'm not even sure that he hears me until I see his visceral reaction to any mention of his sexuality in public. Not that I'd out him like that. Even now, even after this, I would never.

"Do you have any idea how awkward of a position you put me in with Pierce?"

Something inside me snaps, and the furious rage inside me seeps out of my eyes because it can't be held in anymore. Is that why he told him? To cover his own secrets?

"How could you do that, Beck? I kept your fucking secrets. How could you?"

Through the blurry haze of my tears, I see Beck freeze.

"What?" The anger bleeds out of his voice and is replaced with something that sounds like concern, or pity. Maybe my words finally hit him where it hurts. It makes me feel nauseous to admit it, but I hope he feels a fraction of the pain I feel right now.

"Him?" I gesture sharply towards Pierce. "You told *him*? Out of everyone, you picked the one person who would do the most damage? The person whose family ruined everything in my life. Because of what, Beckett? Jealousy?"

His face twists in confusion. "What are you talking ab—"

My voice cracks in a way that humiliates me, but I can't stop now. "I knew you were a pretentious asshole. God knows you work hard to keep that image, but I didn't think you'd stoop this low. You are your father's son after all."

His mouth falls open, hurt and confusion warring on his face, but I can't hear anything he says after that. I'm gasping, dizzy, drowning in the sudden humiliation of it all.

I grab my bag and back toward the exit. Pierce, the fucking idiot, steps into my path. Without thinking, I deck him with a right hook that reverberates up my arm. He goes down hard, and I push through the door.

CHAPTER 27
BECK

No one stops or follows Brody as he steps around Pierce's crumpled body and storms out of the locker room. For a long moment, no one moves or says anything.

The sound of Brody's fist connecting with Pierce's face seems to echo off the red metal of the lockers. A sickening crack, followed by a heavy thud of his body hitting the tile floor.

A pained groan breaks the silence, and I look down at Pierce for the first time. He's holding his face, rolling to the side with blood gushing from his nose, making what I'm pretty sure is an over-exaggerated gurgling sound, gagging and cursing.

"What are you staring at?!" Pierce screams at us in a nasally tone, his voice muffled by blood and his hands cupping his face. "That bastard broke my fucking nose."

Realizing I'm just standing here, staring at Pierce bleeding on the floor in his underwear, I jolt into action. Roman and Cade move in first, trying to help haul Pierce upright, but he fights them off and remains sprawled out on the floor. Grabbing a folded towel from the rack near the showers, I run over and guide his hands away from his face to hold the towel instead, trying to see how bad it is. Pierce bats me away, cursing and moaning.

"Shut up and hold the towel," I tell him. The bastard had it coming, and I don't hate seeing him bleed a little after all he and his family have put Brody through.

Sighing, I look down at the man lying in a fetal position and holding the towel to his face. "What did you do to him?" I ask.

Pierce's eyes flash indignantly, and he pulls the towel away to yell at me. "Excuse me? I'm lying here bleeding, and you're asking what *I* did to *him*?"

Roman steps in, crouching down to take over for me. "Well, it looks like the bleeding has mostly stopped, so it's probably not broken," he says, not sparing much sympathy for our teammate.

"Go get dressed," Roman says quietly, gesturing to my state of nudity with his chin. Right. There's blood on my knees and soaked into the white fabric of the towel still wrapped around my waist.

Just then, Coach McCoy storms into the room with Sean on his heels, nearly tripping over Pierce, who still refuses to get up off the floor. Coach McCoy looks down at Pierce, then at me, rage in his eyes.

"What the hell did you do?" He barks down at Pierce.

"You've got to be kidding me!"

Leaving Coach and the other captains to deal with Pierce as he dissolves into a full-blown tantrum, I step back into the showers to rinse the blood from my knees and calm my nerves. My ears ring like I took a hit to the head. What the fuck just happened? I've never seen Brody like that. And he thought I had something to do with whatever he just punched Pierce out for?

When I'm finally clean again and have pulled on some underwear and a pair of pants, I walk over to where Brody's roommates, Aaron and Jay, are talking in hushed tones with Fish. Cade notices me heading their way and follows.

"Yo, what the fuck was that about?" Cade asks, making the others look up and notice me approaching.

"That was actually what I came to find out, too," I say, my tone serious. "Does anyone know where Brody ran off to? I should check on him."

Aaron's eyebrow lifts, but if he's curious why I'd chase after Brody after he just berated me, punched Pierce, then ran out of here, he doesn't ask. It'd be a normal thing for me to do if I'd been half the captain I should have been this year, but as things stand, I know it seems strange. I can't be bothered to care about what anybody thinks right now, though. I need to get to the bottom of what happened.

"Brody isn't answering his phone," Aaron says. "But Pierce—"

Just as he says his name, Pierce, who has finally made it to a bench and is being cleaned up by one of the trainers, shouts something about pressing charges. "He's going to fucking regret this!"

"Watch your mouth, Pierce," Coach barks.

"I'm not saying Pierce didn't have it coming—" Jay says.

"—but that wasn't like Brody," I finish for him. "What happened?"

"Pierce was talking his usual shit. It started with him making fun of how Brody was flirting with some guy."

That part I know, because I was very aware of the way Brody was so casually affectionate with that pretty boy with the freckles. He taunted me with it all fucking day, and Pierce even commented several times about the way Brody and I were watching each other.

"Yeah, well it didn't end there. Pierce kept on and started saying some fucked up shit about Brody's family and his brother—"

My spine snaps straight. "His brother? How'd he find out?"

Jay's eyes widen. "Don't know. Pierce just said he heard some stuff and made a few calls back home. All I know is something finally struck a nerve. I thought he was going to hit Pierce right then and there, but he went and argued with you in the shower instead. Then he stormed out, decked Pierce, and left."

"Honestly, I probably would have taken a shot, too. That shit he was saying about his family was fucked up," Cade says. "Who does that?"

I swallow hard and bite the inside of my cheek hard enough to taste iron. There's so much I want to say. I want to defend Brody and his family. To tell them that his dad wasn't some drunk monster, that he was a good man who died in a freak accident that the Jamison family exploited for money and attention. That Davis isn't some delinquent. That he was a kid swallowed by grief who went down a dark path. And that the happy, funny, friendly Brody they know has been drowning under the weight of it all this time.

But none of that is mine to share.

Jay taps my elbow and gives me a sympathetic look. I try not to read into it, but it feels like he can see through me. "What happened in there, Beck?"

The look on his face, the betrayal, the awful things he said. The tears. I started seeing past my own blind rage and jealousy the moment I saw the first tear track down his cheek. He wasn't just pissed, he was hurt. Badly.

I nearly choke on the realization. "He thinks I told him," I say, mostly to myself. My spine straightens. "Has anyone heard from him yet?"

They shake their heads as I'm backing away to grab my phone and shoes. I have to find him. Right now. I have to tell him it wasn't me, that I'd never betray him like that. More than that, I need to make sure he's okay.

Aaron gives Jay a look, then chases me out of the locker room. I see Coach talking to one of the officials, and I head across the gym to see if he knows where Brody might be.

"Beck—"

"Not right now, Aaron. I have to find Brody. He seemed really upset."

"I just thought you should know that Pierce has been saying some other things. About you and Brody."

I stop short and spin around, looking down at Aaron, who is a good six or seven inches shorter than me. "What did he say? Wait." I shake my head and resume walking. "Nope. I don't care. I'll deal with that asshole later."

Everyone knows by now that Pierce is a vindictive piece of work and mostly full of shit. Just because he dug up a few truths about Brody doesn't mean anyone will believe him about me.

Why am I thinking about that anyway? Why am I worrying about myself at all, when Brody needs me?

Coach McCoy sees me charging towards him and says something to end his conversation with the official. I hear the official say that a police officer will be arriving soon to take statements.

"Police?" I ask incredulously.

Coach nods and gestures for me to keep my voice down.

"Mr. Jamison wants to file charges for assault."

My face flushes hot with rage. "Seriously? Was his nose even broken?"

"No, he got lucky." Coach scoffs. "Miller obviously held back. Otherwise, Pierce would have been out cold." He gives me a pointed look. "Not that it makes it okay what Mr. Miller did."

I wave him off. "Pierce had it coming. And yeah, I know I'm supposed to be the captain and keep order, but I might have done it myself if I'd been in the room to hear the things he was saying about Brody's family."

"Between you and me, I might have liked to see Jamison get knocked on his ass."

I snort a small laugh. "That part I did see, and it was pretty awesome."

Coach clears his throat and pulls his shoulders back, getting back to business. "Anyway. We've got a shitstorm waiting for us at home. Do you have any idea where Miller ran off to?"

"I was hoping you knew," I say, looking around at the last few Nebraska wrestlers walking around. "His old roommate was on the team. The guy I wrestled, Leo something. And there was, um, a guy with them. Small guy, with sandy hair and freckles. Looked kind of..." I want to say *soft* or *cute* or *pretty,* but change directions mid-sentence. "They looked close," I say, the words tasting like battery acid on my tongue.

Coach nods. "I'll talk to their coach and see what I can find out."

"Coach McCoy, how bad is it?"

"Jamison's parents are already calling a lawyer. I expect the athletics director and the dean will be involved once the assault charges Pierce is filing from the hospital are filed."

"A hospital, seriously?" I feel an entire ocean's worth of rage rushing through my veins. I'm bloated and sick with it. "That's ridiculous, and everyone who was in that locker room knows it."

"I know," Coach cuts in, holding up a hand. "I heard enough about it already, believe me. I've gotten statements from a few of the guys already that Miller was provoked. That will matter, but it doesn't erase the fact that Miller swung first. Unfortunately, Jamison's family has the pull to make things very bad for him. I'm going to do what I can, but this is serious."

I swallow hard. "What's going to happen?"

"For now? He's suspended," he says. "Indefinitely. No practice, no meets, no team activities until the administration decides what to do. I'm going to be straight with you, Beckett." His gaze meets mine, unflinching. "If the Jamison family pushes this the way I expect they will, there's a good chance that Mr. Miller will be expelled. At best, he'll lose his scholarship."

I hear the words, but they don't quite land. They hover in the space between us like smoke.

Brody is going to be expelled. There's no way the Jamison family won't throw their weight around.

If I could have just swallowed my pride and my jealousy and listened to my gut, I could have stopped him. The moment I saw the pain in his eyes and the tears tracking down his face, I knew something was wrong. I should have reached out, held him back, made him talk to me.

But talking was always his thing, and I was too much of a chicken-shit to let anyone see me show another man affection. Because God forbid another man reach out and touch someone's shoulder or comfort them.

I want to be holding him right now.

"Is there anything I can do?" I ask Coach McCoy, hating how small my voice sounds.

Coach studies me for a long moment, something like regret in his eyes. "Right now? Stay out of it. Let me talk to the powers that be. Let things cool down. The last thing we need is more fuel on the fire."

I understand the thinly veiled warning. You don't want to get caught in the crossfires.

Stay out of it.

Right. Sure. Okay.

I nod anyway. "Yes, sir."

He claps a hand once on my shoulder, then lets it fall. "Start rallying the team towards the bus. I'm going to talk to Nebraska's admin about what we can do to track Miller down."

———

Brody still hasn't returned. I was too embarrassed to ask housekeeping for fresh sheets this morning, so I'm lying on his bed watching the minutes and hours tick by on the red glowing numbers of the digital alarm clock. I've been lying here since we got back to the hotel. At some point, the last rays of light disappeared, leaving only blackness outside the window I'm staring out of.

Was it really less than twenty-four hours ago that we were lying here, tangled up together? Less than twelve since I woke up with him next to me.

When I close my eyes, I can pretend I still feel his body heat next to me, especially when I press my face into his pillow and breathe in whatever lingers of his scent. My hand runs over the invisible indentation of where he was lying on his stomach with his face buried in a pillow. He was still asleep when I woke up, so I had time to just look at him, at all his muscle and tan skin on display as I slowly peeled the sheet down his body until it rested just below the perfect round globes of his ass.

My first impulse when he started to stir was to jump out of bed and lock myself in the bathroom to get ready for the day. To go back to pretending there was nothing between us.

Instead, I leaned over and kissed his shoulder, then trailed my lips down his spine.

"I don't think we have time for that kind of wake-up, but I'll most definitely take a raincheck," he said, voice gravelly and eyes still shut. I hummed and caressed my fingers over his skin, lightly dragging my nails around the curve of Brody's butt.

"Do you want to top me next?" He asked, surprising me with such a casual offer. When I could drag my eyes away from the rash of gooseflesh on his skin, I found his eyes, bright and clear, on mine. "You can fuck me if you want to, Beck. Tonight, or whenever we have a night to ourselves again."

My face got warm, but I didn't hide from him even though I wanted to. I was honest, with my eyes, at least. I let him read the truth. That I didn't want to be in control. That I like when he takes me, not just because of how it makes me feel physically, which is beyond comprehension, but mentally and emotionally, too.

Brody is the only person I've ever felt comfortable enough to drop my guard around. I think it's what makes the sex so good.

Will it ever be like that again? Will we get back to where we were this morning, when we laughed while we wrestled for the last clean towel after showering together and making each other come? Will I ever have the thrill of nearly being late because

Brody's mouth on me was suddenly more important than my obsessive need to be twenty minutes early to everything?

I lie awake staring at the ceiling, Brody's words replaying on a loop.

You are your father's son after all.

Rolling to my other side, I reach for my phone again. As I've done a dozen or more times since Brody ran out of the locker room, I check for calls and messages, in case some kind of glitch made me miss a notification. I check that my ringer is on and turned up as loud as it goes, and change his notification tone to something obnoxious so there's no possibility of me missing a message from him.

And then I send him two more texts, and call his number a few more times, it goes straight to voicemail like it has all day. The first time I'm silent, listening to the dead silence of the line before hanging up. The second time I leave another message.

"Brody, baby. Please call me back. I just want to know you're okay. I didn't tell him. I swear to God, I didn't tell him anything. But it might still be my fault, because I snapped at him and told him to lay off. I should have known he'd..." I take a shaky breath. "Just call me back, okay? Please."

I hang up and stare at the black screen until my eyes blur.

He doesn't call back.

———

Becky: I packed your things from the hotel. I'll bring your bag to the airport. You'll be there, right?

Becky: Where are you?

Becky: Just tell me you're okay.

. . .

The next morning, the team is subdued as we climb off the bus and onto our charter flight to go home. Pierce sits up front with team admin, the area beneath his eyes a deep purple and a bandage over his nose despite it being confirmed that it wasn't broken. I overheard the trainer who accompanied Pierce to the hospital tell Coach that all imaging showed no signs of damage other than minor bruising.

The plane fills up, but there's no Brody when the flight attendant pulls the door closed and latches it.

Coach makes his way through the plane, taking a head count and checking in on everyone. When he walks past our section of the small jet, he eyes the empty seat Brody was supposed to be in, then looks around at those of us sitting nearby.

I really thought he'd be here. Why isn't he here?

Brody should be sitting next to Fish, across the aisle and one row down from where I'm sitting with Cade. Jay and Aaron are in front of Fish, and Roman and Sean are behind me and Cade.

"Mr. Miller decided to head back separately," he says, giving us the only information that he can—Brody is safe and accounted for.

I open my mouth to ask for more, but Coach shakes his head. Now isn't the time or place. Before he continues down the aisle to his seat, he nods at the guys behind me. It feels cryptic. I turn and make eye contact with my co-captains, then look around at our friends. His friends, and mine, and the friends we share who are concerned for him.

He should be here. I should be keeping my face pointedly angled away and refusing to make eye contact in case he tries to eye fuck me where everyone can see, not avoiding the empty space next to

Fish because it makes me want to scream and I'm barely holding myself together.

A hand lands on the back of my seat. I turn my head to find Roman leaning forward.

"You okay?" he asks quietly.

I almost laugh. The sound that comes out is closer to a cough. "Yeah, I'm fine." Then I shake my head. "No. This is fucked up. Brody might not be my favorite person, but he doesn't deserve to lose everything like this," I lie.

He nods once, like that's the only honest answer he expected. "Sean and I had an idea that we wanted to run by you. Some of the other guys have mentioned being upset about the likelihood of Brody getting kicked off the team."

"Out of school entirely, you mean," Aaron says, leaning across the aisle to chime in. "If he loses his scholarship, he'll lose everything. He won't be able to continue going to school at all."

Bile rises in my throat. I cut my eyes to the front of the plane where Pierce is leaning back and listening to headphones, watching something on his phone. He looks perfectly relaxed.

"That's right," Sean says, nodding at Aaron. "If there's anything we can do, we want to try. I ran this idea past Coach last night, and he thinks it might help."

"What are we doing?" I ask, impatient to get to the damn point. I'm ready to do something about this. I need a plan, or at least the beginnings of one that I can focus on to keep myself sane.

"Not one person that we've spoken to, even the freshies who follow Pierce around, were cool with what happened yesterday. I saw them physically backing away when he was going off on Brody. So we're going to get as many statements together as possible from teammates in support of Brody, and to confirm the harassment he's been dealing with since the year began." Sean has the kindness not to stare directly at me when he says that, but Aaron doesn't bother holding back his pointed glare. I show him the decency of lowering my eyes and acknowledging his unspoken words.

This is on you, Beckett.

I nod. "I'm in. I'll help any way I can." Thinking of something I might be able to do, I pull out my phone to type out a text message. "My, um, my girlfriend's mom is on the Board of Directors for the school. I'll see if there's anything she can do to help."

"Most of the trainers and admin are willing to speak up in support of Brody as well," Roman adds. "Everyone's sick of Pierce's bullshit, and most of the team really likes Brody."

"I'm in," Matt Young says, turning around from his seat in front of Cade.

"Hell yeah," Cade says, throwing his hand over the back of Matt's seat to give him a fist bump.

Matt's seat partner, a freshman named Sebastian, throws his fist into the mix as well. "Pierce is a dick, and I might know how Brody's tires got slashed," he says, looking uncomfortable. "I'd be willing to report that to admin if it helps keep Brody on the team."

"Thanks, man," I say, as if I've taken the lead on this project. Face hot, I turn back to my co-captains. "What else we got?"

World Wrestling Cup

CHAPTER 28

BRODY

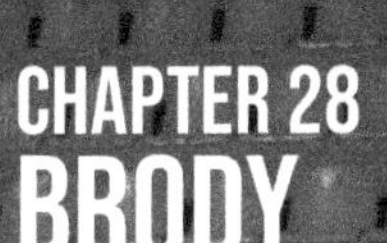

I don't cry much. Not that I have anything against crying. Honestly, I sometimes wish I did it more often. It can be cathartic. It was when I finally released the knot in my throat after realizing I wouldn't be headed back to the University of Nebraska.

But now I can't stop.

This isn't like me. Even the times I've needed to take a step back to reevaluate or process something—my dad's death, my brother's overdose, transferring to a school of people who resented me for sullying their status quo. I've been able to take all that in stride. It doesn't take long for me to stand up, put on the carefree mask I've perfected, and move forward. Even when it still hurts, or when people or circumstances are breathing down my neck, I've just always been able to shut it down and keep going. Compartmentalizing is my lifeblood.

So why can't I pack this up now? Especially when there are people staring at me in obvious concern, I can't pull my shit together.

I cried and screamed my rage out enough yesterday that I don't really have any actual tears left. But I can still feel the sadness and disbelief weighing me down. My body weighs too much. Even the skin on my face feels heavy.

After leaving the sports complex yesterday, I ran straight for the Mabel Lee Fields, where I used to jog and knew I was likely to not run into anyone. I trudged through the frozen sludge that had melted from the night before and stood in the middle of the open field and screamed until my vocal cords gave out, fell to my hands and knees, and heaved.

Eventually, I realized my skin was numb with cold. My knees were red and raw from the sludge I'd been kneeling in for too long. I was still wearing my wrestling uniform with nothing but a zip-up hoodie, in the middle of December in Nebraska. I stood up and walked in my soaked-through wrestling shoes to the residence hall where Leo and Eric live.

Leo was expecting me, although I was late because of the impromptu walk I took across campus. The moment he opened the door, his eyes widened.

"Brody…"

Eric popped up behind him, but the excitement quickly melted off his face as soon as he saw me standing there.

With their eyes on me, and the realization that I probably looked as bad as I felt, I wasn't able to conjure up my usual mask. I haven't been able to get it back since.

"You still look like shit," Leo says, padding across the room with his hair sticking up on one side. It's sometimes hard to tell that Leo and Eric are related because they have different fathers, but when they're sleep-rumpled and disheveled, I can see the resemblance. I've rarely seen Eric rumpled, but looking at his brother now, I see the similarities in the shape of his brow and curve of his neck. That's where the similarities end, though. Leo has dark hair and rugged features, and his body is cut similarly to mine.

"Thanks, buddy," I rasp, my throat still raw from screaming and being out in the cold for so long yesterday.

"How ya feelin'?" He asks, sticking his feet into his shower shoes and tossing a pair of flip-flops at me. I reluctantly push myself up in bed and slide my socked feet into the shoes, wedging the fabric of the socks between my toes well enough to keep the shoes on my feet.

Luckily for me, Leo's roommate isn't an athlete, so he left earlier in the week after finishing his last final. The bed was stripped, but Leo had an extra set of sheets and a blanket for me to use, and I crashed here for the night. I probably should have gone back to the hotel, but I couldn't bring myself to do it. I don't want to be there, surrounded by people who probably legitimately hate me now. Who, at the very least, are going to look at me with pity because they now know the intimate details of my family's private lives.

And I most certainly couldn't handle being in the same room as Beck.

Leo hands me the extra toothbrush we got from the convenience shop downstairs, and I follow him to the bathroom down the hall. The suspicious smell and overflowing shower drains remind me just how spoiled I've been by the ensuite bathroom I share with only two other people in the fancy apartment-style athletic dorms at Huntston.

Shar*ed*, I think, correcting myself. It's not likely I'll be staying there any longer. I'll have to go back to clean out my dorm room and get my car, but I'm probably not a student at Huntston anymore. I knew that before I talked to Coach McCoy last night.

Once I'd been shuffled into the gross communal showers to stand under the hot water for as long as it lasted, I got bundled up in sweats and blankets and told to call my coach. While I was in the shower, Coach Yeardly, the Nebraska team coach, had called Leo asking if they'd seen me. I felt bad for making anyone worry, but Coach McCoy was surprisingly calm about everything.

Since my suspension from the team was effective the moment my fist made contact with Pierce's face, he didn't see any reason why I couldn't make my way home on my own if that's what I wanted. He even offered to help pay for a plane ticket, but I told him it wasn't necessary. Overall, he was incredibly understanding considering I'd decked one of his athletes. He even told me that he'd advocate for me, but we both know the Jamison family aren't going to leave any crumbs when they chew me up. There's a history between us that all but guarantees it. A precedent that will be maintained.

With one swing of my fist, I threw away everything. My scholarship, and therefore my education. My pride. My peace of mind and the guarantee of a better future.

I won't include losing Beck. He was lost to me before I threw the punch. And while my actions are entirely my own, I was actually far more upset with Beck than I was with Pierce. Pierce just happened to step in front of me to try to stop me from escaping before I broke right there in the middle of the locker room.

My chapped lips burn. I lick them and taste salt. More fucking tears.

I pee, brush my teeth, and wash my face while Leo does the same. It's probably a good thing I'm staying with him and not somewhere on my own, I likely wouldn't have gotten out of bed otherwise. As it is, I slump back to cover myself in the blanket the moment we get back to Leo's room. I'm exhausted. Despite lying in this bed basically since I arrived, I didn't sleep much. All I did was stare at the ceiling and cry some more. I keep replaying the look on Beck's face, as if I could go back and change it.

If I could, I'd go back. I'd rewind all the way to just before I told him everything. I wanted him to open up to me, and I wanted to do the same. I never imagined he'd tell anyone. Least of all, Pierce fucking Jamison.

What I can't figure out is why he told him.

You were so fucking obvious, Pierce started asking questions.

Do you have any idea how awkward of a position you put me in with Pierce?

Exactly how did I put him in an awkward position? I knew I was playing with fire by teasing him, but it was innocent. I don't see how my teasing, which was kept just between us, would lead him to spill my secrets to Pierce? I'd told him the night before that I wouldn't be able to handle if Pierce found out about my brother and started talking shit about it.

How could he?

I vaguely remember Pierce making a comment about me wanting Beck, but he could deny any interest or involvement with me without feeding me to the wolves.

I just don't understand.

There's a knock on the door, and a few seconds later Eric walks in, holding a tray of to-go cups from the campus coffee cart and a bag that probably has pastries in it.

"You ready to—"

"No."

It comes out harshly, but I don't have the ability or energy to soften anything right now.

Eric kicks off his shoes and climbs into the bed next to me, snuggling up to my side and rearranging the blanket so it's around both of us. I want to laugh, because even after seven months of not seeing each other, and barely ever texting, it's like nothing changed with him.

Why couldn't I have fallen in love with someone like Eric? Maybe not Eric exactly, because I feel nothing but platonic towards him. But someone like him. Sweet. Affectionate. Not afraid to be themselves.

Wait, what?! Why couldn't I have...

Fallen...

In...

Love?!?

What the actual fuck, Miller? You can't just decide you were in love with someone now that you've lost them. You're just tired and emotional. You're spiraling and need to get a grip.

Except, I knew it was headed that way. I knew I was feeling some sort of way. Even before Thanksgiving, but certainly after...

"You can talk about it if you want to," Eric whispers. "You don't have to. But we're here for you if you'd like to get it off your chest."

My eyes flick up to Leo, who nods from his desk chair.

"There really isn't much to say," I rasp, thankful that it's mostly true. Technically, there's a lot that could be said. But most of it isn't necessary for the overall point to be made. "I screwed up. And I threw everything away."

"I'm sure that's not the case."

"I got myself suspended, expulsion pending."

Leo's mouth dropped open. "How did that happen?"

"I punched Pierce Jamison in the face. I might have broken his nose, although I tried to pull back as soon as I realized my fist was already flying."

Eric pulls back. "*You* punched someone?"

I nod. I know they want more of an explanation, but really that's the only part that matters. I did a bad thing, and I'm going to be punished for it. Which I deserve. No matter where my head was or what my excuses were, I did it. If I'm being very honest, it's something I've wanted to do for a very long time.

"Who is Pierce Jamison and what did he do to deserve getting punched?" Leo asks, sounding almost amused.

"Yes, because I know you, Brody, and he must have done something bad to warrant a teddy bear like you flying off the handle like that," Eric says.

"Maybe you don't know me as well as you think you do," I say.

I can tell by the way his shoulders slump that his feelings are hurt by that, but it's the truth. After all, as close of friends as the three of us were when I went to school here, I never told them anything about my life back home.

"You're Broderick Wesley Miller from Colson Creek, South Carolina. Your first name is your grandma's maiden name on your dad's side because your older brother Davis was named after your mom's family. Your favorite color is burgundy. Your favorite food is any kind of pasta with cheese on it even though it makes you constipated. You're allergic to cats but love them…"

"None of that makes me a good person, Eric."

Eric ignores me and keeps going. "Your favorite color is burgundy because it's your mother's favorite color. You like pasta because it's the only thing your mom had the time or money to prepare very often, and it's the first thing you learned to cook yourself so you could help. You call or text your mama every other day because you don't want her to worry about you. You didn't drink on your own twenty-first birthday so I wouldn't be the only sober one, even though you snuck me into a dive bar and I could have totally gotten away with it," he says pointedly, making both me and Leo chuckle because it's been a long-standing argument.

"Remember the time you fireman-carried my heavy ass across campus when I twisted my ankle?" Leo asks.

"Didn't you twist your ankle because I tripped you?"

"Maybe. But you warned me that if I kept staring at that girl's butt, I'd pay the price for being 'the bear'."

I shrug. "You already look like one, you should take extra care not to act like one."

His lips quirk. "See? Helping humanity one sorry cis straight guy at a time."

"You helped me get switched to an easier ACE-credit math course, then rearranged your busy schedule to tutor me so I wouldn't fail my first semester," says Eric. "And I actually ended up getting an A in that class. I still think you should be a teacher, by the way."

"I saw you apologize to the door frame once when you walked into it."

I snort and swipe a hand over my face.

"Oh! You walked Leo's date home that night he got too drunk to get it up, after you'd been sitting in the lobby for almost an hour to give them privacy."

"You never kicked my clingy baby brother out of our room even though he was annoyingly in love with you, and you still let him latch onto you like a koala even though you spent all day making heart eyes at the Disney prince looking motherfucker that put me on my ass yesterday."

The glare Eric gives Leo would be impressive if he wasn't bundled up in my blanket with only his face sticking out.

Eric sighs and looks up at me. "You moved all the way home, even though it was clear you didn't want to, because your brother got sick."

"You're a good dude, Brody. Whatever happened yesterday doesn't change that."

I laugh to keep from crying, but it doesn't work. My eyes sting and water, and my laughter just sounds cruel, like I'm revealing some kind of deception, nearly three years in the making.

"Brody—"

"If I were a better person, I wouldn't have left Colson Creek in the first place. I wanted out because I hated it there and I wanted to start over somewhere that people didn't know me, so I could pretend to be somebody else. I didn't drink on my twenty-first birthday because I've never had a drop of alcohol and I never will, because addiction runs in my family. It killed my dad and almost killed my brother. My brother is sick because he overdosed. I call or text my mom every day to make sure they're both still alive."

I take a shaky breath and swallow, trying to soothe my sore throat so I can finish. "I punched a guy that I went to high school with because he keeps reminding me of what I am, and that Disney prince I was making heart eyes at is a closeted pretentious asshole who betrayed me because I was using your clingy baby brother to make him jealous."

I barely have enough voice to make it to the end of my rant, but I push through, forcing sound through my abused vocal cords because I have so much more to say. Much like the tears, now that the words are flowing, they don't want to stop. I told Beck, and he told Pierce, and now everyone might as well know everything because I can't hide from who or what I am.

"I'm a piece of shit loser from trash town, USA. My parents bought the cheapest home they could find on the edge of a decent school district so we could get a good education. Davis barely got his GED because he was too fucked up to care about going to a place that reminded us we didn't belong every single day. Where rich assholes like Pierce Jamison tormented us and used our last name as an excuse to pour beer in our lockers and report it to the principal. Or crack open my mom's car window to fill her seats with empty cans so she'd get in trouble with whatever job she'd managed to hold down for more than a week. And you know what I did about it?" I swallow painfully again. "I laughed. They told jokes about my dad, about how I'd grow up to be just like him, and I laughed. I laughed at my brother when the stories about his wild antics got back to my high school. I laughed with them at how haggard my mom always looked, because she worked however many jobs it took to keep us in a house that was falling down, and barely slept because the last time she came home and fell right to sleep, her husband ran off the road and hit a tree that cost more than just my father's life, because a person who thought they were better than us wanted more and didn't mind stepping on us to get it."

"Brody—"

"And when I left home to pursue my dreams, I pretended it was so I could help my family and give them a better life, when what I really wanted was to run away from it all. And then I proved everyone right, and I failed. I threw it away. I threw away a priceless education at a school that could actually make things happen for me, and I did it because a pretty boy hurt my feelings and reminded me that I'm just as worthless as they all said I was."

I stand, grab the coffee I turned down earlier, and chug the tepid liquid. Then I steal Leo's towel and walk down the hall to take a shower and wash away the feelings that keep pouring out of my face. I don't look back to see Eric or Leo gaping at me or to give them a chance to say anything.

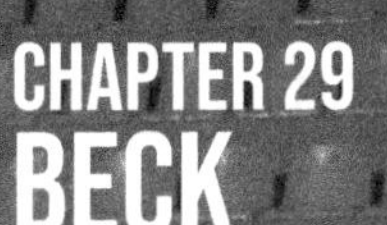

CHAPTER 29
BECK

We've been back on campus for three days, and no one has heard from Brody. Or if they have, they aren't telling me about it. To my knowledge, the last time anyone talked to him was when Coach McCoy spoke to him Friday night. All Coach will tell me is that he was staying with a friend, and said he'd head home separately. He refuses to call Brody's family to ask them if he made it safely, or tell him to please call me or listen to my messages.

Coach McCoy thinks there's something wrong with me, and he's probably right. He told me to go home and have a nice holiday, that we'd take care of 'the Brody situation' after the break. But he doesn't understand. I can't wait. The more time passes that I don't tell him what happened, the longer Brody goes on thinking I betrayed him. The longer Brody goes without knowing that I *care* for him.

I'm not brave enough to come out and say anything to anybody, especially now that I'm not sure I'll ever get him back, but anyone who doesn't realize there was something going on between me and Brody is dense or not paying attention. I've been on a full-on rampage, doing everything in my power to get in touch with him and pull together the plan we made on the flight home.

Even Caty is screening my calls and texting me messages.

> Caty: Take a breath, honey. I'm working on my mom, but you know she's afraid of poor people and the gays, so asking her to go to bat for someone who is both of those things is tricky.

> Caty: Don't you worry your pretty little head, though. I'm working on making her think that you might propose if your team wins the National Championship, and Brody is the key to making that happen. *fingers crossed emoji*

> Caty: Beck, honey. If you call me again, I'm blocking your number. Tomorrow is Christmas Eve. There's nothing anyone can do for a few days at least. You're just going to have to be patient.

> Beck: I can't. He hates me, Caty. HATES ME. I can't stand knowing he's out there thinking that I'm like my father.

> Caty: I'm sure he didn't mean that. He was angry. He'll come back after the holiday break much calmer, and then you two can talk.

> Beck: Calmer because he'll decide he's better off without me, maybe.

What if he's right?

No. No, I can't let that happen. There has to be a way to track him down. He has to turn on his phone at some point. Maybe he'll have blocked my number, but he can't block everyone, can he?

> Beck: Have you heard anything?

Aaron Eros: For the thousandth time today, no.

Beck: Do you have a way to contact his mom, maybe? Or his brother?

Aaron Eros: Why would I have that?

Beck: You're his friend. Don't you have an emergency contact or something?

Aaron Eros: Do you have Cade's mom's phone number saved in your phone?

Beck: No, but I could get her name from his emergency contacts in his file! Good idea, thanks!

No luck. There's no one left in the administration offices, and the janitor caught me trying to pick the lock on Coach's door. If he catches me again, he'll call the police. It doesn't matter anyway, I don't think I was getting anywhere with it. I was just jiggling a bent paperclip in there hoping I'd get lucky.

I'm pacing my empty dorm room when I see it. On the small end table in our living area is a piece of mail. It's a letter from the administration, confirming Jeremy Fisher's enrollment for the spring semester. Inside the letter are his contact details, including his home address.

Bingo.

Three minutes later, I'm banging on Brody's dorm door incessantly. I'm not knocking and waiting, then knocking again. I'm just hitting my palm on the door constantly, calling Aaron's name. I stop for a few seconds, just long enough to peek down at the parking lot at the few cars that are left. I can see my car, Brody's, a handful of cars that belong to other staff or students that haven't left yet or are staying over the break. And I see

Aaron's silver Jetta. Him and Jay have a flight out later this evening, so it's possible they haven't left yet.

I go back to beating on the door. I yell through the wood and metal and whatever this door is made of now that I know they're in there. I'm not going to stop, and if I'm wrong and they don't come out to leave for their flight in the next few hours, I'll pay someone off to either let me in or break in, so they might as well open the door.

Jay finally yanks the door open. I'm not expecting it, so I fall through the threshold.

Jay is red-faced and sweaty. I'm pretty sure he's pissed, but I honestly don't care. I start walking directly to Brody's room.

"What do you think you're doing?" Jay shouts, pulling me back.

Aaron comes out of the bathroom, looking equally annoyed. "What the hell, Beckett? Why are you here?"

"I need to get into Brody's room," I say, trying to dodge Jay, but both he and Aaron stand side by side, blocking the door to Brody's room.

"How do you even know this is his room?" Jay says.

My face flushes, and I can't come up with a good enough reason. "Because you're so adamant I shouldn't go in there."

"You shouldn't," Aaron says. "What the hell is wrong with you?"

For a moment, I'm stunned silent, remembering Brody saying those exact words to me just before he stormed out. I take a few steps back, smoothing down my wrinkled shirt.

"You don't look like yourself, Beck," Jay says with a look of concern.

"I don't feel like myself," I say, backing away from them.

They look at each other, having a silent conversation, probably about my sanity. They're right to be concerned. I've been acting out of sorts since our flight home lifted off the tarmac without Brody.

"Why don't you have a seat? We have a little time before we have to get to the airport," Aaron says.

I take a seat on their small sofa, and Aaron brings me a bottle of water. He sits on the coffee table, facing me. Jay perches on the opposite end of the couch with his arms crossed, likely ready to block me with his ridiculously long limbs if I make a run for the door again.

"I hoped I could look for something that might have Brody's mom's phone number or address on it," I explain, trying my best to sound like my usual, reasonable self.

"And what exactly would you do with an address?"

"I don't know. Show up and see if he's there. See that he's okay. Make him talk to me," I say more quietly.

Aaron's brow furrows. "Don't you think you should give him some space and let him come to you? He'll talk to you when he's ready."

"You don't understand," I say, and almost stand, but I know I'll just start pacing again, and then no one will take me seriously. "He thinks I did something unforgivable, and the longer he goes thinking that I did this awful thing, the more he'll hate me."

"And what exactly happens if Brody Miller hates you? Haven't you hated him since the beginning of the school year?" Jay asks.

"Yeah, I guess. Except, um... Not really."

"Not really?" Jay repeats, his tone flat and unimpressed.

"Jay, stop it," Aaron whisper-shouts.

Jay throws up his hands. "What? He can't say out loud why he's suddenly so interested in Brody's well-being, and I'm just supposed to feel sorry for him?" Jay whispers back.

I watch them bicker back and forth, whispering loud enough for the next dorm to hear, right in front of me.

"Um. You realize I'm right here, right?"

Aaron huffs out a breath and makes a face at Jay. Jay rolls his lips and looks pointedly away from us.

I haven't spent a ton of time with Aaron and Jay outside of wrestling and the dining hall, and I've probably only sat close to them because I was trying to get closer to Brody. They've been good friends to him. And I definitely have not. Especially from their perspective.

"Brody and I are...friends."

"*Friends*," Jay deadpans.

"Will you shut up?" Aaron hisses at Jay. He looks back at me. "Look, Beck, Brody is our friend, and he hasn't called us either. But I did find his friend Leo on Instagram, and I'm hoping he'll see my message."

"Maybe you should try *Eric*," I mutter, and make a mental note to find everyone Brody knows on social media. I didn't think about that because Brody doesn't do social media.

"Maybe you should try being a little less obvious," Jay says, not unkindly. I look up and find him watching me with a soft, understanding expression.

"I love him, okay?"

Aaron gasps. Pulls a hand up to his mouth and everything.

"I know it's a shock. I, uh, I'm gay. And you already know Brody is too, and we—"

"No, we already knew that part," Aaron says. "But you *love* him? Like for real?"

My mouth clamps shut so hard I nearly bite my tongue. What does he mean they *knew*? Did Brody tell them? I don't know how to feel about that. Am I allowed to be angry if I'm trying to get him back?

Does the fact that I am a little angry, but I also still want him back mean something?

"He didn't tell us," Jay says, because I'm transparent. "We figured it out."

"When?"

Aaron clears his throat. "Um, we didn't know for sure until last... Wednesday, was it?"

Jay nods. "Yeah. After finals."

After finals.

My eyes drop to my lap, then dart to Brody's bedroom door. Where we were when we... For the first time.... After finals.

I take a deep breath, and when I'm finally able to meet Aaron and Jay's eyes, they're both smiling. It's a weird smile, though. It's not jeering. It's sweet? Like they're happy for me, or like they approve or something. I don't know. It's weird, and I'm uncomfortable.

"I desperately need to see him. I need him to know I didn't betray him. He thinks I told Pierce those things about his family. Things he never wanted him to know."

"I can't imagine why," Jay says, shaking his head.

"It's so much worse than you know," I tell him, imploring him with my eyes to understand.

Jay flicks his eyes over to Aaron, and they give each other a barely there nod that has me sucking in a grateful breath and almost tearing up.

"We're going in there with you, and we're not going to ransack the room or anything," Jay says sternly.

"You really have a high opinion of me, don't you?"

"Let's just say that no one is more surprised than us that Brody managed to find himself tangled up with you, of all people."

"What does that even mean?" I gripe, following Jay to Brody's door.

"Brody is basically a golden retriever in human form," Aaron says. "And you're…"

"Arrogant," Jay finishes for him.

"Uptight," Aaron adds.

Jay nods like Aaron made a really good point, and then adds, "And kind of pretentious."

"Are we done pointing out my better qualities?"

"I mean, I could keep going," Jay says, but he's smiling at least.

In a low, quiet voice, Aaron tells me, "I had my own experiences with bullies, and I don't like what I've had to watch Brody go through."

I bend my head, ashamed of what I allowed and encouraged, simply because I was insecure. It was dumb luck that Brody always saw right through me.

"It helps knowing that it's mostly some kind of kinky role play though," Jay says.

"Oh my God," I mutter, and start looking through Brody's room, carefully rifling through his things. Aaron starts with his backpack. I open his top desk drawer. Jay walks over to the bedside table.

"Not in there!" Aaron says quickly. "Nobody puts paperwork in that drawer," he says, back to whisper-shouting. "It's for, you know…"

"Oh, he keeps that under the bed," I reply without thinking. It takes a long beat of silence to realize what I just said. Aaron snickers. My cheeks flush as I focus on the second desk drawer, which seems to be meticulously categorized into sections for each of his classes.

"I didn't realize he was this organized," I mutter to myself. Despite going against everything I assumed about Brody, it kind of makes him hotter.

"Probably didn't get a good look around the last time you were in here, eh?" Jay asks, and Aaron snorts.

"Alright. Very funny. Both of you can shut it," I say, forcing myself to keep my head up even though I know my face has to be several shades of red right now. I feel like I'm on fire.

"You know we're just messing with you, right?"

"Yes, well, I'm glad that my arrogant, uptight, pretentious, and very closeted self can bring you joy."

"Beck," Aaron says, making me look over at him. "You realize that Jay and I are together, right?"

"You're what?"

"Together. As in *together*." Jay spreads his hands like he couldn't be more obvious.

I blink a few times. Huh. I don't know why, but a smile spreads across my face. Maybe it's because I'm learning something new.

Maybe it's because I know I'm not alone. Maybe because now that they've pointed it out, it makes a lot of sense.

"That's...Wow. Thank you for telling me."

Aaron smiles and pulls a familiar envelope from Brody's backpack. He hands it to me without question.

"And thank you for this. I promise I'll do everything I can to make things right, and I'll let you know when I see him."

Jay and Aaron walk behind me to see me out, wishing me a happy holiday and assuring me they're going to do everything they can to help Brody.

Just as I'm about to step through the door, a thought occurs to me. I stop and look over my shoulder at the two guys who so obviously fit together so perfectly, Aaron's arm wrapped around Jay's back, with his head on Jay's chest and Jay's arm pulling him close. They're kinda cute.

I look at my watch. "You still have a few minutes before you need to leave, right?"

Jay looks ready to smack me. Aaron looks concerned. "Yeah, why?"

"Well, I just realized why you were so sweaty when you answered the door. So, I hope you have enough time to, er, finish what I interrupted."

Aaron rolls his face almost directly into Jay's armpit to cover his blush. Jay gives me a very pointed look and slams the door, but I can hear them laughing as I walk away.

I wonder if Ms. Delia's "gaydar" would have picked up on all the obvious affection that I missed before.

———

I don't waste time packing a bag and head straight out to my car. I exit the stairwell that I may have taken on purpose for luck, and run into my father about to get on the elevator.

"Lincoln," he calls, stopping the elevator doors from closing and preventing my best chance at pretending I didn't hear or see him.

"Father," I say, the stiff greeting all I'm capable of at the moment. "Can I help you? I'm actually on my way out."

"Are you headed home, then?"

"Uh…" I flinch before I can stop myself. He hates it when I stumble over my speech. He always says it makes me sound weak and unintelligent. Not wanting to let him think that's the case, I straighten my spine and answer more confidently. "No, actually."

"Since when are you not coming home for Christmas? Your mother will be very disappointed."

I'm pretty sure my mother doesn't actually notice if I'm there or not. She gave birth to me, but I'm pretty sure she never wanted to be a parent. I don't say as much, though. I don't want him to think this is a negotiation.

"I have other plans. But thank you for the invitation," I say, as if he asked me to do anything and didn't just expect me to read his mind and fall in line. I'm sure if I'd showed up yesterday, he would have been disappointed that I didn't let him know I was coming. Today he's expecting that I would have already been there.

He made you feel inferior, so you'd never consider rising above him.

The more I replay Ms. Delia's take on my father, the more I think she might be right.

"Where is it that you think you are going?"

"To visit a friend."

"What friend?"

"Brody Miller, you remember him, right? He's actually a really great guy. We've gotten quite close this semester." I let my tone set the stage for whatever insinuations he'd like to make.

The expression on my father's face used to make me feel two inches tall, but for the first time, I realize I'm actually two inches taller than him. A strength I play into, elongating my spine and taking a step closer, accentuating and exploiting whatever I have over him. Just like he taught me.

"You cannot be serious."

"I'm extremely serious."

I start walking, not at all surprised when my father stops me again.

"You won't tarnish my good name by—"

"By what, father? Being gay?"

If glares could burn, I'd be ash, but I'm surprised to find that his expression can't hurt me after all.

"I don't need your acceptance. I don't need your name. I don't need your money." I look at him dead on. "I don't need *you*."

I start walking again, this time not stopping when he calls out again.

"That boy is beneath you!"

Plastering my best Brody Miller smirk on my face, I turn and walk backwards so I can see his face and he can see mine. I don't want him to mistake my words for anything other than exactly what they are. Acceptance of myself.

"Actually, I'm usually the one beneath him."

World Wrestling Clubs Cup

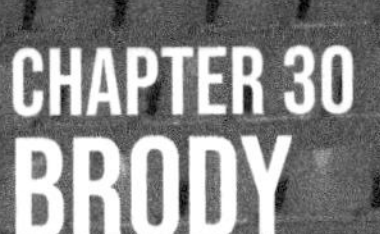

CHAPTER 30
BRODY

The bus ride home is as miserable as the weather. We leave the icy sludge behind after we pass through Kentucky, but it's still cold and grey. Perfectly reflective of my mood.

The bus is depressing. It smells weird, and everyone else looks as depressed as I am. It doesn't feel like a bus full of people traveling to celebrate the holidays with friends and family. Maybe it's just me projecting, but I feel like we're all being transported to the same funeral service.

Forty hours, not including stops, is far too long to be trapped in a confined space with nothing but my own thoughts. I can't use my phone to read or listen to music because the one time I switched it on, it blew up with notifications. The violent, constant buzzing of a hundred notifications exploded all at once, and it was just too much. I switched it off immediately and haven't even been tempted to turn it back on again. I just can't deal with it right now, and nothing anyone can say to me is going to make any of this better. I dug my own grave, and now I'm on a bus to a hell of my own making.

Out the smeared bus window, night turns to pale grey daylight, then back to a purple-bruised dusk. Fields flatten out into highways, highways bleed into the edges of small towns that all look vaguely the same.

People get on. People get off. We cycle through three different drivers and at least a dozen gas stations. I eat the granola bars Eric had the foresight to stuff into my gym bag, and drink enough cheap truck stop coffee that my stomach feels like it's lined with acid.

Along the way, I sleep in fits and starts, neck at a bad angle, knee jammed into the seat in front of me. Every time I drift off, I dream of Pierce's smug face laughing at the mess I've made of things, or of the anguish in Beck's eyes when I confronted him before storming out of the locker room.

Every time I wake up, I'm more tired and sore than I was before. My body feels unreasonably heavy, like I filled my chest full of frozen, wet soil when I was on that field in Nebraska.

When the bus finally pulls into the closest station to Colson Creek, it's after one in the morning. Getting a rideshare in a small town like this is going to be expensive if it's even possible. I consider walking, and probably would if it were morning, but my body is past done, and the thought of trudging an hour along the shoulder of the back roads it takes to get to my childhood home is more than I can face. So I sit on the cold bench and order a rideshare.

I get lucky and find someone working at this hour. The car that pulls up is a faded blue sedan with Christmas lights strung around the dashboard. There's a lot of stuffed cats lining the front and back windshield, and it smells a little like cat pee and stale cigarettes, but the older woman driving seems nice enough. She tries to initiate conversation a few times but doesn't push. We ride mostly in silence, the radio low and crackling through some country Christmas song that's likely to get stuck in my head for the next week.

By the time we hit the long gravel driveway that leads to my childhood home, it's a little after two in the morning. It's dead quiet thanks to not having neighbors, the only sounds coming from random critters in the woods and the creek the town was named for less than a mile away.

I thank Kathy for the ride and tip her more than I can afford to thank her for picking me up. I wait until her headlights have backed out of the drive before turning to the house. Even in the dim light of the one bulb that hasn't burned out on the porch, I can see the peeling paint, the sagging roof, and the half-rotted-out porch for what it is. Home.

"Brody?"

My eyes adjust to the shadows, and I see Davis on the porch, sitting on the middle step with his elbows on his knees, dark hoodie up, breath puffing white in the cold. He stands and nearly trips on a loose board as he bounds down the steps and meets me halfway through the small yard.

"What happened to your car?" Davis is the first to speak, pointing out the most obvious detail. Then his gaze grows more concerned as it flicks from the empty driveway to the bag on my shoulder, then roams over the rest of me. I can only imagine that I look as messed up as I feel, in a wrinkled pair of borrowed jeans, my filthy wrestling shoes, and my dirty Howlers zip-up hoodie that probably smells like several days of old sweat and bus funk. I don't want to talk about how long I've been wearing my compression briefs from the meet. My hair feels greasy. My skin feels grimy. My eyes are dry and swollen, and overall my body feels like I was run over by the bus I rode in.

"It's back at school," I say, voice low and rough. "I'll, uh... I'll go back for it later." *Later when I pack up all the pieces of the future I'll be leaving behind because I'm an idiot.*

I try for a smile, but what I manage is a weird, twitchy grimace that feels like my face forgot its default setting.

"Surprise," I say, holding up my hands in a *ta-da* gesture. It sounds about as defeated as I am, despite trying to cover it up. Davis doesn't need my bullshit right now.

My brother closes the distance between us and pulls me in, wrapping his arms around me in a tight, supportive hug. I freeze at first, not because we aren't an affectionate family, but because of how aggressively I feel like he's holding me up and holding me together at the same time. I don't remember a time when I was able to lean on anyone like this.

Davis doesn't say a word, just holds me for several long moments, until I remember what I'm supposed to do with my arms and all the emotion of the last few days hits me all at once.

I drop my bag and clutch the back of his hoodie, press my face into his shoulder, and do the only thing I seem capable of lately. I cry. Not the controlled, teary-eyed, single-manly-tear kind of crying. I *sob*. Ugly, shaking, gasping sobs that wrench my chest and scrape my throat raw all over again.

Davis doesn't tell me to stop. He doesn't tell me it's okay or that it's not that bad. He doesn't pile me with questions or expect me to do anything.

He just holds me up, feet planted in the gravel, both of us swaying a little under the weight of it.

———

I wake up feeling more tired than when I finally crawled into bed around four, and like I gargled the same gravel I rubbed my eyes with.

It takes a few moments to remember where I am, and something about the tiny circle of water damage in the far corner of my room brings me a breath of relief.

I'm home.

I stare at the spot for a while, deciding if I want to get up at all. I have no idea what time it is, but I stayed up later than I should have for someone who hasn't really slept in several days. I gave Davis the bare-bones version of the story while I shoveled cold pasta into my mouth and talked around the most painful parts. I told him about Pierce. About punching him and getting suspended. My head sagged when I told him about the almost-certain expulsion looming over me.

I couldn't bear to mention what happened with Beck, about how broken I feel that he'd betrayed me like that, about how I should have known someone like that wouldn't care about someone like me.

But when Davis tried to lighten the mood by asking how things went with "that guy you assaulted," my throat closed up so fast I nearly gagged on my food.

"It didn't work out," was all I managed. His eyes sharpened, but he let it go. I think he knew if he pressed, I'd shatter.

After that I had a shower, scrubbing the grime of the last two days off me and standing under the hot water until it turned cold. I almost had a mini breakdown when I remembered that I emptied my underwear drawer the last time I was here, because for whatever insane reason, that feels like a fond memory of a time I won't get back. But finally I fell into bed in a ratty old pair of shorts and passed out hard.

There's shuffling in the kitchen, and I figure I should probably get up and let Davis know I'm not dying, even if it kind of feels like it. When I drag myself down the hall, scrubbing a hand over my face, I find my mom instead. She's standing at the counter in her diner T-shirt and a pair of old sweatpants, her hair piled up on her head. The fluorescent kitchen light makes her look paler than usual, but her eyes are sharp when they find mine.

"Hey, baby," she says when she sees me. "Merry Christmas."

That's right. It's Christmas Eve. Guilt hits again, realizing I was supposed to be here Sunday night. "I'm sorry I'm late, and that I didn't call. My phone has been off." I start rambling, not ready to admit how royally I've fucked things up. I've always prided myself on being the one thing she doesn't need to worry about. "I wanted to be here by Monday at the latest, because I want to get some stuff done outside. I'm going to fix that step today, I think, and—" It suddenly occurs to me that she would have left for work before the sun came up, and it's fully light out, which means she's already been to work and back. "What time is it?" I ask, disoriented.

"It's after noon," she says with a playful smile. "Do you want a sandwich? I brought some leftover bacon back from the diner and I've got a beautiful tomato."

"That sounds amazing." I pull down some glasses and see that she's only making two sandwiches.

"Isn't Davis joining us?" I ask. Tomato and bacon sandwiches are his favorite.

"Oh, he left just before you got up. Took my car when I got back from work. I figured he was heading up to the church early."

Shit, that's right. Davis told me last night that he's getting his six-month chip at his AA meeting today. He asked if I'd like to go with him, and I said I would.

"I was supposed to go with him," I groan with a mouth full of sandwich. "I didn't mean to sleep so late."

"Well, the meetings don't usually start until one," she says, checking the time on her phone. "And it's just down the street. You've still got time if you want to make it."

I nod and take a large bite of my sandwich to hurry through it, but then I remember I don't have my car here. "That bike still in the shed?"

She nods. "That's what Davis uses to get around when I'm at work. Do you want to talk about where your car is? How did you get here?"

I stare at my half-eaten sandwich, the shame spiral creeping up on me all over again.

"I got in trouble at school," I say. "Big trouble."

"Oh, baby." She reaches across and squeezes my forearm. "What happened?"

I swallow. "I punched someone."

Her brows lift. "That's not like you."

I huff out something like a laugh. "Everyone keeps saying that."

"Who was it?" she asks.

"Pierce Jamison." I say.

Her expression hardens in a way I rarely see. "Jamison?"

I nod, and she sucks in a breath through her nose. For a second I brace myself for a lecture, but when she speaks, her voice is thick.

"Are you alright?"

I want to say yes, that I'll be fine. I always manage to figure things out, and this is just another small obstacle. And hey, I've been wanting to spend more time with you and Davis since he got out of rehab. Now I can help more around the house, and...

I guess my expression and lack of answer is enough.

"Oh, honey." She pushes back from the table, comes around to my side, and pulls my head gently against her soft stomach like she used to when I was little and had a nightmare. Her hand strokes the back of my neck. "I'm sorry. I'm so sorry everything has been so hard."

Tears prick again. I squeeze my eyes shut.

She keeps talking, fingers combing through my hair. "I've spent a lot of years wishing I'd done things differently," she admits. "That I'd moved us away when your daddy died. That I'd gotten you boys out of this town, and out from under those people's eyes. But I was so lost when he passed. And then the harder things got, the harder it was to think past just surviving."

I sit up enough to look at her. "I don't blame you," I say fiercely. "All of this is on me. I threw the punch. I knew it was stupid, and I did it anyway."

"I can only imagine how bad it must have been if you finally flew off the handle," she says, giving me way too much credit. "How bad is it?"

"As of right now, I'm suspended indefinitely. But it's likely that the Jamison's will push for expulsion. I'll be lucky if there aren't criminal charges." The word tastes like ash. "Either way, I'll probably lose my scholarship, and it won't matter anyway."

Her hand curls around my shoulder, squeezing the muscle there. "We'll deal with that if or when it comes to it," she says. "One thing at a time. Finish your sandwich and call your brother, see if he can come back and pick us up. I'd like to go, too, now that you're up. We'll figure out the rest after the holiday."

I nod, my throat tight.

"Can I borrow your phone?" I ask in a voice too small for my size and age. "I don't want to turn mine on yet."

"Of course, baby," she says immediately, sliding her phone across the table.

The phone rings a few times before Davis picks up. I hear sirens and immediately stiffen.

"Mom, don't panic," is the first thing he says, which of course makes me want to do exactly that.

My heart stops. "What?"

Mom's eyes go wide. She mouths, *What is it?*

I slap the phone on speaker and set it between us. "Davis, where are you? What's happening." I demand.

There's muffled noise on the other end. Davis's voice shifts, like he's talking to someone else. "I wasn't trespassing, officer," he says, calm but firm. "All I did was knock on the door and ask to speak to Mr. and Mrs. Jamison. They didn't even ask me to leave or anything. They just called the police."

"Oh my God," I breathe. He went to the Jamisons' house? What was he thinking?

"Are you being arrested?" Mom asks, outraged.

Davis sighs. "I don't think so? I don't know. I haven't done anything to warrant getting arrested, but there's an officer here that needs to ask me some questions. I'll call you back."

"Let me talk to him," Mom insists.

There's some shuffling, and then an unfamiliar voice comes on the line. "Ma'am, this is Officer Grant with Colson Creek PD—"

"My son is not a criminal, nor is he dangerous or anything else those awful people surely accused him of," Mom cuts in, her voice shaking but strong. "He is in recovery. He is trying to live his life right. If he knocked on that door, it was to talk, not to cause trouble. Please tell me you are not arresting him for asking for a conversation."

"No, ma'am," the officer says quickly. "We're not arresting him. We just got a call about a disturbance, and we're required to respond and make sure everyone is safe. Mr. Miller is cooperating. We just have a few questions to clear everything up."

Mom takes a deep breath, and Davis comes back on the line. "I'm fine, Mom," he says nonchalantly, like this is all a mild inconvenience instead of a nightmare.

"I'm sure you are. It'll take me five minutes to walk there. Please don't leave until I get there. I'd very much like to talk to Officer Grant some more."

She hangs up before he can argue, grabs her purse and jacket from the hook by the back door, and slips her feet into her sneakers.

"Give me two seconds to get some pants," I tell her, moving towards my room.

"It'd be better if you stay," she says. "Lord knows if they see you there, they'll cause a fuss about that, too. I just want to make sure your brother is handling things alright."

"What if—"

"Stay. Here." There's no room for argument in her tone. "Get dressed and be ready for us to pick you up so we can head to the meeting."

I'm used to being strong. To sucking it up. To taking hits and laughing them off. Right now I feel like a kid again, small and scared and full of anxiety overall all the things that could go wrong.

I nod my agreement even though I don't like it. She's out the door and power-walking down the driveway in moments.

I stand in the middle of the kitchen for a full minute, ears straining for any sign of sirens, my brain conjuring worst-case scenarios like it's on commission.

What if they decide Davis violated some probation term we don't know about? What if the Jamison's embellish the story, as they're known to do? What if Pierce's parents want their pound of flesh and it's easier to start with the Miller who has a record?

What if this pushes Davis too far? What if a night in a holding cell is all it takes to knock his feet out from under him and send him back into the spiral he just climbed out of?

What if I've ruined everything again?

I pace.

From the kitchen to the living room to the front door and back, wearing a path into the thin carpet. I even consider turning my phone on and calling Mom to make sure everything's okay. According to the clock, it's only been three minutes, but it feels like three hours.

I imagine Davis in handcuffs. I imagine Mom arguing with a cop twice her size and getting arrested, too. I imagine Mr. and Mrs. Jamison watching from behind their picture window, clutching their pearls while their lawyer drafts a statement about ongoing harassment by an unstable individual with a history of substance abuse.

My fists clench. I want to hit something, which is exactly what got me here in the first place. *And everyone thinks it was uncharacteristic of me.*

A knock at the door has my heart jumping into my throat.

Instead of answering it, I immediately start overthinking who it could be. If it were the police, it'd be a harder knock. Maybe an announcement of their intentions.

But why would the police be here? Unless the Jamisons' really are charging me to the fullest extent of the law.

The knock comes again, and I shake my head, trying to rattle my brain into its usual level of function again.

Just answer it, idiot.

I cross the living room in a few long strides, wrap my damp palm around the doorknob, and fling it open.

Beck.

Lincoln fucking Beckett is standing on my porch in a dark coat and jeans, his hair mussed by the wind, his eyes wide and bright and so painfully familiar, that for a second, I forget how to breathe.

"Brody." He says my name like he doesn't quite believe I'm real. Like he's not the one who showed up out of nowhere, at my childhood home, without notice or invitation.

All the air in my lungs leaves me in a rush. I think I might pass out.

World Wrestling ... Cup 2016

CHAPTER 31
BECK

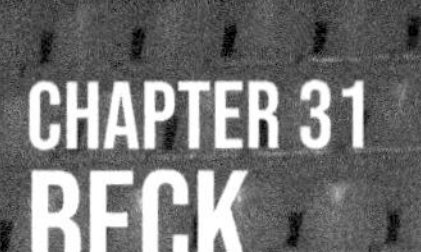

Brody stares at me as though he's looking at a ghost. He's pale and blank-faced.

"What are you doing here?"

His voice sounds rough, like he has a sore throat. Is he sick again? Does it make me a bad person if I hope he needs me to come in and take care of him?

He'd probably like an answer. It's the least I can do after showing up unannounced on his front porch in the middle of the day on Christmas Eve, but I can't get my mouth to form anything but his name. My brain completely stalls out at the relief I feel just seeing him in front of me.

He's standing in the doorway of this tiny home that I can easily imagine a younger version of him running around in, wearing the thinnest pair of cotton shorts I've ever seen, hanging low on his hips and leaving absolutely nothing to the imagination. His legs are bare, tanned even in December, muscles thick and defined. On top, he's wearing a worn blue T-shirt with a faded rainbow Superman logo stretched tight over his chest.

Rainbow. Superman.

It's so endearing I might actually pass out.

"What are you doing here?" he asks again.

My mouth goes completely dry. Every speech I practiced on the drive is gone.

Brody, I didn't tell Pierce.

Brody, I'm sorry.

Brody, I 'm pretty sure I'm in love with you.

My words vanish like dust.

"I, uh…" I start, then choke on nothing.

His eyes harden. The tiny flicker of hope I thought I saw when he first opened the door is snuffed out, replaced by something tired and closed off.

"You really shouldn't be here," he mutters, and starts to pull the door shut.

Nope. Absolutely not.

Panic surges through me so fast I move without thinking. I shove my hand out, catching the edge of the door before it closes, and push it back just enough to slip one foot over the threshold.

He stiffens. "Beck—"

I don't let him finish.

I lean in and kiss him.

It's not a gentle or polite apology kind of kiss. It's messy and desperate and a little too hard, all teeth and atonement and grief. For the briefest moment, I feel Brody melting into me, his mouth opening under mine, his hand fisting in the front of my coat like he's going to drag me inside and slam the door shut behind us.

Then he shoves me. Hard.

I stumble back. My heel hits a weak spot on the porch step, the world tilts, and suddenly there's a crack and my foot goes straight through the boards of the stairs.

My ankle twists and I go down on my ass in the front yard, one leg still half-caught in the broken step. An extremely dignified yelp tears out of my throat.

"Shit, Beck!" Brody scrambles off the porch, bare feet slapping the wood, and drops on to the grass beside me. His hands hover over my leg, my shoulders, my face. "Fuck, are you okay? Did you hit your head? Does your ankle—Don't move. Fuck."

Despite the sharp throb shooting up my calf, I'm absurdly pleased.

Because he's touching me.

"I'm fine," I say quickly, trying to pull my foot free. The board scrapes my shin, and I wince but keep trying to free my foot from the hole I made in his porch. "I'm good. Totally fine."

"Hold still," he snaps, and somehow it still sounds gentle. "You're gonna make it worse."

With careful fingers, he pries the splintered wood apart enough for me to yank my leg out. He cradles my ankle in his big hands, turning it slightly, watching my face.

"Does that hurt?"

"No," I lie, because I can tell he feels guilty that I stomped a hole in his house. It's starting to throb, but I don't want him to feel bad. Then again, if he feels sorry for me, maybe he'll stay with me? I'd rather have him close and worried than standing in the doorway where I can't reach him. "I'm good," I say weakly.

He huffs, almost a laugh, then realizes his hands are still on me. His fingers loosen. He sits back a few inches, palms pressing into the dead winter grass to brace himself.

"You shouldn't be here," he says again, quieter. "Why are you here?"

"I needed to talk to you." I scoot up onto my elbows, ignoring the way my ankle complains. "I couldn't leave things like that. You don't know—"

"We don't have anything to talk about, Beckett." His jaw flexes. "I can't do this."

"I love you," I blurt out.

His whole face changes.

He flinches, eyes going wide, features contorting into something raw and painful and furious. He looks like I slapped him.

"How fucking dare you?" he asks, his voice broken around the edges. "You don't get to show up on my porch and say that. Not after everything. Not after—"

"I didn't tell Pierce anything," I rush out, words tumbling over each other, realizing I probably should have led with that. "Brody, listen to me. I didn't tell him. I swear."

He freezes.

"I don't know how he found out," I barrel on, terrified he'll cut me off. "Aaron and Jay said he overheard you talking to *Eric*." The name comes out sharper than I intend. I might be more jealous than I initially realized. "Then he called someone back home to dig for information. I don't know who he talked to or what they said, but I promise I didn't tell him. I would never do that to you. I... I love you."

The last words leave me on a breath that feels like it scrapes my lungs raw. I didn't plan on saying it, but now I've said it three times. Twice to the man they belong to. It's true though, and it feels good to let it out.

Brody just stares at me. His eyes are shiny in the pale winter light. His chest moves in quick, shallow bursts, like he can't get enough air. There's a long, frightening moment where I genuinely don't know if he's going to scream at me, hit me, or walk back inside and lock the door.

"You didn't?" he asks finally, his voice small in a way I've never heard from him.

"No," I say, leaning in. "No. I swear I didn't tell him. I got mad at him and told him to lay off. He made some comments about me watching you with that other guy, and I put him in his place and pissed him off enough to cause more shit. I thought I was finally doing something right by standing up to him." My throat tightens. "I should've known he'd be vindictive. That's on me. But I never—*ever*—would have fed him anything about your family. Not after what you told me."

A tear spills down his cheek. He swipes it away angrily..

"Fuck," he whispers. "I... I thought you... I thought..." He looks like he's going to be sick.

"I know what you thought," I say, my eyes burning. "You had every right to think it with the way I've treated you this year. But you were wrong."

His face crumples.

One second, we're two feet apart in the dead grass. The next, Brody is hauling me into him, burying his face in my neck, arms banding around my shoulders so tightly I can feel every line of his body against mine.

I wrap my arms around him automatically, fingers fisting in the back of his shirt. My ankle twinges where it's twisted under me, but I don't care. I'd sit in this yard until my leg fell off if it meant I got to hold him.

"I'm sorry," he chokes against my skin. "I'm so fucking sorry I said that to you. About your dad. I didn't mean—"

"I know," I say quickly, squeezing him tighter. "I know. I deserved worse."

"You didn't," he says fiercely, pulling back to look at me. His eyes are red and wet. "You didn't deserve that. I was hurt and I lashed out. God, I've been so fucking miserable, Beck."

"Me too," I admit, because what's left to hide now? "I thought you hated me."

He lets out a half-laugh, half-sob and bumps his forehead against mine. "I did," he says hoarsely. "But I was mostly furious at myself for carelessly falling in love with a rich, uptight douchebag who did everything he could to make my life miserable for three months. I was mad I fell for it. For you."

My heart free-falls through my body. "You love me?"

He lets out a sharp, shaky laugh that sounds more like a sob. "You're still a pretentious asshole," he mutters.

"Yeah," I agree. "But I'm *your* pretentious asshole, if you still want me."

"Obviously," he mutters. A flicker of his smirk plays at the corner of his mouth.

I kiss him again.

This time it's softer, slower. Deeper and dizzy with feelings. Messy, complicated feelings. Love and relief and shame and regret.

He leans into it like he's starving for it. His hand comes up to cup the back of my neck. I make an embarrassing noise against his lips that I'd be mortified by if I had any pride left.

We tip sideways into the grass, bodies tangling, and somehow I end up on my back with Brody braced above me, one knee between my thighs. His hands are everywhere—my chest, my jaw, the side of my throat. I'm pretty sure I'm clinging to him like a drowning man.

"God, I missed you," he murmurs against my mouth.

I can't make words happen, so I sigh against his lips and drag him down harder on top of me. We make out like teenagers who've discovered each other for the first time and think the world ends at the edge of the front yard. It's messy and a little frantic, teeth knocking, noses bumping, my stupid ankle twinging every time I shift wrong. He grinds down and I gasp into his mouth, fingers digging into his hips through those flimsy shorts.

For a blissful moment, I forget we're outside. In daylight. In his front yard. Where just anyone could walk up.

But then a car door slams, and Brody jerks upright like someone fired a gun.

I blink up, dazed, and turn my head just in time to see a small, tired-looking woman and a tall, thin guy with blue eyes like Brody's standing at the edge of the yard. Brody's mom and Davis, I'm presuming.

Well this is a great first impression.

"Uh," I say.

Brody makes a noise that's somewhere between a groan and a whimper and buries his face in his hands.

"Well," Davis says after a long beat. "Guess that answers the question of whose fancy car that is. You could have called and said you got another ride, you know. I'm going to be late."

Brody's mom clears her throat, eyes flicking over our sprawled bodies, Brody's shorts, my very obvious unbuttoned coat. Her cheeks are pink, but there's no anger there. Mostly, I see something akin to cautious amusement.

"We do have somewhere we need to be," she says gently. "Unless you plan to attend the meeting like that." She gestures to Brody's overall state of being.

Brody flails off me so fast he nearly face-plants in the grass. "Oh my God, I, uh, yeah. Right. *Shit.* The meeting. I'm... *shit.*"

His mom discreetly covers a laugh with her hand.

Brody scrambles to his feet and then immediately bends down to offer me a hand, eyes wide. "Are you okay? Your ankle?"

I take his hand and let him haul me up. The ankle protests, but I keep my face smooth because I'm not about to admit weakness in front of his family ten seconds after they found their son dry humping me on their lawn.

"I'm fine," I say. "Totally fine. This is all fine."

No one believes me.

"This is, um, Beck," Brody says.

"*Ohh,*" Davis says. "I see."

"Shut up, Davis."

What does he see?

It occurs to me that two people just witnessed me making out, quite inappropriately I might add, with Brody. Who is a *guy*. Of course he would be out to his family, though. So why do I care?

Do I care?

I don't think I do. In fact, I feel a bit proud of myself, other than meeting my—*is he my boyfriend?*—um, person's family for the first time.

Mrs. Miller steps forward and hugs me. She hugs me. I don't move because I'm not sure how to react at first. "It's very nice to meet you. I'm Brody's mom, Sharon. Welcome to our home." She chuckles a little awkwardly. "I'm so sorry we had to meet like this. Our front yard isn't exactly the height of romance."

"Ma'am," I say, hugging her back tentatively. My heart is still pounding. "I, uh, apologize for that, um… display?"

Brody's brother snorts.

Mrs. Miller smiles, and it's tired but real. She seems surprisingly unbothered by what she just saw. "Oh, honey, if you think that is the most scandalous thing that's happened on this street, you have a lot to learn about this family."

Brody groans. "Can we not?"

Davis claps him on the shoulder. "We really do gotta get going, but I totally understand if you can't make it."

"No, no. I want to go. I want to be there for this." Brody glances at me, torn. "We'll be back. I have to go."

"Go," I say immediately. "I didn't mean to mess up your day. I just—" I swallow and pull him to the side so I can lower my voice privately. "I couldn't let another minute go by without telling you the truth. That I love you. The stuff about Pierce, too, but mostly that I love you."

His lips quirk. He gives me a small, heartbreakingly soft smile. "I'm sorry I ruined everything," he says quietly. "I should've taken a step back and pushed pause or something."

"You didn't ruin anything," I say, stepping closer. "You didn't do anything wrong."

"Well," Mrs. Miller says mildly, "maybe he shouldn't have broken Pierce Jamison's nose. That wasn't good." Brody winces.

"His nose isn't broken," I tell her. "I heard the trainer who went with him tell Coach he's barely bruised."

She scoffs, rolling her eyes. "You wouldn't know that from the way Mrs. Jamison was screaming about it. She said it was broken and that he might need surgery."

"Sounds familiar," Davis mutters. "He'll probably get away with it. Again."

A hot flare of anger spikes through me. "Not if I can help it," I say, surprising myself with how steady it comes out. "The team is putting together a plan. I'm not sure how much we can do yet, but no one is happy with Pierce's bullshit. And no one wants to see Brody go." I look at the man in question. "I don't want to see you go."

Brody blinks rapidly, like his eyes might be burning, too. Maybe we're allergic to the grass, because I can't imagine Brody tearing up.

Davis eyes me. "If you're not opposed to shitty coffee and listening to a bunch of strangers talk about all the ways they ruined their own lives, you're welcome to come along."

"Really?" Brody asks incredulously.

Davis shrugs. "It's Christmas Eve. Might as well drag the new boyfriend into the fun."

Boyfriend.

My heart does something stupid and painful behind my ribs. I think the grin on my face must be manic, because Brody looks at me funny.

I glance at Brody. He's watching me with something like hope and terror twisted together. "Yeah. I'd like that. If that's okay?"

Brody swallows. "It's okay with me if it's okay with Davis," he says, voice thick. "And if you want to come."

"Okay." I'm not sure exactly what we're going to, but from the context clues, I'm guessing it's a family AA meeting or something? I hope I'm not intruding by accepting the invitation, but I really don't want to leave Brody.

Davis stares at me for a long second, then nods, satisfied. "Alright then, fancy pants. Let's go." Then he pauses and eyes his brother. "Speaking of pants..."

———

We eventually make it to the meeting, and I'm kind of blown away by my life right now. If someone had asked me two weeks ago how I'd be spending Christmas Eve, I probably would've said something about a formal dinner, uncomfortable small talk with my father's colleagues, and pretending not to notice my mom drinking too much wine while my father whispers subtle barbs about everyone's net worth.

Instead, I'm sitting in a church basement on a metal folding chair that wobbles, drinking truly atrocious coffee and listening to people tell the worst stories of their lives.

And I am in awe.

People stand and sit and stand again, sharing. Some are older than my parents, hands shaking as they speak. Some are barely older than me. They talk about jail and DUIs, and lost jobs and marriages that survived anyway and kids they're trying to rebuild bridges with. They talk about days marked one at a time. About calling their sponsors instead of dealers, or heading to a diner for coffee instead of the closest liquor store.

No one flinches, or laughs, or judges. They just listen and affirm every feeling and every story. Tears aren't a weakness here, they're strength.

When Davis gets up, I feel strangely anxious for him. I didn't realize this was a milestone meeting for him until I heard it mentioned when we first arrived.

He walks to the front holding nothing but his foam cup. He clears his throat, looks around the room, then zeroes in on a point just above everyone's heads like he's trying not to make eye contact with any one person in particular.

"I'm Davis," he says. "I'm an alcoholic."

The chorus of *Hi, Davis* is warm, familiar, and free of judgment.

He talks about the night he almost died. About how he woke up in the hospital with tubes in his arms and his family around him, worried and crying and remembering the worst day of their lives. He talks about shame, and fear, and the bone-deep exhaustion of wanting everything to stop. *Everything*.

Then he talks about six months. Six months of boredom and rage and cravings and tiny victories like going to the store by himself and not staring too hard at the person in front of him buying wine or beer. Six months without taking any kind of pill at all, even ibuprofen. Six months of watching his mom and brother worry about every sigh, headache, bad day, or mood swing. Six months of his mother's tired optimism and unrelenting patience, and six months of useless texts from his annoying little brother. Six months of them showing up for him when he didn't feel like he deserved it.

"I've done a lot of shit I'm not proud of," Davis says, his voice cracking. "But my little brother still looks at me like I can be somebody again. He moved back home when he was thriving somewhere else, just so I wouldn't be so far away if... if something happened." He swallows hard, knuckles going white around the cup. "And that was my moment. My rock-bottom, when I knew I needed to do better. For my mother and myself, but mostly for him. Because I can't bear the thought of him waiting by the phone to hear if I'm dead. Because he deserves better."

He looks directly at Brody then, and I feel the breath Brody takes as much as I can hear it.

"You're the strongest person I know," Davis says. "You're my inspiration to see this through. I don't know what I did to deserve that kind of loyalty, but I'm trying every day to be the man you think I am under all of this mess."

By the time he finishes and accepts the six-month chip from the meeting leader, my throat feels too tight to swallow. These people are amazing.

When he sits back down, Brody hugs him so hard they nearly topple off their chairs. I slide my hand along the metal folding chair between us until my fingers brush Brody's knee. He looks at me, eyes wet and wondering.

"He's right, you know," I say quietly. "You're the strongest person I know, too."

His gaze drops to our hands. I'm not actually holding his, but my fingers are close enough that I can feel the heat. He shakes his head, looking away.

"I just had a full-blown meltdown in front of our entire team and threw away my future to land one punch," he whispers back. "It wasn't worth it, Beck. It wasn't strong. Neither is laughing off that shit for years or letting them talk about my mom and brother the way they did. Neither is running away from the fallout."

"Maybe not," I say. "But you kept moving forward. You didn't let them break you. Even when you snapped, you were true to yourself. That's strength, Brody."

He doesn't answer, but he doesn't pull his knee away either.

After the meeting, a few people come up to clap Davis on the shoulder or hug him. I stay back, feeling like an intruder in something sacred. Mrs. Miller squeezes my arm as she passes, like she wants to comfort the stranger standing here gawking at them all.

On the way out, Davis stares down at the chip they gave him.

"For whatever it's worth, I think what you've done is really amazing, and you should give yourself credit for it, too."

I duck my head, kind of embarrassed that I opened my mouth.

He studies me for a second, then nods once. "Worth more than you think," he says. "Thank you."

———

Back at the Miller house, Brody and his mom move around the kitchen layering noodles and sauce and cheese in a casserole dish that has apparently held *The Christmas Eve Lasagna* since Mr. and Mrs. Miller were first married. It's seen better days, has a few chips and spots where it's been warped. But it smells amazing, and I think it's a really cool tradition.

Davis and I sit at the small table, ostensibly keeping them company, but mostly just watching.

"You cook?" Davis asks me at one point, lip quirking.

"Not at all," I admit. "Beckett men don't cook," I say, putting on my most pompous voice. "I can make a mean protein smoothie though."

"Brody's a great cook," Mrs. Miller calls over her shoulder. "I don't even know what half the spices in our cabinet are, but he's always been good at making something out of nothing."

Brody blushes, which is frankly delightful. I totally get why he likes getting me all flustered.

The lasagna goes into the oven. Then Davis gets out an old copy of Monopoly that has clearly been played to death—most of the money is wrinkled and worn, corners frayed, the cards are bent, and almost all the game pieces are missing. Apparently, finding your own game piece is part of the tradition. In Brody's room, I steal a kiss and one of his peewee wrestling trophies. He chooses a matchbox car that was displayed on his shelf. Mrs. Miller uses a tube of lip balm, and Davis uses his new chip.

I win, obviously. I'm relentlessly teased for it, but I don't hate it.

Dinner is modest. Salad from a bag, frozen garlic bread, and the lasagna they made themselves bubbling in its dish. It is also one of the best meals I've ever had.

We eat, we talk, we laugh. They tell stories about the boys as kids and include memories of their dad. The whole time, they act as if I'm part of the family. Like I've always been here.

Once dinner is over and I've helped Davis clean up, since the other two cooked, I glance out the window a little forlornly. I shouldn't overstay my welcome, but I really don't want to go. I want to belong here, with these people. With this family.

Mrs. Miller puts a hand on my wrist. "Can you stay?"

"I'm sorry?"

Mrs. Miller gives me an assessing look. "Do you have plans for the rest of Christmas?" she asks. "Somewhere you need to be?"

The honest answer is no. My father's house is not a place I *need* to be. It's a place I've always shown up to for duty, obligation, appearances.

I shake my head, feeling overwhelmed.

"Then you stay here," she says decisively. "We may not have much, but we always have room at the table. And I think it would make Brody really happy if you stayed. He was not himself when he got home. You seem to have brought the light back."

Something in my chest swells, then cracks. "Thank you," I say, because it means a lot that they're willing to share their holiday with me.

We play another board game, then Mrs. Miller says she has to get to bed. She has to be up at some ungodly hour for her job at a diner. I'm surprised she has to work on Christmas morning, but it just shows my ignorance, I guess.

Davis decides he's tired, too, and everyone wishes each other goodnight and starts towards their respective rooms. I shuffle awkwardly for a few minutes, waiting for instruction.

"What are you doing?" Brody asks, and gestures me over.

"Is it okay if I sleep on the couch? I don't want to be in the way."

Mrs. Miller rolls her eyes. "Is this the same man who mauled my son in the yard this morning? We're all adults here, Beck. Brody's bed isn't large, but I'm sure the two of you can make it work."

Davis doesn't miss a beat. "Just try not to let the headboard hit the wall, yeah?" he says, scrunching up his face. "I don't want to hear my baby brother getting railed."

"Davis," Mrs. Miller groans, smacking his arm. "Gross. Boys are gross. Why are boys so gross?"

"That's his job, anyway," I spit out. I'm mortified, but I don't want Brody to think I'm ashamed of anything anymore.

Brody chokes and turns red. Davis doubles over laughing and lifts his hand for a high-five. Mrs. Miller throws her hands up as she walks down the hall.

"Oh great," she calls back. "Now there's three of them."

Later, in his room, with the door closed and the house quiet, we climb onto his bed fully clothed. Then less clothed, but still not naked. We kiss, slow and unhurried, mouths exploring, hands roaming over familiar skin with new reverence.

But we don't go further than that.

We just lie there together. Chest to chest, legs tangled, his hand pressed flat between my shoulder blades like he's keeping me in place.

"You're really here," he murmurs, his breath warm against my throat.

"I'm really here," I whisper back, and fall asleep in his arms feeling more content than I can ever remember being.

———

The entire holiday at the Miller's is nothing like Christmases I've grown up with. There are no mountains of wrapping paper. No carefully curated tree with matching ribbon and glass ornaments. No midnight mass or getting dressed for a family meal like it's a formal affair. No empty gestures in the form of sparkly things that cost too much money and mean less than nothing.

There aren't even any presents under the small artificial tree in the corner. Just a string of lights and a chaotic assortment of mismatched ornaments, mostly handmade from when Brody and Davis were kids.

We sleep late and make a mess of the kitchen making pancakes from a box mix, topping them with artificial blueberry syrup and margarine. Then we have a bubble fight while we hand-wash the dishes because the dishwasher doesn't work.

When Mrs. Miller comes home from the diner, she holds a small ham in one hand and a pie in the other, gifts from her employers at the diner. When she sets her purse down and heads back for a shower, I clear my throat. "I can head out for a while," I tell Brody. "Give you guys some family time." I think about finding a store that's open to get a few things to go with that ham, not that I know anything about cooking.

Brody doesn't even hesitate. He hooks two fingers in my belt loop and tugs me back towards the couch. "You *are* family now," he says quietly. "Stay."

I don't argue. I lay on the couch with him and watch *Die Hard*, because I've never seen it and apparently that's sacrilege. Mrs. Miller and Davis join us.

Brody heats up the ham for a late lunch and whips up mashed sweet potatoes to go with it. After we eat, Mrs. Miller pulls a framed photo of a man who looks a lot like Davis from a shelf near the television. She dusts it off with the sleeve of her shirt, kisses the corner of it, and then sets it in the center of the coffee table like a centerpiece.

I hover awkwardly near the edge of the room. Brody pulls me over to the couch to join them. "Come on," he says. "This is the good part."

I sit. Mrs. Miller pats my leg and explains that when the kids were little, they did a few wrapped gifts, but she and her husband never exchanged gifts. Not the material kind, anyway. When the kids got older, it became a tradition for the whole family to sit around the photo of Mr. Miller and just *talk*.

Mrs. Miller starts. She rests her fingers lightly on the frame.

"I'm grateful for another chance with my oldest son," she says, looking at Davis. "I'm proud of you. So proud. I know how hard it is. I know you could have chosen the easier path, and you didn't. That means more than you know."

Davis ducks his head, brushing his thumb over the coin in his palm.

"I'm grateful Brody came home," she continues, turning to him. "Even though I didn't want to hold him back. I wanted him to have that space. That fresh start we couldn't give him here. But having him closer..." Her voice wobbles. "Selfishly, I'm glad."

Brody leans over my lap to hug her, because I ended up between them.

Davis goes next.

He talks about six months again, but this time it's less about the drama and more about the daily grind. About being thankful his mother didn't kick him out. About being thankful his little brother still texts him a lot.

"I'm thankful neither of you gave up on me," he says, eyes bright. "Even when I deserved it. Your support makes me strong enough to handle this."

The weight of those words lands heavy in the room. I feel like I'm seeing them through new eyes. This tiny, worn-down house is full of people who keep choosing each other, over and over, even when it hurts.

Then it's Brody's turn.

He sucks in a breath, staring at the photo of his dad for a long moment. Then he looks at Davis.

"I'm thankful I get to have my brother back," he says. "I'm proud of you. So proud. Seeing you fight for yourself every day… it's helped me more than I know how to say. If coming home was the price for that, it was worth it."

Davis blinks hard, jaw clenched.

Brody turns to his mom. "I'm thankful for you," he says. "For always accepting us as we are. I know we don't have a lot to show for how hard we all work, but I also know I'd rather have what we have than all the money in the world. And I know I don't need a fancy degree from some prestigious school to succeed." He swallows. "One way or another, I'm not giving up on my dreams. Because you taught us to believe in ourselves."

Mrs. Miller presses her fist against her mouth, eyes shining.

Then, to my utter shock, Brody looks at *me*.

"And I'm thankful for this infuriating, stubborn, uptight guy," he says.

I fake a scoff. "Rude," I mutter, but my heart's pounding.

He gestures to my button-down shirt. "You're wearing a button-up in our living room with only one button undone at the top, Becky. Loosen up a little." He flicks the collar.

Then he looks up at me through thick blond lashes and smiles. "I can't help feeling like everything that's happened led me to you," he says quietly. "In the beginning, you annoyed me and pissed me off. Then I thought you needed me. I thought you were just fun to play with. But somewhere along the way, I fell in love with your pretentious ass."

My lungs forget how to function.

He swipes at his eyes, cursing under his breath. "I think I've cried more in the last week than I have my entire life," he grumbles. "But I don't care about anything else, not really. Knowing I didn't lose you, that's the only thing that matters right now." He looks down at his hands. "I'll work hard and do my best to be patient. And for the record, I don't expect you to come out. Not for me. I know you can do better, you deserve—"

I don't let him finish. I'm already moving before I realize I've decided to. I slide off the couch and onto my knees in front of him, cupping his face in my hands, and kiss him. He makes a soft sound in his throat and leans into me, hands clutching at my wrists.

When I pull back, his eyes are wide and wet and fixed on mine.

"You're the one who deserves better," I tell him. "You're hard-working and kind and generous. You make me a better man. You've been so patient with me—too patient—while I was an unkind, scared coward too afraid to show what I thought was weakness."

I take a breath that feels like it opens up a new chamber in my chest.

"I've realized something, though," I say. "Loving you is the strongest thing I've ever done. It feels like gaining a level of strength I didn't know existed. I am proud to belong to you, Brody. To be *yours*. And I don't care if everyone knows it. I'll wear a collar if it makes you happy."

His jaw drops a little, then he chuckles. "Don't threaten me with a good time," he whispers.

I laugh a little too excitedly and kiss him again. We get so caught up in each other that I don't notice Mrs. Miller and Davis quietly getting up until I hear the creak of the floorboards near the doorway. I break the kiss, blushing so hard my ears hurt, and glance over my shoulder.

Mrs. Miller is standing with her hands on her hips and a smirk that looks suspiciously like the one her son wears when he's planning something wicked. Her eyes are damp.

"Don't let us stop you," she says. "We're going to the Christmas meeting. We'll be home around four."

Davis gives Brody a look that is equal parts *I'm happy for you* and *I'm never going to let you live this down.*

And suddenly, we're alone.

The house is quiet. The winter light filtering through the blinds casts soft stripes across Brody's face. My knees ache a little from the rough carpet, but I don't move.

"I mean it," I tell him. "I don't want to hide. I don't really know how to come out, but I already told my father."

He looks at me as if he might have heard me wrong. "You did not."

"I did," I say, chuckling. "It was pretty epic, actually."

"How'd he react?"

"Surprised and confused, but I'm not sure if that was because I came out or because I stood up for myself."

"That's huge," he breathes, wrapping his arms around my neck. "I'm really proud of you."

"I'm kind of proud of me, too, actually. Not sure I've ever felt that before."

"Well, then we'll just have to make sure you do more of whatever it is that's getting you to come out of your shell."

"Oh yeah?" I say, biting my lip.

"Mmhmm. We've got about two hours if you want to work on your confidence a little."

I can't decide if that's corny or sexy. Or maybe a confusing mix of both. So I kiss him and nip his bottom lip to let him know I'm ready.

"You can start by unbuttoning that ridiculous shirt," he says, then leans into me. "Then you can go to my room, take off everything else, and wait for me on your knees."

I'd like to say I stand up and walk out of the room in a very dignified manner, but I don't. I snap half the buttons off my shirt and trip over my pants trying to run and strip at the same time.

World Wrestling ... Cup 2016

CHAPTER 32
BRODY

We leave earlier than I planned.

Originally, I would have stayed through the end of the holiday break, but Beck has things he needs to do back on campus, and I don't have my car here so it makes the most sense for me to head back with him. And truthfully, I'm greedy for more time alone with him.

I love my family. I love the way Davis laughed and talked with Beck like they were friends, and the way my mom pulled Beck into her arms and treated him like he's always been one of hers. I really, really love watching Beck folded into our chaos.

He was stiff at first, too polite and careful with his words, like he was afraid to say the wrong thing. He was surprised by every hug and show of affection. He held back his laughter and excitement. But eventually, he relaxed into it and became part of the family. He didn't even mind the extra big feelings we all had this year.

On Christmas night, I made an off-handed joke about our poor people Christmas probably being underwhelming for him, and he'd looked at me so wide-eyed I thought he might be offended.

"Are you kidding me? I think this might be the best Christmas I've ever had. Your family is amazing, and the way you all just shared it with me..." He swallowed hard. "It means more than anything my father's money has ever bought me."

It made me sad for the lonely life I realize he's had. It also made me want to jump his bones. Unfortunately for us, my home is small and has thin walls, so those moments were few and far between.

So when Beck said he had to hit the road, I was sad to leave my mom and Davis, but I felt like I should go with him. I'm pretty fucking stoked to have a few uninterrupted days with my boyfriend.

Still getting used to that word.

———

I didn't realize one of the things he had to do was visit Ms. Delia. I'm worried that I overstepped by inviting myself on his trip home, but he seems genuinely excited for me to meet her.

I'm more nervous than I've ever been to meet anyone. This is the woman who raised him. The one person he felt actually loved him in the whole world. She matters a hell of a lot more than the man who gave him his name or his sharp jawline.

The facility is amazing. It looks like a fancy hotel from the outside, with sprawling lawns and walking trails, even a tennis court and indoor pool. There are so many amenities, it seems more like a spa than a care facility.

"I didn't know they made care homes this fancy."

Beck laughs and takes my hand. "It's obscenely expensive," he says. "But it's worth it. Ms. Delia deserves the world, and even my dad recognizes that fact."

"Your dad pays for this?"

"When her mental faculties started showing clear signs of decline, he had her retirement benefits consolidated to provide her with the best care possible. She moved from the UK when she was young and doesn't have any family left."

"Other than you," I say. He squeezes my hand and smiles.

A gorgeous woman wearing a collared shirt with the care facility logo embroidered on the chest stands from a reception desk and lights up when she sees Beck.

"Mr. Beckett," she greets happily. "Ms. Delia said she had a feeling you'd be stopping by today. She said she felt you coming."

"She always does," he says, smiling. "How's she doing?"

"She's been doing well. Having a good day today."

Beck perks up. "Lucid?"

She holds up her hand in a so-so motion. "Not entirely, but she's happy and taking care of her plants and knows everyone's names."

"Definitely a good day," Beck says, then smiles down at our hands like he didn't realize he was still holding mine. He lifts them and kisses my knuckles.

"Jenny, this is Brody."

"So nice to meet you. Ms. Delia has been looking forward to meeting you for some time now."

My eyes widen, and I look up at Beck in surprise. "Ms. Delia knows about me?"

"Of course she does. Ms. Delia knows everything," he says.

We follow Jenny to a set of elevators and up several floors. Then she leads us to what looks like a luxury apartment and knocks on the door.

"Come in, dear," sing-songs an old woman.

We step into a spacious open-floor plan space with bright yellow walls and white wainscoting. There are plants everywhere, on stands and hanging from shelves and hooks. The space is happy and inviting.

"Hi Ms. Delia," Beck says softly, almost timidly.

Her head snaps up. For a second her eyes are cloudy, unfocused. Then they land on him, and it's like the clouds part.

"Linc," she breathes, and I swear I've never seen a brighter smile on Beck. It's relieved and full of so much joy and love.

Oof. That does something to me.

He crosses the room and leans in, kissing her cheek and letting her cup his face like she's making sure he's real, patting his cheeks, pressing a kiss to his forehead. He gets to one knee in front of her so he's not towering over her so much.

"I knew you were coming."

"I'm sorry I missed Christmas," he says. "I ended up somewhere unexpected."

Ms. Delia cackles. "So did I, honey, so did I."

Beck shakes his head and laughs with her.

"Are you going to introduce your young man or just leave him standing over there in the corner? Come on in here, child. I'm a crazy old bat, but I don't bite." She pauses and purses her lips. "At least I don't think I do." She throws back her head and cackles again.

"Told you she was in a good mood," Jenny says, returning to the room with a spray bottle. "Here you go, Ms. Delia. You call me if you need anything," she says, and leaves the apartment.

Ms. Delia turns directly to me and smiles brightly, holding out her hand to take. I step forward and take her hand.

"Ms. Delia," Beck clears his throat. "This is my, um... boyfriend. Brody."

The word hangs between us.

Boyfriend.

I swear my heart does a full Niles Pruitt-worthy gymnastics routine, sticks the landing, then lands in my throat.

Ms. Delia looks at Beck and beams before turning back to me. "Well, it's about damn time," she says.

Beck makes a strangled noise, and I notice his eyes get watery. Ms. Delia nods like she's been waiting years for this exact moment.

"It is so nice to meet you," I say with my whole heart. Because even though I was nervous, it truly does mean so much to meet the woman who made Beck human when his father would have turned him into a machine.

She grills me in her own way. Instead of asking me about my grades or what my parents do, she asks me what my favorite color is and why, if I spend much time outdoors, because she feels that touching nature is the same thing as touching God. She says the same thing about sex, which I wasn't expecting. Sometimes I can't tell what's her quirky personality and what's a potential slip of her lucidity, because she definitely says some odd things here and there. Once she asks Beck if he finished his homework. And another time she looked me in the eye and told me, very seriously, that I get my eyes from my father, but my heart from my mother. Which was weird, because it's scarily accurate and I don't think I mentioned my father at any point.

My favorite part of the day is hearing Beck, or Linc as she calls him, regale her with the specifics of how he shot his father down and came out to him at the same time. She hooted and clapped her hands like she'd never been so pleased.

Somehow the afternoon goes by without time passing at all, and I find myself on my knees next to her chair so this remarkable woman can "love on me," as she calls it.

"You're a special one, Brody Miller. You make sure my Linc takes care of you. And if he wants to do something for you, let him do it. Let him spoil you. Lord knows that child has more money than sense, but he likes to show he cares."

"I'll try," I promise.

I give them a moment alone and wait for Beck in the hallway. When he comes out, he pulls me in for a long hug.

"Thank you for being you," he says, and kisses me before pulling back and looking at me mischievously. "Ready for a surprise?"

———

Beck won't tell me what the surprise is until we're driving into Charlotte. Turns out, he booked a hotel room for the weekend.

I feel like it's too much, but I try to keep what Ms. Delia said in mind and begin making mental plans for something I can do for him. Plus, when I try to argue, Beck mentions a massive king-sized bed and a jacuzzi tub we can both fit comfortably in together, and I'm pretty sold.

I'm confused when we pull into the parking lot of a high-end shopping mall instead of a hotel.

"Why are we here?"

"We need some things. I didn't pack enough clothes, and you have a tragic lack of underwear."

"Whose fault is that?"

He grins. "Exactly. Let me rectify it."

"Does it have to be here, though? This place looks expensive. Doesn't Charlotte have a Walmart?"

He looks aghast. "You would make me enter such a place?"

"I would record you and play it back just for the joy of watching your discomfort."

"Rude. And not happening. Just think of it as a Christmas present."

"Well, that's not fair. I didn't get you anything."

"Brody," he says, making my name sound like an apology and a prayer all at once. "You've given me everything. You gave me something I didn't know I was missing." He glances over, cheeks pink, then focuses back on the road. "I've given you almost nothing but grief and mixed signals."

"That's not true," I protest automatically. "You gave me orgasms. Plural. Some pretty impressive ones, actually."

He chokes. "That's not—" He gives up, laughing. "You know what I mean."

"Do I? Because I can't reciprocate with stuff like this," I say, gesturing to the ridiculously expensive department store.

"I can't reciprocate shitty coffee in a church basement, or lasagna and board games, or any of what you gave me this week, and I promise you that has significantly more value. Maybe calling it a gift was pretentious. I didn't mean it that way, really. But I'm the one who stole most of your underwear. And I knew about the tire situation, even if I wasn't the one physically doing the slashing. So, I owe you. And I want to go into this mall and buy some things that we both need. Underwear and t-shirts, and supplies," he says, emphasizing the word. "Just the basics."

"Supplies?" He nods. "What, like bubble bath for the jacuzzi?"

He laughs. "That too, if you want. I meant like condoms and lube, but anything you like."

Oh.

"Fine. You can buy me underwear and lube. But that's it."

He smirks and opens the door. "We'll see."

"And can we make this quick so we can get to the jacuzzi tub, please?"

———

This department store is worse than I thought. I feel underdressed just walking through the doors.

A woman in heels and lipstick that probably cost more than my borrowed jeans gives us a practiced smile and calls Beck "sir", clearly recognizing which one of us she should be kissing up to.

Beck is in his element, stalking through tables of folded shirts, simply pointing to things that the woman and a sales assistant scramble to set aside in the sizes he specified before we begin. I had to be measured. For t-shirts and underwear. What kind of ridiculous bullshit is that?

He's going way overboard, but whenever he catches me glaring, he grins and says, "basics." As if anyone really needs a shirt that costs more than my family's monthly utility bill. My brain is mentally calculating the tally on the items that are clearly my size and not his, and it's making me sweat.

From the shoe department, I notice some other stores in the interior part of the mall that I'm more familiar with, specifically an adult novelty store that gives me an idea.

"I'm going to run into that store over there. I'll meet you back here?"

"Oh, sure," he says absentmindedly, holding up a pair of designer sneakers. "Do you like these?"

"Sure don't. Be right back."

"Take my card!" he calls after me.

"Eat my ass!" I respond and cackle like Ms. Delia when the sales assistant gasps, scandalized, and Beck turns several shades of my favorite color.

By the time I've returned from visiting two different stores, Beck is only just checking out. My eyes nearly bug out at the total, watching Beck pay without blinking twice. So casually, he definitely didn't have to calculate his bank balance before he handed over his card the way I did when I paid for the three small items I bought. I went into the adult novelties shop because I thought of a fun gift idea, then went ahead and got lube and condoms while I was there to save time. On the way back, I got distracted by something else I decided I had to have even though I really shouldn't have spent the money.

"What'd you get?" Beck asks, gesturing to my tiny bag.

"The supplies," I say. "I figured you were going to take forever and I'm ready for that bubble bath now."

Beck's eyes flash, and he takes my hand right there in front of the salespeople, even after my crass language embarrassed him. He practically drags me to the car, as if I'm the one who's been holding us up. He lets go to stash the bags in the trunk, then takes my hand again as he pulls out of the mall parking lot and drives across the city.

When we arrive at a hotel that looks like a modern art installation, he stops his car right in front of the doors.

"We're staying here?" I hiss as Beck walks around the car.

He hands the valet his keys and tip, then turns back to me, offering his hand like he's escorting royalty. "Come on, Miller," he says. "Let me spoil you."

I'm too busy watching his hand to argue. The hand-holding feels more like being spoiled than the hotel, if I'm being honest. There's something about the way he's holding my hand so casually that is making me feel lightheaded and giddy.

I let him tug me into the lobby. It's opulent in a way I've never experienced before. I'm halfway through wondering what we're supposed to do with all our bags when I realize there's a bellhop behind us with a trolley stacked with all of Beck's shopping bags, including the small matte black bag full of my purchases.

I can't help it. I laugh.

"What?" Beck asks, amused eyes sparkling back at me.

"Nothing," I whisper. "I just... having an actual bellhop carry our lube and condoms is kind of ridiculous, that's all."

He chokes. The bellhop studiously pretends he didn't hear, but his cheeks definitely flush.

———

The second the bellhop has been tipped and the door to our room closes behind us, Beck is on me.

His mouth crashes into mine like he's been holding back all day. His hands are everywhere—my jaw, my back, tugging at my hoodie, skating under my T-shirt to find skin.

I respond in kind, tearing his clothes from him like I'm feral.

We stumble backwards, bumping into the dresser, the edge of the bed, each other. Somewhere in there my hoodie ends up on the floor, his sweater gets half pulled over his head and stuck, and we both laugh into each other's mouths as I help him wrestle out of it.

My blood is buzzing. My brain is cotton candy. I'm seconds away from letting him drop to his knees and take me apart the way he's gotten so, *so* good at. It takes extreme self-control to put some distance between us.

Beck's pupils are blown wide. "Huh?"

"You promised me a bubble bath," I remind him.

"Oh," he says, chest heaving. He licks his lips. "Okay. I'll be right back."

Beck runs off to fill the bath. The moment I hear the rush of water, I scramble over to the pile of bags by the door, digging through until I find mine. My heart kicks up as my fingers brush the small box at the bottom.

When Beck returns, I'm sitting at the edge of the bed with a deep red silicone butt plug in my hand. It's not particularly intimidating, but it's not small. It's large enough that there's no chance of Beck not understanding exactly what it's for.

Beck stops dead in his tracks and stares at the ominous red toy in my hand. "What's that?"

I let the plug dangle from my fingers. "A little present for you," I say lightly.

His eyes widen. His gaze tracks from the plug to me to the bed and back again.

"I, uh," he says, then swallows.

I'd be worried about how apprehensively he's staring at the plug if his cock wasn't practically throbbing with each beat of his heart.

Still, I need to remind him that he does actually have a choice in the matter.

I step closer, tilting my head. "What's your safe word, Becky?"

"I don't need it," he mutters. His eyes are still locked on the plug. "I want to do this. I just... I've never..."

"Do you trust me?"

He looks up at me, really looks, and something in his gaze settles.

"Yeah," he says quietly. "I do."

I smile and step in, pressing a soft kiss to his mouth. "Good," I murmur against his lips. "Then bend over the bed for me, baby."

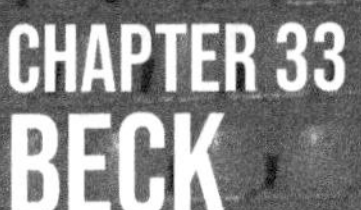

CHAPTER 33
BECK

I lose the thread of whatever Brody's saying somewhere between "The thing about Nationals is," and the way his foot drifts up the back of my thigh.

We're stretched out in the giant hotel tub, him on one side, me on the other. The tub is big enough for us to fully stretch our legs, but my knees are bent and braced against the sides, because straightening them would mean shifting my hips, and shifting my hips would mean...

A groan slowly leaks out of me as Brody's toes slide along the crease where my ass meets the floor of the tub. Then higher. Right over the toy he put inside me what feels like twelve hours ago.

I bite the inside of my cheek and pretend I'm composed.

I am most definitely *not* composed.

The air is heavy and damp, scented with vanilla and sandalwood. Steam fogs the glass shower door and the big mirror over the vanity. It could be coming from the hot water, or my heavy panting as I try to keep myself from combusting.

Brody looks obscene in the soft bathroom light. His broad chest gleaming, blond hair damp and curling in the humidity. There's a couple days' worth of stubble shadowing his jaw that I want to drag my tongue over. I want to feel that stubble on my throat. On my thighs. On my everything.

Instead, I'm sitting here clutching the sides of the tub like it's a lifeboat while my boyfriend pretends to talk about sports logistics and casually uses his foot to torture me.

My breath stutters every time he glances over or pushes on the plug. The pressure is maddening. It's too much and not enough at the same time. Every tease, every tiny push makes my body clench down around it, makes my cock twitch where it's bobbing in the water. A steady stream of pre-cum swirls from the tip.

"Beck."

I blink at him, trying to look normal and definitely failing. "What?"

He raises one eyebrow slowly. "Are you listening?"

"Absolutely not," I say honestly. "I haven't heard a single word you've said since you put this thing inside me and stopped touching me."

Something wicked sparks in his eyes. His mouth curves. Then he presses his toes deliberately against the flared base again.

A strangled sound rips out of me. I slap a hand over my mouth too late.

"Please," I manage, my voice rough. "Stop torturing me."

His grin is sinful. He settles his foot more firmly between my legs, just resting there, like that isn't the worst possible place for him to be. The ball of his foot presses against my balls just firmly enough to cross the line between pressure and pain. A heavy breath hisses out of me.

"Brody. Please," I groan. "I need you. I needed you before, but now I'm pretty sure I'm dying."

It's only a half-exaggeration.

We've fooled around this week, sure. Hands under blankets, sloppy kisses stolen in the dark of his old bedroom, making out on his childhood couch while the TV hummed in the background and we tried to pretend we weren't both thinking about his mom walking in. But there's only so much you can do in a tiny house with thin walls and people coming and going.

Christmas Day was the only chance we had to really be together. To have him inside me. It had been rushed and emotional, and over faster than either of us wanted. It was my fault, because apparently my body decided that feeling safe and loved is a kink now and gave up the ghost almost immediately.

Now I'm stretched and full and simmering, and he's over there playing footsie like I'm not one tickle away from climbing across this tub and humping whatever limb I can reach like an animal in heat.

He nudges the plug again, and my patience snaps.

Fine. If he won't stop being a sadistic tease, I'll just have to redirect his attention.

I shift forward carefully, trying not to slosh too much water over the sides. My thighs are shaking. The movement makes the plug settle differently, and it feels weird. I have to pause and breathe through it, my fingers digging into the edge of the tub.

Brody's eyes track every inch, his playful smirk softening into something hungrier.

I turn onto my knees between his feet and crawl up the slick porcelain, water lapping at my sides. When I reach him, I swing a leg over and sink down onto his lap, straddling him.

His hands fly to my hips automatically, steadying me.

"You good?" he asks, his voice suddenly serious.

"Define good," I mutter, and lean in to kiss him.

The second our mouths meet, the tight coil in my chest loosens. He hums into it, low and pleased, letting me take my time. I kiss him like I've been wanting to all week. Slow and deep and possessive, licking into his mouth, tasting mint and lust and whatever bubble bath was sitting on the edge of the tub when I prepared the water.

His fingers flex on my hips as I rock forward, sliding my cock along the wet plane of his stomach. The angle pushes the plug just right, and I moan into his mouth, my entire body shivering.

"I could come like this," I gasp against his lips. "But I want—"

He cuts me off with a low noise, one hand roaming down to palm my ass, thumb brushing the stem of the toy. My vision whites out for a second.

"What do you want, baby?" he murmurs, teasing. "Use your words."

Right. Words. Those things.

"I want..." My throat works. His eyes are locked on mine, bright and intense, and it feels stupidly like I'm about to jump off a cliff. "I want you to come inside me."

The change in him is immediate. It's like I flipped a switch. His pupils blow wide, the playful edge dropping clean off his face.

"Are you serious?" he asks, his voice rough.

I nod, damp hair flopping over one eye. "Yes. I want it. I want your cum inside me. Now, please."

He laughs once, breathless. Then he moves.

One second I'm straddling him in the water, the next he's standing, and I'm sliding off his thighs. He hauls me to my feet, then bends low like he's going to tackle me.

Bathwater sloshes everywhere, spilling over the sides and splashing across the tile floor as he hauls me up in a fireman's carry. I yelp his name, holding on for dear life as he steps out of the tub and walks across the floor to the bed.

A bolt of electricity shoots straight up my spine with every step, the plug jostling inside me and my cock trapped against his shoulder. He leaves a trail of water all the way to the bed and tosses me down on the mattress.

He crawls over me, bracketing my head with his arms, water dripping from his hair onto my forehead. His stubble scrapes my jaw as he noses along my cheek to kiss just below my ear, and I arch up into him helplessly.

"God, you're beautiful," he murmurs against my throat, turning my head towards the ornate floor-length mirror next to the bed. "Look at you."

"No," I mutter, because if I look at myself right now—flushed, needy, and wrecked—I might actually combust.

He laughs softly. "Yes," he counters. One broad palm slides up my chest, fingers splaying over my racing heart. His thumb brushes my collarbone, then drifts higher, curling around my throat with the lightest pressure.

Every atom in my body combusts.

He kisses me again, slowly and all-consuming. As his mouth moves over mine, his other hand trails down my side, over the curve of my hip, finally slipping around to gently ease the toy free. I gasp into him, the sudden empty ache making me clutch at his shoulders.

"It's okay," he whispers. "I've got you."

And he does.

The rest blurs into sensation. The drag of his stubble along my neck and chest as he kisses down, leaving warm, wet trails in his wake. The way his hands are everywhere all at once, grounding and worshiping and teasing, taking his time with me because for once, we have all the time in the world.

When he finally pushes into me, slow and careful, one hand cradling the back of my head, the world narrows to the heat of him and the way my body yields around him, already open and wanting. I cling to him, breathing harshly against his shoulder, and he goes still.

"Okay?" he asks, voice hoarse.

I nod, fingers digging into his back. "More," I choke out. "Please."

He groans and obliges, moving in steady, shallow rolls of his hips that make my toes curl. There's nothing rushed about it. No frantic edge, no panic. Just us, fitting together, learning each other all over again in this room that feels a little bit like a bubble of universe that's just for us. It's hot and slow and serious and playful and everything all at once.

At some point he pulls me up so I'm upright on my knees and enters me from behind. As he rolls his hips, keeping one hand on my hip to steady me, the other comes around to hold my throat.

"Look," he tries again. This time, it's impossible not to.

Our bodies glisten with water and sweat, reflecting the bright streaks of pink and orange that paint the sky outside the wide-open windows.

Brody kisses down the back of my neck and lightly scrapes his teeth along the back of my shoulder. Then he slowly bends me forward, brushing his hand down my spine and making my back arch just right. My breath catches.

"Right there," he says on a breathy groan as my spine tingles. "Don't stop looking," he says, and our eyes meet in the mirror.

Brody looks fucking dangerous. Holding me just the way he wants me, rolling his hips with each stroke, abs clenching, muscles rippling. He bites his full lip and tells me what a good girl I am for him, how I feel so good, so hot and tight and perfect.

"I can't believe I get to come inside you," he groans. "You're going to have traces of me inside you, leaking out of you. I'm going to mark you from the inside, and you're going to be mine."

My body clenches, and he feels it. He keeps me there, just like that, fucking into me with long, firm strokes that light up every nerve in my body. I choke out his name, eyes glued to his in the mirror, and come undone.

I gasp and heave as the orgasm tears through me, pressing my face into the bedding and screaming when Brody's hand wraps around my cock and strokes me with each thrust, intensifying the sensations ripping me at the seams.

I'm a shaking, shuddering, overstimulated pile of nerves when Brody warns me he's close.

"Oh, fuck. I'm going to—" He groans. "I'm com—Holy Fuck, I'm coming inside you. You're mine, Becky, you're so"—*thrust*—" fucking"—*thrust*—"mine." He thrusts one last time, holding me against him and pulsing, rocking back and forth, until he collapses on top of me, heaving against my back.

Brody is shaking as he lifts himself up, forehead against the middle of my back, still panting.

"I've never done that before," he says, his words coming out between huffs. "That was intense and I... Fuck, Becky, I love you."

"I love you," I echo, boneless and completely spent.

Brody pulls out of me slowly, pulsing the tip inside me a little before he pulls out entirely. I can feel the tickle of liquid spilling out of me. It's an odd sensation and maybe not my favorite until I hear the hitch in Brody's breath.

"Oh my God, that's my—" I worry for a minute that Brody might pass out. He sounds drunk. I don't know how else to describe it. Neither of us drinks, but we are drunk on this thing we just did. On the love between us. Drunk on his cum being inside me, trickling out. Cum drunk, I guess.

I must drift for a minute afterward, because the next thing I register is the weight of a warm washcloth and Brody's soft voice telling me to stay put.

I do, boneless and dazed, while he cleans me up with a tenderness that makes my chest ache. He mutters something about letting him take care of me this time, and I don't have it in me to argue, even though it's still weird to let someone else wipe your butt.

By the time he's done and tossed the washcloth back into the bathroom, I've managed to wiggle under the covers. He slides in behind me, wrapping himself around my back, chest pressed to my spine, one arm heavy over my middle. It feels strangely like crawling into his tiny full-size bed at home all over again, even with the king-sized mattress and high thread count sheets.

At some point, my hands find his face, thumbs brushing over the rasp of his jaw. His eyes flutter closed as I trace the stubble there, then his bottom lip, fascinated by how different it feels. Rough and soft all at once.

"I like this," I whisper when he opens his eyes again.

He huffs a breathless laugh. "Yeah?"

"Yeah." I drag my thumb along his cheek again. "Don't shave it. Ever."

"Bossy," he mutters, but he looks stupidly pleased.

We lie there for a while, just breathing, the hotel's heating system humming quietly in the background. I could fall asleep like this. Easily.

Which is exactly when he ruins it by moving away.

I make a protesting noise and grab for him blindly. "No," I grumble. "Come back."

"I'm not going anywhere," he says, amusement lacing his voice. I hear him rummaging around on the nightstand. "I just forgot something."

"Forgot what?" I ask suspiciously, rolling onto my back.

He climbs back into bed with a small rectangular box in his hand. It's black, with a little gold bow crooked on one corner. He looks weirdly unsure as he settles cross-legged beside me, chewing his bottom lip.

"What's that?" I ask, propping myself up on my elbows.

"I saw it at the mall," he says, staring at the box instead of me. "I, uh, couldn't resist. It felt like it was meant to be."

My heart gives a heavy thud.

He holds it out. I sit up and take it, suddenly very awake, and slide the lid off.

Inside, nestled in cheap black velvet, is a chain. Silver-colored, probably stainless steel. A thin, slightly matte length of links that gleams softly in the low light. At each end is a small heart-shaped ring.

My breath catches.

"It's not fancy. It's not real silver or anything. But it's—"

"It's *perfect*." My thumb moves over the metal, tracing the line of the chain, the curve of one little heart.

Brody shifts next to me, nervous energy rolling off him in waves. When I glance up, he's watching my face like he's waiting for a verdict that might kill him. And I'm overwhelmed with love over this small, sweet gesture.

I can't seem to make my mouth work, so he gently takes the box back, lifts the chain free, and hooks the two heart rings together to form a loop.

Then, with ridiculous care, he leans in and slips it over my head.

The cool metal kisses the back of my neck and settles against my collarbones. The chain lies flat against my bare chest, catching the light. It looks almost delicate against my skin.

My fingers come up to touch it, to feel the weight of it sitting there, just above where his hand rested earlier when he wrapped it lightly around my throat.

I chuckle, full realization of what it is setting in. "You got me a collar."

His mouth curves at the word, but there's something soft and earnest behind the smirk. "It was your idea."

I swallow. The chain tightens infinitesimally as my throat works, reminding me it's there.

"Brody..." My chest feels too full. "I—"

He reaches out and takes one of the heart rings between his fingers, giving the chain the gentlest tug. It cinches just enough for me to feel it, not enough to hurt.

Heat floods me, fast and overwhelming, pooling low and heavy. Every nerve in my body stands at attention.

"Such a good girl," he murmurs, his eyes dark and fond, and a little wicked.

All the blood in my body rushes south at once.

"*Your* good girl," I rasp, dizzy and stupidly happy and absurdly turned on all at the same time. My fingers curl around his wrist where it holds the chain. "Yours."

He smiles, wide and bright and so full of love, it steals my breath.

"Mine," he agrees, and leans in to kiss me again, the chain cool against my throat and his stubble rough against my lips.

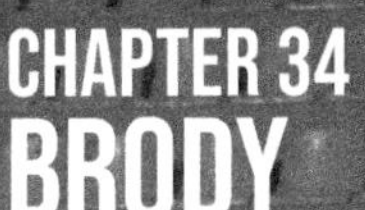

CHAPTER 34
BRODY

It's pretty insane what a difference a week can make. Last Tuesday I woke up in my childhood bed, broken, alone, and with no hope for my future. Fast forward to today, waking up in my dorm room to Lincoln Beckett's mouth on me.

With campus mostly empty, we've been able to ease into being back. Beck seems surprisingly comfortable with allowing himself to be seen with me by the few people around to witness us together. He even held my hand on the way to the fitness center today and didn't get pissed off when I teased him about the boner he was getting while spotting me at the bench press.

"Oh my God, you two are disgustingly cute," Caty says from the screen where Beck is video-chatting with her.

Beck adjusts the angle of his phone so we're both in the frame. I'm using his chest as a pillow, reading the files Caty emailed us with previous examples of harassment cases and Huntston University's diversity initiative mission statements. She's not sure how much her mother is going to be willing or able to help us, but she did a lot of research over the break that we might be able to use.

"So are you two going out tonight? There's a really amazing gay club not far from campus, you know. It's a huge place, with different levels and types of music. There are several dance floors, a karaoke room, a kink room…"

"Kink room?" Beck repeats. "What the hell do they do in there?"

"I actually don't know. But I would love if you two could go find out for me and report back."

"Yeah, that's not going to happen," Beck says, laughing.

I don't particularly want to go out anywhere, even if it is New Year's Eve, but I'd be lying if my stomach doesn't drop a little at the way Beck immediately shuts the idea down.

It makes me worry about what it will be like when the dorm and gym are full of our classmates and teammates. I meant what I said when I told him I have no expectations for him to come out fully, I only wanted him to acknowledge and accept himself and what was happening between us, and he passed with flying colors. I don't really love the prospect of hiding again, either. He wouldn't even sit next to me at the dining hall before, is that going to change now? Is he going to go back to pretending to hate me again?

"Maybe we can all go together after the holiday break," Beck clarifies, shocking me. "I'm not sure I'm up for a huge crowd right now. I'm kind of enjoying the quiet," he says, looking down at me. "Unless you really want to."

"No, I agree. I'm enjoying the bubble too much to leave." I pull lightly on the chain hidden beneath Beck's tank top. He bites his lip.

Caty makes a gagging sound. "Seriously, I can't stand either of you. I'm going to go. Unlike you two lovebirds, I'm going out tonight."

"Oh? Where to?" Beck asks absentmindedly, but all his attention is on the hand he's trailing down my chest.

"Wouldn't you like to know?"

"*Mmhmm*. Have fun."

"I hate you!"

"Love you too, 'kay bye…"

Beck's phone clatters to the ground, and I end up pressed into the mattress as he climbs over me and settles his weight over my hips. My hand dips into the back of his pants, and I circle a finger around his rim.

"Are you sore?" I ask, because I fucked him in the shower less than an hour ago, but I desperately want to be inside him again.

He shakes his head and kisses me, grinding down on my cock. All that separates us are two thin layers of cotton—the pajama pants he's wearing, and the insanely soft fabric of the briefs he bought me in Charlotte. They might be my favorite underwear, and I'm not ashamed to say that I would let him buy me more to be this comfortable. Plus, the way he looks at my bulge makes me feel like fucking Superman.

I help Beck slip his tank top and his pants off. He stays above me, stripping me of my shirt, but only pushing my briefs down enough to free my cock before he's slicking me up and sinking down on me.

"Oh, *Fuck*. Goddamn, Becky."

Beck likes me to take control most of the time, and I love it. It's definitely not a hardship. But I have to say, laying back and watching him ride my dick is probably going on my list of demands to be bossy about. Because *damn*.

"Jesus, you're big," he rasps, but doesn't stop working himself up and down my shaft, using his big, powerful thighs to control the depth and pace, until he's comfortable.

"You feel so good," he moans, rolling his hips and writhing on me like some kind of porn star. His head tips back, hands braced on my chest, and leisurely fucks himself on my cock. I have to flex my abs to keep from coming, to keep this going for as long as possible. It's not just the way it feels, but the way he looks as he loses himself to his own pleasure, taking what he wants from me.

"You're so beautiful," I whisper. His eyes open to blink down at me, and our gazes lock in the most intense eye contact of my life. Beck moves his hips faster, lifting and dropping down on my cock, finding a rhythm that makes his mouth drop open. I raise my hips to meet him, and he cries out.

"Hold on, Becky."

Gripping his hips, I thrust up with purpose. Beck falls forward, bracing himself on the headboard. Once he steadies himself, he pushes back with as much as I give. The springs on the little bed protest, the headboard slams into the wall over and over again, and our bodies clap with just as much force.

Beck bounces on my lap and starts to chant, "Oh, fuck, oh fuck, oh fuck. Brody, I'm going to—"

"Can you come like this?" I pant, nearing the point of no return. "Can you come hands free?"

He nods frantically and lets out a little whine. "I'm going to—"

Wrapping the chain around my fist, I pull Beck down to meet my mouth. "Come on my cock like the good girl you are, baby. Just like that."

Beck sucks in a sharp breath and lets it out in a staccato blend of a wail and a moan, broken by the air my cock drives out of his lungs as he comes apart on top of me. I keep my momentum going for as long as I can, fucking up into him until the last spurt of his cum has splashed across my chest. I thrust up into him once, twice, then a third time before wrapping my arms around his waist and holding him down, shuddering through my orgasm as I empty inside him.

We collapse in a tangled heap of sweaty limbs, damp sheets, and cum, struggling to catch our breaths.

"Fuck, I thought I was an athlete," Beck says, heaving.

"That was… Goddamn, that was something else," I say. I did maybe half the work, and I'm dizzy with it. Beck must feel like he ran a marathon.

I roll onto my side and rub his thighs that I know must be sore. "So what's our story for when your thighs start beefing out?"

"Mmm, new exercise regimen. Not for the weak, that's for sure," he says, chuckling.

I get distracted by a smear of cum on the inside of his thighs and trace it up to his swollen hole. I massage it, too, pushing my cum back inside where it belongs, loving that he's full of me. He's been full of me every day since the hotel, when he asked me to come inside him the first time.

"It's a good thing I can't get pregnant," Beck says with a snort.

"You sure about that?" I say, pulling my fingers out and looking at them glistening in the light.

"Pretty sure," he laughs.

"Hmm, we'll see about that," I growl, pulling him in for a deep, filthy kiss.

"Happy New Year," he whispers. "I love you."

———

Two days later, we're working out, doing squats and being honestly kind of gross about it, but there's no one here to complain about us playing around while we get some conditioning in.

Or at least there isn't at first. We're doing a bastardized version of pull-ups, facing each other with Beck's legs wrapped around my waist, kissing, licking, or nipping at each other's mouths whenever our faces meet above the bars.

I'm fucking giddy, completely at ease in our little bubble.

Then a deep voice makes me jump, almost cracking my jaw on the bar. Beck's legs unwind from around me, and we both drop to the floor, bending over to put our hands on our knees.

"Jesus Christ, you two! This is a gym, not a breeding facility. Now I know I said boners happen, but this is not what I was talking about! Go take a cold shower and meet me in my office in five!" He steps away, and we're both so stunned we don't move right away. "Now!" Coach McCoy barks.

Three and a half minutes later, we're giving each other scared, nervous looks as we speed-walk to Coach's office. We're both still wet from basically dousing ourselves in cold water before getting dressed, although I don't think either of us needed the cold water to calm down. We were both just afraid to not do exactly what he told us.

Coach McCoy's office door is open.

"Come in!"

Shit. We're in trouble. I mean, I'm already in trouble, but I'm really fucked now. And worse, I've gotten Beck involved. So not only is he going to be punished, but he's been outed, which isn't what we wanted.

. . .

Coach is at his desk when we walk in, arms folded, expression like he's smelled something foul. For a second I'm pretty sure *I* am the smell.

"Sit," he says.

I drop into the chair in front of his desk. Beck sits beside me, spine straight, hands folded like he's on trial. Which, to be fair, we kind of are.

"I'd ask if you two want to explain yourselves," Coach starts, "but I've coached long enough to know there's not a single explanation you could give me that I'd want rattling around in my head for the rest of my life."

Heat crawls up my neck. I stare very hard at a scuff mark on the floor.

Beck clears his throat. "Sir, I—"

"Don't," Coach cuts in, lifting one hand. "I am choosing, for the longevity of my career and my overall mental health, to pretend I don't know what you were doing on my pull-up rig. We will consider *that* portion of this conversation closed."

I blink. That's not what I expected.

He leans back, studies us for a long, heavy moment, then he pulls open a drawer, takes out a fat manila folder, and drops it onto the desk in front of me with a heavy thump.

The little metal tab rattles. I feel it in the base of my throat.

My name is written across the top in black marker.

"That's for you," Coach says.

My mouth is dry. "Is... is it expulsion paperwork?"

I knew this was coming. Hell, I've even made peace with it. I decided I'm going to enroll in a community college halfway between Huntston and home so I can finish getting a degree, even if they don't have a sports medicine program. It's something, and I won't have to leave the most important parts of my life behind— my family. My mom, Davis, and Beck, who has already found several apartments that he knows I can't afford but insists on paying for since he plans to be there every night or weekend he has off, and breaks. We have a plan, and I feel good about it.

Still, holding the evidence of my failures in my hands is hard to swallow.

"Open it."

My hands shake a little as I flip the folder open.

There aren't any forms. I don't see a neatly typed letter from the dean or enrollment office, or anything on stark white paper with the terrifying university letterhead I was bracing for. It's something different entirely.

The first page is a printed email, the logo at the top from the Board of Directors' office. I recognize Caty's mom's name, though the subject line doesn't fully sink in before my eyes snag on what comes next.

Concerns Regarding Athlete Welfare

It's a hand-written statement. The page beneath it is the same, another statement. The next page, another.

The stack is thick. Some are typed. Some are messy handwriting. My brain doesn't process individual words at first, just a flood of familiar names at the top of each page. *Aaron Eros, Jay Norman, Roman Bailey, Sean Cabot, Cade Washington, Jeremy Fisher, Matt Young.*

I'm surprised to even see some names of people I was pretty sure hated me. Then I start over and look through the names again. Then I count them. Every single name on our roster, save an obvious one, is present.

"What is this?"

I pick up the first statement. It's from Roman, Sean, and Beck together, an official statement as co-captains. They detail Pierce's ongoing pattern of harassment towards me. Instances where they reprimanded him. Times he ignored them. They describe a lot of what they witnessed in detail, and use words like *targeting* and *hostile environment* and *concern for team cohesion.*

I flip to the next.

Jay's handwriting is cramped and furious. He writes about the way Pierce talks about my family and his blatant homophobia. About how far Pierce took things before I broke and swung. He says he believes I showed restraint for months longer than any reasonable person would.

My throat closes.

"Keep going," Coach says quietly.

I do.

There's an incident report from two freshmen who admit to slashing my tires under the instruction of Pierce, who told them they had to follow through on pranks to earn their place. How he framed it as tradition, as team hazing, and would dole out punishments when they didn't complete the tasks to his approval. They write that they're willing to accept whatever punishment comes their way but feel it's important for the administration to know that Pierce orchestrated the entire thing.

I flip the page and nearly choke.

Someone, Sebastian again, based on the shaky handwriting, details how Pierce tried to spike a drink at a party. One that was purposefully meant for me, to get me drunk. Sebastian details how he purposefully spilled the drink on Pierce and took the heat for it. He writes about being forced to do naked pushups in the hallway of their dorm as punishment.

I flip more pages, and find more accounts from trainers about overhearing Pierce's comments. Notes about reminding him of team policies. Emails from the athletic department documenting past warnings.

Then my heart somehow squeezes tighter when I find a page that's different. Cleaner. It's on official letterhead from the athletics office.

Character assessment: Broderick Miller.

It's a list of my grades, which are all above a B+. My history of volunteer work. My transcripts from Nebraska. Conduct statements from my professors and athletics instructors at both schools, which are full of comments like *consistently on time, well-liked by staff, models positive attitude in workouts and goes out of his way to help others.*

"I—" My voice cracks. I clear my throat. "I don't... understand."

Beside me, Beck is quiet. His knee touches mine, solid and warm.

Coach steeples his fingers on the desk. "What you're looking at, Mr. Miller, is the reason you're sitting in that chair today instead of cleaning out your locker permanently."

I blink, trying to catch up.

"There will still be consequences," he goes on. "You swung and hit another student in the face in front of multiple eye-witnesses."

"Yes sir," I whisper automatically.

"But." He taps the folder with one blunt finger. "Because of your exemplary conduct and rapport with this team, which brought every single member together to take up your case, we have a very different path forward than we thought we would two weeks ago."

My head is buzzing. "What does that mean?"

"It means there will be a disciplinary hearing. You and I will both be there, as will legal, athletics, and student conduct. Mr. Jamison's parents have, unsurprisingly, been eager to pursue charges, but once all this documentation surfaced, they became very aware of how much their son has to lose if the full story is on the record."

He leans back, mouth twisting into something that might be a smirk if he weren't trying so hard to look professional.

"In my professional opinion, with the evidence we have of Mr. Jamison's long-standing behavior, with your teammates and the entire wrestling admin at your back, I believe there's a good chance you'll take a hit with a suspension, but I think you will keep your scholarship. And your spot at this university."

The words land in pieces.

Keep your scholarship.

My chest seizes.

I look back down at the pile. At all those names. All those pages. So many people stepping up for me, when mere months ago many of them treated me like I was less than. Because these statements aren't just from friends. Not just the guys I'd already started to feel anchored to. *Everyone.* Guys I thought barely tolerated me. Guys I assumed sided with Pierce because they laughed at his jokes or didn't step in when he ran his mouth.

They were watching. They were paying attention. And when it mattered, they chose *me*.

I didn't know I was gripping the arms of the chair until Beck's fingers quietly cover mine, prying them loose so he can lace our hands together. I stare at our joined hands for a second.

"Son?"

I drag my gaze back to Coach.

He clears his throat, looking uncomfortable, like he's about to say something earnest and would really rather be screaming at us to do suicides.

"Look," he says. "I knew you were having some growing pains getting integrated into the team. I should have stepped in sooner. That's on me. From where I was standing, it looked like you were making good strides with the majority of the room, aside from Mr. Jamison and, uh," his eyes flick to Beck, then back to me. "Mr. Beckett here."

Beck shifts beside me, ears going pink.

"But I did *not* know the circumstances behind your transfer," Coach continues. "Or everything going on back home. I didn't know how deep Jamison's history with your family ran. That ignorance is on me, and I'm sorry for it."

My throat tightens. I open my mouth to tell him it's not his fault, that I didn't tell anyone, that I wanted to pretend none of it existed, but no sound comes out.

"I also want to say," he adds gruffly, "that I'm proud of you."

My brain short-circuits. "You're what?"

He clears his throat and repeats himself. "I'm proud of you, Miller. And I hope it's okay for me to say that I think your father would be, too. Not just for what you do on the mat. But for the way you handled months of absolute horseshit without throwing a punch." His mouth twists. "Between you and me, and this is *completely* off the record, I think you probably should have laid him out a hell of a lot sooner."

A shocked laugh bursts out of me, half-sob, half-snort. Beck chokes on his own breath next to me.

Coach points a stern finger. "But you didn't. You rose above it. You kept showing up. You did your job. That says a lot about who you are. This," he taps the folder again, "says a lot about who you are. That's why all these people went to bat for you. Don't lose sight of that."

I swipe a quick hand under my eyes. "Yes, sir."

He stands abruptly, as if he's allergic to lingering feelings. "Alright. Get out of here."

Beck and I scramble to our feet.

For a second, I'm not sure what to do with my hands. Shake his hand? Hug him? That doesn't feel right. Coach McCoy doesn't really seem like a hugger.

Coach notices my hesitation and snorts. "Don't even think about it, Miller. That's what you've got Beckett for, apparently." He cuts us both a sharp side-eye. "Just keep it out of my facility. I see enough boners in my line of work as it is. I do *not* need to see *boners with intent* during my workday. They don't pay me enough for that."

My face goes nuclear. Beck makes a strangled noise that might be a laugh or a plea for death.

"Yes, sir," we chorus.

Coach thrusts out his hand instead. I take it, grip firm. He squeezes once, solid.

"Thank you," I say, and my voice cracks, but I don't care.

He gives a curt nod, looking almost embarrassed. "Just doing my job. Now get out of my office before I change my mind and add extra conditioning as punishment for defiling my pull-up bars."

We don't need telling twice.

I stop just outside the doorway to Coach's office, the folder clutched against my chest and lean back against the wall. My knees feel a little unreliable.

Beck hovers close, hand warm between my shoulder blades. "Hey," he says softly. "You okay?"

I let out a shaky breath and nod, though I'm not sure it's convincing. Everything inside me feels squeezed and full and hollow all at once.

Before I can start crying in the hallway like a complete mess, I turn and wrap my arms around Beck, dragging him into a hard, desperate hug. He comes willingly, chin dropping to my shoulder, arms wrapping around my back and pulling me in tight.

I bury my face against his neck and breathe. He smells like my soap mixed with his expensive cologne and the specific, undefinable scent that's him. His hand slides up into my hair, fingers scratching lightly at my scalp.

We stay like that for a long, grounding minute. Maybe longer.

It's only when I can finally breathe without my chest hitching that I realize how silent the hall is. How obvious we must look, two grown men wrapped around each other outside the coach's office. And Beck doesn't seem to mind one bit.

Right on cue, Coach's voice bellows through the closed door.

"Quit fraternizing in my hallway! Don't you two have a dorm room to go to? Take it to a utility closet or something, *damn!*"

I choke on a laugh against Beck's shoulder. Beck snorts, then giggles. It's a ridiculous, delighted sound I've never heard from him before.

"Come on, baby girl," I murmur, pulling back just enough to look at him. His eyes are red-rimmed and shiny, but he's smiling. "Let's go find a utility closet or something."

EPILOGUE—BRODY

ONE MONTH LATER

I'm in the first row of seats at the Duke Alumni Night Dual. It's the last meet I'll be on the sidelines for. The disciplinary board suspended me for three meets and left me with a stern warning that any further violations would result in much more serious consequences. Expulsion was heavily hinted, but it's unlikely to be an issue. I acted out of character, because, as my friends and family have reminded me over and over again, it's not in me to be violent. I've been hard on myself about it. Even with the way things turned out, I still regret my actions.

Although nobody else seems to.

When facing a long list of harassment charges and disciplinary reports that would have made *him* more likely to be expelled than me, Pierce quietly dropped the formal charges against me and transferred to Stanford. As luck would have it, our home dual against Stanford is the first meet I'll be allowed to participate in after my suspension, and although I've joked about trying to drop a weight class to see if we get paired up, I'm not actually that petty. I'd rather just move on.

And that's what we've all done. The team has come together and thrived without the toxicity that lingered beneath every practice and dual. Not just from Pierce, but from Beck.

My boyfriend, Beck.

My totally out and mostly confident boyfriend, who still gets to his knees and crawls to me when I catch him in the showers late after practice. Who still obeys when he's told to meet me in the stairwell with his pants down and his hands on the wall. Who blushes fiercely when we walk out of either of our dorm rooms after I turn him out, but isn't ashamed.

Coming out wasn't exactly easy for him. He was terrified. But even though I assured him over and over again that he didn't have to come out for me, he still did it. My boyfriend stood up in front of the whole team and told them that we were together, and dared anyone to make another disparaging comment about me ever again.

My boyfriend, who is eight points up in the third period of his matchup against a former national champion. I watch as he grapples with the hulking champion, eventually flipping the guy clean over his shoulders and straight to his back. The other guy's face ends up practically wedged between Beck's thighs as Beck clamps down to secure the fall position.

I get a tiny surge of jealous lust and think about giving Beck his Valentine's gift early as a celebration for winning and as punishment for not trying that move on *me* first. I can't wait to see the look of mortification on his face when he opens the box and sees the skimpy satin thong, in the same deep red as the singlet he's wearing right now. He's going to combust.

The ref slaps the mat, confirming Beck's pin, and the Hunston crowd erupts. I'm on my feet, clapping and cheering for my man.

A voice, deep and low, speaks right behind my left ear. "He could've ran it a little tighter on the turn. Would've been smoother on the finish."

I flinch so hard my whole body jerks. Bristling, I turn toward the voice, noting that the mocking tone I've come to expect from Beck's father is suspiciously absent. Then again, it could be that he saves the worst of his venom for Beck alone.

Charles Beckett stands there, hands in the pockets of an expensive coat, expression unreadable except for a slight quirk at one corner of his mouth. His eyes stay on his son as Beck shakes hands with his opponent.

There's something like pride in them. It's faint, but I think it's real. My shoulders relax, if only a little.

Beck catches sight of us. He stiffens instantly, alarm flashing across his face. I subtly lift my hand from my thigh to signal him to hold back.

I wink. *Don't worry, baby girl, I've got this.*

I turn back toward Mr. Beckett. "The half looked fine," I say casually, analyzing his comment about the match. "The guy was already fighting the turn. Running it tighter might've stalled momentum. Beck adjusted for the scramble, and the roll was clean."

He huffs, then gives a single nod of acknowledgement at my assessment. "Fair point."

I hesitate momentarily, then decide to take a chance. I hold out my hand to the man who will, whether he likes it or not, someday be my father-in-law.

"Brody Miller," I say, because we've never actually been officially introduced.

There's a flicker of something in his eyes that looks wary or maybe unsure, but Mr. Beckett clears his throat and takes my hand, grip firm but not unfriendly.

"Charles Beckett. It's a pleasure to meet you."

It's a start. I'll take it.

AFTERWORD

More than ever before, I find myself completely brainless after writing a book. I tend to hyper focus to the point where I don't sleep and ignore the rest of the world until the project is done. This one comes after a year of rapid releases that took it out of me physically and mentally. BUT it was so incredibly worth it, because not only did I have the pleasure of working with amazing people and bringing some of my greatest couples to life, but these releases helped me accomplish a huge goal for the year 2025.

At the beginning of the year, when *that man* was sworn in as president, I felt as many did— hopeless, terrified, and powerless. There is little I'm able to offer in a world that feels as broken as this one has, but I wanted to do something. So I decided that I wanted to give back, and use my platform to do some good, on whatever small scale. I pledged to donate all of my preorder profits and published some dedicated projects to raise money for organizations that were fighting on the frontlines for the rights of the LGBTQ+ and BIPOC communities in the United States. I made an impossible goal of raising $10,000 dollars. But then a friend helped me double many of our efforts through company matching, and one of my short stories went viral, and it became clear that not only would we hit our goal, but we'd exceed it. So we raised the goal to $20,000—which honestly felt insane.

But we did it. WE FUCKING DID IT.

We raised $23,300 in 2025 from this fundraiser alone. OVER $20K went to organizations like The ACLU Foundation, Human Rights Campaign, The Trevor Project, The Transgender Law Center, my local LGBT Center of Raleigh, NC and many others. And it's all thanks to YOU.

YOU helped me achieve the impossible and put good out into the world when it needed it the most. And I can't tell you how fucking good that makes me feel.

Thank you, from the bottom of my heart, for helping me do the work that it will take to move forward. Because I promise you, we're not done yet.

ABOUT THE AUTHOR

Human rights are not politics.

Don't tell me to keep my mouth shut, or to keep politics out of my books. My characters might be fictional, but their struggles are entirely real and often based off true stories.

The United States is backpedaling, falling back into the wrong side of history. The BIPOC and LGBTQ+ communities are not only experiencing an unprecedented attack on their rights, but they're more at risk than ever after years of finally being able to emerge from society's closet.

When we're being force fed rhetoric that trans people are danger-ous, that we shouldn't say gay, or that we shouldn't have autonomy over our own bodies- we need to fight back with our votes. There is no election too big or too small, and big changes start at the local level.

Check your voter registration at vote.gov and make sure you are using your voice to support a future that benefits a beautifully diverse America.

Unfortunately, in the wake of the atrocities happening all around us, **your vote isn't enough**. It's time to rise up, to love loudly and support each other in any way we can.

The powers that be are force feeding harmful rhetoric and trying to overwhelm us with darkness. Don't let them.

ACKNOWLEDGMENTS

I'm so thankful to get to do this- to be a real life author who gets to sit down at my desk every day and give life to all the voices in my head. And I wouldn't get to do this without you.

Thank you for picking up this book, for giving me a chance, for reading even one word that I put out into the world. Just by holding this book in your hand, you are making an eight year old Becca's biggest dreams come true. And I am just so thankful for you.

———

I have an amazing support system that I wouldn't be able to accomplish anything without.

My amazing PA Darcy is the absolute best fluffier in the game, and keeps a raging ADHD maniac like me from completely losing the plot. You put up with SO MUCH BULLSHIT from me, and I am eternally in your debt.

The best editor in the world, the Book Witch herself, who understands my voice and leaves the best snarky comments.

I've recently added a second proofreader to my process, and it has been such a boost to my confidence- Megan (from Feral Fiction Edits) is amazing. Thank you for helping me give my manuscripts that last polish!

My street team- My "Ball Handlers"- you not only support and encourage me every day, but you're helping me put some good out into the world when things feel so bleak. I can't imagine having a better team behind me.

————

My favorite guys! To all of my lovely, amazing, genius friends who not only read my books and make sure that I'm doing my best, most authentic, work- but allow me into their brains and share highly sensitive, intrusive information with me. Without you, I wouldn't feel comfortable writing in this genre and telling these stories. Your opinions, your support, your insight, and our chats keep me going.

————

To my family and in-person friends that put up with my incessant chatter about how a character won't behave, or sit back and smile and nod while I work out plot holes and ideas, and are always understanding of my unhinged cycles of hyper-focus- I don't deserve you. Thank you for putting up with my brand of unique.

I love you. I love you all.